I0692985

The Braided Locket

By

Michael J. Livolsi

W & B Publishers
USA

W & B Publishers

For information:
W & B Publishers
Post Office Box 193
Colfax, NC 27235
www.a-argusbooks.com

ISBN: 978-0-6923010-5-0
ISBN: 0-6923010-5-4

Book Cover designed by Dubya

Printed in the United States of America

Dedication

The Braided Locket is dedicated to my courageous granddaughter Sophia Catherine Livolsi, a young girl with immense courage who is forced to fight each day to live with type 1 diabetes.

Acknowledgment

Writer's need the expertise of certain people when developing their story. I am deeply indebted to family, friends and colleagues who provided input into various aspects of this novel in order for the writer to portray events and situations accurately for the readers, including:

- Shirley Eckhardt, whose editing made the manuscript come alive.
- Elizabeth Zack, BookCrafters LLC., for her editorial critiques; and manuscript assistance.

Prologue

John Adler's life was orderly and predictable until the day he stumbled upon something that would strangely impact him forever. John had always connected with the world in a way few people are privileged to experience. His unique ability to take the ordinary things of life and transform them onto canvas to sought-after pieces of art kept him peacefully centered while everything around him seemed hectic and chaotic.

It all started on what was a perfect day for sailing. The National Weather Service had predicted wind gusts of 15 to 20 knots lasting throughout the afternoon. John aimed the bow of his boat against the wind and sailed on a zigzag course directly into it. He glanced back toward the Coronado coastline about a half-mile away and decided to steer his boat sideways to the wind and the surf. About two hours in, it was time to turn the boat away from the wind and head back to the marina. At that moment, the wind died and there was no airstream for the sails to catch.

John noticed that the few sailboats in the distance were still catching prevailing winds as if nothing had changed, but his boat was now isolated in an area where the water was completely still and calm. Within fifty yards in any direction, the water was as it had been seconds earlier...rough and choppy.

An odd feeling came over him. The sounds you normally hear sailing off the coast of San Diego were nonexistent...gone. There was an eerie silence all around...no seagulls squawking overhead, no whirring of engines as planes took off from San Diego International or North Island Naval Base. He sat still on the edge of the bench seat, bewildered, scratching his head.

As he glanced down into what was normally murky salt water, he was amazed to see it was clear as glass. He could actually see the floor of the ocean below and thought to himself, *How could this possibly be*? He figured that the depth of the ocean at that spot had to be close to two hundred feet, yet he could see coral reefs and sea grasses over a wide area. As he continued to gaze into the water, his eyes suddenly fixed on a flickering, shadowy object directly below him.

At first, he thought he was imagining something that wasn't really there. He blinked several times and suddenly, like magic, the object materialized into the wreckage of a good-sized boat, resting peacefully on the bottom...a portion of it buried in the sandy sediment. Then, amazingly, within a few seconds, the image disappeared.

At that moment, the water became murky salt water again and, without warning, a strong gust of wind filled the sails of his boat and propelled it quickly forward. The jolt whipped him off the bench seat and onto the deck of the boat. From that day on, John's life changed dramatically.

Chapter One

Before I continue telling you John Adler's story and the unusual things that happened to him, I think it only fair to warn you. There will be details that are pure conjecture on my part. Some of the events were personal in nature, and I was not present to witness them first-hand. Therefore, it won't hurt my feelings if you take some of what I say in this story with several grains of salt.

Since I am a part of this story, it is only fitting that I tell you a little bit about me. My name is Manley Fox, but everyone calls me 'Skipper.' Why 'Skipper,' you might wonder? Well...when I was a young boy, my mother used to dress me up in the same old pirate costume every Halloween. My father would burn a cork and draw a curly mustache and goatee on my face. I hated pirates...they always scared me...but I never said anything. As long as I kept away from mirrors, I was OK. My father used to jokingly say to me, "Son...one day you will be the skipper of your own pirate ship"...hence, the handle...Skipper Fox.

At sixty years old, I am no longer scared of pirates, although I do wear a mustache and goatee...both gray. I have a noticeable scar on my face, which might appear as if I had been in a fight with a bear or a tiger...but it did not come that way. It used to give me an edge when competing for girls in my younger years, but now it blends in with the wrinkles I've developed as I have grown older.

Now, you might think that the fun things in life have long since passed me by but, believe you me...I can still raise hell with the best of them. I'm outspoken and, at six-foot-five, I tower over most people, sometimes to the point of being intimidating. I have strong opinions about almost everything...all of which suits me just fine. The women love to talk to me, and I love to watch them listen to me talk to them. I whip up one of the best Blow Job shooters you'll find in any bar around Coronado. I have many friends, but most of them are not 'friend-friends,' so-to-speak. They are just acquaintances who come and go, looking for friendly advice or the point spread or the over or under total scores on upcoming ball games.

You probably guessed it already. I'm a bartender, and I love it. I also own the bar I tend... a popular, local pub not far from the marina in beautiful downtown Coronado, California. I'll bet you can also guess the name of the pub...you're right again...'Skipper's'. Most of the locals have, at one time or another frequented my establishment. They hang out, watch ball games, play darts, or eat the purest beef cheeseburger you will ever find in any restaurant or bar on the Island. I've never been married because, up until recently, I haven't been ready to commit. Sixty and still going strong...I like the sound of it.

As a kid growing up in San Diego, my brother, Frank, took me fishing all the time...and I loved it. We would cast lines from the bank of the Bay into the water next to the Mission Bay Bridge. If we were lucky enough, we'd snag a halibut or two and, now and then, a small hammerhead shark. As I look back, I have accomplished some memorable things in my life, including an unforgettable thirty-day turnaround on a tuna seiner. That trip on the fishing boat really changed the direction of my life.

I was about twenty at the time. A friend I went to school with...an Italian kid named Joe Bataglia, whose father was part-owner of an eighty-five ton tuna seiner named the Starcrest...asked me if I wanted to take a job. I would replace one of their speedboat drivers who had quit and gone to work on a much larger boat.

Of course, I was excited about the opportunity. Wow…to be fishing and get paid a quarter-share of the profits…what a deal! Although I was somewhat apprehensive because I had always heard that working on a tuna boat was one of the hardest and most grueling jobs on earth, I accepted. It was just my luck…the rumor about the hard work was true.

The hardest part was stacking the net and scrubbing the boat down between sets. The fun part was driving a speedboat twenty-five miles an hour out in the ocean's choppy waters, wearing a headset and taking directions from the skipper, who was high up in the crow's nest. The tuna follow the porpoise to find food. The speedboat driver's job was to chase the porpoise into a net spread over a quarter of a mile…a lot like corralling cattle.

As fate would have it, on my first and only trip, I got hurt. I was standing on a heap of net we were stacking, preparing for the next set. A tuna the size of a small refrigerator had become entangled in the net and came through the winch high over my head. The tuna's tail broke loose from the net webbing and the giant fish came down from thirty feet up, almost directly on top of me.

Although I was wearing a safety hat at the time…if Joe had not yelled "heads up," I would have been killed. As it was, I received a scar running from the top of my brow down to the middle of my cheek where the sharp, ridged tail of the fish crossed my face…almost taking my left eye out. I also got a shattered knee and a good insurance settlement out of the deal. Now I walk with a slight limp.

One year later, when I turned twenty-one years old, I used some of the settlement money to attend bartender school. Three months after graduating, I took a job at a well-known Chinese restaurant across from the Grant Hotel…just a block away from the old Horton Plaza in downtown San Diego…and it was several years later when I first laid eyes on Johnny-boy…John Adler.

John was a tall, lanky twelve-year-old kid. He had long, thick, medium-brown hair and seaweed-green eyes. He had the kind of looks that had the teenage girls whispering in the halls at school. However, Johnny-boy was not ready for girlfriends at that stage of his life. He dug into his schoolwork to get above-average grades and spent most weekends at the harbor watching the boats...especially sailboats...sailing around the bay.

Every few days during the week, Johnny would walk from school to the restaurant, climb the steep stairwell and take a table next to the bar while he waited for his mother, Ginny, to finish her waitress shift. He would sit quietly at the table and sketch boats on the back of order tickets. When the bar side of the restaurant wasn't busy, I would stand near the table where Johnny was sitting, lean across the bar and make conversation. To be perfectly honest, at that point, I think Johnny-boy needed a male figure in his life and, well, I guess I volunteered.

Two years earlier, before I met Johnny, his father had died. That was a traumatic event for him since he and his father were very close. John's father used to take him to Shelter Island to watch the sailboats race back and forth in the Harbor, so John developed a love for boats and sailing early on. Over time, our relationship evolved to the point that John would sometimes refer to me as his 'Uncle Skip.'

I will never forget this one day. Johnny-boy came into the restaurant with a brown bag tucked in the crook of his right arm. He was grasping it with his left hand, as if he had taken a hand-off from a quarterback preparing to break through a defensive line. While Ginny was busy serving a party of judges and attorneys, I watched as Johnny, acting somewhat cagy, made his way across the room to sit at his usual table. When I walked to the end of the bar, I noticed the brown bag move a little when he placed it on the floor next to his chair. When I asked him what was in the bag, he smiled and then whispered conspiratorially...'It's a blue-bar.' Well, hell... I didn't know what a blue-bar was so, out of curiosity, I walked around the bar to the table to see for myself.

Johnny took a quick glance around the restaurant to make sure that no one was looking, and then motioned for me to sit down. Just as my ass hit the seat, I heard a cooing sound coming from the bag. At that moment, I knew exactly what was in that paper bag--a pigeon. John reached down for the bag and placed it on the table in front of him. He put his hand into the bag, gripped the pigeon across its back and held its wings against its body. He looked around suspiciously again before pulling the bird out of the bag. I knew that Johnny liked pigeons because he had told me about the small cage with two pigeons he had at home. I gasped, however, when he told me that he had caught that one at Horton Plaza.

He said he used kernels of corn as bait and, when it got close enough, he snatched it up and stuffed it into his empty lunch bag. Back then, it was against the law to catch pigeons in the Plaza, and if Ginny ever found out about it, well...Johnny-boy would have hell to pay. When Johnny pulled the pigeon from the bag to show me the blue bars across its wings, he asked me if I knew how to tell if it was a male or female.

My first mistake was that I didn't immediately tell Johnny to put the damn bird back in the bag and get it the hell out of the restaurant, and my second mistake was that I answered 'no' to his question. That's when he placed both of his hands around the bird's back, with the bird's head facing towards him. The next thing he did, before disaster struck, was to spread the bird's wings apart with his thumbs while telling me that, if the tail points up, it's a male, and if it points down, it's a female.

What happened after that was the disastrous part of this story. The pigeon squirmed loose from Johnny's grip, flapped its wings...almost slapping me in the face...as

Johnny, now grasping only one of the bird's legs, lost complete control. That damn pigeon flew straight for the kitchen at the exact time Ginny came barreling through one side of the double doors carrying a tray of food.

The bird glided right past Ginny without her even noticing, straight through the door and into the kitchen before the door swung shut. That was when I jumped from the chair and high-tailed it back around to the other side of the bar, while Johnny sat there wide-eyed, staring in the direction of the kitchen with his mouth wide open. Now I must say…what was weird is that neither Johnny nor I ever saw or heard anything about that pigeon again. It's something we joke and laugh about to this day.

Chapter Two

Now that I've told you more than I needed to about Johnny-boy and me in the early days, let's get back to the present. John is now thirty-eight years old and a successful local artist on Coronado Island. He paints pictures of boats, mostly sailboats, and displays his work in six local art galleries on the Island. I can't tell you how many paintings John has sold. His paintings are hanging on walls all over the San Diego area…not to mention the homes of many of the boat-loving tourists who have purchased his work to take home with them.

John loves living in Coronado and has no desire to live anywhere else. His condominium near the Glorietta Bay Marina, close to the beach, makes a great backdrop for his artwork…and that's where he docks his own boat. John's sailing instructor had taught him well. The long months of training paid off. For John, sailing became second nature; he knew just about everything there was to know. His instructor, a retired Navy Captain, was the kind who took training seriously and required John to do a lot of it. I'm amazed at how well John can maneuver that boat out there in the water. I've been out sailing with John and his buddies a few times over the years; and no matter how big the swells or how rough it gets out there, I always feel safe when he is at the helm.

Johnny's hair is no longer long and scruffy, but it is still thick and wavy. He combs it back along the sides, covering up the top half of his ears. The front of his hair, just an inch or two above his eyebrows, splits just right of the middle and flows back and down, blending in with the sides...kind of like the way a young Jeff Bridges wore his hair.

Three days a week, John walks to the marina carrying a folding chair, an eight-and-a-half-by-eleven pad and some number 2 pastel sketching pencils. He arrives at varying times during the day to catch the different effects of light and shadows from the sun's rays reflecting off the objects he paints. Sitting in the sun, sketching, has given John a pretty decent tan. If you ask me, however, he doesn't wear enough sun block...and that worries me. I tell him, but it goes in one ear and out the other...oh, well.

When John isn't painting or sailing, he transports himself from reality to fiction by reading sci-fi novels. Me...I prefer looking at the pictures in the magazines stored in the bottom drawer of my desk...if you know what I mean. If you ask me, John's life is kind of boring and uninteresting. However, on the other hand, that's the way he likes it, so...more power to him. I guess painting all the time is the way he gets his jollies, whereas with me...I like gawking at the women that wander into my pub during summer wearing...not much.

Over the years, John has dated a few pretty-good-looking women. If you ask me...he's been too selective, up until recently, that is. He met a woman who finally captured his imagination enough that he became engaged. Elizabeth Humble—a little over the top for John's personality, in my opinion—is just short of a wild thirty-seven-year-old, born from the womb of riches. John met Elizabeth when she pursued him at an art show in downtown San Diego about two years ago.

Now I have to say...John landed himself quite the looker. Elizabeth's high forehead, wide-set eyes, narrow profile, full lips and eyebrows (fairly thick and neatly shaped) and short, blond hair give her a very attractive face...by all standards, a very graceful-looking woman.

Everything about her looks and body hang together very well.

She plays volleyball on the beach with her girlfriends almost every week during the summer, which sustains the pale gold skin tone of her body. What *I* like most, to no one's surprise, are the beautifully-formed breast implants which she has no trouble showing off whenever she gets the chance.

Elizabeth's father, a law partner in a well-known San Diego firm, thought John to be the perfect man for his daughter. He approved of John because of three things...his level head, his talent, and, most importantly, he knew that John had no interest whatsoever in his money.

Elizabeth works for her father's law firm as an event coordinator, so-to-speak. She sets up and coordinates seminars and conferences for the firm's twenty attorneys. Recently, I noticed that John's and Elizabeth's relationship had become a little tenuous. I could see it nearly every time John came into the pub, with or without her. At times, he even seemed distant with me...and that's never happened before. There was something going on with their relationship, and I could see that it weighed heavily on his mind.

I noticed it in Elizabeth as well, but Sakae noticed it first...Sakae (a waitress in the pub, and I'll tell you about her later) noticed it early on. She is very perceptive, you know. Where she comes from...they have this sixth-sense about things. It's not that I didn't believe Sakae, but it took me longer to recognize it...in denial, I guess. I'm sure that Elizabeth's outgoing personality had me fooled, for a while.

Unlike everything else that John and I normally talked about, he was keeping tight-lipped about this one. I do know Elizabeth, however. She never did like the idea that John was satisfied with being a local artist versus going national with his work. It seemed like she continued to press the issue, especially when they were around other people…and I knew John didn't appreciate it. Even though the inferences were subtle, *I* knew what she was doing and so did John…it's called crafty intimidation.

For Elizabeth's own selfish reasons, local art showings were just not enough publicity for her…she wanted more. Red carpet notoriety was more her style. Being part of and growing up in a world where flamboyancy (I guess that's a word) was commonplace does that to people. That's the way her father and mother raised her. Partying all the time with affluent people, vacations in the finest places…that was Elizabeth's life growing up…who's to blame?

I'm sure that Elizabeth loved John enough, but she just couldn't accept his fixation on just wanting to be an ordinary, normal kind of guy. Their relationship was teetering and, in my humble opinion, it would not take much to send their relationship into a fatal downward spiral.

And that happened about a month ago when a storm from the northwest swooped down on San Diego County. It didn't let up for days on end. One of those days, John came blasting through Skipper's doors with squeaky, wet rain booties over his shoes and wearing a plastic rain poncho and hat. Despite the rain, we were quite busy. John headed for his usual table. My waitress, Sakae (meaning *prosperity* in Cantonese, by the way), took John's drink order, which was very unusual for him…especially that time of the day. When Sakae handed me the ticket, I did a double-take. "Tanqueray-on-the-rocks??…are you sure about that?" I said it just that way, staring at the ticket in disbelief, wondering what in the world would drive John to drink liquor at that time of day…especially when he rarely consumed it at all. I poured John's drink and asked Sakae to cover for me while I carried it over to his table.

When I reached the table and put the drink in front of him, John had his forehead planted firmly in the palms of his hands. I pulled out the chair across from him and sat down. He lifted his head up and forced a smile. It was plain to see that he was just short of a basket case that afternoon.

At first, I did not say a word. I just stared at him as he sat there with this pathetic look on his face. I was sure, at that point, that Elizabeth had something to do with the unusual behavior. Finally, I couldn't hold back any longer. I said. "OK, Johnny-boy, it's about time that you and your ole Uncle Skipper have a 'come-to-Jesus' talk. The last time you ordered a drink this time of day was when you celebrated the sale of your first piece of artwork. Now...you've got to level with me...what's eating at you?"

Johnny lifted his glass and took a swig. I watched as the gin almost gagged him going down.

"It's Elizabeth again, Skipper," he replied as he lifted the glass to take another gulp before changing his mind and setting it back down on the table.

"I gathered that," I responded quickly, picking up the glass and taking myself a swig. "I've known for some time, Johnny-boy, that things weren't that great between the two of you; but since you weren't talking, I wasn't asking."

"I wasn't talking, Skipper," he replied sighing, "because Elizabeth and I made an agreement that our personal business would be kept between us...so, even though I wanted to say something, I guess I just was honoring the agreement we had."

"OK, I get that...so now that you've spilled the beans, you may as well share the rest of the story. Because...I'll tell you, Johnny-boy...whatever is happening between you two...its turning you into a boring man to be around."

"Well...that's nice to hear. That makes me feel much better."

"Look, Johnny-boy, to be truthful, boring is putting it mildly. Look...you know that I think of you as a son...but I'm telling you..."

"Uh, oh..." John shot back sarcastically. "Is this the place where I brace myself for another one of Uncle Skip's lectures?"

That's when I decided to put it all out there. "Listen, Johnny-boy. I'm not blind, you know. The fact is...you are one of the nicest people anyone would ever want to know...someone who would never hurt a fly. Nevertheless, a gnat has bigger balls than you do. Listen to me, man...you have to stand up to that woman."

John just sat there taking it from me, but I didn't know for how long so I just kept hammering him.

"Never mind that she has everything any man could ever want," I went on, "looks, money and big manufactured tits...I mean, who could ask for anything more? When you boil it all down, she really is the answer to every boring man's dream. On the other hand, I'll tell you...I'm tired of watching her kick the shit out of you. Look at yourself," I said, staring directly into his eyes, pointing. I reached across the table for his glass again, but John scooped it up before I could grab it. "You are becoming a broken man."

"Now just wait a minute, UNCLE SKIP," John said, sarcastically. "Is all this consoling and love from an uncle supposed to make me feel better? Because...if that's the intent, it's not working."

"I'm just saying, Johnny. Decide what you want and tell her what that is. You haven't finished a painting in weeks. It seems to me...you're reading far-out space stories in an attempt to remove yourself from the real world. Try it. You never know. If you tell Elizabeth how you really feel, she might just love you enough to be more under-standing about what you want out of life...and offer a com-promise. You keep holding all this stuff in and you'll end up in one of those places where you wear a white coat and have your arms tied behind your back."

"It almost sounds like you might be taking her side in this matter," John said, almost gagging on another swig of Tanqueray.

I rose up from my chair, looked into his eyes and said, smiling, "If I were taking her side, which I'm not, it's only because I like big boobs, Johnny-boy. Oh, by the way," I said before turning away, "I noticed that you came in with your folding chair but not with your sketching tools…you know, pad and pencils."

"It's because I left it all at home."

"Left it at home?" I said. "You mean you just sat out there getting drenched in the rain, doing nothing?"

"Y-e-p."

"You see what I mean…that's exactly what I'm talking about. Now pull yourself together, son." At that point, I left John to his thoughts and headed back to the bar to assist Sakae.

Not long after that, I noticed John talking on his cell phone…I suspect to Elizabeth.

Chapter Three

It wasn't long after my heart-to-heart with John that he and Liz apparently patched things up. How it happened, I'm not sure, but I'll tell ya, it made me happy. Johnny-boy was getting to be Johnny again, back into his familiar routine. He was painting, making rounds at the galleries, sailing, and popping in and out of the pub. I know he was getting some because he was wearing a shit-eating grin on his face whenever he showed up with Elizabeth hanging on his arm.

I recently celebrated my sixtieth birthday...I'm a Scorpio...a sign that closely matches my personality...look it up and you'll see. To tell the truth, I actually had forgotten about it until Sakae reminded me of it the day of...you know, who cares after the fiftieth passes. Sakae never forgets my birthday...God bless her. She marks it on the Playboy calendar hanging on the wall by the coat rack in my office in hopes it will remind me; but when I glance at it, my eyes never seem to focus on the days of the month - so guess what? She buys me the new edition every year...and I love that gal for it. The old one goes on top of the stack in the bottom draw of my desk.

One of the things—among many—that impressed me about Sakae when I first laid eyes on her slinging chop suey and gotlet chicken in a Chinese restaurant located off old Pacific Highway was her warm smile but aggressive manner. She knew how to treat customers the way they wanted to be treated, and she got rewarded for it with good tips.

Another thing that was a draw to me as soon as I saw her was her stunning beauty. To me, she was goddess-like. She was forty-five at the time I stole her from that restaurant but looked no more than twenty-five. She is tall, which is unusual for an Asian woman, and her innocent, short, jet-black hair set off her almond-shaped, cat-like brown eyes. One thing about Sakae that everyone notices is that she becomes very emotional at times. I guess I like that about her only because I'm seldom that way…and I consider that balance between us a good thing.

***

John and Elizabeth strolled into Skipper's around eight o'clock in the evening. John carried a large, square package wrapped in brown paper, tied off with twine. He leaned the package against his chair on the floor.

Johnny was always good at making sure I didn't forget how old I was. Last year, he bought me a blue sweatshirt and a baseball hat to match with an 'Old Fart' logo…reminding me that, in one more year, I would officially be one.

Sakae had a handle on the customers sitting at the bar so I made my way around to their table, leaned over…surreptitiously catching a glimpse of the space between Elizabeth's breasts…and gave her a peck on the cheek before sitting myself down. "Would there be a pigeon somewhere inside that brown paper?" I grinned.

John chuckled and Elizabeth smiled…she had heard the pigeon story several times. "No…no pigeon," John replied, lifting the package off the floor and sliding it across the table to me on its edge. "Happy birthday, Uncle Skip."

The package was big and awkward so I stood as I took it from him. I yanked the zip knife from the holder attached to my belt and cut the twine. As I stripped away the paper, I became wide-eyed. It was beautiful, and something I'd asked John for many times…a picture of my own boat to hang over the bar. I even had an antique brass picture light installed six months ago in the perfect spot so that, when I got the picture, it would hang majestically just beneath it. I figured that a light shining on the picture would add some class to the bar area.

A few years back, I gave John a small photograph of the Starcrest…you know, the boat I went fishing on…and asked him to paint it for me. I couldn't figure out what was taking him so long. I guess installing the light on the wall behind the bar motivated him or maybe it *was* because my sixtieth was approaching. Either way…I was ecstatic.

"Damn, Johnny-boy," I said, trying to keep my emotions in check but not doing a very good job of it. "It even has my name painted on the side near the bow."

John said, "I thought I'd give you something special for your sixtieth, Skipper."

"And I thought I'd get a tee shirt with something like 'Over the Hill Gang' on the back."

John and Elizabeth both smiled.

I must admit, there might even have been a lonely tear trying to make its way out of the corner of my eye. The last time I became emotional was at John's mother's funeral last year. The main thing is, however, emotional or not, John knew how pleased I was…and that was good enough.

I asked Elizabeth to hold the painting steady as I rushed around to John's side of the table, yanked him up off his chair and commenced to give him a big bear hug. The excitement had me. I lifted John slightly off the floor before releasing my grip. Once John caught his breath and steadied himself, he reached into his pocket and pulled out a nail.

That's when I really got excited. That space on the wall had been waiting for this very moment. Sakae had a smile on her face that went from ear-to-ear. She knew how badly I wanted this painting. My guess is she knew it was coming and kept quiet about it.

"Let's go, Johnny-boy," I said anxiously as I grabbed the picture with both hands, hurried across the pub and stepped around to the other side of the bar. John followed with nail in hand, all smiles. I shoved the stool that Sakae used to reach for bottles up on the shelves to the middle of the bar and stepped up to position the picture exactly where I visualized it hanging. John handed me the nail while Sakae handed me a hammer she had taken out of the toolbox from beneath the bar. I drove the nail into the spot my eye focused on. I'll never forget it. Everyone sitting around the bar applauded. I finally had my boat, and I was so proud of it.

Chapter Four

The Locket

Now that I've given you a historical glimpse into the relationship between John and Elizabeth, it's time I move on to the bizarre details of what happened to him. OH...there's one more important thing that I failed to mention. John is an avid jogger, and it's important only because that's primarily how all of these inexplicable events started ...with the exception of the strange episode that day when, for no logical reason, his boat stopped dead in the water.

Four days a week, as the sun begins to set, John leaves his condominium barefooted, walks to the beach and heads across the clean white sand to jog four miles along the water's edge. You might be asking why he runs in his bare feet and not in a pair of running shoes.

I asked him that very question one day after he sliced his foot on a small, sharp seashell...a cut that took six stitches. His answer was... "I like the feel of wet sand between my toes." In my mind, I thought it was a little insane. I would think everyone knows the incessant possibility of injury while walking or running at the beach, but what the hell do I know? I can barely walk, let alone even think about jogging.

John was jogging close to the water's edge...you know, where the tide creeps in and back out again. It was like every other day that time of day. The sun was setting, and the cool breeze felt good across his face. John often remarked that, during his runs, he can actually solve the

problems of the world while marveling at the scenic sur-
roundings of the beautiful coastline and the hills of Point
Loma leading up to the lighthouse. I'm telling you...the
way John describes it, it would make everyone want to run
out and buy a pair of Nikes.

As he was about a mile into his run, he spotted something out of the corner of his eye. It was shimmering, moving and swaying in the shallow water as he passed it. At
first, he thought it was a small piece of seaweed shimmering against the warm reds, oranges and yellows created as
the sun set gently across the water. As he got about twenty
yards past the object, something caused him to stop in his
tracks.

Curiosity filled his head and a chill came over him... a
skin-crawling chill...a goose-bumps kind of chill. It felt
like energy leaving his body...possibly like that caused by
some paranormal event. It caused him to turn and look back
to the spot in the water where the shimmering object had
caught his eye.

Breathing heavily, he walked back to take a closer look
and spotted it again...something gold...slithering, washing
in and out with the tide. From his point of view, it reminded
him of a tiny, thin water snake. The closer he got, however,
he realized it wasn't a water snake at all, nor was it a piece
of seaweed. It was a gold chain with some sort of pendant
attached to it. He waded into the shallow water, leaned
down and took the chain up into his hand. The pendent was
in the shape of a heart with small braids around the edge.
As he looked at it curiously, he felt that strange chill come
over his body again.

He stood there as the tide pushed up against his ankles,
higher and higher, and then just as quickly receded. He
gazed out towards the ocean for the longest time, staring at
the breakers as they crashed, one by one, onto the shore. It
was as if he was stuck in some sort of trance.

Finally, he turned towards the shore, his eyes glancing back and forth to see if he was alone in that area of the beach...wondering if the chain might have come loose from someone's neck. Finally, realizing no one was around to confront, he slipped the locket into the pocket of his running shorts and went back to jogging.

After the run, he darted through the door of his condo, grabbed a bottle of water from the refrigerator and headed straight for the balcony to cool down. Grabbing the railing with both hands, he bent over to stretch, and then stood straight up, breathing heavily, his hands resting on his hips. He closed his eyes and saw himself sailing in the ocean on that breezy, sunny day when his sails lost wind and the boat drifted in the middle of calm waters. He wondered how much more would appear in his mind's eye if he continued to keep his eyes closed...so he did.

He recalled looking into the crystal-clear, smooth–as–glass water and spotting the image of a boat sitting on the bottom. It was like reliving it all over again, even the sudden wind gust that hit the sails, thrusting his boat forward. Suddenly, a Navy helicopter, flying low and just off the shoreline as it headed back to North Island Naval Base, disrupted his thoughts.

John gazed at the golden sunset floating just over the unobstructed horizon. He reached into his pocket and pulled out the gold chain. As he held it in the palm of his hand, he felt the same strange sensation he had felt earlier, just before he plucked it from the tidewater...that skin-crawling, goose-bumps chill. Then, in the next second, a feeling very different than a cold chill set upon him. It was a feeling of warmth...an odd sort of warmth in the cool, open air.

At first, I got the impression he was taking words from one of those sci-fi novels he'd been reading. However, as he continued with his story, I could tell there was emotion and realism behind his words...not something he had just made up. Anyway, he stood on the balcony for at least twenty minutes, thinking. His thoughts went from sailing and sunken boats to questions and doubt and a plethora of other emotions dealing with how viable his relationship with Elizabeth really was.

I can tell you that John and I have had *that* discussion many times since their engagement, and the conversation usually goes nowhere. After some intense self-analysis but still coming to no conclusion, he gave up as he made his way into the kitchen, grabbed another water bottle from the refrigerator, and placed the pendant in a key dish on the counter.

Later that evening, around seven o'clock, John walked into Skipper's with Elizabeth. The game had already started. The San Diego Chargers were hosting the Denver Broncos for Monday night football…national television…great for business.

The pub, packed with locals and a few out-of-towners, watched the battle between the two rivals on three huge flat-panel televisions located near the ceiling on brackets. Although I never knew when John would show up, it was always a happy occasion for me when he did. Whether we were busy or not busy, Sakae always made sure she had the reserved sign on his usual table near the far end of the pub.

John was dressed in his usual faded jeans, a Lucky's-brand tee shirt and Van's Half-Cabs…his normal style of dress. Elizabeth, however, stood out in a low-cut, sequined, juicy couture pullover and sparkle-burst skin-tight black pants…causing every guy in the place to lose interest in the game and stare and salivate as she strutted to their table. I sent Sakae over for their drink orders, and she quickly shot me the signal. That meant that John wanted his usual…a tall iced tea, and Elizabeth wanted her usual…a Sex and the City cosmopolitan.

Finally, about an hour later, I caught a break in the action. I tossed the bar towel down and made my way to their table. I walked up just in time to hear Elizabeth tell John she was leaving town for two weeks--one week in Chicago and one in Las Vegas--to coordinate the details of two conferences her father's firm was sponsoring on the subject of tort law or something like that.

I took the liberty, as I always did, and sat myself down. We made small talk until Elizabeth gave me the stink eye...her way of dropping me a hint to give them some space. It didn't offend me at all...I was used to it. It seemed like every time they came into my place, time was her enemy...it seemed to be a strain for her to spend more time than necessary away from her or Johnny-boy's bedroom.

If you ask me, the broad was always horny. I'll tell you, it's a good thing that Johnny-boy is physically fit, given all that running and what not. If he weren't, he'd never be able to keep up with that woman. Nor would I, for that matter...that is, if I was younger and, you know...in his place. Disregard what I just said...I wasn't going to intrude much longer.

Sakae was getting overwhelmed with customers and kept glancing in my direction as if to say 'get your ass over here...I'm drowning.' When I heard Elizabeth say that she had to catch an early flight...that was my clue. I knew she wanted to get Johnny-boy home.

I glanced over at their table a while later and noticed Elizabeth's ankle running up and down John's leg. See...I told you. There is something about the girl's hormones that scientists should study. That woman made no bones about what she wanted and when she wanted it.

Although John was, to a certain extent, reserved and normally shy in his ways, when Elizabeth wanted to have sex, his demeanor changed quickly. Yours would, too, given the same situation--especially with a provocative woman like Elizabeth. After she downed one more cosmopolitan, they quickly left the pub.

***

After two hours of Elizabeth having her way with John, she left his place and headed for hers to pack....clothes and toys and whatever else she takes on her so-called business trips. John stood out on his balcony, taking in the cool ocean breeze and gazing at the reflections of the moon's light bouncing off distant waves as they crashed onto the dark, shadowy, sandy beach.

He thought about the issues regarding their relationship again...issues temporarily erased because of their recent roll-in-the-hay. Now that she had left, his mind began questioning things again. He knew that marriage was a big step, and he was beginning to think that he should have given that a lot more thought before putting that ring on her finger.

Abruptly, John's thoughts then took him back to earlier in the afternoon when he had come across the chain drifting at the water's edge. Finding the chain and locket had slipped his mind. He had not mentioned it nor had Elizabeth noticed it lying in the key dish during the time she was there. That shows you how busy they were. There I go again...assuming things.

I'm sure he intended to say *something* to her...he usually tells her everything...too much, if you ask me, especially when he is under the influence of her spell. It was her way of making the evening with him unforgettable before she left town, making certain that he wouldn't be thinking about anything else but her until she returned.

This might sound a little narcissistic on my part, but who wouldn't mind being on the receiving end of her persuading techniques. Like Dean Martin once said, 'How lucky can one guy be?' When you think about it, why *would* John think about something as trivial as finding some chain when all that was going on?

Chapter Five

It was eleven o'clock, and John had called it a night. Lying in his bed, he stared at the ceiling until he fell fast asleep. Suddenly, there was a loud crack of thunder. He found himself in freezing cold water in the middle of a raging storm. He was treading water in huge swells with surging whitecaps spraying into the dark night high above him. He was taking in and coughing up large gulps of salty water as it cut across his face like a hundred bee stings. He could barely keep his head above water.

He glanced around in a panic, spinning his body in a three-hundred-and-sixty degree motion. He flailed his arms, searching for something to grab onto, anything to save him...but all he could see was darkness and the cold, choppy ocean water enveloping him. His arms felt like he'd bench-pressed two hundred pounds twenty times...aching, throbbing. He panicked, wondering how this could be happening. He kept thinking about his sailboat, hoping to see it, or some remnant of it, so he could use it to save himself.

The water was so cold that his bones seemed rigid and ready to crack; energy drained from his body. The heavy rain was now coming down sideways as the wind blew furiously. John fought so hard for so long that he was gasping just to get a breath of air.

Exhausted and worn out from fighting to stay above water, he was about to give up, relax his body and let whatever happened happen to him. Then, all of a sudden, another loud crash of thunder startled him awake. His eyes widened, and he shot up into a sitting position on the bed and pressed the back of his head against the headboard, sweat running from his forehead to his chin.

Rising to his feet, he made his way into the kitchen for a drink of water. Gulping down the water as fast as he could, his eyes focused on the pendent in the dish. He stared at it as if it were the only thing in the room.

He closed his eyes and had a mental picture of the chain floating in the shallow tidewater as he ran past it. He saw himself walking back to the spot. He focused on the heart-shaped pendent attached to the chain…it appeared to be the size of a real heart and beating like a real heart.

Suddenly the floor shook slightly, the dishes in the cabinet began to rattle and the key dish inched along the granite counter top. What felt like an earthquake lasted only seconds…but long enough to bring him back to reality.

John said too many strange things were happening to believe it was all just coincidence. The image of the gold pendent etched in his brain made him edgy for the rest of that night. The whole story was very disturbing. I've never read books of fantasy, but if I had…I'll bet they would read just like the story John was telling me.

Visions of this and visions of that…I don't know. I have no idea why, all of a sudden, the young man was having these disturbing experiences. The crazy dreams, the images and the earthquake that was never reported the next day in the news bothered me more than I let on.

Normally, John does not dream. I know this because he told me so. We have had conversations about dreams many times in the past because of my dreams. He knows that I dream all the time…vivid dreams. I have taken so many pain pills over the years because of that huge tuna falling on top of me, it is a wonder I am even alive today. My guess is that Johnny-boy has had no dream experiences, at least no dreams he remembered, because he has led such a clean, virtuous life. I must say, I was very surprised when he shared these recent experiences with me.

"I'm telling you, Skipper," John said, describing what it was like. "It was horrifying, I tell you, and still crystal-clear in my mind. It was almost as though I was watching myself on the big screen, in a movie theater, waiting for the moment where I'm dragged under, never to be seen again."

Now, among other things, my hearing isn't that great anymore so I leaned in a bit. I didn't want to miss any of the details. Sakae walked by and pushed a glass of tea past me over to him. Just in time, I might add. John seemed to have a touch of the cottonmouth. How Sakae sees these things amazes me. I often think she has some kind of sixth sense about things.

The way John was acting as he told me what happened made me think he couldn't be making this stuff up...and that worried me no end. When he started in with the heart-shaped pendent pulsating like a real heart, I couldn't be-lieve what I was hearing. At that point, it all sounded like noise to me...my head was spinning...I couldn't process any more of it.

I didn't want to ask John to repeat some of the things I had thought I heard him say for fear he might say the same things all over again. I didn't know whether I should chuckle, feel sorry for him, or try to be serious and under-standing. While he talked, I nodded several times, even when what he said was in the form of a question. I'm sure John wondered if I was even listening to him...or just go-ing through the motions. Finally, I decided to take the high road.

I didn't want to get loud or dominating so I kept my voice at an even level. "Listen, Johnny-boy," I said leaning in. "I hope you will take some comfort in what I'm about to say. I'm haunted...haunted by dreams almost every night; you already know that. It might be because of the pills I take but...whatever. The good news is that I'm functioning just fine. The fact is dreams really don't mean anything in particular...at least, that's what my psychiatrist tells me. So blow it off...it probably won't happen again..."

"Psychiatrist...?" John shot back quickly, bending his eyebrows. "I thought you just told me that you were functioning just fine."

"OK, listen... Johnny-boy," I said. "There are some things I keep private. I prefer not telling people everything...not even you. Besides, the fact that I see a shrink every now and then to cope with my own weird thoughts and dreams is really *my* personal business. But, now that I've opened that can of worms...yes, I've seen a psychiatrist. I've known the guy for years and, believe it or not...he helps keep my mind clear...you know, straight, so-to-speak. He helps me keep the demons away. I think of him as the demon executioner."

"Wait a minute, Skipper...demon executioner?" John, said, pushing off the bar, grinning. "Talk about strange. And your mind has never been clear."

I took a quick glance around and shot back. "Well, young man, that's another reason I've never mentioned it...just because of wise cracks like that."

John wasn't buying any of it. He wagged his finger at me, shook his head and said, "Somehow, Skipper, this whole conversation has turned around, and now we're talking about you. I came here to talk to you about my issue...my dream...or whatever it is. I don't know how real it was or wasn't. Wait a minute...now I've got it, Uncle Skip...maybe some of your demons are finding their way into my mind...how about that?"

His agitation was apparent. John wasn't pleased with me and was quickly losing his patience. I guess I *was* being a little bit harsh with him, but that's me...it's the way I roll and you should know that about me by now. Nevertheless, I realized, however, that I needed to back off before I drove John out of the pub in a complete tizzy. I didn't want him leaving mad at me, either. He already had enough on his plate with you-know-who and that weird dream of his.

"OK...OK," I said apologetically, throwing out the stop sign with the palms of my hands, "Calm down, Johnny-boy. Your dream...now let's analyze for a moment, shall we? You never dream and now you've had one, at least one that you remember. The best advice I can give you is...do what an old friend of mine who lives in Brooklyn always used to suggest that I do about things that bother me...FORGET ABOUT IT!"

"Wow...Uncle. Am I glad I wandered into Skipper's today," John said, spreading his arms wide. "Somehow, this whole experience has made me feel born again. Thanks for the talk...I'll catch you later."

"Now wait!" I said sounding serious enough to command his attention. I've never yelled at him before but there's a first time for everything, I guess. "Before you go running out of here mad...give me a listen."

"Are you sure you want me to hear this?"

"Yes...you can make fun all you want about what I've said to you, Johnny-boy. However, if you could hear some of the horrible stories that I hear from some of the sad sacks that wander into this place every day, you'd understand. Believe me," I went on, narrowing my eyes, looking directly into his..."*Your* life *is* a dream by comparison. You have a gift from God, my boy. You sit in the sun most days, doing what you want to do...making beautiful art. You're healthy, handsome, you have money and you're free from stress... not to mention the fact that you have a hot, sassy girlfriend. One bad dream means nothing...so once again, I suggest that you forget about it and be happy."

After I was finished giving John the 'what for,' I think his conscience got the best of him. I really didn't mean for the things I said to be a tongue-lashing, but he took it that way. He sat his ass back on the stool, sipped his iced tea and stared at the picture of the boat hanging over the bar as

I went about my business. I'm sure he was thinking hard about what I had said and realizing that I was only trying to be helpful.

A few minutes later, John got to his feet. Suddenly, I felt much better about the whole episode. He thanked me for listening to him and for actually making him feel much better about things. I smiled warmly as I wiped my hands with a bar towel and reached my long arm across the bar to gently slap him on the shoulder. "I'm always here for you, Johnny-boy," I said, smiling. "So, then, will we be seeing you tonight?"

"I'm afraid not, Skipper," he sighed. "I've got to finish painting the schooner I started three weeks ago. I committed it to the Shorelines Gallery and they already have a sight-unseen buyer waiting for it. And...now that 'you-know-who' is out of town, I'll have time to do something different, if you know what I mean...get some work done."

I glanced over at Sakae who was wiping the table down behind him, surreptitiously wearing a wide grin. She knew exactly what John was getting at.

Chapter Six

Three days later

It was more humid than normal for an early September afternoon. John returned home, sun-soaked and hungry. He'd been at the marina most of the day sketching out a fifty-foot yacht that had docked a few days earlier. Actually, the owner of the yacht heard about John and had asked him to do a picture in oil for him. John didn't tell me what the guy was paying for it, but I'll bet it was plenty.

He warmed up a slice of pizza left over from the day before. John had a routine. Anytime he craved pizza, he'd leave the island and drive over the Coronado Bridge into San Diego. He'd park near Anthony's Fish Grotto and stroll along the harbor to see if there were any new and interesting boats in the area to sketch. After that, he'd hop back into his jet-black Grand Cherokee and drive east a few blocks to Little Italy and take out a medium pepperoni and sausage pizza from Filippi's Pizza house, one of his favorite Italian restaurants.

According to John, it was around seven o'clock that night when he decided to prime a new canvas. He scooped out two dollops of gesso, put it in a bowl and carried it over to the sink. As he slowly poured water into the bowl, his eye caught the chain and pendent lying in the key dish. Suddenly his priority changed, and mixing gesso was no longer important.

He set the bowl down on the counter and lifted the chain out of the dish, letting the pendent fall into the palm of his left hand. This was the first time he had taken the time to examine it closely. He took the pendent between his fingers and turned it several different ways...studying it...front, back, and front again. It was then that he realized the pendent was a thin locket.

At that point, he carried the locket over to the easel and swiveled the magnifying desk-lamp over it. He could vaguely make out the seam around the perimeter separating two thin wings. He placed the edge of his fingernail between the wings, but couldn't pry it open. It was then that he realized that the locket had likely been in the water for a long time and not recently lost, as he initially thought.

He stood there, staring at it in his hand. It seemed as if, every time he touched it, it gave him an odd feeling. He wasn't sure exactly what the feeling was; but the way he explained it, it was, in a sense, like being separated from reality. Wow! That analogy seemed a little over the top...don't you think?

At the time, I was getting the story from John piece-meal. I'll tell you though, when he mentioned the part about being separated from reality, I had to bite my tongue. Accepting what I was hearing to be true wasn't easy at all. I didn't want to act like the know-it-all, however. If you recall, I offered my opinion before, and John got pissed at me. Although he forgave me then, and I must admit I was a little harsh, I was afraid he wouldn't be so willing to forgive again so soon.

OK...back to John's story. He laid the chain on the pedestal next to the easel and went to the desk to look for something to open it which wouldn't cause damage. He took a small flat-head screwdriver out of an eyeglass kit, went back to the easel and started to gently pry open the seam in different areas until the two wings finally separated.

To John's surprise, cut to fit inside one wing was a damaged, heart-shaped, mostly-faded photograph of a woman. Etched on the inside of the opposite wing was a slightly legible inscription. Centering his attention on the photograph, a sinking feeling came to the pit of his stomach. It was the condition of the photograph that struck him. He knew that whoever lost the locket had lost it a long time ago.

The picture of the woman was faded to the point that he could only make out a few distinct features. He could make out a section of her dark hair, which seemed to be shoulder length. Only the shape of one eye and brow was visible, and the eye seemed to be blue or green, or both. Although the jaw line was nearly faded away, after narrowing his eyes, he could tell that her face was narrow and she had high cheekbones. Her nose, although nearly undetectable in the photo, seemed small and straight. He studied the photograph for a long time. He put all the features of the woman together in his mind and determined that she must have been in her late forties.

John then focused his attention on the other wing. The inscription, covered with a rust-like substance or some sort of solid, murky film, rendered the words indecipherable. John's curiosity was beginning to overwhelm him. He laid the locket down, thought a moment, and then went to a cupboard for a Q-tip and some rubbing alcohol. As he gently brushed the Q-tip soaked in alcohol over the inscription, miraculously, the words began to appear.

'To my darling Anna, keep this next to your heart and I will be with you always'

Once John read that inscription, a feeling of helplessness washed over him. He was holding something in his hand that had deep and profound meaning to someone named Anna, and he had no idea who or where she was. He read the inscription repeatedly until frustration set in. His eyes shifted from the obscure photo of the woman and back to the inscription a dozen times until he finally rose from the stool, walked out onto the balcony and set his gaze towards the ocean…still cradling the locket in his palm of his hand.

As John stood there on the balcony, pictures started forming in his mind…not pictures of boats created on canvas with brushes and paints, not picturesque scenery found in an artist's backdrop…but pictures of two people in deep pain and sorrow. Pictures of two people bound together by the locket he held in his hand and separated by the loss of it.

He squeezed his eyes shut and felt warmth in the hand that held it. He saw himself running in wet sand further along the beach than he'd ever run before. He drew in a deep breath of cool, ocean air. It made him feel like he could run effortlessly, forever.

He said he saw it again…the chain, with the locket attached, shimmering in the water as he passed by. He felt the cold water brush against his ankles then recede as if he and the ocean were one. He stared at the chain shimmering at his feet against the warm reds, oranges and yellows that the sun had created as it set across the water. Suddenly, the phone ringing brought his mind back to the present. He spun around quickly, headed back through the open door into the condo and answered it…it was me.

"Johnny-boy," I said in my somewhat forceful, disconcerting way. "What the hell's wrong, son? Are you alright?"

I could tell the sound of my voice startled him by the way he responded. "Uh…yeah, Skipper…I'm fine. Why?"

"What do you mean…why? I haven't heard from you in three days. *You* know how I get when you don't at least call. I start to get worried, and for an old guy like me, that's not so good. I've been worried that something might have happened to you…like a sailing accident or something. What happened? You get lost in one of those dreams of yours?"

John took a moment before answering. He was staring at the locket he still held in the palm of his hand. I can't remember what got him to talk...something like 'hey you...are you still there?' Nevertheless, after some prodding, he finally said something.

"Calm down, Uncle Skip. I haven't called or been into Skipper's because I've been too darn busy painting my ass off. It's the galleries, *you* know. They have been bugging the hell out of me to get more paintings into play. Apparently, I'm selling out again."

"Well," I said. "I guess that would be considered a good thing. However, I don't like it when you leave me out there hanging. I'm not the only one concerned about you...you know. You've got Sakae in a tizzy. She sees the empty table and continually harps on me to call you...I'm busy too, you know."

"Well...you can just tell Sakae to hold her water," John said with a lighthearted chuckle. "She just misses not getting her five-dollar tip for the free glass of tea she brings me."

John *can* be humorous at times, and that was funny.

Chapter Seven

The angry clouds blanked out the moon's silhouette and poured out the vengeance of the skies. The vicious thunderstorm charged with lightning and ferocious winds blasted John in the face so hard he could barely keep his eyes open. The swells from the squall line were like skyscrapers towering over him.

The storm was violent and lightning zigzagged across the sky before crashing down around him, causing bright electrical arcs to dance on top of the water. John was fighting for his life, taking in more water than air, gasping with every movement of his body. The ocean swells capped and curved into giant white waves, burying him under tons of the foamy water.

He fought with all his strength to keep his head above water but they kept coming, wave after wave, plunging him beneath the dark water's surface. There was no time to think, no time to make sense of why he was there. There was only time to fight for survival. As he thrust his body upward, through the murky, foamy surface, he heard a plaintive sound in the midst of the thunderous noise. Flailing his arms wildly to stay afloat, he heard it again. A girl was screaming at the top of her lungs…crying out for help.

"HELP ME!! HELP ME!! HELP…."

John managed to steady himself, barely keeping his head above water, floating like a buoy over the huge swells that seemed to take him nowhere. His vision was blurred because of the torturous rain hitting his face…stinging like a thousand needles. He couldn't see anything but the dark, murky, foamy water surrounding him, trapping him.

John knew someone was out there. He could hear a desperate voice yelling, but he couldn't see anyone or do anything to help. His fight to stay alive was exhausting and seemingly never-ending. Suddenly, the voice rang out again, echoing all around him from what seemed to be far off in the distance.

"HELP!! HELP ME!! HELP...."

"W-H-O-'S- O-U-T- T-H-E-R-E!!" John yelled at the top of his lungs as he struggled to keep his head as far above the water line as possible. Glancing in all directions, he realized he was losing the battle against the forces of nature and the current that kept sucking him under...exhaustion was going to be his demise. Then, all of a sudden, the clamoring of the phone ringing next to his ear on the nightstand woke him. He couldn't move...he just lay there in a pool of sweat, dazed and disoriented, staring at the ceiling, listening to the phone as it continued to ring.

Just as he reached for the receiver, the voice recorder took the call. He quickly withdrew his hand and listened to Elizabeth's voice.

"Hi, baby," Elizabeth's voice echoed around the room. "Don't tell me you're still sleeping. It's eight o'clock...ten, Chicago time."

John, still a little disoriented, decided to take it and quickly lifted the receiver from its cradle.

"What...ah...oh, Elizabeth," he said in a toneless voice, wiping across his face with the palm of his hand, clearing the sleep from his eyes. "I guess I overslept."

"I should say so, darling," she chuckled. "Let me guess...a late night at Skipper's?"

"Uh...no," he responded, rolling himself into a sitting position, planting his feet flat on the floor. "I haven't been there in a few days."

"That sounds to me like, 'when the cat's away, the mice will play'," she said jokingly. "Perhaps another woman I don't know about filling in while I'm gone, maybe?"

"You know me better than that," John replied monotonously as he rose to his feet and wandered over to the window. He narrowed his eyes and peeked out through the shutters at the gray, overcast coastline.

"You know I'm just joking, darling," Elizabeth replied. "You don't have to get grumpy with me."

"I'm sorry, Elizabeth," John replied, combing his hair with his fingers, "I guess I *am* a little grumpy. I didn't mean to be short, but I've had a lot of things on my mind lately and, over the last few days, I haven't slept that well."

"OK, then, I'll forgive you," she said. "So, tell me…what could possibly be on your mind but little ol' me?"

"Uh…no, it isn't you at all," John responded, walking into the bathroom.

"Thanks," Elizabeth replied, now in a sarcastic tone of voice. "Now *that* was the wrong answer."

John didn't respond. He stared into the bathroom mirror at a face full of stubble…his wavy hair in disarray.

"John..?"

"Look," he said, trying to remain calm. "I'm really not in the mood for a verbal sparring match, Elizabeth. I've got an appointment with the Galleria at nine-fifteen this morning so I've got to get my ass in gear…"

The phone went dead against his ear.

"Elizabeth… Elizabeth?"

Elizabeth was like that. If she didn't like what she was hearing, the conversation would end abruptly. Hanging up without warning seemed to be her specialty. It's the arrogance about her that John keeps giving her a pass on. Another thing that gets under my skin is her lack of compassion. It irritates the hell out of me and baffles me as to why John puts up with it.

John said, that in a brief moment before Elizabeth hung up on him, he considered telling her about the locket and dreams. He thought telling her would have at least provided some justification as to why things had been weighing heavily on his mind. I said she would have only heard what she wanted to hear, wouldn't have given a damn, and suggested it was all a bunch of silliness.

John set the phone down, reached into the shower, twisted the knob and waited patiently for the hot water to come pouring out. He recalled the day I told him to grow some balls and confront the woman. So while he stood there staring into the mirror, he vowed then and there that he would take care of that problem the minute she returned from her trip. Personally, I'd have to see it to believe it.

Now hear me out a second...it's not that I totally dislike the woman...I just don't like what she does to John's psyche. In addition, I must admit, John has to accept some blame here as well. While I completely understand that sex changes one's ability to think clearly, I just needed Johnny-boy to realize that there are other fish in the sea besides sharks...if you know what I mean.

As the hot water flowed in the vacant shower stall, John hadn't moved an inch. He stood in front of that mirror like a statue...staring blankly as the room began to accumulate with mist. It was then that he said the obscure face of the woman in the locket slowly appeared in the mirror as it began to fog over.

John blinked several times and shook his head in disbelief...but the image remained, staring back at him, her features more distinct than the photograph itself. Moments later, the damp, steamy mist began to bead up into little water droplets that began to run down the face of the mirror, causing the image to slowly melt away like hot wax running down a candle.

OK, now here is the deal...I listened without commenting and looked at Sakae's expressions as she was standing there next to me listening, getting wrapped up in all of it: *My* head was about to explode. When John continued to tell bizarre story after bizarre story, I wanted to run into my office as fast as I could. I would have had two choices at that point. Call Joseph Navarra, scream or both…but no, I didn't. I stayed calm and heard him out. Now this part of what he said was really over the top and strange. Just before the image completely faded away, he noticed a locket just like the one that he had found in the water, hanging around the woman's neck in the image.

At that point, even John had to admit the whole thing was weird and unbelievable. I was glad to hear him sort of admit it until he told me *this* part…he said that, out of frustration, he wiped a clear swathe across the mirror with the palm of his hand. He stood there for a few more minutes, hoping the image of the woman would reappear. I told John that he should have, instead, cut the hot water off at that point and jumped into a cold shower.

Even though I knew the whole thing was implausible, John seemed convinced that the image he saw in the mirror *was,* strange as it may seem, the woman's face in the faded photo. I'll tell you… the more I listened to John talk, the more I began to believed that he was trapped inside the twilight zone. How could I not be worried about this kid?

Seeing that locket hanging around the woman's neck in the mirror image freaked John out. When the image didn't reappear, he stood there squeezing his eyes shut in desperation…an attempt to lock the image of the woman, exactly the way he saw her in the mirror, permanently inside his mind. As an artist, he did that sort of thing all the time.

That's what they say about talented people of the arts…like artists who paint or musicians creating songs…they can naturally recall things in their mind that normal people can't. In any event, in this case, it didn't work. He was only able to retain some of the detail and not all of what he saw before the image melted away.

John went on to say that another odd thing happened that morning after he saw the image in the mirror. Instead of climbing into the shower, some strange feeling made him to go to the locket. He turned the water off, hurried to the kitchen and went straight for the key dish. The locket lay in the middle of the dish with the two wings spread apart. He stood there scratching his head, wondering how that could possibly be. He was absolutely certain, without any doubt, that he had put the locket in the key dish with the wings closed.

It was just another thing that had John convinced there was something strangely real behind all this. I wasn't convinced by any means, but what did it matter...it was real to him. John rested his butt on one of the three captain's chairs in front of the kitchen's island, taking on the position of Auguste Rodin's 'The Thinker,' trying like hell to make sense of what was happening.

Assembling all the pieces in his mind was easy. The first part was how he stumbled upon the locket in the water. After that, it was the dreams...dreams of being caught in the ocean in raging storms. He was certain that, in his dream, he heard a woman's voice crying for help while he was fighting to save his own life. Just the thought of seeing the image of a woman in the mirror who resembled the woman in the photo with that locket hanging around her neck gave him chills.

On top of all that, he was sitting in his kitchen staring at an open locket which he was sure had been closed when he saw it last. How much more of a case can I make? John needed help...and he needed it fast. What could I do other than worry how all this was going to end?

Chapter Eight

The meeting which John told Elizabeth he had was with Kate Sutter, the proprietor of the Galleria (the biggest art gallery on Coronado Island). Kate loved John Adler. Every time he walked into the Galleria, her eyes lit up like a kid opening that first gift on Christmas morning.

Kate, a wealthy woman, lived in a house on Coronado's Spinnaker Way...one of the most prestigious homes in the neighborhood. Her husband was a well-known plastic surgeon. Unfortunately, he died tragically at the age of sixty from prostate cancer.

Kate, now sixty-five, had been diagnosed with cancer herself...breast cancer...fifteen years earlier. Fortunately, it didn't get her. She continues to be in remission and highly involved in raising money for the National Breast Cancer Foundation as well as other fundraisers for the same cause. She is a well-known figure on the Island...a celebrity of sorts.

If you see Kate, you would guess she was no more than fifty-five years old...a mature but always elegant-looking, refined, sophisticated woman. It didn't matter the day of the week. Working or at home, Kate could class-up the environment around her with her sheer chiffon blouses or cashmere fitted sweaters in mostly dark jewel-tone colors. Her light-brown hair, done in a simple, symmetric, wavy style, added to her youthful appearance. Like I said, she was the picture of elegance.

Kate never had any children and regarded John as the son she never had. She single-handedly put John on the map in Coronado as an artist whose paintings of boats were a must-have. His renderings, displayed in the windows on each side of the entrance leading into the gallery as well as in every corner, never remained on the list of inventory very long...his paintings sell out quickly. Although John had paintings in other galleries, Kate promoted John's work as if she was his personal agent...and John didn't mind that at all.

What John didn't know when he walked in was that an art dealer from New York City was vacationing with his family on Coronado Island for a few weeks. This dealer had wandered into Kate's gallery and admired John's work. He asked Kate to set up a meeting with John to discuss placing some of his work in popular galleries in the New York City area. Kate liked the man and wouldn't have done it if she hadn't.

John spotted Kate sitting on a sofa towards the rear of the store, just one of the several antique pieces she had positioned throughout the gallery. A heavy-set, middle-aged man with a shiny noggin, sporting a slightly gray, bushy mustache was seated next to her. The man was wearing dark-rimmed glasses, shorts and a Hawaiian-print, short-sleeved shirt...very eclectic-looking.

When John told me that Kate neglected to mention there would be a stranger from New York waiting there to greet him, that didn't surprise me. Kate knew how John felt about placing his paintings in any galleries other than those local to Coronado. If Kate had told him the truth, she knew he might not agree to the meeting. Nonetheless, the meeting was on and that was that.

I must say...Kate was definitely in Elizabeth's corner on this one...and I agreed with both of them. Even though it was the source of many of John's and Elizabeth's disagreements, the fact remains that John is a great artist and should take greater advantage of his talent. Kate feels strongly that John should go national with his paintings and makes no bones about it.

As John made his way towards them, Kate nudged the man and they both stood to greet him. Kate gave John a warm smile and a hug before introducing Thomas Conlin. It was then that John realized something was up. Kate was making another attempt to convince John to rethink his stand in that regard and I, being a betting man, would have given big odds that, whatever the man's persuasion techniques...it wouldn't work. Just so you know, I was right...no deal with the man wearing the dark-rimmed glasses. If I bored you with this story about a gentleman from New York trying to sign John up, I apologize. I couldn't think of a better way to introduce you to Kate Sutter.

Chapter Nine

The morning after John's meeting at the Galleria. I noticed his Jeep pull into one of the spaces behind the pub. He dragged himself into my office looking haggard...beat-down...worse than I had seen him look in a long time. I could tell quickly that something was bothering him. I tried to get him to open up about it, but he wanted no part of it. I reverted to small talk but he just sat there like a bump on a log staring blankly in the direction of the Playboy calendar hanging on the wall.

I went back to doing what I was doing. Five minutes of that and he rose from the chair as if I were not there and made his way out the door back to his car. As much as I wanted to, I didn't say anything to stop him from leaving. I just bit my tongue and watched him go. He stayed away from the pub that night, probably a good thing.

Around ten the next morning, John shows up again looking like he did the morning before. I'm behind my desk adding up the receipts from the previous day, and he plops himself in the chair across from me. This time I didn't say anything.

Suddenly he spoke. I was hearing it all over again...those God-awful dreams. He started in about the run on the beach. Next, it was that blasted locket. He rehashed the dream he had had that same night...the one about treading water in the ocean, smack in the middle of a storm. He described the obscure picture of the woman that was inside the locket and mentioned the inscription again. The story about the woman's image appearing in his bathroom mirror and, let's see, what else...blah, blah, blah. The whole thing still sounded just as wacky as it sounded before. I was a sounding board but I couldn't remain one for very long. I finally shuffled him out of the office and out to the front where Sakae was rushing around trying to get things done without me. We were now pushing against the time we open for lunch...eleven. Time was my enemy...and John kept talking.

Now you know me by now...I don't pull many punches...I just tell it like it is. However, listening to John...a man of his intelligence telling that kind of tale...I felt like he was losing his grip on reality. He was in an uncontrollable tailspin.

I glanced at the clock then looked him straight in the eye and said, "Now listen to your old Uncle Skip, Johnny-boy. You've had a lot on your mind lately...and you know exactly what I mean...the uncertainty of your engagement with Elizabeth, who is continuously pressing you to do things that you don't want to do just to feed her ego...and the untimely death of Ginny just a year ago. I know that you dearly miss not having your mother around. I know things like that would tend to make one wonder what's coming next around the corner, but adding to your anxiety by thinking that finding a chain on the beach and a few repetitive dreams might really mean something...I tell you...it's just ain't natural."

At that point, I spotted the ever-inquisitive Sakae glancing over at us. She knew that John and I were engaged in some sort of deep, serious conversation. She had eavesdropped on some of it as she passed by several times. Then, wouldn't you know it, just when I was about to deliver the speech of the year, several customers with a hankering for my famous hamburger and a beer came through the door like cattle through the gates, breaking my concentration. It seemed like they all knew each other...a small group of business folks. I hate when they do that without calling ahead.

Now I knew I had to get to work. Sakae started to seat customers and I said what I needed to say. This is where I suggested to John that he ought to see my psychiatrist friend in San Diego.

"A psychiatrist...?" he shot back, scoffing. It was obvious that the suggestion stung him like a wasp. "What? You think I'm crazy now...is that it?"

"No, no, Johnny-boy..." I said holding up the palms of my hands in front of him in an effort to calm him. "I'm not saying that at all, but perhaps it would help if you talked to someone who knows about these things. Believe you me...Joe Navarra is a good guy, and besides, everything he hears stays right in his office...you know...client confidentiality."

"Joe, the psychiatrist...I think not, not ever. Save that advice for one of your patrons who hangs around the bar too much, Skipper," John, said shaking his head. "That ain't going to happen."

Well...that didn't go well, did it? At least I said my piece and was happy that I did. We sparred a while longer but I could see I was losing the fight. Sakae ran out of patience and shot me the signal. I decided to go another three-minute round and gave up just as John's cell phone rang...it was Elizabeth. I forced myself to stand there and listen in. There was a verbal sparring match that wasn't going well...you know...trading barbs like politicians. She apologized for hanging up on him earlier. He said, "Don't worry about it...you do it all the time." She refuted the comment. He said, "It doesn't matter." They were going on as if they were a couple of schoolchildren when I'd finally had enough.

I hurried into my office, shuffled through a bunch of papers in the desk drawer and found what I was looking for...Joe Navarra's business card. I hurried straight back to the bar where John and Elizabeth were still going at it, stuck the card in a frustrated John's shirt pocket, shook my head then scrambled to help fill Sakae's drink orders, most-ly beer.

John walked out with the phone still stuck to his ear. Sakae motioned for me to take two drafts of Bud from her hands, and then nodded towards the end of the bar. Before letting go of the second one, she made the comment "Frosty conversation?" referring to John's phone call. My reply was something like, "Cold as that glass of beer you are holding, baby."

That night, John had another dream. It was a bad one, the straw that broke the camel's back, if you will. The next morning he informed me that he had set up an appointment with my friend in San Diego, the psychiatrist.

Chapter Ten

One week later

The elevator doors slid open to the third floor, but John couldn't move. Although his brain said 'go,' his feet said 'no.' He felt as though his shoes were glued to the floor of the elevator.

John just stood there, deep in thought. He hesitated so long that the built-in timer activated, causing the old elevator doors to rattle and slide closed. John flinched and took a quick guess at which button to push. He quickly stabbed at it with his finger and watched the doors open again.

John stood motionless in the elevator a moment longer, gazing at the white frosted glass on the door across the hallway directly in front of him. A sudden knot developed in the pit of his stomach. His eyes narrowed as he stared at the black lettering embossed in the middle of the glass...Dr. Joseph Navarra, Psychiatrist.

As he stood there, a scary thought kept flashing through his mind. He was afraid that, after this shrink evaluated him, he might say John was going crazy and that he needed to be in some quiet place where ominous-looking people in white uniforms hold patients down on tables for shock treatments. Leave it to John to think up this crazy stuff.

As the elevator doors began to close again, he mustered up enough courage to quickly squeeze into the narrow hallway onto the dated carpet. At that point, John tried to rationalize a way out by thinking psychiatrists are for people with real problems...certainly not him. As soon as he told me that, I thought the next words out of his mouth would be that he beat feet down the stairwell and into the street, running as far and as fast as he could from that place.

The building John had reluctantly walked into was located on Sixth Avenue, just off the I-5 freeway, in a run-down section of downtown San Diego. John said just walking into the building gave him the creeps. He wasn't used to being in that part of town anyway, and just the thought of meeting with a psychiatrist in *that* neighborhood made him extremely antsy.

The hallway smelled old and musty and was as quiet as a church between masses. I chuckled when John told me he stepped up to the door, leaned in and put his nose against the frosted glass…squinting, trying to make out something on the other side. I thought it even funnier when he said that, suddenly, the door knob rotated and the door opened into him, startling him backwards.

An older, thin man with bulging eyes, whom John described as a character out of a zombie movie, walked through the door. The man took the few steps to the elevator, pushed the button and turned back to look at John as he waited for the doors to open. John gave him a furtive look and quickly grabbed the office door before the spring mechanism pulled it all the way shut, yanking it back open and quickly stepping into the waiting area.

Once inside, he just stood there, again questioning why he was there in the first place. Across from him, John spotted an older woman with thin-framed reading glasses sitting behind a pane of sliding glass in the middle of the wall. In the upper right-hand corner of the glass was a sticker which read…'No checks accepted - cash and credit only.'

Feeling anxious, John finally mustered up enough courage to approach the woman. Waiting in front of the narrow counter, he rubbed his hands together, glancing around at nothing in particular. Finally, the woman looked over the top of her glasses, slid the glass pane to one side, and instructed him to sign the appointment sheet and take a seat. That is when it really kicked in...he was on the waiting list.

The waiting area was approximately ten-by-ten with five wooden chairs positioned along three of the walls. John took the chair adjacent to the door. Across from him sat a young woman blotting tears from the corner of one eye. A young boy, about six years old, sat in the chair next to her clutching a small blue and orange blanket with a teddy bear pattern. He leaned against her with his thumb shoved in his mouth all the way up to the knuckle.

To John's right, an extremely large man in a plaid shirt noisily sucked in oxygen from the wheeled tank next to his chair. John watched as the man pulled a Snickers candy bar from his shirt pocket, ripped the wrapper off halfway, and bit off a big chunk before shoving what was left of the bar back into his pocket. Now sweat was beading on John's forehead. He was hoping the fire alarm would go off, making it mandatory for everyone to evacuate the building.

The longer he sat there, the more apprehensive he became. Suddenly, an inner office door opened and out came someone who looked like a character out of 'One Flew Over the Cuckoo's Nest.' At that point, John had seen enough. He leaped out of his chair and fled the psychiatrist's office like a robber leaving the scene of a crime. I shook my head in disappointment when he told me what he had done.

It pissed me off that John didn't keep his appointment with the psychiatrist ...and the way he did it...storming out of the good doctor's office like that without a word, well...that pissed me off even more. He had his chance to get himself on track, and he blew it.

However, who am I to judge a person who seems to be emotionally unstable? Moreover, how am I to know how a person will react to certain pressures? That's the psychiatrist's job.

It was Friday night...my favorite night of the week... and despite what John told me, I was happy. The place was getting crowded, and Sakae was raking in tips. Around seven-thirty, the pub was getting pretty damn noisy. Loud voices, music...the commentators spewing out play-by-plays of games showing on the flat screens was so loud that it was hard to hear yourself think...just-the-way-I-like-it.

There was one empty stool at the bar until a beautiful angel dropped in from Heaven and sat down right in front of me. The only thing missing was her wings. She looked right at me and, for a long moment, I forgot who and where I was. Sakae squeezed by me and jabbed me in the ribs with her elbow; I must have looked like I was salivating.

The angel wore a white, long-sleeve silk blouse that had small, diamond-like sequins running down next to her breasts, coming together at her belly, and a small collar tucked beneath her auburn, shoulder-length hair. She had incredible cat-like, deep-blue eyes peering through semi-rimless glasses that sat up on the bridge of her perfectly straight-to-convex nose. I couldn't take my eyes off her full lips, lightly painted with something in a berry color. I stood there, staring like some old pervert, until she opened her mouth.

"Hi," she said loudly, trying to break through the acoustical turbulence. "I'll have a screwdriver with Kettle One, please."

I heard what she said and watched as she fiddled in her bag. It was as if I were still in a daze. I see plenty of beautiful woman come into my pub, but she was truly amazing. I was stuck on the heavenly sound of her voice. Her smile was warm and inviting, and I couldn't move fast enough to mix what she wanted. Sakae squeezed by and whispered near my ear, "You're old enough to be her father...close your mouth...you're drooling."

I whispered back as I took the top off the bottle of Kettle One, "Thanks for the vote of confidence."

I parked the drink on a napkin in front of her and asked, "You new around these parts, young lady? I know pretty much everyone on this Island, and I've never laid eyes on you...what's your name?"

Sakae squeezed by again and gave me another poke; this time in the back.

The angel smiled widely and shouted over the noise, "Sabrina, Sabrina Harper... and I *am* relatively new in these here parts, cowboy."

Sabrina. What a fitting name for such a beautiful woman. In addition, the way she responded to my question...a beautiful woman with a sense of humor, I thought to myself...she *must* be an angel. "OK," I said smiling. "I like that name...Sabrina."

Sabrina said, "And what should I call you...other than a handsome, distinguished man wearing a captain's hat and an intriguing beard?"

At that point, bells went off in my head...she had me at 'handsome.' "You, *young lady,* can call me anytime," I said with a grin. "However, as far as my name goes, people who know me call me Skipper."

"Skipper...an interesting name for an interesting man," she replied. "So this neat little pub is your place?"

"Good guess, Sabrina Harper," I replied as I twisted the top off a bottle of Bud and handed it to the guy sitting on the stool next to her...who, by the way, had his tongue hanging out like a dog in heat since the minute the angel sat down.

I leaned in closer, anticipating the next moment when her luscious lips would move. "What brings you to Coronado?"

"I'm visiting here from Joplin, Missouri," she replied as she reached into her handbag. She pulled out a business card and slid it across the bar to me. "But I'm not new around here...well, not new-new, that is," she went on, flicking her eyes between me and the creep sitting next to her...who thought he was being discreet as he slobbered over her every word. "The last time I was in San Diego, I drove over that enormous bridge of yours to the Silver Strand and spent the day hanging out at the beach with a friend."

After hearing that, the first thing that crossed my mind was, *I'd give my right arm to see this one in a bikini*. I'm sure the creep sitting next to her was thinking the same thing. I lifted my reading glasses from the pocket of my Jimmy Buffet parrot-head Hawaiian shirt and took a glimpse at the card. "I see...'Sabrina Harper, Journalist'. You work for a newspaper. That must be an exciting job."

"Uh...yes...you could say exciting. But it is more in the category of interesting. I work for my uncle. He owns a small magazine in Joplin. I do research and write human-interest stories. The magazine does quite well; it's been in circulation for years."

"Human interest stories, huh? So what brings you to Coronado this time?"

She lifted the drink glass to her lips and took a sip...I couldn't help but stare. "I'm doing an article about the Del Coronado," she replied, having to raise her voice.

"Interesting place, the Del," I said, as Sakae tapped me on the arm, scoffed, and passed me three mixed-drink or-ders. "That old hotel has lots of history to write about."

"I'm finding that out," she replied.

Much to my dismay, over the next twenty minutes, I was forced to tend to other customers while Sabrina sat there, tolerating the guy next to her. He was trying to put the make on her...as if he were worthy. I glanced over and spotted her holding up her empty glass. I broke away from another conversation and hurried to rescue her.

"So how do you like the way I mix a drink, Sabrina Harper?" I asked.

"Best screwdriver I've ever had, Skipper!"

"I guess that means you want more of the same?"

"Most definitely, one more" she said, smiling. "That's usually my limit."

I turned for the bottle of Kettle resting on the shelf behind me and, as I turned back to mix her drink, I spotted John walking in the door carrying one of his thick sci-fi books. He glanced at me, gestured with a salute and walked straight to his table. I set a new napkin in front of Sabrina and placed the drink on it.

She said, "I've been admiring that boat painting up there on the wall...it's beautiful...and I see that your name is on the side of it. Is it your boat?"

"Nah..." I replied shaking my head. "I wish it was...I went fishing on a boat just like that years ago."

At that point, the place was so loud I almost had to yell the words. The flat screens on each side of the bar were the main source of the racket. I couldn't do anything about it; my customers like it loud. "That picture is a birthday present from an artist friend of mine," I said, elevating my voice. "In fact, speak of the devil, he just walked in and sat down at his private table over there in the corner." I nodded in the direction of John's table.

"His table?" she asked, glancing in the direction I nodded. "Does *his* table mean he is some sort of part owner in your pub?"

I shook my head. "John...? OH...hell, no...that's John Adler; he's like family. I've known him since he was a pup. His table is always reserved...over there...out of the way. He comes in sometimes and just sits there drinking tea, reading sci-fi novels. When we are a little slow and I get the chance, I sit with him and we shoot the breeze. Anyway," I went on as I poured Bud Light from the tap into a tall, frosty glass, "it doesn't matter if the pub is busy and loud or quiet and empty; he either reads or puts finishing touches on his sketches. It's strange to me how nothing distracts him. It's a gift that artists have; they don't distract easily. By the way, he's pretty popular around Coronado."

Sabrina glanced in the direction of John's table again and, for a second, I detected a slight twitch of her beautifully curved, dark eyebrow. I'm guessing, of course, but I think she liked what she saw.

By now, the guy sitting next to Sabrina had a look of frustration on his face. I could tell he wanted me to shut my trap so he could make another futile attempt to move in on her...but I wasn't having it. I knew the guy. He thinks he's God's gift to women. He tries to put the make on unsuspecting young ladies but always fails...he's just downright annoying. At that point, I went around to the other side of the bar and whispered into Sabrina's ear.

"I'd like to introduce you to John...would that be alright?"

Sabrina, taken aback, glanced in John's direction again, then back at me. She shrugged her shoulders and said, "Uh...OK...I guess so...but why?"

It didn't take me long to answer. It gave me a chance to get her away from the creep sitting next to her. "Well...number one, you probably won't find a more interesting human-interest story in the whole of Coronado Island." I leaned in close to her ear again. "And number two, the guy sitting next to you is bugging me, and I'm sure you, too...so now would be a good time to lose him. Are you game, Sabrina?"

Sabrina grinned, shrugged her shoulders once more, grabbed her bag and slid off the stool. I picked up her drink and we moved between tables to where John was sitting. He had his nose buried in the book. I knocked on his table as if it was a door to get his attention; it was enough to startle him back to reality.

John looked up and saw Sabrina standing next to me. He smiled curiously...no wait...it wasn't just a smile, his face lit up like a beacon. I said, "John, Sabrina. Sabrina, John." I moved the chair out for her and scooted it back in when she sat down. I set her drink on the table in front of her, turned and walked away…just like that.

For a moment, John stared at her like a deer staring into the headlights of an oncoming car. He took a quick glance around as if to say what-the-hell-just-happened? He was shell-shocked, tongue–tied…and I was enjoying it. I thought I'd give him the chance to converse with a woman who wouldn't dominate the conversation, like someone else I know.

Sakae took me to the side and wanted to know what I was doing. She said I was trying to start trouble. Obviously, she meant that, if Elizabeth found out I introduced her man to a beautiful woman like Sabrina, she'd go on some sort of a rampage…but I didn't care. It's not as if they were on a date or anything like that. My intentions were innocent…really.

The two of them stared at each other for a moment. "Skipper wanted me to meet you. He just rushed me over here," Sabrina said, loudly. "I don't mean to intrude…would you prefer that I move?"

John said, "Intrude…? No…Move? Uh…no," he went on, raising his voice each time a word came out of his mouth, baffled at what just happened. "Quite the contrary...one never knows what my Uncle Skip might do at any given moment…or why, for that matter. He's what I call a spontaneous type-A personality, an enigma. I should be apologizing for his behavior."

Sabrina chuckled at John's characterization. "No apology necessary," Sabrina said over the deafening sound in the pub, leaning in. "Skipper seems like a nice person. I like him. I think it was his way of saving me from the guy sitting next to me at the bar. I was sitting there, looking at the picture of the boat hanging on the wall…admiring it. He told me you painted it for his birthday. You walked in and, the next thing you know, here we are."

John thought for a moment and said, "It's true, Sabrina. I do paint boats, and I did paint that one for him. I love the man...I really do, but right now I'm a little miffed at him," John continued with an anxious sigh. "He can sometimes get under my skin...but that's another story and my problem. I don't need to bore you with those details. I must say...Sabrina...that is a beautiful name. It reminds me of a movie I once saw starring Harrison Ford and Julia Ormond entitled, umm..."

"Sabrina," she interrupted. "I love that movie."

"Ahh...something we already have in common," John said, smiling.

Sabrina smiled back, "Painting that boat for his birthday was a wonderful gesture. I could tell after talking to him that he really cares for you a lot, John."

"Yeah..." John replied with a suspicious sort of headshake. "But sometimes Skip can be a major pain in the ass...believe me, if you knew him like I do, you'd understand."

"I know exactly what you mean," Sabrina offered, elevating her voice above the noise again. "My boss is like that. He's my uncle and the owner of the magazine I work for...and he feels content to be in my business or just overprotective all the time. I'm not sure why that is. I'm over twenty-one and I keep telling him that, but it doesn't matter. He says he loves me too much to back off. I'll tell you...it's not easy living in a small town like Joplin, Missouri. Everyone is in everyone's business."

"And what do you do for this...magazine?"

"I'm a journalist. I investigate and write human-interest stories. That's why I'm here in Coronado. I'm doing a story on the history of the Del Coronado"

"Interesting occupation--journalist," John said, grinning. "As I think of it, we are almost in the same line of work. I paint and you write. I use pencils in my work and you use pencils in yours. I create pictures and you create words…interesting. So far, about the only thing I can think of that we don't have in common is the fact that I've never been to Joplin."

"Well, then," she replied, as she lifted her glass to take a sip, "it's final. You should put Joplin on the top of your vacation bucket list. The people are real friendly, as evidenced by yours truly," Sabrina went on, lifting her glass again as if she were toasting. "And…in case you are interested; they have the most popular figurine factory in the world…Precious Moments."

"In that case…" John replied, his gaze unconsciously falling to her lips, then back to her eyes. He reached across the table with the glass of tea Sakae had set in front of him as soon as he sat down. "Here's to Joplin. When I'm in the market for a figurine, I'll make sure I find my way there." They both laughed.

It was comforting for me to know that John was finally having an honest-to-goodness two-way conversation. In my mind, Sabrina was just what the doctor ordered to keep John's mind free of those stupid dreams and, hopefully for a while, off his fiancée, who was probably preparing for a wild time in Nevada. You know, what goes on in Vegas, stays in Vegas.

Whether they wanted it or not, I mixed Kettle One and orange juice in one glass and poured one shot of Tanqueray in another glass. I skewed a green olive with a swivel stick, dropped it into the glass of Tanqueray and instructed Sakae to deliver the drinks to their table.

It didn't take long for me to figure out what I really liked about Sabrina…besides her amazing good looks. When I compared her personality to Elizabeth's, Sabrina seemed centered…down to earth…attributes Elizabeth did not possess.

I learned this by talking to her for only a short while…I should be some sort of profiler. Some women are like chameleons; they can change colors at any moment in time. This Sabrina...I tell you, she's different. What you get with Elizabeth is confrontation, questionable morals and secrets...basically, a chick not to be trusted. I'm only expressing *my* opinion here. I'm telling you...this woman is as genuine and sincere as they come.

After Sakae delivered the drinks, John and Sabrina glanced over at me. I gestured thumbs up. Sakae hurried back to the bar with a smirk on her face. 'What's with you, girl?' I said.

Her reply was somewhat funny...she said the only thing I was missing was a bow and arrow.

***

"Usually, John," Sabrina said, fingering the rim of the glass, "two drinks and I've reached my limit. This is number three."

"You don't have to finish it," John responded. "I struggle to get one down. I must confess...I've never been much of a drinker, especially this stuff. It's almost pure alcohol...tea is my drink of choice."

John gazed at Sabrina somewhat tensely as their conversation came to a screeching halt. They were both cherry-picking in their mind what to say next. It was an awkward situation, to say the least. I threw them together when they had no clue it was going to happen. Being at a loss for words in this situation is unnerving... believe it or not, I've been there. First, you start off talking like crazy...and then you suddenly space it for no good reason. Finally, Sabrina broke the silence first.

"If you don't mind my asking, just what did Skipper mean when he said there wasn't a better human-interest story on Coronado Island than you?"

"He actually said that to you?" John answered, creasing his brow.

"Yep..."

"Oh, that's just great. That's one of the reasons I'm a little miffed at him. Sometimes he talks too much. Just exactly what did he say about me?"

"Honestly, John," she replied. "He didn't divulge much. He just made a general comment about you being some sort of human-interest story…and, well, quite frankly, I did find it a bit odd that he would say that."

"*He* is odd," John said, with a stunned expression. "Did he mention anything about dreams?"

"Dreams…? No," she replied curiously. "But would you like to share? It sounds pretty interesting."

For a moment, John was still. He just looked at her, wondering if he should answer her question or just avoid it. "Look, Sabrina," he said, shrugging. "This whole thing has caught me by surprise…you know, Skipper bringing you over here out of the blue like that. If I did tell you about the dreams I've had, you might think *I'm* a little odd. I wouldn't want you to get a wrong impression of me over something that probably means nothing. After all, that would be no way to start a relationship. Furthermore," he went on grinning, "you might get bored and go take a seat on the bar stool next to that guy again."

Sabrina smiled. "No," she said grimacing. "No bar stool, especially not next to him. Look, John…you don't have to worry about that. In my line of work, I'm used to hearing all sorts of things. I promise…I won't judge."

Chapter Eleven

I popped the top off a beer and handed it to the guy who was still holding a grudge against me for dragging Sabrina away from the bar. I then glanced over at John, who was glaring back at me with this strange look on his face...probably thinking, 'What did you tell this woman about me?'

At that point, it didn't matter to me what John was thinking. I figured that if he spent some time having an intellectual conversation with someone besides Elizabeth, it would do him a world of good. On the other hand, the thought crossed my mind that if Elizabeth ever found out that I introduced a woman who looks like Sabrina to John, she'd have my nuts on a chopping block.

John sat there, staring, as if he was the only one in the pub...zoned out.

"Would you prefer not to discuss the dreams?"

John snapped out of his funk then took a small sip of his drink. "Are you sure you want me to bore you with details about my dreams when, the fact is, everyone has dreams, even strange one now and then? I'm thinking there must be other, more interesting things we could be talking about...like figurines or something. Besides, according to old Skipper over there...who believes he is some kind of authority on dreams...dreams really don't mean much anyway."

"I'm not so sure that Skipper is correct about that," she replied, smiling. "Greek philosophers might have something to say about it as well. Nevertheless..." she continued, "you never know, I might be able to offer some unofficial analysis. What I mean is...I can't pretend to be as smart as Skipper on these matters...and even though I'm not a philosopher or psychiatrist, I..."

When Sabrina said the word psychiatrist, a pain went straight to John's temple. At that point, John wasn't sure what I had told her. He was questioning her motive for even mentioning the word. "Just exactly what *did* Skipper tell you about me?" John broke in crisply.

Sabrina, stunned by John's abrupt manner, wondered what she might have done that set him off and shrugged. She thought for a moment, and then smiled again as if nothing had happened. "Well...let's see now...to answer your question, he said you were very handsome and very rich, that you loved to dance...oh, yeah...you like tea, and you paint. Yep, I think that's about it."

John told me that after Sabrina's light-hearted response, he felt stupid and a little guilty for what he had said and the way he said it. He reset himself.

"I guess I'm lucky that I didn't scare you away. You have a good sense of humor. I apologize for being short with you. I had no right to do that. Forgive me?"

Sabrina gazed at him and smiled, "You are forgiven."

John said, "I will tell you this, however, Sabrina Harper. About the only accurate things on Skipper's list that you can take to the bank with certainty is that I *am* a tea drinker, and I very much like to paint. The other stuff you mentioned is debatable."

"I don't know about the rich part," Sabrina replied warmly, "or the part about you loving to dance. You know? Now that I think about it, John, he may not have mentioned any of *those* things. I am sure of one thing, however," she continued, her gaze fixed on him. "That part about you being handsome...he didn't have to mention that...I figured that part out on my own."

***

While mixing a dry martini, I glanced over and noticed John squirm a little in his chair. Sabrina was saying something that was making him nervous. This was new territory for John. I didn't know whether I should rush over to his table with a dry cloth and wipe the beads of sweat off his forehead or make him another Tanqueray...even a double, perhaps.

John moved his chair around to the adjacent side of the table. I wasn't exactly sure what was happening but, then again, why speculate? Much easier to communicate with each other over the noise, I suppose. Sabrina didn't shy away from him, so all was good.

***

"OK, then," John said. "You asked for it, so here goes. It all started a few months ago when I was jogging on the beach. I found a chain in the water with a locket attached to it and..."

Sabrina held up a finger to stop him. "Sorry to interrupt, but... are we now talking about dreams and is this where the dream starts...by you finding this chain?"

Sabrina's question threw John's thought process an unexpected curve ball. "Uh, no... not exactly," he replied. "Well, actually, I did find a locket, so you might say everything unofficially started then, I guess."

"Oh...OK. Again...sorry for interrupting."

"Don't apologize," John said. "Believe me, there is more confusion coming your way. Anyway..." he went on, getting a strong urge to reach for the Tanqueray and chug-a-lug. "Actually, it was that night after I found the locket I had the first dream...a dream about being caught up in a violent storm in the ocean."

Sabrina's eyes narrowed. The term 'violent storm' caught her interest, something like the hook in the beginning of a mystery novel.

"Before you ask if, in the dream, I was in a boat," he went on, "the answer would be no, I wasn't. I was just out there. In any event, it I was unable to save myself. To tell you the truth, it was pretty damn frightening."

"That does seem scary," she said, sitting on the edge of her chair, taking it in. "What happened after that?"

John shrugged. "Nothing... I just woke up."

Sabrina took in a long breath then let out a sigh. "Hmm...well, then," she said, seemingly disillusioned after anticipating more, "if that's all there *was,* John, I wouldn't worry too much about it. As you know, people *have* dreams, similar dreams...maybe not exactly like that...but dreams like falling endlessly from a high place or dreams of being chased down some dark alley."

"Sabrina," he responded, leaning in close. "I've had that same kind of dream many times...at least three times in the last four days."

"Oops..." Sabrina said, scooting back in her chair. "Now that does seem to be a little peculiar."

"For some strange reason, Sabrina," he said, "I think that locket has something to do with the dreams."

"And you are thinking that – why?"

"Gut feeling, I guess," he replied, taking in a deep breath. "Believe me, Sabrina, I know it sounds strange, and obviously there is no real basis for suggesting it, but I feel like the dreams and the locket are linked together...pardon the pun."

"What kind of locket is it?"

"It's a gold, heart-shaped locket."

"Heart-shaped, huh?"

John nodded. "Yes. And, inside the locket, there's an obscure picture of a woman on one of the wings and a rather sentimental and touching inscription on the other wing."

"What does the inscription say?"

"Well, first...let me tell you about the picture. It's of a woman who looks to be in her late forties. I only say that because she looks mature and has dark hair with no sign of gray. The picture is a little water-damaged which leads me to believe that the locket had been in the water for what may have been a long time. I can only make out her left eye, a partial outline of her chin, part of the nose, part of the cheekbone, a portion of an eyebrow, and half of her shoulder-length hair."

Sabrina was now resting her right elbow on the table with her chin and cheek tucked squarely in the palm of her hand, staring directly into John's eyes...now fascinated by what she was hearing. "Well... I must say, John," she said as her hand fell away. "Wow...so far, this is not in the least bit boring."

John narrowed his eyes and leaned in as if he were telling a secret. "Now here is the part that's really been bothering me. The inscription reads...'To my darling Anna, keep this next to your heart and I will be with you always'."

Sabrina sighed then touched his forearm. "How sad is that? So *you're* thinking," she went on, "...since you found the locket in the water and suddenly you're having these dreams of being *in* the water...that the two together add up to some significant meaning?"

"I'll bet the whole thing sounds a little crazy to you," John said, placing the palms of his hands on the table, leaning back. "Skipper certainly thinks so. I'd be interested in your thoughts?"

"Well, John," she replied, taking in a deep breath. "In one sense, the dreams and everything you've said does sound a little bizarre. On the other hand, however, the story is also sad. Right this minute I feel sorry for the person who lost the locket. Trying to make sense of it all must be difficult, I agree. I guess...if I were a trained psychiatrist...I could...."

"Sabrina…" John said, kindly. "Please don't mention that word."

"What word?" she responded with a blank stare.

"The P word…psychiatrist. Old Uncle Skip over there," John said, nodding in the direction of the bar, "talked me into going to his shrink friend in San Diego. It was very uncomfortable being in that office so, before I even saw the guy, I freaked out and left."

Sabrina couldn't hold back a chuckle. "I'm sorry, John," she confessed. "If I had known, I wouldn't have thrown the P word out there. But, I will say, in case you are worried about those kinds of doctors…they really don't bite, and some of them are very good at what they do."

"I know that," he said, sitting straight up. "It's just the thought of letting some stranger dissect my brain…well; it just gives me the creeps. Look, Sabrina," he went on crossing his arms and pressing his back against the chair. "That's enough about silly dreams…tell me something about Sabrina that I don't know."

"Well, now…" she said, taking on the appearance of forming some deep, profound thought, with one elbow resting on the table and her chin resting between her thumb and index finger, eyebrow raised. "Something about me, you ask. Hmm…let's see. You already know that I work for my uncle's magazine in Joplin, and you already know that I'm a journalist. Oh, *I've* got some interesting stuff you don't know. How about this…I like dogs and pizza, and I jog most mornings around the park near my house. I enjoy a good book or a movie and most anything else that normal people like to do…how about that for some interesting stuff?"

John chuckled. He was becoming fond of her sense of humor. "What about friends?" he asked, smiling.

"Friends…?"

"Yeah. like boyfriend… You know… husband friend, friends… that kind of thing."

"Never been married…and boyfriend…? Not today," she replied, smiling back at him.

Suddenly, John realized that he had failed to mention that *he* had a girlfriend. He felt like kicking himself for not disclosing this fact sooner…or even bringing it up with her at all. He said he thought some more about it and decided, why should it matter? After all, they were only talking…a friendly conversation. He then felt so conflicted about it that he made the decision to say something before she quizzed him about the same thing.

"I HAVE A FIANCEE!" he blurted out, as if he were in a race to declare the next word. Once he did that, he said he felt like an ass putting it out there like that. I told him I would have done the same thing. I think it made him feel better about feeling like an ass, even though I really would not have brought it up then. I…would have waited for her to ask.

What John said and the way he said it really caught Sabrina by surprise. It caused an uncomfortable moment between them. Sabrina, taken aback by the word 'fiancée,' tilted her head slightly and nodded. "Oh…that's nice…congratulations," she said, forcing a smile.

Then John really felt stupid. He knew he had to recover quickly. Without hesitating, he said. "How is it that a beautiful woman like you has no boyfriend?"

Sabrina, as smart as she is, didn't answer what was an obvious touché on John's part. Instead she turned it on him. "And where is your fiancée tonight?"

The game was on, so-to-speak. John was going to play it his way. "Uh…out of town on business. Doing some work for her father's law firm."

"I see," Sabrina replied. At that point, Sabrina thought that it might be a good time to make her exit. She glanced at her watch, then said with a smile, "Wow, John. I didn't realize it was getting so late. I've got some editing to do on my story before I call it a night. I really should go."

John said, at that point, he had to scramble for words. He didn't want to drive her away like that. "It's only nine o'clock," he countered, glancing at *his* watch. "Can't you stay a while longer, Sabrina. I like talking to you… and besides, a potentially out-of-his-mind guy like me who probably needs to see a shrink shouldn't be left alone in a place like this."

Sabrina smiled wide. "Nice joke about your state-of-mind, and it *was* funny, but," she went on, taking hold of her bag, "I really do have to go…I'll tell you what, though. I do find your story about the locket and the dreams intriguing. It would be nice if you could return that locket to its rightful owner. I can see how something like this might make you wonder how sad this person, Anna, might be…having lost it and all."

"You're right, Sabrina. That's exactly what I told Elizabeth and Skipper, but *they* don't seem to get it."

Elizabeth… Sabrina thought. "Well, John. I'm sure they all mean well," Sabrina said, reaching into her bag. "Here is my card with my phone numbers. I would appreciate a call if something else develops about the locket. Who knows…there could be a story my magazine might like me to follow up on."

At that point, John took a card from his wallet and handed it to her. "Since I've got your card, you may as well have mine. You know… just in case, uh…you know… if…"

"Got it," she replied quickly, hoping to put his obvious display of nervousness at ease. As much as she hated to, she forced herself to get up out of the chair and offered her hand. "It was really nice to meet you, John Adler."

"Likewise," John said, standing at attention. He took hold of her hand and felt a sudden surge of warmth rush through his body. He held on, gazing directly into her eyes. As the moment got awkward, he reluctantly let go and said,

"It was nice meeting you, too, Sabrina Harper. By the way…how long are you in Coronado?"

"Just a couple more days, unfortunately," she replied. "I really like it here, but you know how work is…Joplin awaits my return."

Sabrina turned on her heels and made her way over to me at the bar. "So long, Skipper," she said yelling over the noise. "Thanks for the Kettle screwdriver…best I've ever had!"

***

I hated to see Sabrina leave, and I was certain John felt the same way…how could he not? When I looked over at him, he was standing there looking like a lost puppy, watching the angel spread her wings and fly out the door.

Chapter Twelve

I watched Sabrina walk out the door and wondered if I would ever see her again. When you meet someone like Sabrina, it changes your whole perspective on things. John was experiencing the anxiety you feel when you suddenly let someone get close that grabs your emotions. Sabrina did just that to both of us.

When John walked into the pub with that book in his hand, he had no idea his life was going to take another turn. Even though I may have had something to do with it, life, in and of itself, does that to people when they least expect it. If a rainbow suddenly appeared outside, it would extend from Coronado to Joplin, and Sabrina would be standing at the end of it. In a way, that may sound corny to you...but not to me. That woman is pure gold.

All of the things that had been affecting John's life negatively...the horrid dreams and the rollercoaster relationship with Elizabeth...disappeared during the time he sat and talked with Sabrina for that short period of time.

After Sabrina left and things had settled down in the pub, Sakae tended to the bar which gave me the opportunity to mosey over to John's table. I wondered if he might be sore with me for forcing Sabrina on him the way I did.

I sat down in the chair Sabrina had vacated. Sitting close to John at that point was a little uncomfortable so I took charge and motioned for him to move his chair back to its original place...I wanted him sitting across from me, especially if there were ill feelings about the way I forced Sabrina on him.

After dragging his chair back around to the other side of the table, he plopped himself down and stared at me through squinted eyes. At that point I felt I needed to break the ice, you know, at least say something. Before I could utter a word, John suddenly developed a wide smile.

Much to my surprise, he thanked me for playing cupid. He didn't exactly put it *that* way…that was Sakae's equivalence. Nonetheless, John thanked me, and I felt so relieved. Just to be clear about this, any dozen alpha males in the pub would have offered up their right arm to have the opportunity to meet a woman like Sabrina…she's that desirable. I accepted his thanks…I deserved it.

Over the next five minutes, he couldn't stop bending my ear about the angel. He described how beautiful she was, more than once, and how humorous and appealing her personality was…and on and on as if I didn't already know all of that stuff. I had assessed her attributes before he did, remember?

What I did was to create a situation which caused John to lose the ability to think clearly. I didn't intend for that to happen, it just did. I had to do something quick; damage control was in order. If for no other reason than to bring Johnny-boy back to some sense of reality.

"Now listen, Johnny-boy," I said as compassionately as I could, placing myself directly out of my comfort zone. "I can't blame you for being overwhelmed with joy right now... *I* would be if I were thirty years younger and not old enough to be Sabrina's father. But the way you seem to be gushing over your new-found friend is…well, it's almost like you have forgotten that there is a woman wandering around Chicago, doing who knows what with who knows who, whose finger has an engagement ring wrapped around it with your name on it."

John shook his head. "Leave it to you to spoil things," he said as he folded his arms tightly across his chest, defiantly. "One minute, you're telling me to dump Elizabeth and be on my way. The next minute, when someone like Sabrina suddenly peaks my interest a little, you try to make me feel guilty. You can't have it both ways, you know. Is that why you are over here?" he continued, scoffing. "Because, if this is one of your 'Uncle Skip's come-to-Jesus talks' again, my brain will explode. After all, this *was* your doing, you know."

"Whoa...son, no... that isn't it at all." I said. "I just want you to keep e-v-e-r-y-t-h-i-n-g in perspective. You know what I mean. You just met the girl and have no idea what's going through *her* mind. However, there is something that you do know is for sure...and that is the wrath Elizabeth can wield if there is a hint of your feelings heading in another woman's direction. You just have to be logical about this and play it cool. Did Sabrina say she wanted to see you again?"

"Not exactly...and why does it matter?" John replied, with an obvious look of frustration. "She left once I told her about Elizabeth. That's all there was to it. Besides, you act as if I'm about to go off half-cocked about a girl that I just met a few hours ago..."

"Now that's what I'm talking about, Johnny-boy," I said evenly. "That's exactly the point I'm making. I want you to take a deep breath, take your time and think about the next step. Whether you admit it or not, Sabrina had to have left her mark on you. Now...you have to access the feelings that you have for Elizabeth, and where you go from here. Have you heard from her since she left town?"

"As a matter of fact, yes...this morning. She hung up on me again."

"Again? Well, that's not unusual...and it's a bad habit, *isn't* it?"

"Yeah..." John replied, as he lifted the glass of Tanqueray, looked at it and set it back down without taking a drink. "And it pissed me off more than usual, too."

"Hooray for you, Johnny-boy," I responded as I picked up his glass and emptied it down *my* throat. "Now you're growing some cojones. This is a good start. If you and she are going to work, you have to let her know that she can't get away with that kind of bullshit any longer."

"I intend to do just that the next time she calls…unless, of course, she hangs up on me before I finish giving her hell about it."

"Well…if that's the case, and she doesn't let you vent and be honest about your feelings, then you'll know it's probably time to think hard about breaking off the engagement. She will be enraged and her father won't be happy…but so what? Life can be pretty tough when you're stuck in a screwed-up marriage you don't want to be in."

"Gee…" John said, drawing in a breath. "I wonder if your psych friend would give me the same advice if I went to see him about *this* problem."

"You just listen to old Doctor Skipper Fox. The advice I'm handing out is golden. It's only because I love you like a son—you know that."

I could tell that John's mind was starting to whirl. He stopped talking and just sat there, looking dazed. Actually, for a moment, I think he forgot I was still sitting at the table. I decided to leave him to his thoughts and went back to the bar to help Sakae.

A while later, I saw John with his cell phone pressed against his ear. I wasn't sure at the time if Elizabeth had called him or if he'd called her. It was her he was talking to, though…I was sure of that. Moments later, with the phone still stuck to his ear, John picked up his book, made his way past the bar, glanced over at me and strolled out the door.

***

Around 9:00 the next morning, while I was lying in bed waiting for Sakae to bring my coffee…OOPS…that's one cat out of the bag I was not prepared to disclose... Oh well, John called me. Before he could say much, I asked him point blank and I was right; he *was* talking to Elizabeth as he left the pub the night before.

He said that Elizabeth had gotten back to her room late, called, and admitted to having drinks with some chump from a law firm in Chicago who was trying to get cozy with her. If you ask me, she tried to make it sound to John that she blew the guy off when I would have bet a C-note that she was the aggressor from the start.

Anyway, even though Elizabeth had no idea that before she called John was having a drink with Sabrina; the question of honesty might come into play. The way I see it, John was sitting in a public place, having an innocent conversation with another woman; completely justifiable with no requirement for disclosure on his part.

John did dodge a bullet, I guess. If Elizabeth called while Sabrina was at the table it would have been disastrous. He would have been as nervous as a cat and she would have sensed that something was wrong; John is a horrible liar. None the less, that didn't happen. As far as their relationship goes...status quo. She didn't hang up on him and he didn't bring up the subject as he said he would...go figure. I guess I could rationalize why he didn't confront her tendency to slam the switch hook down in the middle of their conversation. Too many things were going through John's mind at the time...you know...the locket, the dreams, the fact that lately I've been all over his ass and now throw Sabrina Harper into the mix. Who could blame him for not wanting to start a war? In that state of mind, he probably would have lost the battle anyway.

Now to the real reason John had called me at home and couldn't wait until I was open for business at the pub. He just had to burden me with another one of those damn dreams; am I sounding too harsh? This would be the fourth or fifth in, I think, as many days. I could tell that he was on the brink of insanity. In so many words, I got the impression from the sound of his voice that *he* was now questioning his own state of mind; and by all accounts, that cannot be a good thing. Actually, I was glad he had me to talk to.

I listened quietly, took another shot, but it didn't go over well. I brought up Joseph Navarra's name again but John wasn't having any part of it. Once I suggested it, he suddenly cut me short, making up an excuse. He wasn't rude and defensive like he was when I brought it up before. He calmly said he was heading to the marina earlier than usual to sketch...and to clear his mind. I didn't press the issue and gave him a pass. Johnny-boy was in over his head with all this. I really hate to admit it but sketching, reading sci-fi books or running as fast as he could on the beach wasn't going to change anything...he needed help.

***

When I arrived at the pub that morning, I took it upon myself to give Joseph Navarra a call...just to ask a few questions, mind you. Joe and I go back several years and, just in case you are wondering, I'm not going to go into any of those details. That's another story...and that cat will definitely stay in the bag.

Anyhow, I should have seen this coming. When Joe's assistant put me through to him and I started to talk about John Adler, Joe let me know he wasn't happy about the way John darted out of his office after having a legitimate appointment...and I agreed. After a brief tongue-lashing, we moved on to John's problem.

In the time Joe had to listen, which wasn't much until he would be forced to put me on the clock, I tried to rush through John's issues. Joe mentioned a few things that made me quickly realize that fixing John's problem wasn't going to be that easy. Joe suggested that John might have subconscious issues that go back a ways... maybe even before his father died and perhaps including the death of his mother. Joe was talking about stuff that was going way above my head...stuff like psychoanalytic treatment and psychoanalysis. That's when I stopped him.

Just before hanging up, Joe strongly encouraged me to try again to convince John to reschedule another appointment, sooner than later. For some strange reason, I got the impression that Joe was thinking that John would be a good test case for a thesis or something like that. I told him that I would try...but I also said it wouldn't surprise me if, after trying, John's response would be...'fat chance of that ever happening.'

Deep down, however, I was not so sure about Joe's sight-unseen diagnosis about John. That's because I thought that I knew John better than that. So the long and the short of it is...I didn't tell John that I had called Joe...but I did tell Joe that, if I determined that John was really at the edge of insanity, I would drag him down to his office myself.

Chapter Thirteen

Let us get back to John and his most recent dream. John said he had no idea how long it lasted, but indicated it seemed like forever. He found himself back in the ocean, fighting to survive another raging storm. The swells were high above his head, just like before. They formed huge whitecaps that crashed over the top of him, forcing his body beneath the water.

With the rain coming down sideways in buckets, the wind was blowing at gale force. It took every bit of energy he could muster just to keep his body above the water. Huge bolts of lightning burst into giant balls of electrical flashes as they slammed into the water within yards of him before dispersing back into the sky.

Then he heard the same plaintive voice he had heard in the previous dream...calling out for help again. 'H-E-L-P M-E!' the voice cried out just before another wave took him under. He fought his way back to the surface, struggling to raise his head above the water line for another gasp of air. In the distance, he could see what looked like a pole with a small white flag at its top moving up and down, swaying back and forth violently with the raging wind, just above the whitecaps.

As the swell he was riding took him higher and higher, he saw two sails attached to the pole. The big one was intact but the smaller one was torn to shreds, flapping in the windy gale. He knew at that point that he was looking at the mast of a sail boat tipping and leaning back and forth, in and out of his view, as if it were about to capsize. He tried desperately to swim toward the boat but couldn't fight the strong undercurrent, which kept him from moving in that direction. John knew there was a boat there, just over the next few monster swells, but could only see its mast and sails.

I must admit, even I took in a deep breath or two just listening to him tell this story. Just then, a giant wave crashed down on top of him, driving him underwater again. This time, as he struggled with all his strength to get to the surface, his alarm clock (set for seven o'clock) went off...and startled him awake.

As the clock's annoying sound continued, he just laid there with beads of sweat running down his temples, staring blankly at a thin fracture, which now seemed like a crevasse, running diagonally across the bedroom ceiling.

He shook his head a few times to clear his mind and forced himself to sit up on the side of the bed, planting his feet flat on the floor. Feelings of frustration and confusion brought a strong realization that he just might be going bananas.

At that point, John said he almost lost it. He didn't know whether to smack the alarm clock off the nightstand or put his fist through the wall to relieve the stress that had his stomach in knots. After taking several deep breaths to steady himself, he moved the switch on the alarm to the 'off' position, pushed himself up off the bed and headed straight for the coffee maker.

As he stood like a statue leaning against the kitchen counter with his arms crossed, thinking, waiting for the coffee to finish brewing, his eyes fixed on the key dish. He reached for the locket, lifted it out and gazed at the inscription. 'To my darling Anna, keep this next to your heart and I will be with you always.'

Holding the locket in his hand, he closed his eyes...his thoughts transported him back to the day he found it drifting along the tide's edge. That's when it hit him. He was certain, at that point, that there had to be a connection between the locket and the dreams plaguing him.

I listened quietly as John tried to get me to swallow this stuff. Inside, my stomach churned. Trying to force myself to buy into what he was saying was not easy. In fact, it made me think that Joe Navarra's psychoanalysis was in order after all, to extricate whatever demons had infiltrated John's mind...or whatever it was that was controlling his thoughts.

***

"I know this all seems crazy, Skipper," John said, with a confounded look of despair on his face, "but it's driving me nuts. I can't think straight. I'm afraid to sleep for fear I won't recover from one of those fucking dreams! It's that bad, Skipper," he went on as he slammed his fist down.

That's it. When John said that, I knew there was some serious issues going on in that head of his; and at this point, they were becoming a *real* problem. He was obsessing about this stuff all the time and it was taking over his already confused state-of-mind. As if the thing with Elizabeth wasn't complicating things enough, John was on a slippery slope and teetering on the edge of having a mental melt down. Just last week, four galleries had called to see if John had finished any of the paintings he committed to - and guess what? John still hadn't even returned the calls much less deliver the paintings!! I've never seen him so obsessed about anything. John was becoming a different person altogether...and I was beyond worried.

***

Lying next to the key dish, Sabrina's business card caught John's eye. He picked it up, carried it into his work area and sat down on a stool in front of one of the canvasses...one foot resting on the bar between the legs of the stool and one foot flat on the floor. The raised, embossed lettering of her name made him smile. For a moment, a feeling of calm came over him. He thought about the good time they had together...the way they laughed and talked openly about, well, just about everything and anything.

In his mind, he began to make a comparison between the two women...Sabrina and Elizabeth. It wasn't hard at all to distinguish between the two of them. Sabrina was beautiful, inside and outside...warm and centered. She was happy with herself and the life she lived. She was content to live in a small city where people cared about who you are and not who you pretended to be.

Elizabeth, on the other hand, was cold and mischievous...always wanting something more than what she had. She was pretty, yes...but inside, not so much. She could turn her passion on and off like a light switch, making it difficult to understand where she was coming from.

He got up from the stool, went to the window and opened the shutter. A small seagull perched on the railing of the balcony heard the noise and fluttered its wings before leaping into the air and soaring away, cawing. As John turned to head back to the kitchen to pour a cup of the freshly-brewed coffee, his eyes centered on the picture of him and Elizabeth at the Galleria's party the previous year. The picture sat on the computer desk in plain view. It was taken the same night that he had proposed. It was a wonderful night in his memory, but it now seemed to be a mistake in his life.

Given everything that was happening in John's life now, things were much simpler for him back then. He didn't have too much to think about. Painting, jogging on the beach, hanging out at my place and...oh yea, bumping uglies with his hot new fiancée pretty much rounded out his daily activities. Every man should be so lucky. Now, everything in John's life seemed unclear. Someone else who was not as stable as John might have walked out onto that balcony and tossed himself over.

***

Later that morning, around eleven, John decided to drive to the Hotel Del Coronado. He didn't call Sabrina, but he had her card with him just in case fate wasn't on his side. She had two more days left on the Island before returning to Joplin, and John felt compelled to see her again.

When John walked into the lobby with its majestic vintage staircase and extravagant ballroom crystal chandelier, he looked up and spotted her on the second level talking to someone in a gray pinstriped suit...the hotel manager, he guessed. His brain went into panic mode. Should he or shouldn't he?

He froze in place and felt very nervous about the whole situation. I thought it was brave...absolutely the right thing to do...but then again, I'm Sabrina-biased. He wondered what she might think if she saw him just standing there, unexpectedly, like that. The thought ran through his mind that Sabrina was most likely working on her Del story, interviewing the person she was talking to...or whatever.

He said that he felt like an intruder. He was just about to turn and book it out of there the way he came in when their eyes simultaneously met...it was kismet. He didn't need the business card after all; fate took a powerful hand. She looked at him, smiled, and the nervousness he was experiencing dissipated.

He smiled back. It didn't take long for her to excuse herself and make her way down the staircase to the lobby floor. John moved over to the large, oval glass table, situated directly beneath the chandelier showcasing a huge, opulent flower arrangement, and watched her descent. She reminded him of the Kate Winslet character, Rose, as she elegantly descended the spiral staircase in James Cameron's 'Titanic.'

Sabrina walked up to John and they stood there silently, looking at each other as if they were the only two people in the world. "This is a pleasant surprise," she finally said, smiling.

"It's been a while, hasn't it?" John grinned, kidding. "I had hoped that I would find you here."

Sabrina chuckled at the 'it's been a while' comment. "Well, I'm glad you came looking. Wait," she went on, checking herself..."was that too forward of me to say?"

"Not in my estimation," he replied, sheepishly shoving his hands into his pants pockets.

"Another dream?" she asked.

"How did you know?" he replied, raising a brow.

"That was one of the things that came into my mind when I saw you," Sabrina responded, laying her note folder on the oval table. "Believe it or not, I woke up about three in the morning for a drink of water and, for some reason, I immediately thought of you...and look, here you are. How do we explain such things," she said shrugging, grinning.

"Now that is interesting. I probably had the dream around that same time."

"I'm not so sure that we should make much out of the coincidence, John. My internal clock is still on Joplin time," she said, delicately adjusting her glasses.

"OK...I'll give you that, but I'd rather think it was some kind of a synchronized calling..."

Sabrina creased her brow. "What was that you just said?"

"Hell...I don't know...just some crazy stuff that flew out of my mouth."

"Well...anyway, I thought it was cute," she smiled.

John said, "Are you hungry?"

"Not real hungry," Sabrina replied, "but it is going on noon and the Sunset Bar does have great braised chicken with oysters."

"Hmm...I'm for that..." John said. "Tea and oysters...my favorite."

"Are you sure?" she added as they walked together. "We can always go to Skipper's or somewhere else, for that matter. When I walked into Skipper's the other night, I noticed the sign at the end of the bar. It raved that Skipper's has the best pure beef hamburgers on the Island."

"That they do...trust me. You should have one sometime...but no...really. The Sunset Bar is great... I've been there many times with my..."

You see...there he goes again...opening his mouth before his brain shifted into gear.

"Oops...sorry... I didn't mean to bring her up. Force of habit, I guess."

"No problem," Sabrina said, looking straight ahead as they walked, hoping to avoid another uncomfortable moment. "You have a perfect right to...after all, she is your fiancée."

John said that he made a mental note as they passed through the doors leading into the restaurant. He would not say another word about Elizabeth unless Sabrina brought the subject up.

Chapter Fourteen

John and Sabrina sat outside on the patio at a table which had a breathtaking view of the ocean. Just as they settled in, ordered tea and started to peruse the menu, John's cell phone rang.

John lowered his menu, glanced at Sabrina and reached into his pocket. "Probably one of the art galleries," he said.

He stared blankly at the phone touch screen as the phone rang. It wasn't a call from any gallery...it was Elizabeth. He felt his heart rate elevate with each ring, flicking his eyes between the phone and Sabrina. He couldn't think fast enough to come up with the right thing to say once he answered...or even if he should answer at all. His mind drew a blank wondering how he should play it.

Sabrina, a very perceptive woman, knew at once what was going on as she witnessed the uncomfortable look on John's face...a business phone call it wasn't. Having reason to believe his fiancée was on the other end of that call, she saved John any embarrassment. All in one motion, Sabrina scooted her chair back, stood up, took her bag, pointed across the patio towards the restroom and hurried off.

"Hi... Elizabeth," John said, answering just before his voice messaging kicked in.

"Hi, baby, where are you?" Elizabeth asked. "I called the house, got the machine and left you a voice message you might find stimulating. You can listen to it before you go to bed tonight. It will make you miss me, I promise."

Ordinarily, John might have found that amusing; however, now was not a good time for that sort of thing. John had to enter into territory he very seldom entered...he had to lie. Because he's such an honest person, he wasn't very good at it. Pressing the phone against his ear with one hand and nervously massaging the back of his neck with the other, he told her he was sitting at the marina sketching a schooner.

After several minutes of small talk, Elizabeth told John that she was flying out of Chicago late that afternoon. She made note that, once she arrived in Las Vegas, she had several meetings scheduled. She also told him that the meetings would most likely continue late into the evening; therefore, he would likely not hear from her until the next day.

When he told me this, I quickly concluded her story was bogus. Even though John didn't get it at the time because of the immediate pressure he was under to make up *his* story, all one had to do was put two and two together.

When a girl like Elizabeth is in Vegas, any meeting lasting late into the evening only means one thing... screwing around with someone. I could have voiced my opinion about this, but it wouldn't have done any good...so I didn't. He would have said that it was only fact less speculation, and I was sticking my nose in places where it shouldn't be.

The phone call ended on a peaceful note. Sabrina lingered around, waiting...waiting for John to finish. When the call ended, several things passed through John's mind. His life was now moving in a direction that only brought more confusion and uncertainty.

That is one thing that John wasn't used to... uncertainty. Things weren't so bad until he found that damn locket. Then, when Sabrina popped into his life (I guess I'll take credit for that), things really became confusing. If you ask me, the real problem he was now facing was Elizabeth. The locket and his crazy nightmares were definitely a drag, but those issues he could probably deal with.

Elizabeth's jealous nature, however...well... that's where things get very sticky. Just a hint that John might be spending time for any reason with another woman would not go down well at all. So, yes, Elizabeth…and the way she treats him…is his biggest problem.

It reminds me of the time when this hot-looking blonde art dealer picked up John's business card from one of the small galleries and called him. He subsequently met her for an innocent lunch to discuss his paintings. They were sitting in the Brigantine when Elizabeth walked in with one of her girlfriends. Before John had a chance to explain the circumstances, Elizabeth went ballistic. In front of everyone, she accused him of cheating, called him a bastard, and abruptly left the restaurant.

That memorable afternoon happened shortly after they had made their commitment to become engaged. When John told me about Elizabeth having that conniption fit in front of God and everyone while he just sat there and said nothing, I remember my reaction wasn't very amiable. It was then I suggested he needed to start growing some balls.

Once Sabrina returned to the table, it took a moment of uncomfortable silence to get the conversation jumpstarted. John figured it was his place to speak first.

"Wow…that was a little awkward. Sorry for making you feel like you had to leave…but…"

"No…really, John," she broke in. "I really did have to use the ladies room. Besides, maybe I should apologize. Given your circumstance, I probably put you in an uncomfortable position. Knowing that you were engaged before I left Skipper's last night, giving you my card may not have been the right thing to do…do you think?"

John gazed into her deep blue eyes, eyes that seemed to sparkle as the sunlight danced across the Sunset Bar patio. "Sabrina," John said with a slight headshake, "you're just so darned accommodating, and I really like that about you. Of course, you didn't put me in…how did you put it…an uncomfortable position? Things are just the way they are right now. Nothing is your fault."

Sabrina smiled and wiped a hand across her brow. "Boy, that's a load off."

"See," John, declared, "there's that humorous side of you coming out again. And why is it that you are so darned nice about everything?"

"I guess," she confessed with a grin, "and it might sound a little cliché, it's because my mother raised me that way."

"Kudos to your mom," John said, staring at her. "Do you know what I'm thinking right this minute, Sabrina Harper?"

"Would you like me to guess?" she replied, smiling curiously.

"No, not really" he promptly replied, "...only because I'm thinking about more than just one thing, and it wouldn't be fair. I will share one thought crossing my mind, however," he continued as he put his palms on the table and leaned forward. "Your mother deserves a medal for raising such a compassionate, beautiful woman."

Sabrina smiled and said, "Now you're the one being nice."

The server stopped at their table with pad in hand. "Are you guys ready to order?"

"How about I speak for the both of us?" John said. Sabrina nodded. "Braised chicken with oysters and tea?"

The server jotted it down on her pad. "Excellent choice," she replied before scurrying away.

"OK, then." John said. "Now would be a good time for me to tell you the reason I came looking for you..."

"Wait," Sabrina interrupted, eyeing him, grinning playfully. "You can't get off that easy," Sabrina said, wagging a finger in front of him. "What was the other thing you were thinking about before you said my mother deserved a medal?"

John hesitated. He thought for a moment, listening to himself breathe. "Ah...ah...you know what?" he replied cagily. "It seems we've changed topics so many times in the last few minutes, I just can't remember. I'm sure, however, that there will probably come a time when it will enter my mind again, and then I'll be sure to let you in on it."

Sabrina smiled as she replied, "You only get away with doing that once, you know."

John returned the smile, "That's a deal. Anyway," he went on, sitting up straight in his chair. "I came here to tell you that I had another dream last night."

"The same one...?"

John didn't answer her right away. He sat there, deep in thought. It was strange...the way he described it to me. He said he was witnessing the obvious contrast between Elizabeth and Sabrina. It was all about being comfortable in conversation...no verbal conflicts.

Sabrina watched him curiously. It seemed as though he were looking right through her...as if she were invisible. "John," she said. "Are you alright? Is there something wrong?"

"Huh? What did you say? Oh...the dream...of course," he said, regaining focus. "Well...basically, it was the same dream, but this time there was more going on. Like in the other dreams, I was fighting for my life in the ocean. The storm was raging all around me; and, as I was trying desperately to save myself, treading water, I spotted the mast and sails of a boat."

"Hmm," Sabrina said wide-eyed. "What about the voice...the voice you heard before crying out for help...did you hear that again?"

"Yes...far off in the distance," he replied, shifting in his chair. "And it made sense to me. The boat was off in the distance, and the voice seemed to be coming from the same direction. I tried to swim towards the boat, but the more I swam, the further the boat drifted away from me."

"OK...now this is getting a little bizarre," Sabrina said, just as the server set both glasses of tea on the table. "Let's see now," she went on as she lifted the glass of tea to her lips and took a sip. "If I remember what you told me last night, this would be the fourth dream within the last week?"

"Actually, I've lost count," John said. "But this is the first time I've seen the sails of a boat, one of which was ripped to shreds," he went on, sighing anxiously. "I'll tell you, Sabrina, the whole thing is starting to get the best of me. I have no idea where this is going to end, unless it ends with me sitting in a grassy yard at a nut house watching butterflies land on flowers all day."

"I know you are joking about the nut house...but I must say...the dreams are getting more interesting. A boat, huh?" she said, her eyes wide, staring. "And tell me...what about the locket?"

"That's the other thing," John replied, squeezing a slice of lemon into his glass. "If it isn't the dreams, that darn locket is consuming me... especially the picture of the woman."

That's when Sabrina took the leap of faith. She took matters into her own hands and opened the door to what would enhance the uncertainty of all John's issues. It went something like this.

Sabrina said, "I sure would like to see this locket."

John said, "Why don't we go to my place after lunch and I'll show it to you."

I have to say...I have to give the boy credit. Whatever his motivation was at that point, locket or otherwise, asking her to his place was definitely ballsy.

They left the Del Coronado in John's car and arrived at John's place around one o'clock. This would be the first time any girl other than Elizabeth had stepped foot in John's condominium in the last two years.

Chapter Fifteen

John and Sabrina took the elevator to the fifth floor of the eight-story complex to John's condominium located down a long hallway on the northwest side of the building. All of the condominiums on the west side had views of the ocean, while those on the east side overlooked San Diego Harbor and the downtown skyline.

After punching a code into the keypad, John grabbed the knob and effortlessly pushed the door open into the spacious, open living space.

"Keyless entry," Sabrina remarked. "Impressive."

"Technology," John replied, holding the door open for her.

Sabrina took a few steps inside, glanced around and said. "Very nice place you have here, John."

"*I* like it," he replied, closing the door behind them. "This room, two bedrooms, two bathrooms, a dining room and a nice-sized kitchen…perfect for me."

On the left is a leather sectional, perfectly placed against two walls, and a stone fireplace with a beautiful painting of a boat hanging on the wall above it. A flat screen hung on an adjacent wall over a walnut console with glass doors that housed the television and stereo equipment. An oval coffee table, strategically placed on a decorative area rug accenting the hardwood floor, rounded out the living space.

On the oval table, next to a stack of coasters and a half-empty glass of tea with a slice of lemon floating at the bottom was a picture in a small frame. John watched as Sabrina slowly made her way over to the table. She turned and looked at him, pointed at the picture and said, "May I?"

John nodded and stood there feeling very uneasy as Sabrina picked up the frame and studied the picture of John and Elizabeth sitting on John's sailboat, which was docked at the Marina. "Elizabeth?" she asked.

John angled his head a bit and again nodded. "Yes...taken about year ago on my sailboat. She doesn't really like to sail that much so the picture was more of a photo-op."

"I went on a cruise ship for a week with a few friends, but I've never had a chance to go sailing...seems like it would be a blast."

John smiled. "You'll just have to put that on *your* list of things to do."

Although the conversation was light-hearted, John felt an uneasiness up until Sabrina set the frame back down on the table.

Sabrina moved to the opposite side of the room which doubled as John's art studio. There were two stools, two easels, and a long table with palettes, primer, oil paints, pencils and brushes strewn about. There were clean canvases leaning against a table leg. Studio lighting hung conspicuously from the ceiling...a set-up you would not normally see in someone's home.

"Impressive studio," Sabrina said making her way over to one of the easels to admire an unfinished painting. "And this is a beautiful painting."

"It's nearly finished," John replied, stepping next to her. He took her slim hand in his. "Come...walk over here."

He guided her across the room to a corner in front of curtains covering both the windows facing the ocean and the windows to the right, facing north.

"I am about to show you something really beautiful...if I may?" he said, gently passing his hand over her eyes. "Now close your eyes and don't open them until I tell you to."

John hurried back to the entrance of the condominium. He pressed the switch on the wall next to the door and, automatically, the semi-sheer curtains drew open. He made his way back to stand beside her. "OK...you can open your eyes now."

Sabrina's eyes opened to breathtaking views. John's condominium provided a spectacular view looking straight out to the ocean as well as a panoramic view of the north coastal shoreline.

Sabrina just stood there; for a moment, the view rendered her speechless. "It's breathtaking," she said, in a loud whisper.

John opened the sliding-glass door to the balcony, reached for her hand once more...and guided her through the opening.

As she stepped past him, she lightly brushed up against his shoulder, allowing him to subtly bury his nose in her hair. In that moment, he could feel his testosterone level rise. He released her hand as he followed her out onto the balcony and stood alongside her.

"I'd be willing to guess that you don't get a view like this in Joplin."

"That would be a good guess," she murmured, taking in the gentle ocean breeze. "It makes me want to stand here forever, in this very spot. I love the way the breeze caresses my face and lightly brushes through my hair."

If you ask me, Johnny-boy was putting his loyalty to Elizabeth to the ultimate test. I don't know if it was Sabrina's beauty, her kind nature, her intelligence, her obvious morals, or a combination of all that was causing the emotions. I know for sure, just by listening to him talk, he was becoming increasingly conflicted about his engagement to Elizabeth.

Although Sabrina wanted the moment to last forever, reality was pulling her apart inside. It was her nature...the way she was raised. John was engaged to be married, and she needed to respect that. It felt right being there, standing next to him, but she knew the temporary nature of it all. She decided at that moment that it would be best if they circled back to the original premise for her being there.

"Uh, John," she said, nervously adjusting her glasses. "Shouldn't I look at the locket? After all…that's why you brought me here…isn't it?"

"Oh, sure," he said, turning to her, making eye contact, nodding. "It's just that, for some reason, the locket doesn't seem that important anymore. Since you like it out here, though, you stay and I'll go get it."

I have a feeling that Sabrina revisited John's words in her head, 'Didn't seem that important.' She must have wondered what he meant by that.

John made his way into the kitchen, lifted the chain and locket out of the key dish, returned to the balcony and placed it in her hand. "Be careful," he said grinning. "I might be passing on to you the curse of my dreams."

Sabrina chuckled. "That's funny," she replied, shaking a finger at him. "But I wouldn't worry about that, John. I don't curse easily."

After examining at the locket in the daylight, she turned and walked back into the condo to sit down on the leather couch. John followed and sat next to her. She studied the locket as if she were picking it out in a department store to buy for herself. She managed to open it and read the inscription inside.

Chapter Sixteen

John watched as Sabrina examined the locket, inside and out. She studied it for the longest time, concentrating, moving it between the fingers of both hands. She even closed her eyes for a while as she held onto it. "Well... John," she said, "I have to tell ya...I'm not getting any vibes."

John looked at her oddly. He furrowed his brow and said, with a grin, "Sabrina, if you are trying to make it disappear, it won't work. I already tried that."

Sabrina chuckled. "No, John," she replied in a heartfelt tone, placing her hand on his arm. "I guess I was conducting some strange, unscientific experiment. I was hoping to get the same feeling about this locket that you get when *you* hold on to it, but nothing is coming through...you know, the chills and stuff. I am, however, feeling really sad about the circumstances the more I hold on to it." She gently laid the chain and locket down on the table. "It breaks my heart that someone, somewhere, has lost something very dear to them."

Sabrina could see that John felt the same sadness. They both gazed at the locket lying there on the table.

"That's the same feeling I get every time I pick it up...along with the other feelings you mentioned," he confessed, shaking his head. "Only I've got dreams to go with it. I think of the person that lost it and wish there was some way I could return it."

"I've got an idea that might help relieve some of the anxiety," she said, shifting her eyes towards his. "Maybe you should just put it somewhere and see how you feel about it later...you know...'out of sight, out of mind.' If you try that…who knows…" she went on, feeling something hopeful or encouraging might come from her words. "It might change things."

"You're probably right," he replied evenly, nodding his head in agreement. "I should just put it in the back of a drawer somewhere and forget about it. That's a good idea. The thoughts and the dreams might vanish just like that…who knows? There is, however, one more part to this story that I forgot to tell you."

"I'm all ears," she said as she leaned back on the couch, crossed her legs and sent an inquisitive glance his way. "How much more interesting can the story get?"

John almost lost his concentration. Noticing the way she positioned herself on the couch hit an emotional chord. "Maybe a little," he said, taking in a breath, exhaling it completely. "But that I'll leave up to you, once you hear me out. I can promise you one thing for sure. It will add more intrigue to the story of Adler's dreams."

"Will it change any of the things you have already told me?"

"I doubt it," he replied, "but again, you can decide after you hear it. You tell me if it all ties together," he said, settling back on the sofa. "Well, here goes nothing! It was about two-and-a-half months ago, before I found the locket. I was sailing alone on a windy day out there on the water when the boat suddenly slowed until it hardly moved. The wind abruptly died, and the boat suddenly stopped dead in the water, as if it had no sails. It was bizarre, to say the least…anyway…"

"I don't know much at all about sailing," she broke in, "but that does sound unusual…the wind dying all of a sudden like that. Oh, and I just interrupted."

"You're right," he replied, "very unusual…especially on a day when the wind was blowing hard. Now here is the strange part. I looked down into the water, and it was as clear as glass. When you are that far away from the shoreline, in salt water, it should have been dark and murky. As I gazed down into the water, a boat suddenly appeared at the bottom of the ocean directly below me...how is that for bizarre?"

Sabrina uncrossed her legs and inched towards the edge of the couch. "What kind of boat?" she asked as her voice dropped to a softer tone. "You mean like a...sunken ship or something?"

John shook his head and pointed at the picture over the fireplace. "Not that big," he replied flatly. "More like the size of the sailboat in that picture. I only caught a glimpse of it, you know. Just like that," he went on, snapping his fingers, "...it vanished right before my eyes."

"Well..." Sabrina said, reaching for the locket, "*that* puts a different twist on everything...now doesn't it?"

"Now you know the whole story, including how it all started. I just wish I knew what the ending was going to look like. In the meantime, Sabrina Harper," John continued, perching on the edge of the couch, "you, Skipper, and probably Sakae, are the only ones who know about this."

Sabrina smiled and put her hand on his hand. "I feel privileged. I mean that in a good way."

"When I string all the things that have been happening to me since that day out there on the ocean, it makes me wonder if I'm on to something, or if I'm just flat-out going crazy."

"Crazy...??" she said, with a strained laugh. "I don't think so...maybe just a wee bit paranoid."

"OK..." John replied with a smirk. "That's another word Skipper's psych might use to describe me. I'd rather think of myself as a 'little crazy,' thank you." They both chuckled.

Sabrina reached for the locket. Her eyes narrowed as she set her gaze on the picture inside. It seemed to John that she was studying it as she had before, but this time, she seemed to be waiting for some clairvoyant reaction.

"You know what, John," she said, curiously touching the picture with her index finger. "Forget what I said before about putting the locket away somewhere. You are an artist. You have the ability to create images...isn't that right?"

John nodded. "I think I know what you are about to say, Sabrina...you want..."

"Can I suggest it?" she carefully broke in. "I was merely going to say...don't put the locket away. Leave it where you can look at it frequently. Try to recall the image that you saw in the mirror; and when you feel that you are ready, paint a picture of the woman. Let your heart and your mind become your guide," she went on as she leaned close to him and placed the locket in his hand. She gently closed his fingers around it, leaving a portion of the chain dangling from his fist. "Paint her on one of those canvases you have leaning against that table over there."

John was amazed at how articulate Sabrina was, and how soft and warm her hands felt when she closed his fingers around the locket. He could feel her breath close to his cheek. She said what he was thinking and in a way that made all the sense in the world.

Why hide the locket...embrace it. It made him think that maybe that is what he was supposed to do...paint the picture of the woman. That might put an end to the whole thing...bring the mystery to a close. All the dreams of fighting for his life in the ocean, hearing voices and seeing sunken boats might finally end if he did that.

There was silence between them. They stared at each other for a long time, both seemingly lost in another world...a world where lockets, boats and pictures no longer mattered. For that moment in time, the only thing that made sense was the two of them sitting next to each other.

Suddenly, a ring tone startled them back to reality. Sabrina's bag was lying on the coffee table next to the picture frame. She grabbed her phone from the bag, rose from the couch and walked towards the sliding glass door leading to the balcony.

While Sabrina talked on the phone, John sat there facing a different kind of reality. He eyed the picture of Elizabeth in the frame on the table in front of him. Over the last few hours, it seemed as though there was no other girl in the world but Sabrina. The fact is, however, there was another...Elizabeth. Moreover, for the time being, she was a reality he had to accept.

He pressed against the back of the couch, holding the locket in his hand with a look of confusion on his face. While his head was spinning, his brain churning, he listened to Sabrina's one-sided conversation. As near as he could figure, it was someone calling from her office in Joplin. By the time the conversation ended, he knew that something was definitely wrong back home.

Sabrina walked back to the couch with a somber look on her face. John said, "Is everything all right, Sabrina?"

"No..." she said, shaking her head. "I mean...it could be worse," she went on as she lifted her bag from the table. "That was the office. My boss...rather my uncle... has had a mild stroke. It seems that he is OK, but I need to get my things from the hotel and catch an earlier flight back to Joplin."

"I'm very sorry to hear that," he offered as he stood up next to her. "Is there *anything* I can do?"

"Yes," Sabrina replied, swallowing hard. "If you could get me back to the hotel, I'll get my things together, check out and catch a shuttle to the airport."

"Are you sure...? Can I at least give you a ride to the airport?"

"Honestly, John," she replied. "It really won't be necessary. Just to the hotel will be fine. I have to make a few calls before I go."

John stood alongside the car in front of Sabrina at the entrance of the hotel. "I hope that your uncle recovers quickly from this," he said in earnest.

"Thank you, John," she replied, warmly. "This is his second stroke. He made it through the last one OK. He is a tough old bird who does not listen well. His doctor recommended that he retire from the magazine at that time, but he wouldn't. He's a very stubborn man. He will recover from this, but he still won't retire."

"Will you come back to Coronado anytime soon?"

"I'm not sure it will be anytime soon," she replied, smiling as she took hold of his hand. "That is, unless I get a craving for one of Skipper's finest Coronado hamburgers. But," she continued, "if anything materializes further with the locket, you have my card…please call me."

John wasn't about to let her get away that easy. Before she could react, he pulled her into him and they willingly held each other close for a moment. Sabrina arched her back and looked into his eyes. Why John didn't plant a kiss on her lips right then and there, I'll never know. He said they held each other until, reluctantly, she let loose, turned and walked away.

Chapter Seventeen

The tipping point

Two weeks later

Elizabeth was back, Sabrina had returned to Joplin...and no one was the wiser. I won't say that John was totally over Sabrina, although what man in his right mind would be? Things seemed somewhat normal, although Elizabeth was once again Elizabeth. John hadn't been in during the day as he was painting his ass off playing catch-up. They dropped by the pub a couple of nights...which gave me the opportunity to witness Elizabeth falling back into her dominating ways.

John finally had further discussions with Elizabeth about his dreams and the locket...but he said he felt the more he brought it up, the less she wanted to hear about it. Unlike Sabrina, Elizabeth did not take John's struggle seriously. I'm a witness to this truth. The other night, I was sitting with them. We were chatting about nothing in particular when John brought up the subject. Even though I'm a little down about the topic, at least I did listen.

Elizabeth, on the other hand, ignored him. She fiddled with that damn i-phone of hers the whole time, texting or something. I wanted to grab it out of her hand and toss it across the pub. Believe you me, if I were in John's shoes at the time, I would have excused myself and left her sitting there alone the rest of the night...big boobs and all. I would have understood his motive for doing so and applauded him for it.

The fact is everything was starting to take a toll on Johnny-boy again, including you know who. I'll tell you one thing… if Sabrina, with *her* caring personality, had been sitting with us when John opened up about that recent dream of his, she would never have ignored him, not for one stinking second. She would have listened to what he had to say and at least tried to help him through the struggles and uncertainty.

Anyway, that's enough about Elizabeth for now. It was on a Thursday afternoon around three o'clock when John made it back to his place after spending three hours parked at the marina, sketching under overcast skies. He said he poured himself a glass of tea, walked out onto his balcony and plopped down in one of the two wicker balcony chairs. He took a long swig of tea, set the glass on the small wrought-iron table next to him, and closed his eyes, falling into what he described as a deep sleep.

This time, the dream was different. Instead of John fighting for his life, he was suddenly knee-deep in the surf…wading deeper into the ocean with every step until his body became completely submerged. In what seemed to be slow motion, he found himself walking along the sea floor. He wandered along the ocean bottom, over ridges and valleys, rocks and sediment…scanning, searching.

All of a sudden, through the mass of marine life surrounding him, he noticed in the distance the obscure wreckage of a sailing vessel, a portion of which was buried under the sediment. As he made his way closer, he could see the mast and boom leaning almost parallel to the ocean floor, the headsail torn and shredded, moving slowly with the sea current.

Through the murky water, he could scarcely make out the name painted on the stern of the boat…"Solitude One." Then, in the blink of an eye, he found himself standing next to the boat, his gaze slowly washing over the entire structure. Small fish, scurrying about, were stirring up the sediment that filled the stern.

The rest of what John said sounded like a scene from a horror film. He told me that something on the deck, barely covered by the sediment, caught his eye. He leaned over across the structure into the deck area to get a closer look. With his hand, he took a swipe at the sediment, sending up a flurry of dirt and small pebbles. It was the glimpse of a skull and the remnants of chest bones that startled him awake.

John sat straight up in the chair, looking one way and then another...realizing he had been dreaming again. That's when the real paranoia set in. If you ask me, John was at the point of no return. Distinguishing between what is and what is not real was becoming a big problem. My friend, Joseph Navarra, calls that 'altered perception of reality.' I know this because he used that terminology with me one time...he was kidding, of course.

Anyhow, John made his way into the kitchen and picked up the locket. He gently pried it open and stared at it for a moment before backtracking to the studio. There was a clean canvas propped up on one of the easels. He sat down on the stool, read the inscription several times and then shifted his gaze to the picture of the woman. Thoughts of Sabrina and what she had suggested he do filled his head. 'Paint a picture of the woman. Let your heart and your mind become your guide'.

John shut his eyes and focused on recalling the image of the woman that had appeared in the vanity mirror. Some of her features began to materialize, but the image he was seeing wasn't complete. The whole experience was frustrating, discouraging. He squeezed his eyes shut even harder in an effort to force his mind to recall the image; but for the life of him, it wasn't working. After trying like hell to reconstruct the necessary elements of her features to complete the puzzle, he finally gave up trying.

He read the inscription on the other wing of the locket, wondering how much more depressing it could be, then glanced at the time. It was four-fifteen and time to go for a run. It was perfect timing as a good run on the beach would help curb his frustrations.

***

This was the day (or night, however you want to describe it) that her father's law firm was having a black-tie dinner at the Sheraton Harbor Island for the firm's clients, and Elizabeth expected John to make the grand entrance with her. John was hoping to wiggle out of it but had no good excuse to put out there. He was supposed to pick her up by seven o'clock so, given that, there was still time to run.

The air was brisk, just the way John liked it. As he set out on his run, there were only a few diehards left on the beach that time of the day...two couples in shorts and tops playing volleyball...and an older man in rubber wading boots, whom John had seen many times, standing knee-high in the surf, fishing. The man gave John a look as he passed by and John waved.

Halfway through his run, and in about the same place where he had found the locket, John heard a faint cry for help...twice. He stopped in his tracks, scanned the beach and the water, but saw nothing. He looked upward just as a lonely seagull flew overhead and out towards the ocean. It led him to believe that what he really heard was the faint squawk of a gull in the distance.

Chapter Eighteen

Joplin, Missouri
two weeks earlier

It wasn't fifteen minutes after Sabrina sat down at her desk that her phone rang. She knew exactly who was on the other end of the line, Karla! Karla Madison, Sabrina's associate and best friend, couldn't wait to get the scoop about the mystery man named John Adler. A mere summary version of Sabrina's encounter with him during a phone call, lasting only a few minutes while Sabrina was in Coronado, in no way satisfied Karla's curiosity.

Karla was the type of girl who wasn't satisfied until every single detail was exposed. You know the type. She is one of those women who can't handle being left out of the loop when it comes to her girlfriend's men. If you ask me, based on what little John knew about her, the woman could be downright nosey.

Let's see. How did John describe Karla, based on Sabrina's description of her? Oh, yeah. Karla is an average-looking, thirty-six-year-old single woman with a grudge against other women who have it all. That's the best I can do. Oh…and one more thing, she's very protective when it comes to Sabrina. She considers Sabrina to be the younger sister she never had. I draw these conclusions based solely on hearsay. By the way, I have no problem with someone being over-protective, if you know what I mean.

Karla worked in the cubicle next to Sabrina's at the office. Sabrina had called her before checking out of the Hotel Del, just to let her know she was heading back to Joplin.

While talking to Karla for those few minutes, Sabrina made one critical mistake. She made mention of meeting a nice guy by the name of John Adler.

You might guess that Karla didn't waste much time once Sabrina got to the office. She couldn't wait to press her for more information about the guy Sabrina met in Coronado. It didn't matter that the likelihood of Sabrina ever seeing him again was questionable; Karla still tried to drag the information out of her.

Karla started asking questions as if she were some covert operative. In low whispers, she shot off questions as if they were coming out of a machine gun. 'How tall is he? Is he handsome? Is he rich?' See what I mean when I say she is nosey?

Sabrina waited for Karla's mouth to stop, which it didn't. She kept going, repeating. "Well, girlfriend, out with it," Karla said in a low tone of voice. "What's he like? You know...let's have it..."

"Karla, stop," Sabrina broke in, whispering. "I haven't even had enough time to get myself organized this morning, and you're already on the hunt."

"And your point is...?"

"My point is," Sabrina said, sighing anxiously, "my uncle...your boss, is in the hospital and I'm only here for a few, then I'm heading to Joplin Mercy. But, I'll tell you what...since I won't be back to the office for the rest of the day, let's meet at Club 609 tonight for drinks...and we can talk then."

"If you insist, damn it" Karla said, sighing deeply, then lightly punched the carpeted cubicle divider between them. "I guess I can wait until then, but it won't be easy, you know! A real friend would give me something to chew on before leaving for the hospital, you know...just some little detail. Is he handsome...? Is he...?"

"See," Sabrina interrupted sharply. "There you go...being overly curious to the point of... Please stop.

You'll just have to wait until tonight. Besides, if I stick around here too much longer, by the time I get to the hospital and navigate my way around to my uncle's room, they'll probably want him to take a nap."

***

When Sabrina arrived at Joplin Mercy around nine in the morning and entered her Uncle Phil's private room, he had just finished breakfast and was complaining to one of the nurses that the scrambled eggs were too cold and overly done.

Sabrina smiled at the nurse, who moments later left the room. It was obvious that she was annoyed with the antics of the patient. Sabrina knew that, even if the eggs had been cooked to perfection and were piping hot, her Uncle Phil would find something else to complain about... he hated being around hospitals.

At sixty-two, a widower, and somewhat of an enigma, Phillip Carson had started his magazine in Joplin in the small print shop his father handed down to him. He is an English major who turned freelance writer after graduating college.

Even though the magazine's main circulation was the Missouri area, the magazine had a reputation outside of the state with an extremely high online readership. The magazine is all about human-interest stories, travel ideas, local cooking, restaurants and home decorating.

Phillip loves his niece, Sabrina. He has watched out for her ever since his sister's husband, Sabrina's father, died in a tragic accident fifteen years earlier. Assessing the suitability of every guy Sabrina dated was a responsibility he took seriously, even though Sabrina had problems with it. However, she knew that her uncle had her best interests at heart so, for the most part, she heeded the advice he gave her.

"You sure are chipper this morning, Uncle Phil," Sabrina said, stepping over to the side of the hospital bed. She leaned over and kissed his forehead.

From the minute Sabrina walked through the door and even though he was still giving the nurse shit, his eyes widened. He was surprised and happy that Sabrina was back in town.

"These people around here have no idea how to treat their patients," he said, scoffing. "They don't smile or talk. They just scurry around, making noise and moving things. If they are not doing that, their poking the hell out of me with needles and who knows what else. They won't let me get up...even to take care of my duties. No compassion I tell you...no compassion."

Sabrina smiled as she pushed an armchair up next to the bed, sat down, and rested her arms on the metal bedrail. "Now, Uncle Phil...if Aunt Millie were still alive, she'd say that you are being overly critical. After all, this *is* a hospital...and they are very busy around here. I'm sure they are taking very good care of you."

"That's my girl," he said, grinning. "Leave it to you to put a pretty dress on the proverbial pig. Even at that, Sabrina," he went on, squirming and fiddling with the mechanism that adjusts the movements of the bed, "these places still give me the creeps."

Sabrina snatched the control from her uncle's hand and adjusted the bed to his liking. "So... tell me how you are feeling," she said in a serious tone of voice. "This is the second time this has happened to you. I'm worried there might be another episode, and you won't be so lucky. I don't want to lose you."

"Oh...you worry too much," he replied, grasping her hand. "You are like your mother in that regard. I promise...don't you worry your pretty little head...I am going to be just fine. Rest assured...I'm not going anywhere. As a matter of fact," he went on, putting on an unusually wide smile, "I'll be back at the office before you know it. I hope things are running smoothly. You know how things can get when I'm not cracking the whip around there."

"That is exactly my point, Uncle Phil," Sabrina shot back. "You should start letting the office take care of itself. You have trustworthy, smart people working for you. It is time for you to find a companion and take some vacations or something," Sabrina continued, speaking softly and squeezing his hand. "Whether you like it or not, the office is functioning just fine without you, so don't you go expending all kinds of energy worrying about what's going on there. You need to get better and out of this hospital as soon as possible."

"You are right, young lady. However, I'm not sure about that companion thing. I might be a little old for that," Phil replied, grinning. "So…now tell me about your trip to Coronado. Did you come up with a good story for the magazine? How did you like the Del?"

"As a matter of fact, I did," she said. "The Del Coronado is a wonderful place with a lot of history, and our subscribers will love to read about it. Oh…and for your information, I also met an interesting man…an artist."

Sabrina inadvertently let that slip. She probably shouldn't have mentioned John; she just couldn't help herself. It slipped out as the thought of him popped into her head. Those thoughts started happening the minute she left him standing outside of the Del Coronado. As overprotective as her uncle is, she could only hope it wouldn't get him overly excited and elevate his blood pressure…hoping didn't do the trick.

"What kind of artist?" Phil said, giving her a look.

"Huh? Ah…he paints boats…you know…sailboats, yachts."

"And…" Phil said, sensing a touch of embarrassment, "did you spend some time with this man?"

"Uncle Phil," she replied anxiously. "Don't start grilling me yet; it wasn't like that. We just spent a lot of time talking, that's all. Besides," she continued cagily, "I had to rush home to Joplin to be with my uncle."

"Talked? Talked about what?"

Sabrina paused before answering. "See...I knew you'd start doing this if I said something. I shouldn't have said a word until you got out of here. Anyhow," she went on shaking her head, "since I did, I can tell you that he had a strange kind of story to tell...a story about finding a locket on the beach...an intriguing story that caught my interest."

Phil looked at her curiously. "That doesn't sound too strange to me, finding a locket on the beach. People lose things all the time when they are at the beach. It seems the sand has a way of swallowing things up."

Sabrina shifted a bit in her chair. "That's not the half of it, Uncle Phil," she said cautiously. "He started having all these crazy dreams...dreams of being caught up in the ocean in violent storms and seeing sailboats..."

"Wait, Sabrina," he said, slowly angling his head looking directly at her. "The man's an artist. He *paints* sailboats. People frequently dream about the business they are in or things they do a lot. Just like me...I dream about magazines all the time."

"But this is different, Uncle Phil," she said quietly. "The locket has an inscription inside that is sort of haunting. The inscription makes you feel something when you read it."

"Feel something?"

"Yes, Uncle Phil...it's hard to explain. The inscription inside the locket reads like this, *'To my darling Anna, keep this next to your heart and I will be with you always.'* Like I said, it is a long story."

"That is a little sad," he replied, suddenly drawing in two deep breaths.

"Are you OK, Uncle Phil?" Sabrina said, flicking her gaze between her uncle and the heart monitor.

"Yes…I'm fine, Sabrina. I'm not ready to have the big one yet, you know. I'm just a little tired, I guess."

Just then, a heavy-set woman with a white smock came through the door, pushing a cart in front of her with towels, a sponge and a pan of water. It was Sabrina's clue to leave. She stood up, leaned over and kissed her uncle on the forehead again.

"I guess it's time for me to leave you two alone," she said with a smirk.

Phil narrowed his eyes. "I'll pay you back for that. I told you…no compassion."

Chapter Nineteen

When Sabrina walked into the Club, she spotted Karla sitting across the room near the stage at a small table along the bright-blue back wall. Club 609 is one of the most popular spots for young people to congregate who like to listen to live jazz music. It just so happened this was the night one of the best small jazz ensembles in the Joplin area would start playing around seven. The place was packed and the crowd was anxious…the noise was not very conducive to having a quiet conversation about the subject matter Karla was most interested in.

Karla, off in her own world, had a frozen margarita in her left hand and was fiddling with her i-phone in the other. She looked up and saw Sabrina standing at the opposite end of the small table, looking down at her. It didn't matter what bar or restaurant, Mexican or otherwise, Karla always ordered frozen margaritas with salt around the rim. Sabrina placed her bag on the table next to the wall and sat down.

Karla said, "Well…how did Phil look?"

"He looked fine." Sabrina replied, lifting the appetizer menu from the rack next to her bag. "But he wasn't *doing* fine. Just like the last time…complain, complain, and complain."

"That's your uncle," Karla said, licking salt from the rim of her glass. "Ornery as hell lately, but we all love him just the way he is, don't we?"

"I guess two strokes in two years would make anyone ornery…especially if you have that tendency to begin with," Sabrina said with a grin, shrugging her shoulders.

"So…" Karla said, gesturing with her hand.

"So…?" Sabrina said, mimicking Karla's hand gesture and grinning.

Karla gave her a look. "Come on, girlfriend…you know exactly what I mean. Give me something before the band starts playing, and I have to continuously ask you to repeat stuff."

The server stepped up to the table. "Hi, Sabrina," she said. "Shall I bring you your usual?"

"Yep," Sabrina said with a smile. "Kettle One and orange juice."

Just as John was in Coronado, Sabrina was fairly well known in Joplin, partly due to the fact that the magazine displays her picture at the top of the page featuring her human-interest stories.

"OK…no more stalling. Talk to me…you know I have to know."

"Yes…" Sabrina said. "You do, don't you? Well…to start off with…the guy's engaged…her name is Elizabeth."

"Oops…didn't like hearing that to start off with, but I'm sure we can get past that minor detail."

"I'm sure glad that *you* think it's a minor detail," Sabrina chuckled.

"OK…enough with the funny. Tell me more."

Sabrina thought for a moment. The whole idea of discussing John was bringing back the memory of him pressing up against her body before they said goodbye after dropping her off at the Del Coronado. She also envisioned in her mind the two of them standing close out on his balcony, gazing out towards the ocean. Sabrina wasn't talking…lost in her own thoughts. Karla shook her head and waited patiently until it was annoying. Sabrina wasn't being too accommodating. Karla, tired of the silent treatment, finally piped in.

"Since you are not talking, should I start asking questions?"

"Huh...?" Sabrina said, blinking back to the present. "Oh...no...I'll tell you everything," she went on as she put the menu back in the rack. "I warn you though...if you are thinking there is a juicy story in this, you are mistaken."

Karla shrugged. "Let me be the judge of that."

Over the next hour, Sabrina talked about John. She told Karla the story about him finding the locket, which had set off the strange chain of events in his life. She told her about the photograph of him and Elizabeth, all cozy on a boat at the marina. The part about the two of them alone in John's condominium and the way they said goodbye outside the Hotel Del Coronado is the part of the story that really kept Karla on the edge of her chair.

"The picture..." Karla said, referring to the photograph of John and Elizabeth on the boat, "the picture...is she pretty?"

"Darn, girl...you're really getting weird about this," Sabrina said, shaking her head. "The picture was taken from a distance with the two of them sitting on his boat...but, if you must know, yes she looked pretty. Are you happy?"

"Not about that...but I'll bet she's not as pretty as you are," Karla offered, fluttering her lashes jokingly as she sipped on her third Margarita. "It sounds to me, based on what you've told me, this John fella might be having second thoughts about this Elizabeth woman...which might just cause him to waver a little with respect to the engagement."

"Why would you say that?"

"Well...you know," Karla said in an encouraging tone of voice. "It's the way he acted towards you. He didn't want you to leave the pub. The way he held you when he dropped you off at the hotel...you know...all of those things are a sign."

"A sign, you say?" Sabrina said, laughing softly. "What are you...a psychic all of the sudden? Believe

me...nothing that happened between us would even remotely qualify as a sign. Yes...I think that John is a little
confused right now, given what's been happening to
him...but no sign."

"It may seem that way to you, but not to me," Karla
said flatly. "Something more than meets the eye is going on
with that girlfriend of his. You should call him."

"Are you crazy? That's the last thing I need to do. I'm
not going to meddle in his affairs."

Karla downed the last drop of her Margarita. "You do
like him, don't you?"

"I didn't say I didn't. It's just that...well, there is a line
and I'm not first in it."

"Now you're the one who is crazy. You need to fight if
there is an opening...and I think there is one here."

"You know me...I'm not that way, and you know it."

"Save it, Sabrina," Karla said, staring at her. "If you
ask me...I think you better start thinking differently. If you
don't, you'll end up an old maid like me."

Sabrina laughed aloud. "Old maid...I'm barely over
thirty. Listen...I've been out there. I just haven't met the
right guy yet."

Karla laughed back. "When was the last time you were
'out there'?"

"You know," Sabrina replied, taking a moment to
think. "Richard...you know, the salesman...remember
him?"

"Richard...?" Karla countered with a chuckle. "That
was six months ago. A girl that looks like you and is as
smart as you should have guys lined up, beating down her
door."

"We live in Joplin...remember. Besides...look who's
talking..." Sabrina said. "How come there is no one beating
down your door?"

"This is about you...not me. Besides, I see it as apples and oranges, girl. Look at me. Compared to you...I'm homely-looking."

"That's just not true and you know it," Sabrina countered, leaning back in her chair, pausing for a moment. "I gave him my card and told him to call if anything new materializes regarding the locket."

Karla's eyes widened. "Oh, yeah, that locket thing you mentioned over the phone. OK...that's it...now we're talking. That was a great move on your part. I bet he'll call soon."

Sabrina reached for her bag. "I'm not betting, but I doubt that he will."

"I'm just saying," Karla said in a serious voice. "Guys like this John don't come around very often so don't, whatever you do, screw this up and let him get away...you remember the 'Message in a Bottle' thing."

"That's a little morbid...don't you think?" Sabrina shot back. "Kevin Costner died in that movie."

"I'm just saying, Sabrina...you could lose him forever if you wait for nature to take its course."

"I still don't like the comparison."

Chapter Twenty

Coronado

John had just finished picking up art supplies at Blick Art Materials in downtown San Diego. It was close to noon, and he craved the walnut chicken salad at Arrivederci's restaurant in Hillcrest. Blick Art Materials is located about two blocks from the law firm where Elizabeth worked.

John decided not to call her. Instead, he thought he would take a stroll to the building, head up to the sixth floor, and surprise her with a lunch invitation. Surprises were on the list of things Elizabeth loved...jewelry heading up the top of the list.

Just down the street from the law firm, John stopped at Horton's newsstand to pick up the latest issue of *Artists and Illustrators* magazine. He paid for the magazine and continued on until he spotted Elizabeth a half block down...walking out of the building arm-in-arm with this guy named Gary Moberg, a young but long-time associate of the firm. John had met him twice before at the firm's annual parties. He recalled Elizabeth yukking it up with him as everyone mingled about, but never thought too much of it. John stopped in his tracks when he spotted them and watched curiously.

Just down the street from the law firm is the Red Fox Steak House and Piano Bar...mostly a popular dinner spot, but they do get a substantial lunch crowd. With Tudor paneling, a large fireplace with a finely-carved mantel, dark leather booths circling the walls, and a few tables filling out the interior of the room, the decor represents an old, dimly-lit inn in Surrey, England…a place where people go for a quiet, romantic experience.

As John watched the two of them dart into the restaurant, questions about what was really going on between them raced through his mind. He recalled that Elizabeth had mentioned Gary several times in the past, but he couldn't remember in what context. Although John doesn't have a jealous bone in his body, he said he wondered if this Gary person was on the recent business trip to Chicago that winded up in Vegas.

He stood near the newsstand, contemplating whether he should head straight for the restaurant and walk in on them…you know…act ignorant, say he saw them go in and decided to invite himself to join them for lunch. After giving it more thought, however, he felt it would be a foolish ploy on his part just for the purpose of satisfying his curiosity. He concluded that the whole thing…them being together…could turn out to be an innocent lunch meeting after all. Without giving it another thought, he turned on his heels and headed west to the Waterfront Bar and Grill for a chicken caesar salad. It wasn't Arrivederci's, but it was convenient.

Now I don't claim to know everything, but one thing I am for sure is a good judge of character. After a while, most bartenders do acquire that ability. Since you already know the gut feeling I have about Elizabeth, what I'm about to say won't surprise you. There is nothing that woman can say or do that will make me feel any different about her…she's deceitful to the core. I just wish John could see it. Deep down, I wanted Johnny-boy to break it off and be on his merry way.

It was Friday night and the anniversary of their engagement. John and Elizabeth had plans to take a dinner cruise around Mission Bay on the Bahia Belle, the place where he had proposed to her. As the sun was setting, John drove the Strand towards Coronado Cays to pick her up, calling to let her know he was heading her way.

As soon as Elizabeth answered the phone, the thought of her and that Gary fella darting into the Red Fox for lunch popped into John's mind. He decided to put her honesty to the test. I do have to give the boy credit. I was thinking he'd give her a pass, but he didn't.

He mentioned to Elizabeth that, earlier, he had thought about surprising her for lunch...but the way his day went, he ended up not having the time. Elizabeth's response was very telling...at least it was to me. She told John that she had a lunch meeting with one of the associates and some clients and would not have had the opportunity. I forgot to mention another one of her attributes...she is quick on her feet.

John decided not to ruin their special evening with speculation by pressing the issue. Believe me...if John had shared this information with me before their date, I would have advised him to get right up in Elizabeth's face that very night and confront her about this Gary Moberg guy...special evening or not. However, you know John by now. It's going to take heavy prodding by me, or some special, undeniable circumstance that Elizabeth can't bluff her way out of, to get him fired up. I guess the lunch with Gary wasn't it. He got close to going to battle with her over the phone hang-ups...but begged out of that fight as well. He put the events of the day out of his mind; what a wussy!

According to John, the dinner was romantic, and the weather out on the bay made it a perfect night for a cruise. It was the next morning that John said things went south. Actually, I should rewind a bit. After the cruise ended around ten-thirty, they drove straight to John's place.

Elizabeth's condominium was another fifteen minutes south along the Strand and she couldn't wait to get John into the sack. If I were to guess, John had a hard time concentrating during the drive over the Coronado Bridge with

Elizabeth's hands all over him. It's some scary maneuvering one has to do...believe me...I've been in that situat...uh...never mind.

Anyhow, Elizabeth had had much more to drink than John so she was primed for having her way with him. Once in the condo, Elizabeth disappeared into the bathroom to do whatever women do to freshen up before sex. John, on the other hand, walked out on the balcony, set his gaze towards the ocean and took in a deep breath.

For a split second, Sabrina crossed his mind. The thought of her stepping past him onto the same balcony and the scent that overwhelmed him aroused the memory of that day. The breeze hit his face, reminding him of what Sabrina had said...how she loved the wind caressing her face and blowing her hair. He could hear her soft voice in his head.

Without warning, Elizabeth, wearing nothing but a towel tied around her body, stepped up behind him, startling him back to reality. She whipped him around to face her and started tearing his clothes off right there on the balcony. She grabbed him by the arm and almost dragged him into the bedroom. She pushed him back onto the bed and straddled him. Elizabeth was on a mission. Before John knew what hit him, she released his belt, jerked his pants to his knees and slowly went down on him. The rest I'll leave up to your imagination.

Now it's morning, and this is where things went south with the relationship. Elizabeth was sitting at the kitchen island while John poured coffee. She spotted the locket in the key dish. She had known about the locket and John's dreams but had never really taken an interest. After being out of town for two weeks and caught up in who knows what, this was the first time she'd been to John's condo since the locket was found.

As she reached for the locket, she noticed a corner of Sabrina's business card sticking out from under the key dish. She lifted the key dish, took the card into her hand and studied it. A moment later, when John turned to hand her a cup of coffee, she let him have it.

"Who in the hell is Sabrina, John?" she demanded loudly, tossing the card across the counter at him.

John, caught off guard, hesitated. "Uh…she's a woman I met at Skipper's. She is a journalist and…"

"I can read, John," she said sarcastically. "Why are you keeping her card and what were the circumstances surrounding your meeting up with this woman at Skipper's?"

John refrained from telling her that I was the one who introduced them. Thank God for that. I wouldn't want those long fingernails of hers anywhere near my face. He said he set his coffee on the counter and said, "If you want to talk about this, you're going to have to calm down, Elizabeth."

Elizabeth did no such thing and replied viciously, "I'll calm down after you tell me what the hell went on when I was away."

"Nothing went on," John countered. "I told her about the locket and the dreams and she was interested in the story…that's all. Look, Elizabeth," John said. "Sabrina writes articles for magazines. She thought there might be a story behind the locket and my dreams. She left her card here just in case I…"

"What do you mean, she left her card here?" Elizabeth interrupted. "Was she here…in your house?"

Now this is where it really gets ugly. John had to answer honestly…but in a way that wouldn't get a cup of hot coffee thrown at him.

"She came only to see the locket…"

Elizabeth didn't let John finish. She started yelling and calling him a liar and a cheater and other names I'm not too comfortable repeating. John was cool, however. He really surprised me. He took the rapid fire from her and, when she was finished, he calmly said, "Why did you lie to me last night?"

"What the hell are you talking about?" she replied loudly…shooting daggers directly at him.

"You told me that you didn't have time to have lunch yesterday, but I happened to see you go into the Red Fox with your friend, Gary."

Elizabeth stood up and stared at John in silence. She was like a mouse in a trap. John stood there as calm as a priest in a confessional. He said he was surprised at how calm and cool his demeanor was. I didn't think he had it in him.

After a long pause, Elizabeth said, in a calm voice, "For your information, Gary wanted to tell me something in confidence…that's why we went to the Fox. He is thinking about quitting the firm."

"And this caused you to lie to me?" John said. "First, you said it was lunch with clients…now some confidential thing with this guy, Gary. That doesn't say much for our relationship, now does it? Trust is important; and right now, I'm having a hard time believing anything."

Elizabeth's eyes narrowed. "So what are you trying to say?"

"I'm saying we ought to break off the engagement. Listen, Elizabeth," he went on. "Who are we kidding? You and I both know that the way I want to live is too boring for you. You want much more…so I think you should go find it."

Well…after several more words between them, that was the end of that. No surprise there…I predicted that it would eventually happen, didn't I?

Chapter Twenty-one

Things seemed to be back to normal for John. His break-up with Elizabeth didn't appear to affect him that much. She had called him a few times in an attempt to patch things up, but John wasn't having it. I had to pat the young man on the back for that. If you ask me, I think having Sabrina on his mind the whole time helped him get past it. To me…that would be the only way to explain away the easy transition.

Time went by and, for a while, John was dream-free. Any dreams he may have had, whether he would share or not, would have been about the girl from Joplin…I would bet my bottom dollar on that. Like I said, John seemed to be back to normal. He was hanging out at the marina during the day…sketching and painting…and then showing his face at my place every few days…pretty much back to his boring lifestyle. To tell you the truth…I was happy with what was going on in John's life again…until the other day.

He wandered into the pub round three o'clock in the afternoon with his head hanging down. He left his folding chair and sketchpad in the usual place and headed directly for his table without even so much as a peep when he passed the bar. Sakae noticed him come in first and nudged me. We both sensed something was wrong so I finished stocking one of the shelves and made my way over to his table to sit down across from him. What initially crossed my mind was that Elizabeth had something to do with the attitude, so I took a chance and went with it.

"This look you are wearing worries me, Johnny-boy," I said. "Don't tell me you are back with Elizabeth…because if…"

John cut me off.

"It's not that at all," he said, with a long deep sigh. "I had another dream. I'm telling you, Skipper, this shit is really wearing me out."

"OK," I said in an encouraging tone of voice, "It's not Elizabeth. That's a good thing." I turned and signaled for Sakae to bring John a glass of tea. "Same dream as before?"

"Yes and no," he answered, brushing a hand through his hair.

John told me that he finally took the advice Sabrina gave him the day she left for Joplin. He took the locket out of the key dish and tucked it away in a drawer. She thought out of sight out of mind and no more dreams. Instead it sparked another one that night.

What John told me that afternoon peaked an interest in me I didn't have before. Usually, when he talked about those dreams of his, I would be polite and act interested even if the words only stuck with me for a nanosecond. This dream was different, more complex...you might even call it perplexing. What he was describing to me now seemed to weave all the previous dreams together...seemingly playing out like some fiction novel. The thought actually crossed my mind that maybe he should stop painting for a while and become a novelist. To be honest, the whole thing was now getting really weird for me.

As he talked, it was eerie. His eyes were wide and shifty. His voice even cracked a little...somewhat of a stammer as he talked. It was as if he didn't want to tell me...almost as if he was embarrassed to lay it out there...but he did it anyway. After all, who else would he tell to get it off his chest?

He said he was wading into the ocean until he was submerged and walking on the ocean floor. This time, as he reached the sailboat, he looked up and saw the silhouette of a girl in a white flowing gown, free-floating deep beneath the ocean's surface directly above the sunken sailboat.

At that point, John lowered his voice to a whisper, and I don't know why...the pub was quiet and almost empty. For a moment, he even had me looking around. He said the girl in some suspended animation turned her head and looked down directly at him. He went on to say that looking into her eyes was like staring at lasers getting brighter with every passing second...her eyes were wide open and strangely eerie. The way John described it, the girl looked terrified. John said she actually reached out her hand in his direction, as if he was supposed to do something...but all he could do was watch...he couldn't move.

The water began to bubble up and swirl around the girl's body. Her gown was still flowing as if she was in a gentle current in the middle of it all. Suddenly, the water began to produce millions of tiny bubbles that swirled rapidly around her body like a tempest until, suddenly, it swept her up and she vanished. At that point, he said, the boat vanished too...and he woke up.

When he finished, I sat there shaking my head. What could I say at that point that might offer him comfort? Offering up any advice, besides suggesting that he take another go at my psychiatrist friend, I'm sure would have been futile. I really had no other legitimate ideas to put out there...I was stumped.

John took a sip of tea before taking in a slow, deep breath. I could tell there was definitely something churning deep in his mind. Suddenly, just like that, he snapped out of it.

"I'm going to do it," he spat out, feeling hope swell up in his chest, sounding calm all of a sudden.

"Killing yourself is not the answer, son." I said in a joking manner, trying to keep the mood upbeat.

John chuckled softly. "No, Skipper...I'm going to do what Sabrina suggested."

Ah...Sabrina. Now that would lighten up any mood. "OK..." I said, crossing my arms. "I give up...what is it that Sabrina suggested besides sticking that locket in a drawer somewhere?"

John sat there in silence again, thinking. I waited until he brought his mind back to our conversation. "I'm going to paint the woman in the locket."

"Paint the woman?" I said. "First off...you said that the picture of the woman in the locket is hardly recognizable and, secondly...what does that accomplish?"

John heard the question but didn't respond immediately. I presume he was trying to find an answer that might make some sense.

"Right now, I'm not really sure," he said, shrugging, letting his exasperation show. "Sabrina thought it might somehow do some good. Maybe bring closure...who knows? I've got to do something...otherwise, if I keep having these dreams, I'll end up wrapped in a straightjacket in a padded room somewhere. She suggested that I put the locket in a drawer and then changed her mind and told me to paint. I tried putting it in a drawer anyway and that didn't work...so this time, I'll paint."

I wasn't buying any of it, even though that beautiful angel had suggested it. What could he possibly accomplish by painting the portrait, other than extend the drama? Oh, well. I guess if it makes John feel better, I should be all for it...so I said, "How will you compensate for not having a full likeness of the woman's face to work with?"

"I have to go back and try to reconstruct in my mind the image I saw in the mirror."

"Ah, yes...the steamy mirror," I said, straining to keep my tone positive. "I remember you telling me that. That would be a good title for the book when you decide to write it."

John didn't laugh at my comment, and I couldn't sit with John much longer. Not only was it getting depressing for me, but it was time to finish setting things up for the Friday night crowd. Juan Mendoza, my cook, was back in for his second shift of the day. He's been with me forever. He cooks for the lunch crowd, cleans up and leaves, and then returns for the evening shift. I glanced at my watch and then at John. "It's four o'clock…are you coming back tonight?"

"I don't think so, Uncle Skip," John said, taking the last gulp of tea from the glass. "The woman in the locket, remember?"

"Oh…yes," I replied with a strained laugh. "The woman in the locket and the steamy mirror. Remember what I said about a good title. On second thought, you ought to ask Sabrina to write a novel about this…she's the writer. It would be an interesting four-hundred-pager…don't you think? You can collaborate and have a best seller."

"I get it," John mused. "Humor relaxes the mind. Where did you learn that…in your physiotherapy session?"

"OK…you got me there." I replied. "That…was funny. How about I have Juan rustle up some rolled tacos with guacamole for you to take home?"

John smiled. "No thanks, Uncle Skip…but I appreciate it. I have some left-over pizza waiting for me in the refrigerator."

Chapter Twenty-two

John laid the sketchpad on the table next to the stand with the magnifier lamp attached. He took the chain out of the drawer and opened the wings of the locket. He laid the locket on the stand next to the sketchpad and lowered the frame with the thick glass to rest just above it.

Two hours went by. He began to transform a blank sheet of paper into the essence of a woman's face. Even though he used a combination of the obscure picture and the visual memory of the face that materialized in the misty mirror, he wasn't satisfied.

Disappointment became his enemy, making it difficult for him to concentrate. His attitude turned negative. The frustration of it all was killing him. He suddenly subconsciously convinced himself that he couldn't possibly draw all the details of the woman's face.

John didn't want to just capture the facial structure; he wanted the many unique nuances that went with it. Without those particular characteristics, it wouldn't be a portrait. It would just be two eyes, a nose and a mouth.

Here is the problem, as John explained it to me. Although he was a gifted artist, he did not have the high level of memory required to extract and develop the tiny details necessary to create an exact likeness of a person.

The visual detail an artist gains from looking at a live image of the subject they are painting enables them to capture the personality and other unique characteristics of the person. Because of his lack of what he described as "total recall memory," such as absorbing in his mind's eye what he had witnessed in the mirror that morning in that room full of mist, drawing the exact facial features of what he saw would be difficult.

The harder he tried to recreate the image, the more frustration set in. Although the magnifier lamp helped to enlarge the photograph, his eyes grew tired from focusing on it. In addition, and to add more stress, he had promised Kate Sutter that he would deliver a new painting to the Galleria in the morning and, unless he got moving, he would not be able to fulfill that promise.

It was now eleven o'clock. Frustrated and tired, he glanced over at the unfinished painting of the thirty-five-foot cutter on the easel across from him. The staysail located in front of the mast was the only thing missing. His gaze moved back to the incomplete sketch of the woman on the pad in front of him, then shook his head. He decided he was finished sketching or painting anything for the rest of the night.

John stepped onto the balcony just as a light rain started falling on the overhang above and the metal railing in front of him. He said it actually felt good. It made him think of Sabrina. He didn't know why, other than the cool breeze brushing his face reminded him how much she enjoyed it when she was standing on the balcony next to him. He thought again about contacting her. It seems that, over the last few weeks, that's all he did…think about it…I told him it was procrastination.

Eleven o'clock in California was one o'clock in the morning, Missouri time. He wasn't about to call her that time of the morning. He asked himself again if enough time had passed since his break-up with Elizabeth, but was only confused about what the right answer should be. He asked me the same question days ago and…well…I think you know what I told him.

It started raining pretty hard, forcing John back inside. He was fighting to stay awake. For some silly reason, it crossed his mind that if he went to bed now, the rain crashing against the bedroom window might toss him into another stormy dreamscape...right where he didn't want to be. He picked up Sabrina's card and thought about shooting her an email.

Three ways to contact that beautiful angel...office phone, cell phone, email, and the man hadn't used one of them! Can you imagine that? Going back to a few days ago when he, for the umpteenth time, asked me if enough time had passed...he also brought up his options for contacting her. I told him to stop dallying around and do something before some other guy grabs her. Did he listen to his Uncle Skip? No.

***

The night passed without restlessness. Not so much as a muscular impulse occurred. A still, quiet night's sleep was just what the doctor ordered. John woke up around seven-thirty in the morning, fully rested and ready to finish the painting of the cutter.

He poured himself a cup of hot coffee, sat down on the stool in front of the desk and, for a moment, stared at the incomplete sketch of the woman he'd started the night before. What he really wished for was another shot at seeing her image again in that misty mirror. However, he accepted the reality that that would most likely not happen, and he'd just have to do the best he could once he got back into the drawing. For now, his priority was to finish the cutter for the Galleria.

***

I arrived at the pub around eight in the morning. It was the paperwork part of the business that I hated, but there it was in front of me. Juan left the food list on the top of the desk, and Sakae was responsible to keep the inventory on booze.

I sat in my office and called in orders to Associated Wholesale Grocers and my liquor distributors. I took a moment to clear my head and leaned back in my old leather swivel chair. Suddenly, John crossed my mind...so clearing my head wasn't working. I opened the desk drawer to throw the pen I was using back in and noticed Sabrina's card lying on the bottom of the drawer next to some scattered papers.

It was as if I was supposed to see it. It was the right thing to do, and I didn't think twice about doing it. I had already convinced myself that, if John didn't take action, *I* was going to call her. Maybe it's just me, but for whatever reason, I had to let Sabrina know that John and Elizabeth were no longer a couple. Why shouldn't she know? I'm sure you would have done the same thing under similar circumstances. There is a downside here, however. John probably would not speak to me for months if he found out that I had made a call like this to Sabrina.

Why John was dragging his feet with this woman, I have no idea. It was irritating the hell out of me...can you tell? *He* wouldn't admit it, but I knew better; I knew how much not calling her was eating at him.

It was plain to me that John wanted to contact her but he hadn't...so I decided to take matters into my own hands. I'm now beginning to think it's just a matter of having some guts. Apparently, John has none. What else is a man supposed to do in my spot? As Sakae said, I'm Cupid with the bow and arrow...so I used it. Personally, I'd love to see that angel again.

Some operator answered the phone. "Sabrina Harper, please," I said.

After a moment and a click or two, I heard her voice. "This is Sabrina."

"Sabrina...Skipper," I said.

Once I said 'Sabrina...Skipper,' I could have counted down five seconds of silence.

"Uh…Skipper? You mean, Coronado Skipper?"

"Good guess, lady. You *are* good at guessing things, aren't you?"

I could have counted down another five seconds. It was an awkward silence.

What Karla said to Sabrina at Club 609 popped into Sabrina's mind…'*Message in a Bottle*'. Then, suddenly, the words came rushing out of Sabrina's mouth. "Is something wrong? Did something happen to John?"

That response tells me a lot about her feelings towards him. "What? Oh, no, Sabrina. It's not that at all…John's fine. A little messed up in his head right now, but you already knew that, didn't you?"

"You're talking about the dreams he has…I hope?" she said, as her voice dropped several octaves.

"You guessed right again…see what I'm saying? You're a good guesser."

Sabrina chuckled loudly. Meanwhile, Karla, in the cubicle next to Sabrina, had caught wind of one side of the conversation. She heard Sabrina mention John, and her antennas shot straight up. I could hear her in the background asking Sabrina, "Is it John…Sabrina? Is it him?"

"Shhh…" Sabrina whispered, pressing her palm over the phone handset. "No, it's not! Sorry about that, Skipper," she went on. "That was my nosey cohort, Karla. Anyway…Skipper, I told John to call me if he had any more interesting dreams but he hasn't called yet so I just assumed, well…you know…no call, no more dreams."

"That's really not why I'm calling. I'm calling, Sabrina Harper, to let you know that John broke off the engagement with Elizabeth."

There was another moment of silence. I got the feeling that Sabrina, caught off guard with the news, was searching her brain for some response to the news I just handed her.

"Hmm…how long ago and why?" Sabrina asked.

I could tell she was trying to maintain a calm composure...you know, try not to sound too excited.

"Well, let me put it this way," I said, frankly. "The break-up was inevitable...and it happened a while ago. I know he hasn't called you, but I do know for a fact that he wanted to. That's just the way John is."

Sabrina said, "Skipper, there is no reason for me to expect that John would call. I mean, well...you know what I mean."

"Listen, girl. Right now, John has mixed feelings about everything in his life...the problems with Elizabeth, the crazy dreams...and you. I'm at my wit's end with all this, I tell you. I don't know what to do with him. I have to be honest, Sabrina. I think you are the only one that can save him from himself...I'm convinced of it. Oh...if he knew that I called you, he wouldn't speak to me for a very long time so..."

"I would never tell him you called me," Sabrina interrupted in a serious tone of voice, nudging Karla, who had made her way around the cubicle, to move back and stop breathing down her neck. "Are you suggesting I call him?"

I heard Karla whisper in the background, 'Call him. Call him now'. I thought for about half a minute to find an answer to Sabrina's question but drew a blank. It was one of the few times in my life when I was at a loss for an answer.

"I guess you'll have to figure that one out on your own. As it stands now, Sabrina, I wouldn't count on him taking the first step anytime soon. You have to know I am very worried about him. Otherwise, I wouldn't have called you. You might be just the medicine he needs. I have to get my ass in gear. I'll be opening the doors soon, and this call has put me a little behind. I hope to see you soon, Sabrina Harper."

Sabrina replied warmly, "Maybe you will. I've been craving one of those famous Skipper's hamburgers."

***

Sabrina and Karla walked the North Park shopping mall. It was three days after my 'plea for help' call. Christmas was a week away and the mall was wall-to-wall people searching for last-minute deals. Sabrina needed to buy a few small gifts to send off with her mother to Florida. Karla wouldn't shut up about John. Ever since that phone call I made, it seemed to Sabrina that every other word out of Karla's mouth was 'John this and John that.' She was really getting on Sabrina's nerves.

"Did you call him last night like you said you would?"

"Will you stop it with the John thing...no, I didn't," Sabrina replied, glancing through a window outside of Abbey's Hallmark. "Let's go in here."

"Damn, girl...that guy, Skipper...he told you that you'd have to initiate! What is the holdup?"

"No holdup," Sabrina replied, as she made her way past shoppers and headed for the figurines. "But if you mention John's name one more time today, I might scream. I know what I'm going to do."

"Yes!! What's that?" Karla said anxiously, pumping her fist.

"Send him a figurine," Sabrina replied nonchalantly.

"Are you crazy?" Karla replied, tugging on Sabrina's arm. "Men don't want figurines...they want real things, like shirts, pants and...sex."

I guess Karla has a sense of humor as well. She just might be OK in my book, after all. Even though she is a nosey one, at least she was on my side.

"It represents a kind of joke between us...believe me, he'll love it. Oh...now, would you look at this one?" she continued as she carefully lifted a porcelain sailboat with a boy and girl sitting under an umbrella. "I'll mail it to him for Christmas."

"Mail it to him?" Karla spat out. "If you insist on giving him that thing, you take it to him!! Your Mother is going to visit your sister in Florida, and you're not going this year. The way I see it, you have two choices," she warned. "You can either spend Christmas with me or your uncle… and how exciting will that be? Or, you could spend Christmas with John."

Sabrina chuckled as she examined the small porcelain sailboat closer. "You mentioned his name again…should I scream now and send everyone in the store into a panic?"

"Go ahead," Karla warned. "I'll keep mentioning it until you come to your senses."

"So let me get this straight. You want me to tell John…a guy I only saw twice almost two months ago…what he's going to do for Christmas? Is that it?"

"Sure…why not?" Karla said in an anxious tone of voice. "I heard what that fella, Skipper, said to you over the phone…John's a basket case. You said yourself that his father and mother had passed away. He might be spending Christmas alone or sitting in some pub. What kind of Christmas would that be? You'll never know until you ask."

"How about a compromise," Sabrina offered. "I'll FedEx this figurine with a general note attached. If he calls me…and we talk about Christmas…well…then…we'll see what happens."

"I don't like it," Karla said, vigorously shaking her head. "Leaving it up to an "if it happens by chance" scenario is risky. My vote is you take it to him."

"You don't get a vote. How do you like it?" Sabrina asked, holding up the figurine.

"Cute," Karla replied. "Take it to him."

Chapter Twenty-three

John spent what seemed like another futile hour on the portrait, studying the picture, racking his brain to recall the image he saw in the mirror. It was exhausting, and he couldn't get it right. The composition...finding his way around the drawing...it wasn't working yet. Sketching for a painting is like reading a good book...even though it was good, you don't particularly want to go back and start over again. He developed images in his mind, erasing and re-drawing repeatedly. It still didn't look or feel quite right.

At two o'clock in the afternoon, he gave up. It was cool out...around fifty-five degrees. John decided to take a walk to the marina, just to clear his mind...you know. He lifted his jacket off the hook inside the closet. He glanced at the portrait one more time, shook his head, zipped up his jacket part-way and headed out the door.

The marina was full of boats tied to the dock, tucked next to each other, bow to stern. The lines of boats reaching to the end of each floating concrete boat slip were rocking to different rhythms as the tide washed in and out. John walked along the shoreline's concrete walkway. He thought about how great it would be to have Sabrina walking next to him. He pictured in his mind the two of them, arm-and-arm...Sabrina wearing some sort of warm jacket with fur around the collar.

Coming from the opposite direction, a man and woman walking their fluffy white poodle smiled as they passed...as if they didn't have a care in the world. It was exactly the position in life John was in before he met Elizabeth...and before he came across that annoying locket. If only Sabrina had wandered into Skipper's two years ago instead of two months ago, things might have been different for John to-day.

The breeze crossed John's face as he walked along the path. He felt Sabrina's presence even though she was far away in Joplin. He said that it felt so real that a range of emotions transcending understanding took hold of him. I had no idea what that meant when he said it, but I played along and nodded. For a moment, it struck me that he might have gone downtown to see Joe Navarra without telling me.

You can't imagine what was going through my mind as he told me this stuff. Though we are very close, Johnny-boy and I, it surprised me that he would even share this kind of personal information. It just goes to show you how messed up he was at the time we had this conversation. To tell the truth, I had been getting bored with the whole thing, especially anything having to do with that locket.

Apparently, the call I made to Sabrina hadn't helped the situation either. She hadn't called him or attempted to contact him at all. I'm sure I made myself clear by insinuating that she had to be the one to make the first move...but she hadn't. I tell you...it is confusing. I thought I was pretty darn good at reading people.

Again, I don't understand it. I thought for sure Sabrina would jump at a chance to call him, especially since Elizabeth was no longer in the picture. At night, I tell all this stuff to Sakae while we are lying in bed and...oops...oh, what the hell. You already know what's going on there. Even Sakae was getting somewhat bored with it all. Maybe it was because she wasn't hearing a lot of it from John; it was coming from me.

The loud screech of a hungry, low-flying seagull caught John by surprise. He reacted by ducking his head at just the right angle, allowing him to catch sight of a red sailboat in a slip docked between two bigger boats half-way down the side of one of the ramps. He blinked several times to make sure he wasn't seeing things…he needed a closer look.

The name painted along the bow caught his eye. He needed to make sure that he wasn't seeing a name that looked somewhat familiar, but was actually different. He made his way down the walkway to the entrance of the dock, all the while keeping his eyes locked on the red sailboat. A closer look verified what he thought he saw. Seeing that name painted on the boat raised the tiny hairs on the back of his neck.

The name painted on the boat spelled out the words, 'Solitude Two.' Right away, John flashed back to the dream he had had where he was making his way along the ocean floor. It was the exact same dream where he spotted a sailboat lying there, partly sunk in the sediment, with the name…Solitude One. He wasted no time hurrying to the unattended boat…and when he reached it, he just stood there, staring blankly.

After snapping out of the momentary trance that suddenly struck him, John made his way towards the stern of the boat get a look at the CF registration number. He locked the numbers in his brain…J21364465. It didn't take long for him to get back to his condo to fire up the computer. Getting the name and some information about the boat's owner was easy, especially when you've registered your own boat in the system.

Ron King. That's the owner. John was elated to have discovered this. He didn't know if it would lead to anything, but at least it was something for him to go on. He sat at his computer, gazing at Ron King's address. The phone number is confidential but the address is readily available. The house was located just off Orange Avenue. John could literally walk fifteen minutes from his condo to Ron King's house. The address was also quite close to my pub.

John said he contemplated rushing right over to the address, knocking on the door and coming straight out with the reason he was there. It didn't take long, however, for him to shake off that thought. Instead, he slipped his jacket back on, shot out the door and made his way over to see me.

As soon as John walked through the door, I could see the excitement on his face. He wasted no time getting to a stool at the bar. I must say, he caught me by surprise...and Sakae too. John never breaks his routine. He comes in and heads straight for his table, and that's it...every time. It was still early...in between the lunch and dinner crowd. There was no 'hello,' 'how are you?' ...nothing...for me or Sakae. He just started spewing information that really didn't make sense. I finally had to slow him down a bit.

"Whoa..." I said, thinking about shoving a bar towel in his mouth. "Slow down and start from the beginning. I know you think whatever you're saying is important, but saying it at a hundred miles an hour isn't going to work."

John held out the palms of his hands. "OK," he said, taking in a deep breath. "I just was walking the marina. As I was walking, I spotted a sailboat that seemed curious to me. To make a long story short..."

"Thank you," I broke in. "So there will be an end to this story?"

John looked at me funny when I blurted that out. Well...I couldn't help it. I had a lot to do and didn't have a lot of time for more stories of dreams and such.

"Anyhow," he said in a calmer tone of voice. "I spotted this boat, walked out on the boat dock to get a closer look and... guess what name was painted on the stern?

I looked at him. "No clue," I said.

"Solitude Two!" he said.

I glared at John, thinking...*so what*? Before I could articulate that thought, he said, "Remember, Skipper? That is the name of the boat I saw sitting at the bottom of the ocean in my dream...with one exception. The boat in the dream was Solitude One.

"Ok," I said, as wiped off the draft beer towers. "Sorry that I didn't remember that little detail in all the dreams you've had."

"No problem," John said quickly "And listen to this, I got the owner's name off the registration site and..."

"Wait...Johnny-boy." I interrupted. "You're not *really* going to contact this person, are you?"

John looked at me oddly...like I was wearing a skirt or something...apparently having a hard time believing that I would question his plan of attack.

"Sure I'm going to talk to him," he replied with con-viction. "I need to find out if they know anything about Solitude One."

"Great, I can't wait till you come back here and tell me that they thought you were a loony for even asking the question...especially if you start off by telling them you came up with this as a result of some dreams."

"Thanks...Uncle," John said, now returning fire. "Do you think I would really start the conversation off that way?"

"That's just it...Johnny-boy. I don't know. You have been a little reckless with your thinking these days and you must admit..."

"OK...OK," John said, interrupting again. "You are right...I must admit that I haven't been thinking that clearly as a result of all this, but I'm settled in now. I'm going to first inquire about the name of the boat and if they were aware of another boat named Solitude One. If they have info on Solitude One and, depending upon what that infor-mation is, that's when I will decide if I need to go into the strange dreams part."

I thought for a moment about what he had said. "OK, Johnny-boy," I said. "If you really must talk to whoever owns that boat...the plan sounds like it might work."

John said, "I'll go to their house tomorrow, but not too early. If they are working, they might not be there. If that is the case, then I'll go back just before supper. The name on the registration is King...some guy by the name of Ron King."

"Wait... I know him," I said proudly, as if I were solving some mystery. "He is a long-time San Diego detective. He comes into the pub now and then...nice man...tall man. You'd have no trouble picking him out of a crowd. He doesn't live far from here."

"You see...Uncle Skipper," John said, sticking his chest out. "Everything might be coming together."

This is where I have to bring Johnny-boy back to reality. I looked directly into his eyes. "Now please, Johnny-boy... you listen to me on this one. You do know the story about the dreams might be construed by some as bullshit, including yours truly. No one is going to believe the 'walking on the bottom of the ocean' stuff or the girl floating in a white gown business. You really have to come to grips with that...and stop thinking you are involved in some fairy tale. You do realize that...don't you?"

John didn't like it, but all in all, he is a smart guy. He really didn't challenge what I said. He smiled politely, said goodbye to both Sakae and me and made his way out of the pub. At that point, I kept my fingers crossed...hoping that, after he met Ron King, he wouldn't end up being more confused than he was before going to see him.

Chapter Twenty-four

The very next afternoon, John did what he said he was going to do. Around two o'clock, he knocked on the door of an average, quite modest house just off Orange Avenue. A pleasant woman, who looked to be in her middle fifties with short graying hair, opened the door. John said it was a little awkward at first, primarily because he just stood there a moment without saying anything.

He had a hard time recalling the rehearsed words that he planned to use to start off the conversation…a conversation he thought he was going to have with Ron King. It put John a little off guard when a woman answered the door instead of the expected Mr. King.

"I'm sorry to bother you, ma'am," John said with a smile. "My name is John Adler. I happened to be walking the marina yesterday and noticed the name on your sailboat…Solitude Two."

"Yes," she replied, looking somewhat concerned that some stranger was inquiring about their boat. "That's my husband's boat…why? Has something happened to it?"

"Oh, no, ma'am…"

"Please…call me Millie," she said, switching to a warmer tone of voice.

"Thank you," John said. "Anyway, I was just wondering…since the name of the sailboat is Solitude Two…is Solitude One his boat as well?"

As soon as the words 'Solitude One' left his mouth, a look of surprise washed across the woman's face.

"Solitude One was my husband's brother's boat, dear."

John was stunned when he heard that. He wasn't expecting that kind response. He quickly tried to process what it meant. At a loss for words and feeling somewhat stupid, he merely stood there, dumbfounded. He was the one who started the conversation, and she was the one left hanging. As he finally gathered his wits, a dark-colored Crown Victoria cruiser pulled into the driveway.

Millie said, "Oh…there's my husband now. I'm not sure what it is that you want, uh…you said your name is Adler?"

"Yes ma'am. John Adler."

"Well, John," she said smiling, "I'm sure my husband can answer any questions you may have about his boat and his brother's boat. Did you want to purchase Solitude Two or something like that…because it's not really for sale?"

"Oh…no," John replied, giving his head a shake. "I have my own sail…"

Before John could finish the statement, Ron King quickly made his way up the steps, curious about the stranger standing on his porch, talking to his wife.

"Ronald," Millie said without hesitation. "This is John Adler; he's inquiring about your sailboat."

Millie retreated back into the house, leaving Ron and John standing alone on the porch. Ron extended a hand that seemed to John to be at least half-a-hand larger than his own.

Ron was tall…towering over John by about three inches. His face was rugged, like that of an action star you might see in the movies…the Arnold Schwarzenegger-type but with a dark, bushy mustache which was slightly graying. John described him as a gentle, yet imposing figure. I reminded John that Ron wandered into the pub every now and then for a hamburger so, based on his description, he was one and the same.

"It's very nice to meet you, John," Ron said, peering down at him. "Now, what is it about my boat you'd like to know?" he continued as their hands fell away.

"Well...to tell you the truth," John replied, nervously jamming a hand in his pocket. "I'm not sure how to put this...and...quite frankly, I feel somewhat awkward saying what I'm about to say. I was actually asking your wife about Solitude One."

"Solitude One?" Ron said curiously. He was now just as confused as Millie was to hear this stranger mention his brother's boat.

"Yes, sir," John said respectfully. "I know you'll think this sounds crazy, but I saw the boat sitting at the bottom of the ocean."

"You **w-h-a-t**...! You saw my brothers' boat? When? Where?"

John gathered his thoughts. "Well...I can't pinpoint exactly where in the ocean I was when I saw it. I have a sailboat of my own. A few months ago...I was sailing off the coast, quite a distance from the shore, maybe a half mile. All of a sudden...just like that...strangely, the wind stopped blowing and I started drifting. I glanced down into the water and could see the boat directly beneath me. I know it might sound..."

"Excuse me, John..." Ron interrupted, with a confused look on his face. . "I've sailed all my life. It would be impossible for you to see a boat let alone recognize it to be Solitude One sitting on the bottom that far out in the ocean...you know, needle in a haystack sort of thing.

"That's the reason I came to see you. You see...um, this is going to be hard-to-believe. I hardly believe it myself. The only way I know anything about Solitude One is that I saw the name embossed on the stern of the sailboat in a dream."

After hearing that, Ron gave John a different kind of look. He probably was thinking about sending John on his way, thinking he was crazy or delusional...I would have. Instead, he invited him in.

"Come, John...we can sit in the house and talk. It will be more comfortable than standing out here on the porch. I'd really like to hear what you have to say. You see..." he went on, gently taking John by the arm and leading him into the house. "My brother, Steve, went sailing one afternoon many years ago on his boat, Solitude One, and never made it back. It was a horrible time in our lives...and is still difficult to this day."

When Ron mentioned his brother went missing when sailing Solitude One years ago, John's knees buckled slightly and an anxious feeling came over his body. In that moment, all the dreams, wrapped together, flashed through his mind. Seeing the boat beneath him on the bottom of the ocean, fighting for his life in the ocean storm, witnessing the bones inside the boat as the sediment lifted, and watching the woman in the white gown disappear right before his eyes.

Ron noticed John looking as if he were hypnotized...standing there in a daze. "John," Ron said, "are you feeling OK? You look a little disorientated."

"Huh?" John reacted, giving his head a quick shake. "Fine...yes...I'm good."

Actually, John was also trying to quickly sort out in his mind how much detail about the dreams he would tell the Kings.

Ron guided John into a warm, comfortable living space with photographs everywhere. The photographs were hanging on the walls, sitting on end tables, the coffee table, the mantle over the fireplace, on top of a walnut cabinet with glass doors, and inside the cabinet as well. John said it seemed like a room set up to memorialize something or someone.

In addition to all the photographs, John did a double-take when he saw one of his boat paintings hanging on the wall over a recliner in the corner. He also noticed several small model sailboats scattered around the room on shelves, and a few behind the glass in the walnut cabinet.

Millie walked into the room carrying two glasses of tea. After handing one to Ron and then one to John, she sat down in the chair under the boat painting. John smiled and said, "I sure like that painting hanging on the wall above you, Millie. You folks must really like sailboats."

"Ron is a fanatic about sailboats," Millie said, grinning at her husband. "His brother was the same way, rest his soul."

Ron said, "Wait just a minute...your name is Adler...John Adler?"

John smiled, glanced at both Ron and Millie. "Yep...you guessed it," he replied. "That is my tiny signature near the frame in the bottom right-hand corner."

"Well, I'll be," Ron said, sitting straight in his chair. "I'm familiar with your name. Every time I walked into a gallery looking to buy a boat painting, the salesperson in every store mentioned your name...you're a popular guy."

With a humble smile, John said, "About as popular as I want to be."

"I bought that one five years ago at the Galleria on Orange. Millie, looks like we have a celebrity on board," he went on, giving her the thumbs up. "I'd like to purchase another one, but Millie won't allow it," he continued, a grin across his face. "She said we don't have room in the house for one more picture...can you imagine that?"

John looked at Millie and chuckled. "Wait a minute here. How am I supposed to make any money if you don't continue to buy my paintings?"

They all had a good laugh, and the ice was broken. It was now time to get down to the business at hand, the real reason John was there in the first place. Ron got up and went to the walnut cabinet. He reached in and took out a five-by-seven picture frame, went back to the couch and handed it to John.

Although the color of the boat John saw sitting at the bottom of the ocean had faded from the elements and the wood showed signs of deep decay, John felt sure that the boat he was looking at was the boat he saw in his dream. There was a man standing in the boat who clearly had Ron's features.

"That's my brother," Ron pointed out. "That picture was taken just before he and his friends went missing."

"How many friends were with him?"

"Two of his college buddies,"

John thought for a moment. "You mean three people were lost?"

"Yes," Ron replied, shaking his head. "Like I said, it was a horrible time...not only for us, but for the other families involved as well."

"If I might ask," John said evenly, "when you say there were three people lost, were there any women on board?"

"As far as we know, it was only a couple of his college friends. We knew them. The authorities investigating the case talked to a boat dock worker. That person had recalled seeing a woman get on board. After further investigation, however, no one knew for sure how many people were aboard Solitude One. The Coast Guard searched for days...with no luck. My brother was two years younger than I was at the time...twenty-two. That was thirty years ago last April."

What John found out from the Kings that day didn't resolve any of his unanswered questions about the existence of the locket. The fact that Ron had no idea if there was a woman sailing with his brother the day he went missing led John to decide it would be best not to tell Ron the rest of the bizarre dreams. What good would come of that information?

Ron and his family had grieved the loss of his brother for all these years, it would be cruel to open up more wounds over things he could not prove were real, no more real than his sighting of a boat deep on the ocean floor. Saying anything about how he knew it was Solitude One in a dream while strolling along the ocean floor would only sound more bizarre.

Then what? Would he tell them about the bones buried in the sediment or the girl in the white flowing gown...I think not. In any case, John made the right decision that day. The fact is, John was sure that Ron and Millie thought it odd enough that he even approached them with his strange story. Stirring the pot with the rest of it at this point would only cause more confusion. If, at some point, if he ever made sense about whatever has been happening to him, he might go back and tell them the rest.

One thing is for sure, however. Now that John had found out that there actually *was* a Solitude One, it made things even more interesting. It added still another element for him to mull over...become more confused about. I must admit, although I wouldn't say it to John, the information about Ron's brother disappearing at sea has definitely increased the drama of it all for Sakae and me.

Credible? I wouldn't go so far as to say that, but interesting...yes. You can bet your bottom dollar that I won't be telling any of this to Joseph Navarra any time soon. I'm now what you would call a person sitting on the fence...in a "wait and see" mode. I'm not ready to buy into any theory that John has some super, intellectual powers just yet.

Chapter Twenty-five

Three days before Santa drops down millions of chimneys with his sack full of presents, Christmas came early for me. We were cleaning up after the lunch crowd cleared out. Sakae was wiping tables, and I was on my knees behind the bar changing a five-gallon, ball-lock soda canister. I said something to Sakae and then heard the whisper of an angel's voice. It didn't register at first until I heard the voice again. It was coming from in front of the bar.

"Hey, Skipper."

I quickly rose up, coming within inches of smacking the back of my head on the rim of the cupboard. Once to my feet, much to my surprise, there was my early Christmas present! Sabrina Harper was standing on the other side of the bar, holding up a small gift bag with the most perfect smile on her face. I placed both hands flat on the bar top, shook my head in disbelief, smiled and tried to speak…but all that came out was babble. I was tongue-tied, something that never happens to me. She placed the bag on the bar and pushed it over to me.

"Merry Christmas, Skipper."

I opened my mouth once more and, finally, something audible came out. "I am so glad to see you, girl!" I said, as if I'd been waiting for years to reunite with a long-lost relative. I didn't say 'hi,' 'hello,' 'how are you doing?'… nothing that a normal person would say under the same circumstances. What I said was…"I knew that you would come. John? Does he know you're in town? If he doesn't, he's going to lay one big golden egg when he finds out." I went on and on as if I were the only one allowed to speak…can you imagine that?

Sabrina laughed. "You mean he's going to shit a brick when he sees me...is that it?"

"That, too," I said.

"I hope that means something good," she said, jokingly. "And, to answer your question...he doesn't know I'm in town. I'm counting on what you told me over the phone to be true...remember...your 'how much John misses Sabrina' speech?"

"I guarantee it," I said, curiously eyeing the gift bag. "Uh...is that for me?"

"I know it's not Christmas yet, Skipper...but go ahead. Yes...it is for you."

I reached into the bag and pulled out a small box similar to a sizeable watchcase. When I opened the box, my chin must have dropped at least an inch. Sabrina noticed and smiled wide. Inside the box was a magnificent-looking master compass. The compass, encased in sterling silver, lay majestically in the walnut box. I'm telling you...now I'm the one laying the golden egg. I was speechless...not tongue-tied, but truly speechless...another thing that seldom, if ever, happens.

"I got that just for you Skipper," Sabrina said, smiling, "so that when you get your own boat, you won't have any trouble navigating the high seas."

That was just the incentive I needed to beat-feet-it around the bar and hug that beautiful angel. I held her close and thanked her for the gift. I wanted to keep her in my arms forever but that would have appeared inappropriate to Sakae, who was watching. In any event, *that* kind of embrace would surely be up to Johnny-boy to give once Sabrina surprises him as she did me. I asked her where she was staying.

"Glorietta Bay Inn," she replied.

"Perfect," I said. "It's right next to the marina. So what's your plan? Will you call John or just go knocking on his door?"

"I was hoping you could help me with that one, Skipper," she confessed. "After all...you're the one playing Cupid."

I glanced over at Sakae, curiously. "By any chance... have you been talking to Sakae? She made a comment to me that night you wandered into the pub...when I hooked you up with John. She said the only thing I was missing in my antics was a bow and arrow."

Sabrina laughed softly and glanced over at Sakae, who heard what she said and was now smiling. "She knows you pretty well, Skipper. Am I sensing something here?"

"The only thing you are sensing is the fact that I l-o-v-e the compass. Sakae's my helper around here." I figured I'd spare Sabrina the details about Sakae and me. I'm sure that, at some point, John will fill in the blanks on that one.

"Let's see now," I said, checking my watch. "It's two o'clock. If John is not at his house painting, he will be sitting in a spot at the marina sketching some boat for a new painting. So... the way I see it, you have a couple of options. One, you can take your chances and wander down to the marina. If he's there, you can sneak up behind him and surprise the hell out of him. Or, two...you could take a chance and head straight to his condo, knock on the door and surprise the piss out of him. If he's not home...well...you can park your tush on the carpet outside his door, lean back against the wall and, when he comes strolling down the hallway, you can hold up a sign that says 'surprise, it's me'."

Sabrina thought the whole thing funny. We were really starting to develop a great relationship.

"On the other hand," I continued, "you could do it the easy way. You can call his cell phone and tell him you're in town. I would take the easy road."

Sabrina smiled. "Not on your life, Skipper. That won't be any fun. Come on now...it's Christmas," she continued with a chuckle. "Everyone likes surprises...don't you think?

That's the Sabrina-sense-of-humor that John was telling me about, and I love it!

"What the hell am I thinking," I said, tossing aside the option to take the easy way. "You're right...go on...go out on a limb and do it up big. It will be something you guys will talk about well into your nineties."

"Aren't you jumping the gun a little here...Uncle Skip?" Sabrina said with a grin.

"Time will tell, Sabrina Harper," I replied, grinning back. "Time will tell."

Well...I was wrong on both counts. John wasn't at the Marina or at home. He had gone to the Galleria specifically to deliver a painting. I had not been in the office for a while; otherwise, I would have noticed his Jeep parked in the back. Instead...I sent Sabrina on a wild goose chase to find him.

John was at the Galleria longer than he wanted to be. When he got there, Kate did what she always did. She dropped what she was doing, gave him a big hug, and then forced him down on the antique couch. Kate wouldn't let him up until he told her everything about his breakup with Elizabeth.

John had called Kate a short time after the break-up occurred as a courtesy, but didn't have the time to provide her with the details. She made him promise to tell her everything the next time they were together.

Kate actually liked Elizabeth but had no idea the difficulties the two of them were having. The fact that she was aware of the breakup but knew nothing of the details had been eating at her since the day she found out. Kate was certainly sad to hear John's explanation of the circumstances surrounding the breakup but didn't question the motives. She sympathized with him and what he had gone through... and that was that. Kate is a class act.

It was around three o'clock when John came in through the back office door and parked himself on a bar stool in front of me. I cringed as soon as I saw him. I had no idea where he had been, and I was sure he hadn't laid eyes of Sabrina yet. I couldn't say anything to him about Sabrina showing up earlier although it was difficult for me to keep tight-lipped about it. I couldn't imagine me spoiling any surprise that she had in store for him. Sakae avoided us like the plague.

You know the bartender's drill. You start by making small talk. You ask a few questions such as…'Where have you been?' or 'What have you been doing?'…that sort of thing. You also learn in bartender's school how to look busy while you chat so they can't pin you down. It's an old trick…primarily to keep them drinking. But in this case, I just needed time to think. That's right…time to devise a plan and somehow covertly communicate to Sabrina.

Since I brought the whole thing on by calling her in the first place, I figured it was now my responsibility to figure out a way to get the two of them together while honoring Sabrina's wish to surprise John. I was playing cupid again…so to speak. Sakae finally walked up and set a glass of tea down on the bar in front of John and quickly walked away. I could tell by the look she shot me that she wanted me to fess up and tell John that Sabrina was in town…I knew that look. It was the…'enough with the games already' look. She knew, however, I was not going to do any such thing.

John and I shot the shit for almost thirty minutes…and I was antsy, wondering what Sabrina was doing. During that time, I quizzed him about his plans for the evening. He didn't have any and that didn't surprise me. He said he was going to run the beach around four–thirty and then try again to work on the portrait of the woman. I shook my head and told him he should give up on that project and concentrate on living again. He smiled to humor me. I knew he wouldn't let it go.

I continued to make small talk all the while hoping Sabrina would waltz through the door at any minute to put me out of my misery. I started saying stupid things, such as reminding him how cold it was going to be as he ran the beach that time of the day...as if he didn't already know that... he did it all the time. 'Just the way I like it,' he said, giving me a curious look.

I finally ran out of options. My only choice was to tell him that I had to make a quick call. I put a small bowl of shelled peanuts in front of him, left him to his tea and hurried into my office to call Sabrina. I shuffled through the messy desk drawer again, grabbed her card and dialed her cell number.

"Sabrina," I said anxiously. "It's Skipper here. Where are you now?"

"Still wandering the marina...I've scoured the entire place and no John-sighting. I guess he's at his condo."

"Wrong guess," I said. "He's here... sitting at the bar drinking tea and eating peanuts."

"What about me? Does he kn...?"

"I haven't said a word," I quickly replied. "Should I...?"

"No, Skipper," she said anxiously. "Keep him there, and I'll casually walk in."

"Will do... just hurry. I don't know how long I can keep him here, though. He said he was going to run the beach so he's liable to walk out at any time."

This was going to work out fine, I thought as I tossed her card back into the drawer. Sabrina walks in. John spots her and falls off his chair. At that point, she'll have to administer mouth-to-mouth resuscitation.

This is what I pictured in my mind as I opened the door to head back to the bar. I froze when I noticed that John wasn't sitting where I left him. Shock set in and panic overcame me until I glanced at Sakae and she pointed towards the restroom. Damn…was I ever relieved to find out that bit of refreshing news! Who would have thought that I'd get so excited finding out that someone went to take a pee.

I quickly motioned at Sakae to refill John's glass of tea. A minute later, John made his way back to the bar but didn't sit down. He lifted the jacket he'd hung over the back of the stool and, as he did, I had to think fast on my feet. There were six boxes of booze, two canisters of 7-up and one canister of tonic water in the storeroom which we needed up front.

I said. "Johnny-boy…before you leave, I need a quick hand. Do you mind?"

"Sure…anything, Uncle Skip," he replied cordially, tossing the jacket over the back of the chair again.

"Thanks," I said. I thought fast and told him that my knee had been acting up and that there were a few things in the store room that I needed to bring to the front. How's that for acting out of panic? I surprised myself with that one. I'm a genius, quick on my feet.

I glanced at Sakae, who sensed I was up to something. John followed me into the storeroom. I figured that by the time Sabrina got to her car, her estimated time of arrival would be about fifteen minutes. I was going to hold John until she got here…even if I had to hog-tie him.

John was behind the bar, on his knees, hooking up the last canister. I stood next to him on the engineered wooden blanks running the length of the bar on top of the concrete floor and kept my eye on the entrance. I expected she would have arrived by then. I started to worry that my calculation for Sabrina getting to the pub might be off and I'd have to figure out another story to keep John from leaving.

Luckily, John finished attaching the dispenser to the bottle just when Sabrina walked in. At that point, I could rest easy…my job complete. I took in a breath and moved away, towards the south end of the bar and then motioned to Sabrina to position herself in front of the bar in the exact spot where John would pop his head up and get the surprise of his life.

Two surprises in one day--one for me earlier and one big one for John. His eyes lit up as soon as he saw her. He was tongue-tied, similar to the way I was earlier. They stood in silence, staring at each other. It reminded me of another movie...the one where Tom Hanks and Meg Ryan finally meet on top of the Empire State Building. You know the one...'Sleepless in Seattle.' It was Sakae's favorite movie.

I looked at Sakae...who was tearing up. I walked completely out of the picture. Who would want to spoil a moment like that? Sakae and I stood together near the office door, wondering which one of them would make the first move to say or do something.

Just as she had with me earlier, she was holding a gift-wrapped box in her hands... somewhat bigger than the one she gave me.

Sabrina said with a warm smile, "Merry Christmas, John," as she placed the gift on the bar top and slowly pushed it over to him.

John still seemed dazed and confused. He took in a deep breath, let it out slowly and smiled. "How did you know that you were on my wish list?" John said, gazing into her eyes.

On my wish list. How brilliant of John to come up with that one. It couldn't have been a better time. The pub was completely empty. Sakae and I were almost embarrassed to stand there and watch it unfold...but we weren't about to miss it.

John slowly made his way around the bar...never taking his eyes off the angel. He stood directly in front of her. He remembered how she smelled when he held her close after dropping her off at the entrance to the Del Coronado.

He took Sabrina into his arms like there was no one else on the planet...not even Sakae and me standing awkwardly watching it all.

"I've missed you," he whispered in her ear.

"You didn't call me."

"You have no idea how much I wanted to," he replied, drawing in a deep breath. "It's just been so hard trying to sort everything out in my mind. Elizabeth and I broke up," he said quickly...wanting to get that news out of the way.

I could tell by the look on Sabrina's face that she wanted to tell him she already knew, but she held my confidence as she promised. Still holding each other tight, "Don't explain," she said. "When you want something bad enough, you go after it. *I* should have called you."

John pushed her slightly away but still kept her close. He looked into her eyes. Their lips came together. They shared a kiss that seemed to last forever. Sakae tugged on my sleeve...and we stopped watching for that moment. John looked over at me and smiled. I would only be kidding myself if I believed John didn't know that I set the whole thing up. He never brought it up, and neither did I.

"Let's leave," John said. "My car is parked down the block."

"My rental car is parked out front, at a meter," she said.

"I have an idea," John said. "I'm sure Skipper won't mind if I keep my car in the back lot for the night. We can take your rental to my place.

"I like that idea," she said, smiling softly. She handed him the box wrapped in Christmas paper.

John sighed. "I'll put this under the small tree I put up," he said. "Only I don't have anything for you."

"Oh...I'll think of something," she whispered, looking nervously around. "Don't let it worry you."

Before I knew it, they were gone. They didn't even say goodbye. Could you really blame them?

Chapter Twenty-six

Time was standing still for both of them, but they didn't waste time trying to make sense of it. Being together again seemed to have negated the few months spent apart. How the two of them met was simple, but the reason that fate brought them together in the first place would always be a wonderful mystery. Yes...partly a mystery and partly because of me. I have to take some credit, after all... remember the bow and arrow? He needed her, that's for sure. In some way, she needed him. Why else would a woman like Sabrina still be single in her thirties. All that didn't really matter; they were together.

As soon as they walked through the door of John's condo, the canvas with the unfinished portrait of the woman propped up on the easel caught Sabrina's eye. She made her way over to it and noticed the locket lying opened on the table in between the two easels. She picked up the locket and studied it closely before switching her gaze to focus on the likeness on the canvas.

"Well...what do you think?" John asked, stepping alongside of her.

Sabrina took a step back to get a wider angle. "The portrait makes her a very pretty woman, but to tell you if it's an accurate portrayal of the photograph in the locket, I can't quite do that," she went on, shaking her head. "I mean...don't get me wrong, John," she continued. "You could have captured her looks accurately, but I didn't see the face in the mirror like you did, so I don't have the same reference points that you do...I wish I could be of more help. To me, it's a sketch of a woman's face...and a darn good one, I might add." Sabrina studied the photograph even closer. "I do, however, now see more of a resemblance to the photo in the locket. It takes a while to really compare the two," she said, pulling the magnifier glass over the top of the locket.

John had no idea that Sabrina already knew from the conversation with me that John had had another dream…she couldn't wait for him to tell her about it.

To be honest, I didn't like keeping secrets…especially from John. I went behind his back and wasn't feeling that great about it.

Calling Sabrina without him knowing...breaking the news that he had had another dream, and then sharing the news about his breakup with Elizabeth…it just didn't feel right. I fought the urge inside to confess. How can you blame me? You know that I had no choice. If I hadn't taken action…who knows where we'd be at this point. Sabrina might still be in Joplin and John…well…who knows where he'd be.

Sabrina walked over to the window and gazed out towards the ocean. "Any more dreams," she asked softly, turning towards him.

John, still concentrating on the portrait, heard her say something but didn't catch it. "Huh? I'm sorry," he said, suddenly refocusing. "I didn't hear what you said, Sabrina."

Sabina walked over to him and took his hand. "I just asked if you had any more dreams," she repeated in a soft voice.

"I've got an idea, Sabrina," John said, without answering her question direct. "I have hot chocolate. Do you like hot chocolate?"

John wasn't ready to delve into that just yet. He wanted to treasure the time with her. He figured that there would be time when they settled in for the other stuff.

"L-o-v-e hot chocolate," she replied, smiling, then rubbed her palms together.

"OK, then," John said. He hurried to the closet and took a wool blanket off the shelf. He handed it to her. "I'll make some hot chocolate and we can sit on the balcony. I'll push the two patio recliners together. It's cool out there, but we can keep warm under this blanket. I do have a lot to tell you, and we may as well be comfortable while I do it."

"Super," Sabrina said, nodding her head. "I love a good camp-out...and on the balcony...no ants or bears... perfect plan."

"Not only do you look beautiful," John said stepping onto the balcony, "you look warm wrapped in that blanket. Can I join in?" he went on, smiling. Sabrina smiled back. He handed Sabrina her cup and held onto his while he moved the empty recliner next to her.

It was then that John told Sabrina everything about Elizabeth and the break-up. He held nothing back... I was proud of him. He explained Elizabeth's moods and eccentricities, her desires for John to be something he didn't want to be. He told her how I had warned him about her from the beginning of their relationship and that I was right. I'm telling you...the guy opened up like a clam in boiling water. He said it was his way of cleansing his soul. He wanted there to be no secrets between them.

John told Sabrina about the day he spotted Elizabeth sneaking into the Red Fox and how that was really the straw that broke the camel's back. He also admitted that, if he'd never met Sabrina that night in the pub, things might have been different regarding that situation. The outcome might have been different.

I think he may have even disregarded my advice and possibly forgiven Elizabeth for lying to him about the lunch she had with that Gary Moberg fella. Who knows for sure...Elizabeth's story may have had some half-truths in it which surely would have given John the option to call it a misunderstanding and the breakup might never have happened. Thank God for the little things.

After John loaded Sabrina up with all that information, they made a pact. They promised each other that *their* relationship was going to be transparent...no secrets. It was now Sabrina's turn. I might have known this was coming. After all, how could a beautiful woman like Sabrina remain single? I would think that every eligible man in Joplin would be sniffing around trying to land her.

Sabrina told John she was in an engagement once but it had fallen apart a year earlier. She had known the guy in junior high school and had innocently dated him a few times over the years and then he proposed. In Joplin, being the small town it is, you never really lose touch with people. John said that Sabrina told him the guy is a salesman by the name of Mark. She graduated high school with him. She didn't expand on too much detail regarding their relationship, or how long it really lasted...and it didn't matter that she didn't. He was out of the picture, and that was all that mattered to John. Sabrina told John emphatically that she realized early on in the engagement that Mark wasn't her type, so that was the end of that.

In addition to this Mark fella not being her type, he traveled so much it caused too many holes in their relationship. She said that they thought they loved each other enough to compensate for the time spent apart, but that just wasn't the case. Sabrina also told John that her Uncle Phil harped on her constantly to break it off with the guy...so she did. Again, thank God for little things. It seems as though Uncle Phil's role in Sabrina's life is much like the role I play in John's life.

Sabrina also admitted, thinking back on it (which raised John's ego when she told him), that even though this Mark was a stand-up kind of guy, being away from *him* didn't produce the intense yearning that developed in her gut for John after she left Coronado to return to Joplin. Can you imagine that? You know someone for less than forty-eight hours, almost three months earlier, and sparks fly to the point that a yearning burns your insides? See…this shit doesn't just happen in the movies. We are talking a real love story here.

Sabrina went on to tell John that the last time she went out on a date had been six months ago. He was another good guy, but again, not the right one…so she declined a second date with that fella. I guess John didn't need to share all this with me; but since he did, I thought I'd share it with you. What is important to note out of all this, however, is that the very fact that Sabrina travelled back to Coronado tells me that she thinks that John *is* the right guy.

Before they knew it, it was six o'clock in the evening. A lot of time was spent exploring each other's life up to and until the time I pulled out my bow and arrow…everything they learned only brought them closer together.

John never did go for his run on the beach nor did he ever say a word about the dreams or his visit with Ron King. That conversation seemed trivial compared to what they were learning about each other. It was a fresh start, as John explained it. Not everyone would have the guts to put it all out there the way they did. Clean living gives one that opportunity. If I did that, who knows what Sakae would think about me.

The sun had set, and even though John and Sabrina were all snuggly under the blanket, feeling the warmth of each other's body, it was too cold to stay out on the balcony.

"Let's go in, and I'll tell you about my last dream and what happened after that. Are you interested?"

"Am I interested?" she said, lightly digging her finger into his ribs. "I can hardly wait. But as much as I want to hear about it," she added, "I really need to freshen up. The flight was long, and I haven't had much to eat…just a protein bar I threw in my bag before leaving for the airport."

"Damn, Sabrina," John said, annoyed with himself. "I should have thought about that."

"Oh, no, John," Sabrina said warmly. "I could have said something earlier, but being alone with you out here on this balcony has been in the back of my mind ever since the last time we were here together."

Sabrina leaned over the arm of his chair slightly, placed a hand on his cheek and brushed her cold lips against his. The kiss literally ignited their passion for each other. Flooded with arousal, the arms of the two chairs separating them received the pressure of John's weight as he shifted his body over on top of her. Their lips were no longer cold from the elements. The kiss was now so warm and passionate that they could feel the wet caverns of their mouths take them to breathless exhilaration.

With both of them on the one balcony recliner, it seemed unsteady. Sabrina relaxed her body, and John slightly loosened his grip. "Do you think the chair will hold both of us?" she whispered in his ear, breathing heavily.

John thought a moment and then murmured, "I'm not sure."

They lay still. Sabrina whispered again, giggling slightly, "I don't think we should move much...do you?"

John said, "I don't like that idea."

"I don't like it either," Sabrina whispered again.

"OK...don't move a muscle. I'm going to get up very slowly so the chair doesn't collapse beneath us."

John moved ever so gently, sliding off the end of the chair onto his knees. He got to his feet and stood there, holding the blanket out. Sabrina pushed herself off the chair and stood directly in front of him. He pulled her close and wrapped the blanket around both of them until they could hardly move ...almost as if they were competing in a sack race. They looked into each other's eyes and started laughing aloud.

John said, "I have another idea."

Sabrina lifted up on her toes, touched her lips to his, and then said, grinning, "I hope it's better than this one. I can hardly breathe. I'm ready...out with it."

"We shuffle into the house and you relax. I'll take a shower and get dressed. After that, we go to your hotel so you can do the same. And then, we'll go get something to eat."

"I love it when a plan comes together."

While John was getting ready, Sabrina perused through sketches John had lying on the table. The true extent of his talent amazed her. She noticed that the frame with the picture of John and Elizabeth in the boat was no longer on the oval table...that delighted her. Being in the condo again gave her a warm feeling of entitlement, like she truly belonged there.

She could hear John in the bathroom getting ready and thought about how it would be to hear the sound of him doing that every morning in the future. She made her way back to the table in the studio, switched on the magnifier light situated over the locket and took another look at the inscription. She thought to herself, 'How sad the person must have been at having lost it.'

Suddenly, the doorbell chiming broke her concentration. John was still in the other room getting ready. "I'll get it!" Sabrina yelled out. The bell chimed again just as Sabrina peeked through the peep hole in the door. "Uh, oh," she said softly. Now *this* will blow your mind.

Standing there face-to-face with Elizabeth was very awkward. She could have just not answered and waited for John's ex-fiancée to turn and head back down the hall but decided not to...there was nothing to hide. On the other hand, the ratings on Elizabeth's personality were not that great, so she opened the door cautiously. Elizabeth was holding a box in her arms. Sabrina's eyes opened wide, and Elizabeth's eyes narrowed, looking past Sabrina into the open room.

"John here?" Elizabeth asked...her voice just short of a sneer.

Sabrina played it cool. "He's in the shower."

There was pause... almost a stare-off. Finally, Elizabeth pushed the box into Sabrina's hands. "This is John's stuff that he left at my place," she said.

Without so much as a 'hi,' 'bye' or 'Merry F-ing Christmas,' Elizabeth turned and walked away. Sabrina put the box down on the coffee table and headed into the bedroom. The bathroom door was cracked. She knocked lightly then took the liberty of peeking in. John was standing in front of the mirror shaving, towel around wrapped around his waist.

Sabrina cleared her throat. John turned and smiled at her. "You just had a visitor," she said.

John bent his brow, "A visitor? Who was it?"

"Well," Sabrina said, "I'll give you two guesses, and it wasn't a delivery man with pizza."

"Don't tell me," John said, his voice serious. "Elizabeth?"

"Yep..." Sabrina replied. "It sure was. But I have to tell you, it really wasn't that uncomfortable. She brought a box with stuff that you left at her place...a small box, I must say," she went on, shrugging slightly. "It was a little awkward, but like I said...not bad. She handed me the box, kind of huffed, and went on her merry way."

"I had no idea that that would hap..."

"Really, John," Sabrina interrupted. "It was really no big thing. As a matter of fact, my friend, Karla, will get a laugh out of it. By the way," she continued, eyeing him up and down and smiling mischievously, "you look nice wrapped in that towel."

John smiled, "Could be Christmas wrap if you want it to be."

Chapter Twenty-seven

John and Sabrina sat at a small corner table in Arrivederci's restaurant. The waiter delivered two glasses of red wine and lit a small candle set in glass next to the wall. John recommended the walnut chicken caesar salad and that's what they ordered, along with calamari and zucchini fritti for an appetizer.

Sabrina glanced around, admiring the Mediterranean décor. Beautiful scenes of Italian villages, vineyards and streets were hand-painted on the walls and the inside of old half-brick mantle frames. Wine bottles of all shapes and sizes lay in dark wood racks everywhere. Quaint wooden tables, perfectly situated around the floor, with small red-and-white-checkered tablecloths and candles set to the side provided the ambiance for a quiet, romantic dinner.

John said he couldn't take his eyes off her, and she noticed him staring. He focused on the small sequins circling the neckline of her sweater in the flickering candlelight. The low lighting set off the natural beauty and silkiness of her fair skin. They sat quietly, both of them. He found himself lost in deep thought, contemplating how wonderful it would be to spend the rest of his life with the wonderful woman sitting across from him. I assume she was thinking the same thing.

Sabrina broke the silence and said, "You can't find this kind of authentic Italian restaurant in Joplin...this is very nice...thank you for bringing me."

"I like this place a lot," he replied, sighing contentedly, thinking even more so with Sabrina sitting there across from him. "It's not over-the-top fancy, but the food is delicious...I mostly come here for lunch."

After gathering her thought's, Sabrina said, in a warm tone of voice, "I can tell that you really like California, John. I can also understand why you're not big on traveling. I'm sure it would be really hard to leave this city for any length of time."

John nodded. "This place is one of the reasons making it hard to stay away or leave the San Diego area," he said. "And there are many more reasons," he added, "...the beaches, the authentic food choices, the entertainment, the climate...and especially Coronado. Anything anyone could ever want is right here. Besides all that, there is one more thing." Sabrina angled her head curiously. "Don't laugh after I tell you this."

"I promise," Sabrina, said crossing her heart.

"I'm a little afraid of flying."

"You mean you are afraid of heights?"

"Nope..." he replied. "Flying. It's not that I won't fly," he went on. "It's just that I try to avoid doing it. It happened years ago when my mother and I flew to Long Island. I was young at the time. We were going to see my aunt in Blue Point. We hit a storm over Chicago and lightning shot through the cabin. That, along with terrible turbulence, scared the hell out of me."

***

John said he worked hard on Sabrina to sell the idea that California was the only place to live during the course of that dinner. When Sabrina had gone back to Joplin, John thought about her all the time. He knew right away that he wanted a relationship with her, but he also knew that a long-distance relationship wasn't going to work...he and I both knew it. This dilemma somehow had to work itself out...that's what I told him. On this day, however, what really mattered was that both of them were together...in a place that he frequented many times, with a girl he wanted to be with.

The waiter placed the salads in front of them and, after Sabrina took one bite, Arrivederci's was now on the list of her favorite restaurants. John lifted his wine glass and proposed a toast.

"Here is to the beautiful girl from Joplin."

Sabrina lifted her glass and lightly touched it to his. "And, here is to the handsome, compassionate guy who made me ache inside as I was trapped on an airplane flying away from him."

John held his gaze on her, smiling as he reached across the table and gently took her hand. "Now that was one of the nicest things anyone has ever said to me."

***

You see, this is what I'm saying. During the entire time John and Elizabeth were an item, he had never heard anything like that from her. While John is obviously a type B personality, Elizabeth was the dominate one...the type A...the part of the relationship that commanded all the attention. In my opinion, mind you, polarizing personalities are a definite "no, no." Now...whether Joseph Navarra would agree or disagree with that, I don't know and really don't give a shit.

The good news is that what Sabrina said to John came straight from her heart. This was way different compared to what John got from Elizabeth. The bad news is that this might be another thing to take John over the edge... complications. It isn't enough that he's got the dreams and the locket to confuse his mind. Now he's falling in love with a girl from Joplin, and the mere fact that the girl from Joplin lives in Joplin, well...that is a major complication.

OK, I've done enough babbling. It was now time for John to bring Sabrina up to speed...to let her in on the latest events involving the locket and his dreams. I must say...he almost had *me* on board...believing there might be something to this whole dream/reality theory after he told me about Ron King and Solitude One and Two. I'm not quite there yet though. Let's see how Sabrina reacts to the latest developments.

***

Halfway through dinner, John asked Sabrina if she was ready to hear about the latest adventure into dream land. As much as she was interested, she asked him if he would hold off until later...later meaning when they were back at his place...or her hotel, for that matter.

Being with John in that time and space...in that restaurant having a quiet, memorable dinner...was all she wanted to think about. John said that it didn't bother him at all; he was content talking about other things...such as their relationship. So the dream stuff would have to wait until another time.

Having dinner together...or lying together out on his balcony...or walking on the beach with him in Coronado was all she thought about from the minute her plane took off towards Joplin over two months ago. I can't blame Sabrina for wanting to hold off on what had happened in a dream. This was a much-anticipated "wow" moment for both of them. Why spoil it? That's my view too.

***

After leaving Arrivederci's, they headed over the bridge towards Coronado. Sabrina looked north towards the San Diego skyline.

John said, "Isn't it beautiful...downtown San Diego?"

"From way up here, it's breathtaking," she murmured, her eyes fixed on the city lights.

"Think you could live here, Sabrina?" John said in a curious sort of way.

Even though the question caught Sabrina off-guard, I think she knew where he was going with it. She tried to think fast and formulate the right answer, something other than 'maybe…or under the right circumstances.' That would, however, only lead to more questions that I think neither one of them was prepared to address, yet.

I have to give John props, however, for throwing the question out there. After he asked her that question, for the next minute or so, all you could hear inside the car were the tires howling over the blacktop at sixty-five miles an hour across the bridge.

"You know, John," she said, in a low tone of voice, slightly chuckling. "I was thinking. I could ask you if you would consider living in Joplin instead of Coronado, but I know that the big differences between the two places, you know…like the obvious ones…the beach and the incredible weather out here versus Joplin where I live…well, it wouldn't be a fair question."

John took his eyes off the road for a moment and faced her. She glanced at him and grinned. John focused his attention on the road again. When John told me this, the first thing that came to my mind was…that was an interesting back and forth. John needed to find a way out of that one until another time…and he did by quickly changing the subject.

"You mentioned earlier that the exchange between you and Elizabeth at my front door would be something that someone by the name of Karla would get a laugh over. Tell me about Karla."

Sabrina played along. She *also* thought that changing the subject at that point was a good idea on John's part. "Karla?" Sabrina chucked loudly. "Karla is a hoot. She's my nosey girlfriend and coworker. Right now, she is probably biting her nails, waiting impatiently for me to call and give her the scoop."

"Scoop?"

"Yes…the scoop," Sabrina said, laughing softly. "She has to know everything…you know the type…every little detail."

"Sounds like Skipper to me," John countered with a chuckle.

"Much worse, I promise you," Sabrina said in a serious tone.

"How is that?"

"Karla is a modern-age Hedda Hopper. She loves to gossip and, in order to *be* a gossip queen, one must first get all the info. Believe me…getting information is her specialty."

"Huh?" John said. "Somehow, it still sounds like Skipper to me."

"I'll tell you, John," Sabrina said, "other than that one fault of hers, which I'm willing to overlook, Karla is a compassionate, loving, good friend."

John said, with a smile, "That still sounds like Skipper."

"What worries me, though," Sabrina said, placing her hand on John's shoulder. "She's single. She thinks she will remain that way for the rest of her life. I've told her it doesn't have to be like that. But the truth is, John," she went on in a serious, concerning tone, "it seems that every time she meets a guy who takes a liking to her, she talks him to death. Two-way communication seems to be a foreign language to her."

"Well," John said, smiling, as he pulled into his parking spot at the condo. "Let's see what we can give Karla to talk about once you return to Joplin."

Sabrina chuckled, and lightly punched John's arm. "I've got news for you. She will want to know details long before that. She is a text-messaging freak."

Before Sabrina could open the car door, John put his hand on her forearm. She looked at him. He leaned in towards her and gently placed a hand on her cheek. Sabrina melted as he gave her a long kiss for the second time that day. When their lips came apart, John whispered, "I want to open the door for you, so don't you dare move."

John quickly stepped out of the car and hurried around to the other side…opening the door and offering his hand.

""Why, John," Sabrina said coyly, "how gentlemanly of you."

John looked into her eyes and said with a huge grin, "Oh, it's nothing. I just wanted you to have one more interesting thing to add to all the other juicy stuff you will be telling Karla when you talk to her."

Sabrina lightly slapped him on the arm again.

Twenty-eight

The romantic dinner at Ristorante Arrivederci offered the perfect ambiance to set the stage for a man and a woman to transition into a night of passionate lovemaking…two lovers ripping each other's clothes off in the heat of passion.

But no…what does John do when they walked into his condominium? Instead of lighting a few candles, pouring Sabrina a glass of wine and rushing to cuddle up to her on the sofa, he offers up more hot chocolate. This guy must really be comfortable in his skin, I guess.

"How about I brew us up some hot chocolate?" he asked.

"L-o-v-e hot chocolate," she replied, smiling.

John chuckled and made his way into the kitchen. Sabrina went to the sofa, sat down and ran her hands along the top of the soft leather on each side of her. She leaned back and let a deep sigh of satisfaction escape her body.

Moments later, John walked in carrying two cups of hot chocolate with a few miniature marshmallows floating on top of the foamy mixture. "I hope you like marshmallows," he said.

Sabrina laughed. "I l-o-v-e marshmallows…how did you know?"

John smiled, "I just took a wild guess. Besides…who doesn't love marshmallows?"

I could only smile and nod so many times after John went on and on about how great the two of them got along and how wonderful and funny Sabrina was. I was happy for the both of them—happy, I tell you. However, enough already with the 'l-o-v-e hot chocolate and marshmallows stuff.

John sat on the sofa next to Sabrina and told her he waded into the ocean until he was walking on the sea floor as if it really happened.

"It was the strangest thing, Sabrina," he said. "It was one thing to be fighting to stay alive above water as I was doing in previous dreams, that was scary stuff, but walking on the ocean floor was another thing altogether...it felt so real. It was almost like a walk on the beach on a calm, hazy day. There I was...walking on the bottom of the ocean without any trouble breathing or anything. Crazy stuff, huh?"

"Sounds pretty strange alright." Sabrina said anxiously. "So, let me understand this," she went on. "You remember walking straight out into the surf until you were completely submerged?"

"I remember it all. Just like that," John replied, shrugging.

"WOW! Then what?"

"I saw rocks and fish and algae and coral, as if I were staring into some giant fish tank at Sea World...but in this case, I was in the middle of it. It was then that I spotted the sailboat. It was stuck sideways in the sediment along the bottom, a portion of the boat buried. The only thing I wasn't sure of was how far out in the ocean it was. But it was definitely there."

"Sailboat, huh...?" Sabrina murmured. "Was it the sailboat you saw in a previous dream?"

"Well..."John replied, gesturing with an open hand, shrugging again. "I assume it was the same boat...but obviously, I can't be certain." John slowly rose to his feet and wandered over to the sketch of the woman. "It looked like the boat had been there for a long time, so I just don't really know...but here's the interesting part," he went on with his back to her as he fiddled with something on the desk. "The boat had a name painted on the stern…Solitude One."

Sabrina began to feel the mild euphoria, a release of the feel-good chemicals in her body from the glasses of wine she had had earlier at dinner. She got up from the sofa feeling relaxed with an urge to be sensual. She walked up behind John, placed her hands gently on his shoulders then began to massage lightly.

"I can tell this has been hard for you, John," she said, slowly turning him around to face her, taking charge. She put her arms loosely around his neck and gazed into his eyes. She stood slightly on her toes and gave him a soft, tender, romantic kiss. "Wouldn't you rather continue telling me about this a little later?" she said softly as she kissed him again.

With both hands around her slender waist, he held Sabrina at arm's-length. He gazed into her deep blue eyes leading her to believe he would defer talking about dreams and pull her in but, no…not John. Instead, he comes back with, "I'm on a roll here. Trust me…you're going to want to hear the rest, now and not later…and the dream gets even more weird."

Sabrina sighed. It was the last thing she wanted at that moment, to hear anything being defined as weird. There was a pause, and then she shrugged lightly, grinned and said, "Well…if you insist. Since you put it that way…OK, I guess. Should I head back to the sofa and sit for this?"

John grinned as he gently took her hand and led her away from the sofa and into the bedroom. Sabrina felt confused, a little anxious, *the wine playing tricks maybe, she thought.*

"This is a long story," he said, letting go of her hand once in the room. He propped the bed pillows up against the headboard, stood at the side of the bed and bowed at the waist like a gentleman as he motioned with his hand for her to climb on. "We might as well get comfortable," he said. "Is that OK with you?"

Sabrina slowly batted her eyes and said, "And you have to ask?" John smiled.

She kicked off her shoes, playfully leaped up backwards onto the bed and scooted over, all the while gazing at him, starry-eyed. She leaned back against a pillow and held out her hand.

"I will only agree to this," she said with a wide grin, "if you promise to hold me tight in your arms once you start telling me the scary, weird parts."

"That is a promise you can be sure I'll keep," John said. "Cross my heart and hope to die."

He took hold of her hand and positioned himself next to her on the bed…close enough that their bodies touched. He put his arm under her neck. She snuggled against his shoulder and rested her hand on his chest.

"OK…I'm ready," she said. "Tell me everything."

It wasn't easy for John to get his thoughts together. The mere sight and feel of Sabrina being there, lying provocatively next to him in his bed, gave him a sense of content excitement. He was now anxious as she was earlier. He could start talking about dreams and lockets or even Ron King's brother if he wanted to…but holding Sabrina in his arms seemed now to be much more important than any of that. He brushed her hair towards the back of her head with his fingers, exposing her delicate ear and neckline.

"If your intention is to get me to relax while you tell me what happened, it's working," Sabrina said softly.

"I'll try to concentrate, but it won't be easy," he replied as he gently stroked her silken hair, refocusing his thoughts. "Let's see. Where was I? Oh, yeah," he went on, shifting his hand to gently touch the side of her neck, causing a warm sensation to run down to her hips. "I walked up to the boat and peered into the deck portion towards the stern…layers of sediment covered most of it. That's when I noticed something sticking out of the sediment…something half round. I leaned in and brushed over it with my hand, stirring the sediment. Suddenly, I was looking at a partially-decomposed human skull."

Just the thought of it changed Sabrina's demeanor for a split second. "Holy shit!" Sabrina said, making a fist, crumpling the material of his shirt in the palm of her hand. "Are you sure it was human and not the bones from some sort of fish?"

"Positive," John replied. "And, not only that… there were bones lying next to it, like a shoulder blade and upper arm bone."

"That must have been a horrible sight."

"Like you might see in a horror film," he said.

Sabrina ran her hand around to his side and tightened her grip. "This is starting to get creepy so I get to hold you tighter," she said, in a humorous tone of voice, smiling as she slightly lifted her head to look into his eyes.

At that moment, the mood shifted again. The subject of dreams suddenly became insignificant. Their lips came together, touching just enough to make them want more. At that point, John said, the stars lined up, the room became silent. No more talking about dreams and boats or lockets or anything that prevented them from pressing up against each other.

Now, both confident in each other's intentions, John used his strength. In one continuous motion, he rolled her onto the top of him. He moved his hands to the inside and up the back of her sweater, touching the warm crevasse of her back in a gentle and loving motion until she quivered.

He slowly kissed her warm lips, keeping his desire to devour her in check. He kissed her ear lobe, her neck and then her shoulder, slightly pulling down the neckline of her sweater. They began removing each other's clothes in a slow and enticing manner, one article at a time, until their skin melded together. They continued kissing and caressing each other…their warm bodies moving in a rhythmic motion.

***

It may not have happened the way that I explained it but in my mind it did. The rest of this is you using *your* imagination. Whatever happened, however, given the dribbs and drabbs that John gave me, he was a lucky man that night.

***

Anyway, when it was all over and they lay motionless in bed on damp sheets staring at the ceiling, John began to tell Sabrina about Solitude Two.

"I just happened to be strolling the marina," John said, "when a sailboat protruding out between two other boats caught my eye."

Sabrina nestled in the crook of John's arm moving slightly onto her right side. She let out a deep sigh of satisfaction then murmured something John couldn't make out. Within seconds, she was fast asleep.

John was content just to let her sleep peacefully. The long flight from Joplin combined with wine, dinner and intense lovemaking…he knew she was exhausted. He slowly removed his arm from underneath her neck, pulled the blanket up to her shoulders, laid back and fell fast asleep.

Chapter Twenty-nine

The woman was alone, sitting in a chair in an unfamiliar, dimly-lit room, sobbing uncontrollably. John was looking straight at her, but she had no idea he was there. The room and everything in it, including the woman, seemed to move around him like moons orbiting a planet, as though suspended in some strange time and space, was how he explained it.

He looked curiously at the woman, mentally noting every feature and detail of her face. On the table next to the chair was a small frame, holding a picture of two women standing arm-in-arm, one younger than the other, both smiling...seemingly during a happy time.

Suddenly, John found himself back on the ocean floor looking directly at the silhouette of the girl in the white, free-flowing gown floating just above the sailboat. The girl extended her arm towards him and, just as before, millions of tiny bubbles appeared, engulfing her body.

***

"John, John," Sabrina said softly, afraid that she'd startle him. She gently placed her hand on his shoulder, moving him slightly. "Wake up, John."

"What...? Huh...?" John opened his eyes.

Sabrina sat on the edge of the bed and rubbed his arm. "You must have been dreaming," she said as sunlight seeping through the shutters danced across the room. "You seemed very restless."

John thought for a second, struggling to get his bearings...and then quickly grasped the reality of Sabrina being there with him in his bedroom. He smiled at her, took her arm and gently pulled her down next to him. "For a moment, I thought that I had two dreams," he said, holding her close, taking in her delicate scent.

"OK," Sabrina said, kissing his cheek as she abruptly sat up on the side of the bed again. "Now that one you'll have to explain to me."

John gazed at her beauty. He rolled to his side and positioned himself on his elbow, resting the side of his head in the palm of his hand. "For a moment, Sabrina," he said smiling, his gaze washing over her, "...at first, when you woke me, I thought I had dreamt you and I were clutching each other, making mad passionate love, but that wasn't a dream at all. Mind playing tricks, I guess."

Sabrina laughed with some restraint. "I'm really glad it wasn't a dream; reality works much better in those circumstances, don't you think??"

John nodded and pushed himself to a sitting position next to her. He brushed his fingers through his hair and leaned forward, resting his elbows on his knees and his forehead in the palms of his hands. "Dream number two was one of those."

"You mean...one of *those*?"

"That's exactly what I mean," John replied. "I saw her clearly."

A small furrow appeared across Sabrina's brow. "Who did you see?"

"The woman in the photograph, you know, inside the locket," he replied, smiling, turning to her with a confident look, then tapped his index finger on his temple. "And it's all right in here, locked away...her image."

Sabrina said excitedly, "You can finish the sketch!"

Sabrina, draped in a white towel, rose from the side of the bed to stand directly in front of him. "I hope you don't mind, but I took the liberty of using the shower while you were sleeping."

John looked up at her and smiled. He placed a hand on each of her perfectly formed thighs, slowly moving them upward, underneath the towel. She gently put one hand on his shoulder and the other on the back of his head...the towel fell to the floor.

***

Much later, as John and Sabrina sat on the sofa together having coffee, Sabrina noticed John was being particularly quiet. He gazed for the longest time at the artificial Christmas tree standing in the corner. There was one gift underneath it, the gift Sabrina had placed there for him the night before.

Christmas was two days away. What was really on John's mind wasn't the fact that he didn't have a gift for Sabrina...there was plenty of time left for that. What was heavy on his mind seemed much more important than gifts, dreams or lockets...even paintings for that matter.

At some point during the night before, Sabrina had told John that she was flying back to Joplin the day after Christmas. At the time, it seemed rather a matter of fact. Now, thinking about the reality of it put John in a solemn mood.

He told me how hard it was for him not to bring the subject up. On the other hand, in his mind, if he left it alone, it might be too late to discuss it in depth later. The reality was, and they both knew it, Sabrina would be flying away to Joplin again soon.

Gently taking his hand in hers, she looked into John's eyes and said, "You are being awfully quiet. Are you thinking about that dream, the woman in the photograph, or something else? It seems that something is bothering you."

"It's not the dream or the photograph," he replied, gazing back at her. "It's you, Sabrina."

I knew they couldn't hold out for very long before bringing the subject up. You can't just let those things fester. If they didn't tell each other what they were feeling, who knows what may slip through the cracks later.

"I wonder if you are thinking the same thing I'm thinking," she said, softly, reluctantly. "If we *are* thinking the same thing, I want you to know that I was thinking about it while I was showering this morning."

After a pause, John said. "You leaving?"

Sabrina replied. "Yes... When I woke up, I laid there and watched you sleeping next to me for the longest time. It made me wish I could wake up every morning in the same way for the rest of my life."

John turned to her and said, emphatically, "I have to say it, Sabrina. Thinking about you leaving Coronado is making me feel empty inside, and the hard part is I know I have no right to try to do anything about it," he continued as he gently lifted her chin and lightly kissed her lips. "Your home is in Joplin, and your work is there. My work is here, and I'm not willing to change that. I could tell you that I love you and you could tell me the same…but what comes of it?"

A lonely tear made its way down Sabrina's cheek. "Right now…this minute," she said, "this is my dream…and in this dream, I do love you. I believe in such a thing as love at first sight and that could have happened in Skipper's when I first saw your handsome face and those sincere eyes. But…"

John quickly put his hand against her lips and wiped away the tear running down her cheek. "Don't say another word," he said. "Let this be OUR dream. I want you to know that, in this dream…I'm madly in love with you. Since we only have a few days left of this dream of ours, let's take advantage of every minute," he went on as she listened intently, staring at him the whole time. "I know it's going to be heartbreaking and painful when you leave, but I believe that this world of ours sometimes works in strange ways. In the end, some dreams do become reality, you know. I read a quote once by some fella by the name of Richard Bach. 'True love stories never have endings.' I consider our being together, here and now, just the beginning."

John wiped away another tear trickling down Sabrina's face, took her tightly into his arms and kissed her hard and long.

Chapter Thirty

Sakae and I knew this was very hard for John and Sabrina to deal with, even though they both made it sound easy…you know…her loving him and him loving her in some sort of fantasy dream world. We all know that only works in the movies…not in real life.

Love and togetherness takes serious planning, especially when two people live worlds apart. I told John that adding another dream to his life wasn't a good idea…more complications, if you get my drift. Besides, you'd think John would have had enough of dreams already.

Using a dream to explain away the fact that they had fallen in love with each other in a very short period of time wouldn't work for very long. They still had three days together. They needed to make decisions quickly before it was too late. Three days would seem like three seconds and, before they realized it, reality would set in. She was still going home, and he wasn't going anywhere.

All of that translated into John being even more miserable after she leaves and me carrying the burden of having to cheer him up every time I saw him. I would have recommended they reconcile their dilemma post haste…before she goes, not after. After all, the way I see it… people do have options… and when love is involved, anything's possible…even for an older man like me. Oops, there I go again.

OK…since you already know about Sakae and me, I'll let you in on another little secret about us. Even John doesn't know this tidbit of information. Sakae and I are planning to get married! How about that…me…over sixty and getting married! Sakae is a few years younger…but who's counting! Like I said…when you are in love, anything is possible.

It was going to be a small ceremony… We even talked about getting married in Vegas, that would be a hoot. In any event, it *was* going to be a month or so from now. We wanted to surprise everyone that had a need to know…which isn't that many.

Sakae's parents live in Japan and are too old to travel so, with John (and now maybe Sabrina), a few of Sakae's friends, and maybe a few folks who frequent the pub that I'm kind of close to.

Once again, and this time unintentional, I've turned this story into something about me…but I felt it was important to mention it. I just can't, for the life of me, make this a happy occasion when the young man that I hold so dear has so much emotional turmoil in his life.

The wedding will have to be postponed a while. Sakae and I both came to that conclusion. Sakae has worked for me for years, and our relationship has been the same for about that long. Waiting a while longer for the sake of John's mental stability is really no big deal...and Sakae agrees.

***

Let's get back to John and Sabrina. After doing whatever they did, fawning over each other about how much they loved each other in their fantasy world, he started telling her the rest of the Solitude Two story.

"OK…where was I…let's see now," John said as he scratched the back of his head, thinking of where he left off. "Oh, yeah… the sailboat…the one docked at the marina. The name of the boat is Solitude Two. I was stunned when the name, painted in yellow and red, just jumped out at me."

"How strange is that?" Sabrina murmured.

"I thought it very strange," John replied. "So I made my way down the ramp and out to the boat to get a closer look. For a moment," he went on, thinking back to that day, "I thought I was seeing things because the boat was moving and swaying on the water between two other boats. However, as I got closer, it *was* true…there it was… tied to the dock…Solitude Two. I was certain that I was looking at the sister boat to the sunken Solitude One."

Sabrina inched to the edge of the sofa. "What crossed your mind at that point?"

John thought a moment. "I can't remember…I was dumbfounded, I guess. I stood there staring directly at the name for maybe…two minutes. I suppose all kinds of things were passing through my mind at once. It was as if I were in a daze, staring at the name on the boat. Perhaps the remote possibility of now finding the owner of the sunken Solitude One was one of those things I thought about."

A light went off in Sabrina's head. "You know what, John?" Sabrina said, leaning forward and getting to her feet.

Before John could respond, Sabrina quickly makes her way to the table as if she were on a mission. She stood there awhile, her eyes scanning the table. Finally, she picked up a pad and sketching pencil and quickly returned to the sofa, plopping herself down next to him.

With a curious look on his face, John asked, "You going to draw something?"

Sabrina laughed softly. "Write something," she replied evenly.

John gently took hold of Sabrina's wrist as he took the sketching pencil out of her hand and laid it on the coffee table. He then pulled open a small drawer, took out a number two pencil and handed it to her. "That sketching pencil will run the letters together if you are not careful…here, use this."

Sabrina smiled. "You are so smart," she said.

John nudged her shoulder with his elbow. "OK…I give up," he said, eyeing the pad resting on her lap. "What is it you plan on documenting…how crazy you think I am?"

She laughed, and he smiled. "No, silly," she said, pressing her index finger against his lips. "This story is getting too interesting…time for me to start making notes. I didn't tell you this; but just before I left Joplin, my Uncle Phil told me to use my judgment as to whether I thought your dreams might make for a good human-interest story for the magazine."

John cringed at the thought of anyone else knowing about the weird fantasies conceivably made up in his head or, for that matter, his crazy dreamscapes.

"Oh, no, you don't," John said shaking his head from side to side. He snatched the pencil out of Sabrina's hand, twirled it around twice between his fingers as if he were a drummer twirling a drumstick then tossed it back into the drawer. Sabrina eyed the sketching pencil and quickly snatched it off the top of the table, held it behind her back and giggled slightly.

"Now, John," she said grinning. "I promise…I won't print anything unless I have your permission. I just want to make notes so we don't have to, at some point, hash out all the details again in case you do find the rightful owner of the locket."

"This is really a stretch, you know," he said evenly.

"What stretch? No stretch," she replied, shaking her head.

"So you are thinking that all this will lead to the mystery woman in the locket and, eventually, to Anna?"

Sabrina replied, "Well…don't you?"

John wavered a bit and gave her a small shrug. "Can we forget about all of this for now and go back to talking about how much we love each other?"

Sabrina thought for a moment. "OK…" she replied, putting on a bright smile. "I'll say it… I love you, John.

Now I'll say it for you…I love you, Sabrina." She glared at him. "Now that that's done…and by-the-way, I truly meant what I said, speaking for both of us… now…answer my question, please…don't you?"

John shook his head at her antics and grinned. "OK…I'll play along. The answer is, uh…yes, yes."

"'Yes' that you love me?" she said grinning. "Or 'yes' that we'll find who the locket belongs to…or both? Which is it?"

John made out like he was going to reach for the sketch pencil again but, instead, grabbed her around the waist, pulled her in close and planted a kiss on her lips. She gave in.

***

Here we go again. All of these games they were playing with each other were taking time away from John telling her the good part of the story…the part about Ron King. I then began to wonder if I was getting too involved in their lives *and* the dreams.

Sakae said I *was* too involved. Telling Sabrina about Ron King, or anything else for that matter, was probably the last thing on John's mind. She said they were just having fun with the little time they had left…and that's all that *really* mattered. I thought about what she said, when she said it and she was probably right.

Chapter Thirty-one

Around to the back of the building, off the alley, there are three parking spaces reserved for my pub. The other six spaces belong to the boutique and antique store located on each side of me. Normally, when I show up to start my day, all the other spaces are usually empty.

John's Jeep still occupied one of my spaces and that's how I knew the two lovebirds stayed the night together. John would have to come back to get his car sometime, which indicated to me that they would be in sometime during the day…and I wasn't wrong. They walked in through the front entrance around lunch time.

I didn't know where they had spent the night, John's house or the Glorietta Bay Inn. I guess that detail wasn't really important. One thing for sure, however, I could tell by the glow on their faces that they were definitely together. Thinking about it made me want to grab Sakae and take her in the back room. Unfortunately, we were too busy for that. I'd have to hold on to that thought until we lock the doors later tonight.

I remember John telling me what Sabrina had said to him the last day he saw her; the day he dropped her off at the Del Coronado Hotel two months ago. She said she'd come back to Coronado if she got a craving for one of Skipper's finest pure-beef hamburgers…so guess what?

I knew how John liked *his* burger cooked, but I didn't know how Sabrina liked hers. I instructed Juan to cook them both the same…medium-well. As they sat there at the table, talking, drinking tea and laughing it up, John made another attempt at telling Sabrina the rest of the Solitude Two story. Before he could get two words out of his mouth,

I walked up carrying two oblong plastic baskets lined with red-and-white-checkered paper. In the baskets were the purest beef hamburgers found anywhere on the Island...with golden french fries sprinkled around.

As I set the baskets in front of them, Sabrina looked up with eyes widening, and said, "Mmm, Skipper... how did you know I was craving one of these?"

I shrugged and told her that I was clairvoyant. The comment drew a laugh from both of them. I suggested that they enjoy their burgers and hurried off. I would have preferred to sit down in one of the two empty chairs to visit for a while, especially since the angel was there, but the pub was getting busier by the minute.

Juan's wife, Andrea, a part-time worker, scurried from table to table. She set clean napkins, forks, knives and newly-filled squeeze bottles with ketchup and mustard on recently vacated tables. I had to get back behind the bar where Sakae was pouring draft after draft...which was primarily my job. I'll tell you what... if it weren't for Sakae... the place would be complete chaos.

***

"This hamburger is delicious, but way too big for me to eat by myself," Sabrina said, holding the hamburger with both hands, the juice beginning to drip down her wrists. "I hope I don't offend Skipper if I don't finish it."

John said, "Believe me...most people who come here for a hamburger know right away they won't be able to eat the whole thing. The exception would be the guy sitting over there," he went on, as he nodded towards a table over in the corner before dipping a fry in ketchup and popping it in his mouth. "His name is Mahoe...born in Hawaii, lives here on the Island. He weighs about two-seventy-five and eats two of them. I don't know why Skipper makes them so massive. I suppose, in some way, it's a novelty thing to draw crowds. 'Big and juicy burgers at Skippers.' I'll tell you, though…it works. Look around this place…it's packed."

"To be truthful… I'm not really a big hamburger person," Sabrina said, wiping her hands and wrist with a handful of napkins. "But I must admit… it's the best I've ever had."

As John worked his way through three-quarters of his burger, he leaned back in his chair and let out a sigh of satisfaction. Sabrina only made it half-way to the finish line before rubbing her hands together anxiously.

"Well…I'm done," she said. "Now I want to hear more about Solitude Two."

John sipped his tea and thought for a moment. "You *know*, don't you, Sabrina," he said cagily. "Every time I try to tell this story, we end up getting distracted by something else."

"Look around, handsome man," Sabrina countered, giving him a cunning look while at the same time feeling for his leg beneath the table with her foot. "See all these people? You'd never try something like that in here, right now…would you?"

John angled his head slightly and glared as if he would really attempt something just to get a reaction. The look on Sabrina's face quickly changed. She questioned in her mind if John was really contemplating something that the people sitting at the table next to them might start whispering about. John glanced around before laughing softly. "OK…pretty girl. You've made your point"

I love that about these two lovebirds. There's no end to their flirting and joking and laughing. They're a match made in heaven. John put it all out there, this time with no interruptions except for Sakae refilling their empty glasses.

John told Sabrina that he had investigated the origin of Solitude Two by using some internet search engine, as he explained it to me…as if I knew what the hell he was talking about!

I have a hard time using the automatic teller...I still write checks. Sakae tells me to stop living in the past. Well, it so happens, I like living in the past...you know...Sinatra, the Bee Gees, Colombo...that sort of thing. Whoops... here I go...making the story about me again.

***

John explained to Sabrina just how he located the owner of Solitude Two...with my help, I might add. Well...I at least knew the guy. He told her how the registration number of the boat led him straight to the owner and how awkward it was just showing up at a stranger's house. He felt even more awkward when the man pulled up in an unmarked police car while he, John, was asking personal questions of the guy's wife.

"How old were these people?" Sabrina asked curiously, her elbows planted on the table, her chin resting in the palms of her hand.

"Let's put it this way...retirement age."

"Darn it...I should have brought the pad and pencil," she said, mad at herself for not thinking of it before they left John's condo.

"I thought you reporters had tiny little tape recorders hidden somewhere," John said, chuckling. "Maybe I should get you one for Christmas."

"OK," Sabrina said, "that's funny. Just continue...and I'll shut up."

***

You see what I'm saying about these two. Did I say earlier that they were a match made in heaven? Now I'm starting to think it might be just the opposite. God might strike me down for saying that, but all the joking...it's getting to be a little annoying...don't you think? Sakae thinks it's what makes them the perfect couple. She even reminded me that I used to complain about John and Elizabeth being too serious. OK. What do I know?

"Listen to this," John continued as his tone became serious. Sabrina's eyes narrowed as she listened. "They invited me into their house and their living room was filled with pictures and small models of sailboats everywhere you looked. I've never seen such a display. There was even one of my sailboat paintings hanging on the wall."

"You're joking," Sabrina said. "Did you let them know it was your painting?"

"In so many words…yes. Actually…the man…Ron King is his name…put two and two together and figured it out.

"Wow…how exciting is that? You're his artist of choice."

"I don't know about that," John replied, grinning. "However, he did say he wanted to purchase another one of my paintings; but his wife, Millie, said there was no room to hang even one more picture in their home."

Sabrina laughed softly. "They seem to be nice people."

"Believe me…they were. To tell you the truth, I felt bad about bringing up the past."

"Past…?" Sabrina questioned.

"Yes…the past," John replied, nodding. "Believe it or not, Solitude One was this Ron King's brother's sailboat."

"Holy shit!" Sabrina spat out…then quickly put a hand over her mouth as she glanced at the people sitting at the table next to theirs. Her fair skin turned a shade of red and she leaned in and whispered, "Gosh…I'm sorry for the outburst."

"*I* can't blame you," John said. "It caught me by surprise just *like* that when I found out."

"So you told the Kings about the dreams?"

"Not really," John replied. "Trust me. Once they realized that I knew there was a Solitude One…well, I didn't have a choice but to be tight-lipped about the crazy stuff. After all, his only brother was lost at sea. I could tell it still really affected both him *and* his wife, and I didn't want to add to that."

Sakae returned to their table with a fresh pitcher of tea to top off their glasses, smiled at Sabrina, and subtly winked at John before scurrying off.

"Did this Ron King say if there were any witnesses who might have seen his brother's boat go down?" Sabrina said, squeezing a slice of lemon into her glass.

"That's the sad part. Ron said the Harbor Police searched the bay and the ocean for hours, maybe even days, with no success," John went on with a long sigh. "Just like that... his brother and two more people were gone forever."

"Two others ...?" Sabrina said curiously. "Was one a girl?"

After a long moment, John responded to Sabrina's question with a somber look on his face, shaking his head from side to side. "If there was, it couldn't be substantiated at the time ...only two other guys."

"I don't get it," Sabrina said, her eyes fixed on his. "How do Anna and the locket fit into all this?"

"I wish I knew," John replied. "I wish I knew..."

Chapter Thirty-two

The fact that Ron King had told John that Solitude One went down with three men aboard made a bad situation even worse, leaving more unanswered questions. It only added extra confusion to the mystifying, and thus far, un-solvable puzzle of dreams. Although nothing at that point was certain, John felt deep inside his belly that the locket did have something to do with Solitude One sinking on that stormy afternoon.

With Christmas only two days away and the fact that Sabrina was flying back to Joplin the day after, sitting around my place discussing dreams was eating into the lit-tle time they had left together. As compelling as the story was, they both agreed to let it go and discuss it another time. I couldn't blame them for that, wanting to skedaddle out of Skipper's and make a day of it together, minus the dreams.

They said adios to Sakae and me, climbed into separate cars and headed for the rental car return facility. After dropping off Sabrina's rental, they headed to the Westfield Plaza Bonita Mall where John had something in mind but kept it from Sabrina.

Being together at that time and place felt right for both of them. As they strolled through the mall holding hands, they noticed others holding hands, walking arm and arm. They fit in perfectly as a couple. John spotted the Star-bucks.

"Do you like and are you up for a latte from Star-bucks?"

You are not going to hear me say it. Let's just say Sa-brina liked the idea. They sat at one of the small, round tables outside Starbucks drinking caramel lattes and watching the hundreds of scurrying shoppers looking for last-minute gifts.

John's plan all along was to buy Sabrina a nice piece of jewelry, a reminder of the time they spent together. Directly across from Starbucks is Daniel's Jewelers. Daniel's was the jewelry store where John and Elizabeth shopped for her engagement ring. It made John feel a little uncomfortable but it didn't deter him. There really was no need for Sabrina to have that information.

"I wish we had a mall like this in Joplin," Sabrina said, marveling at how big the mall was and the number of well-known outlets.

John put his latte down on the table, reached across, took her hand in his and pointed over towards Daniel's jewelry store. "I'm going to buy your Christmas gift right over there," he said.

As Sabrina watched John point to the jewelry store, an obvious question may have crossed her mind. I asked John if he considered that possibility. Did she ask herself the question that would perhaps draw a conclusion...do you hear what I'm saying here? You know...the-love-story-in-the-dream scenario. Would she then think an engagement ring was in order?

I guess we won't know that answer until John asks if that was in her mind at the time. Does what I'm saying add anything to this story? I think not. I just thought, if that were the case, her nosey friend Karla would certainly have a field day spreading that around the office.

"You don't have to do that, John," she smiled. "What *I* got you is just a little something I thought you'd get a kick out of...and it wasn't at all expensive."

"Are you saying you don't *want* me to buy you a present?" John said with a silly smirk. "Is that what you're *really* saying?"

"Well...uh...no... I'm not saying *that* but..."

"Well, then… no 'buts,' Sabrina," John interrupted, grinning widely. "In this dream of ours, how many times have I told you that I love you?"

Sabrina grinned. "Not enough, as far as I'm concerned."

"I'll say it again…I love you."

"*Oh*… I see," Sabrina replied with a smile. "I get it…you're going to *pretend* to buy me something since we are dreaming all this up."

John narrowed his eyes and gave her a naughty sort of look in response to what she had said. He smiled and slowly pushed his chair back. She watched as he stood up and made his way around the table to stand directly behind her. He slid the chair back with her in it, and before *she* stood up, he gently brushed her hair aside, softly kissed her neck and whispered, "Does that feel like I'm dreaming this up?"

Sabrina inhaled deeply. "Do it one more time just like that, and I'll let you know."

"Now you're asking for it," John said. At that point, John slid her chair to the side, took Sabrina by both hands, yanked her up into his arms then planted a kiss on her lips in front of God and everyone. How much more real can this love story be, I ask you?

Sabrina put her arm around John's waist as they made their way over to the glass display case just inside the store entrance filled with all kinds of jewelry. The rings, lined up in rows like tiny little soldiers in white velvet display trays, caught Sabrina's eye.

"Wrong case," Sabrina said, chuckling.

"How do you know what my intentions are?" John replied as he gazed into her eyes.

Just then, an older saleslady with stylish reading glasses attached to a silver chain around her neck showed up on the other side of the case in front of them.

"We have some beautiful rings on sale for the holidays," she said with a warm smile. "You two look like a couple in love," she continued, as she removed a flex-band with the key to the case attached from her wrist. "Shopping for a ring...am I right?"

There was a pause as John and Sabrina looked at each other and chuckled. Sabrina turned to address the lady.

"That we are, shopping that is," she said boldly, smiling. "But we're not quite ready for rings just yet."

The lady glanced at John. He pointed a finger at himself and smiled. "I am...she's not."

Sabrina poked John in the arm with her elbow. The saleslady thought the whole episode was amusing and could hardly hold a straight face.

Suddenly, right out of the blue, John said, "How about an ankle bracelet?"

Sabrina turned to look at him again, lifting an eyebrow. "I l-o-v-e ankle bracelets," she replied in a reedy tone.

When John told me, she mentioned 'love' again in the same way...'l-o-v-e'...I almost gagged. I know they were having fun with it...and it's cute to a point, once or twice. But...come on...give me a break already...am I the only one feeling this way?

Anyhow, John bought Sabrina a beautiful gold ankle bracelet with two small hearts on it. The store etched a 'J' on one heart and an 'S' on the other before gift-wrapping the box so John could have something under the tree for Sabrina to open Christmas morning.

After leaving the mall, they headed straight for Sabrina's hotel so she could check out. Why keep the hotel room when she was sleeping in John's bed?

John had something special planned for Sabrina. When he suggested it as they were driving back to Coronado, she became really excited about the idea. In John's mind, with only a few nights left together, Skipper's (with all the beer drinkers and noise) was not among the options considered for a romantic evening. It was going to be an intimate dinner at Primavera Ristorante on Orange Avenue. John was ahead of the game. He had called for reservations while he was waiting for Sabrina to get her things packed.

When they finally got to John's place, it was four o'clock in the afternoon. Time was counting down for dinner, and John wanted to go for a quick run. If you remember, running was one of the things Sabrina said she liked to do. She figured that, at some point, they would jog the beach so she had prepared in advance by packing something warm to run in and a pair of Nikes, just in case.

Now, you see...this is what I'm saying. On the weekends, Elizabeth played volleyball all summer long on the beach but would never jog with John when he asked her to. He'd seen other couples do it all the time and thought how great it would be if they ran together...but no.

Don't ask me...because I don't know why...the woman was in great shape and could have easily shared that kind of time with him. Now...he had Sabrina who couldn't wait and came prepared. This is what I mean...and I'll say it again...match made in you know where.

As they ran along the shoreline at an even, slow pace heading north, the cool breeze felt refreshing against their faces. They talked continuously as they ran. John talked about his mother, Ginny, and how much of an influence she had been in his life. Sabrina told John how her father had met with a premature death five years earlier.

John listened to Sabrina's voice crack as she explained the circumstances. John said it was very hard emotionally for Sabrina to relive the memory of that time. He slowed their pace down until they stopped, then turned to her.

"We don't have to talk about this now if you don't want to," John said, putting his hands on her shoulders.

Sabrina felt warmth in his tone and smiled. "I'm OK," she said. At that point, she took hold of John's arm and they started walking. "I want to finish telling you about it," she continued. "Two days before he died, a major storm hit Joplin hard. My father worked for an airline. The snow on the ground turned to ice, and my father slipped on the tarmac while doing a routine inspection on a regional jet before take-off. The back of his head slammed hard onto the tarmac. He received a major concussion that took his life."

John turned to her again and took her into his arms. "I'm sorry, Sabrina," he said whispering in her ear. "I know how hard it must have been for you to deal with that. It is still hard for me to imagine my mother and father not being a part of my life today. I'm really sad now," he continued. "I wish they could have had a chance to meet you."

"I know one thing, John," Sabrina said, sighing happily. "If they were as loving and compassionate as you are…then in my heart, I *have* met them."

As John told us, Sakae and me, what happened during that run, Sakae ran off to get a tissue…the tears were streaming from her eyes. I guess by now, you have figured out how emotional Sakae can be. After getting past all the sad emotions, John and Sabrina continued their run.

They talked about almost everything imaginable during that run, including their likes and dislikes. They compared what it was like growing up in different areas of the United States. They talked about how John got interested in painting, and even how he came to know me. Yes… John even told Sabrina the story of the pigeon in the brown paper bag.

It was about thirty minutes into the run when, without warning, John suddenly stopped in his tracks. Sabrina, who was a few steps ahead, wondered why John had stopped so abruptly. She put on the brakes, turned to look back curiously…and then walked back to where he was standing, still and quiet.

When she walked up to him, she noticed that he had this strange look on his face and wondered if he had hurt himself…pulled a muscle or something. She put her hand on his arm. "Why did you suddenly stop like that? Are you alright?" she asked, breathing in and out heavily.

John didn't answer. He looked around as if trying to get his bearings. He, too, was breathing heavily. Suddenly he blurted out, "This is the spot, Sabrina."

"What spot?" she asked, curiously.

"The locket," he replied, brushing a hand through his hair, nodding, his eyes narrowing. "This is where I found the locket floating, right there, in the shallow water."

Sabrina said, "How do you know for sure this is it, John? There's lots of shoreline here."

"I just know it, Sabrina," he said, then took a few steps into the water, looking down, pointing. "It was right there, floating in and out in the shallow water. This has to be it. I didn't stop intentionally," he went on, glancing in all directions. "Something *made* me stop right here...some strange feeling that I have felt before."

At that point, Sabrina couldn't think of what to say. She had no words to express what she was feeling. According to John, it was all so weird for her, and he couldn't blame her. She knew how passionate he was about finding that locket, yet she had a hard time being in the same place mentally that he was about it. Sabrina wished she had been with him when he found the darn thing. That way, they would both be experiencing the same emotions.

Now I cannot and will not get into Sabrina's subconscious. After all, I'm not Joseph Navarra. But... if it were not for the fact that John was so adamant about seeing Solitude One sitting at the bottom of the ocean in a couple of his vivid dreams, and then actually finding Solitude Two at the marina, she might have agreed with me...you know, thinking that John needed some kind of professional intervention.

I think it really happened after that run on the beach. Sabrina, for the first time, became convinced that there might be something bigger, something very strange and inexplicable happening to John. And even though it was difficult to grasp, she had to try and be more supportive now than ever.

Sabrina watched as John stood in ankle-deep water, silent again for the longest time, wondering what he was thinking. He gazed at the water, seemingly in some sort of trance. He said the locket captivated his thoughts. Finally, he took in a deep breath and let out whatever tension was holding him captive in the moment. He put his arm around Sabrina and said, "I'm sorry about all this. If it's alright with you...let's head back."

Sabrina put her arm around his waist as they headed back in the opposite direction, towards the condo. "There's nothing to be sorry about, John," she said, leaning her head against his shoulder. "Somehow it will all work out...I'm sure of it...although..." she went on as they made their way across the sandy beach, "I *am* kind of wishing you had never found that locket. Is it wrong for me to say that?"

John gripped her thin hand. "I was thinking the same thing. It would make things a lot easier, wouldn't it?" he said with a sigh.

For the first time in John's life, he felt a real connection with someone. Although I don't really know for sure, I could probably say the same thing about Sabrina. The way these two were acting, if they ever thought for one moment that they were in love with someone else in some other time and place the way they were in love with each other in this dream of theirs, it was only an illusion, in my opinion.

This was real for both of them, something very different. John knew deep inside that, if *his* feelings were that compelling, then this person he craved, wanted, felt so strongly for, and was in love with had to have the same feelings.

The fact is, however, these strange interruptions...the dreams and events related to them disrupting their ability to concentrate on each other...can't be helpful. I'm sure that Joseph Navarra would agree with me on this one.

Anyway, with Sabrina holding on tightly to John's arm, the walk back to John's place suddenly met with an overwhelming, uncomfortable silence. It was a silence *they* were not accustomed to during their short relationship. Deep inside, John was getting angry at the circumstances. He was upset with himself, and although he tried hard not to show it, it wasn't easy.

When they walked into the condo, Sabrina could see the annoyance in John's eyes. He pulled off the damp, hooded sweatshirt he was wearing, tossed it on the floor behind him and headed for the bathroom. She bent down, picked up the sweatshirt, laid it over the back of a chair...then quickly followed.

John was standing in front of the mirror with his head down, both hands tightly gripping the rim of the sink. Sabrina grabbed a towel that was hanging over the shower door and gently started wiping the dampness from John's back and shoulders. After a moment, John turned around and took Sabrina by the shoulders. His gaze shifted to her mouth. He kissed her with all his passion. She stiffened with anticipation...then gave in.

Placing her hands flat against his bare, upper body, she could feel his chest move in and out heavily with each inhale and exhale. Suddenly, he pushed her to arms-length and held her there. He looked at her silently. Sabrina stood there...her breath accelerated...she didn't know what to think or do.

"I can't do this to you, Sabrina," John said in a frustrating tone, letting his hands fall away. "Can't you see," he went on, now massaging his temples with his fingers. "The dreams, the ghosts...that damn locket...it's all driving me crazy. All I want is you, Sabrina, and I've put you right in the middle of my nightmare. I think its best that you *are* going back home. That way, at least *your* life can get back to normal."

Sabrina eyes began to tear up. She gently placed the palms of her hands against his cheeks. "Now you listen to me, John Adler," she said gazing at him, turning his face with her hands so he would look directly into her eyes. "I don't want normal. Forget about those bad dreams and concentrate only on *our* dream...remember?" she went on, rising slightly on her toes. "I love you. Isn't our dream the only dream that really matters...isn't it?"

John studied her intently, then relaxed his body, put his arm around her waist and gently pulled her close until they were one. He gazed into her deep blue eyes. "So..." he said with a warm smile, "in this dream of *ours*, what do you think we should do next?" Smiling cautiously, Sabrina took a step to the side, reached for the rain-patterned, glass shower door and opened it.

Chapter Thirty-three

John and Sabrina never made it to the Primavera Ristorante. I guess that should be no surprise to any of us. All John told me was they got busy doing other things and that was the reason his plan for a romantic dinner out fell apart. I would say it was a few hours of fun and games that caused the change in plans. They did eat, however. John drove to Peohe's and picked up to-go orders of shrimp cocktail and peppered, seared Ahi tuna.

John also told me that Sabrina looked fantastic with a towel wrapped around her body. Now why would the kid put that into an old man's mind other than just to be vindictive? He knew that, at my age, jealousy wasn't really my game; besides, he knows I'm family. He chuckled when he told me that only because he wasn't going to give me any other details which might pollute an old man's mind. Sakae, I'm sure, would have thanked him for that.

***

John walked through the door and set the bags of food on the dining table. He headed for the kitchen, happy to find Sabrina's body still wrapped neatly in the towel.

You see what he's doing here, don't you...vindictive?

Sabrina had kept herself busy since John left for the restaurant. She found two candles that John had stored in a cupboard in the case of a power outage and placed them on the dining room table along with napkins and utensils. John commented on the preparation...the beautiful setting on the dining table. That, I presume, is another one of Sabrina's knacks for doing things. I keep adding up all the positives about this gal and have yet to find a negative.

With the heater set on low and the fireplace adding additional warmth inside the condo, she decided to lose the towel and put something on before they sat down to eat. She shopped in John's wardrobe closet for something to wear while John lit the candles and poured white wine into two glasses.

Meanwhile, after scanning John's closet, Sabrina picked out one of his Ralph Lauren cotton button-down, long-sleeved shirts and let the towel drop to the floor. Now I can only picture in my mind's eye when John told me exactly how she looked as she walked into the dining area wearing an oversized shirt, opened to the forth button, with only lace-lined underwear underneath. After hearing him describe it, I might just have to take back that what I said about not being the jealous type. I asked myself later, when I thought about his description of her, why did I feel somewhat uncomfortable hearing it? Sakae wasn't around at the time...so why did it matter? I guess I have to go back to what I said earlier...he's family.

According to John, when she walked in and stood there in his oversized shirt...her perfectly-formed legs exposed up to her thighs and four of the seven buttons on the shirt undone from the top down...it made him want to put the bags of food in the refrigerator for another day.

A candlelight dinner with the most beautiful girl in the world was more than John could ask for on Christmas Eve. They sipped white wine from a half-full bottle Sabrina found in the refrigerator. I don't recall John ever, at any time, drinking wine alone so you can conclude that the other half bottle had been, at one point, shared with Elizabeth. I hope that isn't bad luck.

John used the term 'magnificent' as he described their dinner together. They sat at the table for the longest time, sharing stories about their past...as if each one of them needed to know every little detail about the other before Sabrina went back home to Joplin.

John pointed at the picture of his mother, Ginny, hanging on the wall near the hallway. She was dressed in white, wearing a thin tiara and holding a small trophy. The picture was taken when Ginny won Queen of Trays--an award given every year to the most popular waitress in San Diego by the San Diego Tribune. It was John's favorite picture of her.

Sabrina rose from the table, made her way to the picture and studied it. "Your mother was a beautiful woman, John," she said, turning back to him.

"Everybody who knew her said the same thing...Hollywood-starlet-type," he replied with a sigh. "I miss her terribly; especially around this time of year...she loved Christmas."

"I miss my mother, too," Sabrina said. "Only *I* get to call her tomorrow," she continued as she walked back to John's side of the table. She leaned down and softly kissed him on the lips. "I wish with all my heart that you could call *your* mom this Christmas."

This girl has a heart of gold... how could anyone not love her...dream or no dream. It was now eight o'clock Pacific Standard Time...ten o'clock in Joplin. Sabrina had promised Karla that she would call her on Christmas Eve. She grabbed the cell phone from her bag, looked at John and motioned towards the bedroom.

John smiled. "I suppose that Karla is going to get her Christmas wish...the scoop?" he said, smiling.

Sabrina chuckled at the joke, made her way into the bedroom, and sat on the edge of the bed. Nano-seconds after Sabrina touched the display for Karla's number, she answered on the first ring...as if she had been sitting there, waiting to press her finger on the send key. At the same time, Sabrina inadvertently touched the speaker key and, before she could switch it off, John heard Karla's voice echo out...'What the hell took so long, girl!' Sabrina instinctively shot up from the bed, went to the door, peeked out at John, and shrugged her shoulders. John laughed as he waved with his hand for her to close the bedroom door for privacy.

While Sabrina sort of satisfied Karla's need to know everything that was going on, John moved from the sofa to stand in front of the sketch of the woman. As he worked to conjure up the image he received from the last dream by squeezing his eyes shut, his retrospective memory began to kick in. He opened his eyes, picked up the 2B sketching pencil from the thin shelf at the bottom of the easel and started making changes to the previous sketch.

Continuing to reference the image in his mind, closing and opening his eyes, he narrowed the bridge of the woman's nose. That, in turn, indicated where the inner corners of her eyes should go. He studied the picture in the locket just to confirm, and then briefly closed his eyes again. He slightly lifted the eyebrow over the right eye, erasing the original brow line, and then repeated the process with the other eyebrow.

He briefly closed his eyes again to specifically recall the woman's cheekbone and the shape of her chin. He gave her a slightly stronger chin and lifted her cheekbones a touch. He closed his eyes again and saw the hair on the right side of the woman's face, the damaged side of the picture; it looked somewhat wavy near the top. His only choice was to sketch it the way he saw it in his mind's eye.

Fifteen minutes had passed when the door to the bedroom opened. According to what Sabrina told John, Karla didn't get all there was to tell. Some things at this point need to be left unsaid. You can bet, however, the way Karla is…she will press until she gets enough to write a book.

Sabrina crept up alongside John and watched as his artful motions worked the canvas. He glanced at the small clock sitting on the worktable before shifting his eyes back to the canvas. "Wow…only fifteen minutes? I'll bet your girlfriend didn't like that," he said, keeping his eyes centered on the canvas. "There is no way she got what she wanted out of you."

Sabrina chuckled. "Huh…fifteen minutes," she replied running her hand up underneath his shirt. "Seemed like I was away from you an hour. But to answer your question, I left out the juicy stuff. She knew I was holding back, so you know she'll try again."

John backed away from the portrait and shut his eyes for a moment before opening them again. "Not finished yet…but what do you think?"

Sabrina looked at the locket through the magnifier again, and then took a step back to gaze at the drawing.

"Well, now, let's see," she said, focusing on various areas of the drawing. "With my inexperienced eye, it seems you've managed to fill in many of the blanks…" Squinting a little, she took another look at the locket and then fixed her gaze on the sketch. "I noticed that, in the picture, her hair is almost straight…yet you've sketched it wavy on the right side near the top of her head?"

"Apparently," John replied as he began to apply some shade to the drawing with the side of the pencil, "and I really don't know why for sure, but I'm thinking that's the way she wore it. I saw it that way in the image that popped up in my mind. I also saw some sort of mole or beauty mark just above the corner of her lip on the right side." He sharpened the lead to a point and marked a spot with the pencil just above and to the left of the upper lip, meticulously enlarging the circle to about a 1/6 of an inch. "Like that."

Sabrina admired what John had done. After examining the picture of the woman in the locket once more, she could now see a sharp resemblance to the sketch.

"I've looked at the photograph so many times, I'm getting snow blind," she said, setting the locket back down. "I can't imagine what you have been going through."

John said, "I'm used to it."

"The woman is pretty," she said.

"She'll be prettier once I put oil to her."

"Are you going to do an actual oil painting?"

"Yes," John said, placing the pencil back on the shelf of the easel. "I had an idea while I was sketching...and while you were spilling to Karla," he went on grinning. "I'll do an oil painting of the woman and display the portrait in Kate Sutter's Galleria."

"But I don't understand, John," Sabrina said, looking puzzled. "You mean you're going to sell the portrait like you do your boat paintings?"

"Not quite," John replied, taking her hand, leading her to the sofa.

Sabrina could tell something specific was going through John's mind and she couldn't wait to hear it. She sat patiently waiting for him to explain. He started rubbing his hands on his thighs somewhat nervously.

"OK, Sabrina," he said, looking at her. "This may sound a little crazy, but what about this idea? I paint the picture as best I can. It might be a little difficult for me because...well, boats I know how to paint. I'm not sure about a portrait. But anyway," he went on, "if Kate will let me display the portrait in her store...not for sale, you understand...just leave it there a while. Maybe someone will see it, recognize the woman, and inquire about it."

Sabrina's eyes opened wide. "Brilliant, my dear Watson...I love the idea! At least that way you are doing *something*."

John leaned back and took a breath. Sabrina had a second wind, pushed John down on the sofa and straddled him. "I think we are getting way too serious...don't you think so?

I must say I wasn't too receptive about John's idea to display the portrait of the woman in the Galleria. When he talked about it, it sounded far-fetched to me. Not only did I not *like* the idea, even though the angel did, I thought the idea was stupid and a waste of time. But... did I express my thoughts about the matter, no, I did not…and here's the reason.

When he told me about this crazy idea, we were sitting at his table…John, Sakae and me. It was before lunch and the place was empty. I had asked John to come early that day because Sakae and I had some breaking news. We were going to tell him that we were getting married. Before we had a chance, however, he sprung this crazy scheme on us.

Sakae knows me well. She watched my expressions while John was explaining what he was going to do. She could see I was ready to pounce on him, express my strong opinion about the whole thing. However, the minute I started to open my mouth, Sakae gave me a kick under the table so I ended up biting my tongue once more, nodding and smiling. I didn't want to get on Sakae's bad side, I guess.

By the time John was finished with his portrait revelation and other things, it was time for Sakae and I to prepare for the lunch crowd and too late to tell him about our plans to get married.

Chapter Thirty-four

Christmas Eve for John and Sabrina was a night filled with stars and fireworks. Bear in mind, however, this is not me talking...it's exactly the way John described it to me. That night was the kind of special evening two people spend together which remains locked in their memory for the rest of their lives...he said that too.

The look on John's face was telling. Regardless of what happens to their relationship in the end, John said, as wild and sex-reckless as Elizabeth was, she was no match for the memorable sensation of tenderness and intimacy that Sabrina gave to him that evening. When he shared some of the details with me about that evening...not the "details" details but some of the things that gave him hope that their relationship would be everlasting...I knew he was really hooked on this angel.

I must admit...when John told me they had spread out a blanket on the floor in front of the fireplace, lit some candles, put on soft music...he had me wanting more. Instead, he left it up to my imagination as to what took place the rest of the night...and I felt a sense of wild abandon. At that point, I couldn't wait to shut the pub down and get Sakae home! We didn't have a fireplace, but that's just a minor detail.

***

John awoke Christmas morning feeling fully rested for what seemed like the first time in a very long while. There were no dreams of unknown faces and boats and fish scurrying about as he marched on the ocean floor...he said that he felt reborn, whatever that means.

He said he reached across the bed and found that the space next to him was empty...Sabrina was missing. For a moment, the thought crossed John's mind that *she* was some sort of dream--a wonderful dream to counteract the others he'd had. I chuckled loudly when he told me that. He said that a smile crossed his face when the aroma of freshly-brewed coffee filled his nostrils.

He figured, since it was Christmas morning, there was nothing to do but relax so he rolled out of bed and into lounging pajamas. He went into the bathroom, stared at himself in the mirror and smiled. There were no dreams during the night and no images of anything but him in the mirror. It was the makings of a perfect morning.

Lying on the vanity was Sabrina's toothbrush and a tube of Crest. He couldn't exactly explain to me how it felt when he placed her toothbrush in the wall mount holder next to his. He said, at that point, all he could picture in his mind was all of Sabrina's things being next to his...like her clothes in the closet, her deodorant on the shelf next to his in the medicine cabinet, the breakfast cereal she liked next to his in the pantry...and so on. After replacing *his* toothbrush, he took in a deep breath, brushed his fingers through his hair and made his way into the kitchen.

Sabrina had shopped in the refrigerator for something with which to make breakfast and was holding onto a skillet, flipping over a delicious-looking vegetable omelet. The toast popped up at the same time as John put a hand on her shoulder, moved her hair aside and gave her neck a gentle, slow kiss.

"Mmm...smells wonderful. I can butter the toast, if you want me to," he whispered.

Sabrina said, moaning slightly as she angled her head back, "Would buttering the toast require you to stop what you're doing?"

"Probably," he answered.

Sabrina's shoulders dropped heavily as she let out a deep sigh. "Well...if you can't do both, I guess you'd better butter the toast before it gets cold."

"*OK...*" John drawled, reluctantly. "But be assured, you don't know what I'm capable of this time of the morning."

"And you have no idea how good my omelets taste," she said, cutting the omelet in half and transferring one of the halves to another plate.

They sat across from each other at the small oak table. John took one bite of the omelet and declared Sabrina the best cook in the world. Sabrina accepted the compliment...and then, according to John, there was silence at the table for what seemed like an eternity.

It was extremely awkward...the silence between them. Up until that time, they couldn't stop talking to each other. In fact, communicating was one of the things that made them good for each other. Their time together should have been no less than euphoric, but they both knew things were going to change, one way or the other, within the next twenty-four hours. As much as they desperately wanted to enjoy their last day together, it was hard doing so.

As John nibbled on his omelet, all of the attributes Sabrina possessed flashed though his mind...and the list was long...how pretty she was, how sweet she smelled, how smart and compassionate she was, and on and on. To top it off, he now had to add one more thing to the list...she was a very good cook as well.

The reality had set in for both of them. They were fully aware that the next day would be heartbreaking. John couldn't help but wonder what he was going to do. Being forced to say goodbye to the girl sitting across the table from him for a second time would be difficult. Sabrina couldn't stop thinking about how far away she would be from him.

John couldn't take his eyes off her. She wore no makeup, and she didn't need to. She hadn't spent time gazing into a mirror, thinking she should do something to herself before John woke up...because she didn't have to. In John's eyes, she was nothing short of sheer, raw beauty.

Finally, John broke the ice. "I know what's going on here, Sabrina." John said, leaning back in the chair, crossing his arms over his chest.

Sabrina took her last bite of omelet before looking up at him, gazing directly into his eyes. "And you think I don't?" she said softly, leaning in and reaching across the table. "The world implodes tomorrow."

"Don't put it that way," he said evenly. "Somehow, we are going to figure this out."

Sabrina thought for a moment. "You're right, John," she said in a serious but warm tone of voice. "I'll try to dismiss the negative thoughts I'm thinking and be thankful I have this time with you. It's hard, though...I'm scared and unprepared."

"Almost impossible for me," he replied, gently taking her hand in his. "But let's don't let the inevitability of tomorrow ruin this day for us. After all, it's Christmas Day. Like I said...we'll figure it out."

John's words helped to relieve some of the tension. He lit the fireplace, opened the curtains to the view of the ocean, cracked open the door leading out to the balcony, stepped out and took in a deep breath. The crisp air rushed into the room, sending a chill to Sabrina's shoulders. She took the throw blanket left on the sofa from the night before, wrapped it around her body and went out to stand beside him. He put his arm around her.

"Smell that?" he asked, as he took in another breath. "This is another reason I like it here...the smell of salty ocean air."

Sabrina took in a deep breath. "I could do this every morning," she said, feeling the chill of the breeze brush across her face.

John felt something hopeful in his chest after hearing that. Just a hint of something they might be able to share for more than just that moment. Unfortunately, the moment was fleeting. The curse of sadness crept slowly back into his head, even though they had decided earlier to put negative thoughts aside.

John did his best to hide the sadness that once again overwhelmed his thoughts. Instead, he led Sabrina back into the house and to the sofa. She sat down, but he didn't. He stood there admiring her, admiring her every feature. She gazed into his eyes, wondering what he was thinking. He leaned over and kissed her warm, waiting lips.

He let go of her hand, made his way over to the tree and picked up the two small gifts that were lying on the floor beneath it then made his way back to her. He sat down just to her right and placed the gifts on the table in front of them.

"*OK...*" he said smiling, rubbing his palms together. "Who goes first?"

"Ooh, boy...!" Sabrina said, perching on the edge of the sofa. "This is exciting... I get to open a gift."

"It would be more exciting if you didn't already know what it is," John said chuckling.

Sabrina gave his shoulder a slight nudge. "Don't spoil it for me," she said grinning, fluttering her lashes at him amusingly. "I'm like a little kid when it comes to opening presents."

Sabrina reached for his gift, lifted it from the table and handed it to him. "Since I know what mine is," she said, "you open your gift first."

John smiled and gave her another kiss before he carefully unwrapped the gaily-wrapped box. On the outside of the box was a picture of a boy and girl sitting under an umbrella in a sailboat. He opened the box, took out the porcelain boat and held the figurine out in front of him.

"I like this a lot," he said, marveling at the detail molded out of the porcelain. "How did you know I like sailboats," he said, smiling widely.

Sabrina closed her eyes, pretended to think about his question, and then said. "Duh...I don't know...a good guess...I suppose," she replied, smiling back at him.

John rose to his feet and crossed over to the fireplace. "How about up here?" he said placing the figurine on the thin mantle.

"Perfect..." she replied, nodding. "Right where I pictured it."

"Now it's your turn," John said, grabbing the beautifully-wrapped, thin anklet box off the table.

Sabrina took the small box from him and pressed it up against her heart as if it was so precious she wouldn't let it go at any cost. She gazed at John then a tear began to glisten in the corner of her eye. "This will be as important to me as Anna's locket was to her," she said softly.

He looked at Sabrina and was in awe of her sincerity. Here they were exchanging gifts that had a certain meaning to only them and, at the same time, Sabrina had a heartfelt moment about someone who lost something dear to them. Sabrina tore away the wrapping on the little box, opened it and once again admired the beauty of the gold chain with the two hearts.

From the moment they had walked out of Daniel's jewelry store, John couldn't wait to fasten the anklet around her slim ankle. Although it wasn't a wedding ring, it was something she could wear forever, regardless of what happened in the end.

"May I?" he said, holding out an open hand.

Sabrina removed the anklet from the box and laid it in the palm of John's hand. "As much as I like this," she sighed happily, "I want you to know that, in our dream, this anklet would really be a ring."

The statement totally knocked John for a loop. For John to hear that coming from Sabrina's lips, well…it even shocked *me* when he told me she said it. The things they were saying to each other were just getting them into more hot water in that they were making the next day's goodbye even harder.

I guess for the two lovebirds to consider the consequences of their words would be expecting far too much. The way they saw it, however, was that this Christmas would always be a Christmas to remember, no matter what.

Deep down, John said, they both knew it would be an impossibility to consider engagement at this point for two reasons. One would be the reality of knowing each other for such a short time, and the other would be figuring out how to deal with the distance between them. I wonder if they only continued the charade because they figured it was fun doing the 'pretend' thing.

John kneeled down on one knee and Sabrina raised her foot up in front of him. "You do know, don't you, Sabrina," John said, in a serious tone of voice, "it's OK to make a wish, whether in a dream or in a fairy tale."

"So we are making up the rules as we go along," she replied. "Is that it?"

"You are damn straight we are," he said, grinning as he wrapped the chain around her slim ankle to fasten it. "Let's do…let's pretend that this ankle bracelet *is* a wedding ring."

Trying to understand all this is starting to make me feel older than I am. How can two adults talk about fairy tales, even if they are, for the moment, obviously in love? Although Sakae claims that she understands it well. She said they just couldn't commit to anything other than the *thought* of love.

In Sakae's way of thinking, the time John and Sabrina have spent together wasn't time enough for them to figure everything out. She said that they just needed more of it. She was convinced that, even though they would again be far apart, the unforgettable memories of the time they shared, the time spent making love together, would be the things that help guide whatever happens in their future. I guess I should give Sakae credit for being the realist here.

Chapter Thirty-five

John and Sabrina spent part of the day leisurely lying around the condo, talking. They were still fulfilling that need to know every little thing about each other before she boarded the plane to Joplin the next day.

They talked about several things that were important in their lives. John's father and mother had both passed away, and he had no siblings. He told Sabrina that his family was pretty much just me now. When he told me he actually said that to Sabrina in that way, a warm feeling came over my heart. I guess, in that regard, you could consider me an old softy.

Sabrina had her mother, sister, a niece, a nephew and Uncle Phil. John was thirty-eight and Sabrina thirty-five. Sabrina loved pistachio ice cream and so did John. They both liked to jog...but you already knew that. I guess I could go on and on about all of the things they talked about, but my head is still spinning from the run down. It was around twelve-thirty on Christmas Day. The sun was high in the sky, and its rays periodically sliced their way through the massive cloud cover which meant that the marine layer had almost burned off. Admiring the view of the ocean through the windows in John's place was one more thing that made Sabrina wish the next day would never come.

They *both* wished the next day would never come. They said that to each other several times that morning. With the passing of each hour, the certainty of the next day became more real to them, haunting the time they had left.

I had to laugh when John said that Sabrina performed magic again in the kitchen, fixing lunch. It was then that I figured it out. To John, no matter what Sabrina did, it was magic. How hard could it have been to smack peanut butter and jelly on two pieces of bread and open a bag of Fritos?

John had decided to take Sabrina on a ride to Shelter Island. The temperature was around sixty-five degrees, perfect sweater weather. John had a favorite bench on the Island positioned in a perfect spot. From that particular bench, there was a clear view of the boats moving in and out of the harbor and a wide-ranging view of the downtown San Diego skyline. John had told me about this spot before and how he and Elizabeth used to sit there when they were together. I will guarantee you that he will never share that factoid with Sabrina.

In my opinion, taking Sabrina to that spot was another attempt on John's part to sell Sabrina the beauty of being in San Diego. Can't blame him for doing it. Sabrina made hot chocolate, filled a thermos and off they went, heading over the Coronado Bridge towards San Diego. Once off the bridge, John headed north on I-5 to Hawthorne Street West, to Harbor Drive North. The signs over the roadway caught both their eyes. They were driving past the airport, Lindbergh Field. It was the one place neither of them wanted to think about at that moment.

Shelter Island was one of the spots where, on a clear day, you can see the Old Point Loma Lighthouse at the end of the peninsula that separates the bay from the Pacific Ocean.

According to John, the boats moving in and out of the harbor were few but the view of downtown San Diego and the Point Loma Peninsula was the same as always...spectacular. There were a few people fishing off the jetty but, other than that, it seemed to them that they had the whole Island to themselves.

Even on a warm day, the breeze from the southwest brushing the bay always made the Island a little chilly. John sat with his arm around Sabrina, her head resting on his shoulder, as they watched the tide slap against the rock-covered jetty and shoreline. They sat there as peacefully as two lovers could possibly be.

"I could get used to this," Sabrina said as she nestled up next to him, "How often do you sit out here?"

"About twice a month...I usually pick up a coffee and a sprinkled chocolate cake donut from Dunkin Donuts and..."

"Hmm...I l-o-v-e donuts with sprinkles," she broke in, grinning.

Sakae made me promise not to say anything else as I tell this story regarding their childish dialogue. Sakae's exact words were, 'If you do, everyone will think you are becoming an old, miserly Ebenezer Scrooge.' Sakae maintains they are just having fun and that I should just go with it...oh, well...what the h-e-l-l.

***

Getting back to the story, after two hours of sitting and strolling up and down the shoreline, they headed downtown to the Gas Lamp District. Again, with very few people out on the holiday, they felt like they had the historic district to themselves as they did out on Shelter Island.

Sabrina had seen that area of town before when she had visited San Diego with 'you know who'...the nosey girlfriend from Joplin. Revisiting the historic district, holding hands with John as they walked, gave being there a whole different meaning. According to Sabrina, strolling past Sevilla, Bandar, Gaigin Noodle and Sake House, and Petco Park was much different than being downtown with Karla...whose only interest was to frequent the bars and clubs to, as Karla put it, 'troll for the single guys.'

They walked around for an hour past clubs, restaurants, shops, and the Hard Rock Hotel with Sabrina holding onto John's arm as if she would never let go. I'm telling you...someone should write a book about this love story. Unfortunately, however, this chapter will soon be ending.

Sabrina's plane, scheduled to take off for Joplin within the next seventeen hours, will not have John strapped into the seat next to her.

It appeared as though the sun was sitting on top of the ocean like a huge candle on a never-ending table as they drove back over the bridge towards Coronado. Darkness would arrive in the next hour, which made John and Sabrina count down the hours silently in their heads.

Even though there were dinner bells ringing everywhere as people celebrated the end of a wonderful Christmas Day, the anxiety of the next day suppressed their appetites. Sabrina sliced two different kinds of cheese while John retrieved crackers from the cupboard and the rest of the wine left in the refrigerator from the night before.

It was inevitable that the subject would come up...but when? They both knew that, at some point, they couldn't avoid it any longer. The cheese and crackers sitting on the table in front of them was almost untouched and the wine glasses remained filled to the halfway mark. The silence was deafening.

They both seemed lost in their own thoughts. Neither of them wanted to broach the subject of being apart again. John and Sabrina knew the inevitability that lie ahead. The wheels were turning in both their heads and none of what developed made any sense. Finally, it was John who broke the ice. He took the glass of wine in his hand and lifted it above the table towards Sabrina.

He gazed into her eyes, smiled wide, and said, "Here is to the most wonderful fairy tale two people could ever have."

Sabrina touched her glass to his. "A fairy tale that doesn't have to end tonight," she said as her lower lip began to tremble.

John set his glass down without taking a sip. Sabrina held onto her glass and watched John make his way over to her side of the table. He leaned down and took a few soft bites of her lower lip. Quickly longing for the next step, Sabrina kept her gaze on him and blindly set her glass on the table.

She lifted her hand and placed it on the back of John's head then pressed her lips against his, adding the extra touch of intimacy before their tongues twisted together in a sensual motion for the longest time.

***

Now here I go again...pure speculation. John said it was the best kiss he'd ever experienced so I just assumed it went the way I explained it, or the way a dirty old man such as I am would have craved it.

***

The kiss, however, didn't...at that point...lead to the bedroom. It was just a warm-up. John returned to his chair and held up his glass again. Sabrina followed suit and they sipped simultaneously, finishing off the toast John had made.

Suddenly, the room went uncomfortably silent again. John spoke first. "I guess I should get you to the airport around eight-thirty in the morning."

"Yeah...about then would be alright," she replied softly, staring hard, trying not to face the subject.

After a long pause, John said, "When do you think we'll see each other again?"

"I don't know," she answered in a serious tone. "I'll be working on the February issue, and it will take a while to get it prepared for print. Meanwhile, though," she went on, "we can talk over the phone or even 'Face Time' each other. At least our iPhones will let us see each other and that might be fun, depending on when we do it," she chuckled.

John smiled. "I guess that's better than nothing. At least that way," he went on, taking in a deep, sighing breath as he reached for a cracker, "I can look at your beautiful face."

Silence fell once more. They both sat there like kids who had lost their favorite toys, nibbling on cheese and crackers. When you think about it…what *could* they say to each other that would solve anything? He was here and she was there. That is how the real world turns…unless, that is…one or the other is willing to make some sort of sacrifice.

***

I already had explored all these speculative options with John before Sabrina made her surprise visit to Coronado, unannounced, as she did carrying that nice gift for me. Before, when she left, I knew that in John's mind he had some strange premonition that he would someday see her again. This was a different story, however. Neither one of them knew what the future would bring.

Sakae and I decided that, if there was going to be a next time, it would mean something more significant… more final. You can bet your ass that, if there were a next time, it wouldn't be because someone craved one of my all-beef hamburgers.

Let's look at the big picture. Sure…John could ask her to get married, but what happens next? She says 'yes' and still goes away. At what point do they work out who lives where? They could visit each other…that wouldn't be a problem…with the exception of John and his dislike for flying. Sabrina could take several vacations from her place at the magazine and see John here…but, realistically, how much time can a person take away from their job until it becomes a real problem, even if she is the boss's niece?

On the other hand, even if love at first sight sounds more real than it is, without having the time to get to know each other, jumping into a permanent relationship could be the mistake of their lives. I discussed this whole thing with Sakae and she tells me I'm making too much of it…analyzing too much…I don't think so.

Something will happen, one way or the other. In view of the fact that I really haven't talked to John a whole lot since Sabrina arrived, I was hoping they would agree to a wait-and-see scenario...see how they feel during this separation...and just remember the great sex they had the last night they were together.

Guess what? I got my wish. They agreed to stay in their fairy-tale dream, speak as much as they could while apart, and then see where the emotions lead them.

Chapter Thirty-six

Morning came sooner than John and Sabrina wanted it to. With little sleep and the reality of having to say goodbye for a second time, the mood was somber, to say the least. By the time Sabrina showered and packed her suitcase, she had no time to fix John her now-famous vegetable omelet.

John said he tried to lighten the mood that morning. He even cracked a joke about how painful it would be to wait for an omelet until the next time they were together...but couldn't get Sabrina to play along. When I think about how miserable those two were at the time, eating breakfast was probably the furthest thing from their minds anyway. To make things worse, he said he heard Sabrina sobbing in the shower and felt helpless to do anything. She was going back to Joplin...and that was that.

John put her bag in the Jeep, and they headed for the airport. He was determined not to let silence become their enemy on the way. I thought that was a good strategy. After all, they had a wonderful time together and had committed to seeing each other again...why not part ways on a happy note?

Talking now was difficult, however. Not because they couldn't think of anything to say; they never had a problem with that. Talking at this point was difficult because any-thing either one would say meant just another thing to think about when they were apart. There was enough already to keep their mind occupied for a very long time, or at least until they saw each other again.

What was needed was one of them to lighten things up a bit in the little time they had left together. Nothing too complicated, something that might make them smile. John went first.

"Do you think there will be enough scoop about us to satisfy your friend, Karla, when you get back to Joplin?" John said with a smile, looking straight at the road ahead of him as he drove.

Sabrina chuckled, placed her hand on his shoulder and lightly massaged. "I'll cover just enough around the fringes to make it interesting for her," she replied. "She'll have to fire up her imagination for the rest. All the juicy stuff is confidential between you and me; deal?"

John moved a hand from the steering wheel and placed it on Sabrina's thigh. "I hope your Uncle Phil fully recovers from the stroke he had," he said in a warm voice. "I'd really like to meet him some time, you know. From what you've told me about his personality, I'll bet he and my Uncle Skipper would get along just fine."

"Who knows," Sabrina replied, "maybe one day my uncle will escort me down the aisle where he will meet up with Skipper standing next to some handsome guy waiting to put a wedding ring on my finger."

"Still dreaming…aren't we?" John said, smiling.

"Maybe," Sabrina countered, gripping John's hand softly, "…maybe not."

***

Listening to this story was getting to be a little too painful. Here we have two grown people, living far apart, who want each other so badly, yet the reality of life is making it so difficult to be together. There must be some way to describe their situation, but damned if I could come up with one.

I know one thing for sure, however. There is no such thing as being far-away lovers. These two had to find a way to be together. If not, each passing day will be crippling. They will fantasize every waking moment about the way things could be and not the way things are. That can't be good for anyone's mental state of mind, especially John's, given the dreadful nightmares he's been dealing with.

Dreaming about lockets and sunken boats is one thing, but Sabrina is a real person and not a figment of John's imagination or some character in a dream. They had to find a way to make it work, sooner rather than later. I was emphatic about that when I talked to John. Sakae was sitting next to me, and this was one time she didn't kick me in the leg for butting in.

**

* * *

John left the Jeep in short-term parking, grabbed the suitcase from the back and walked Sabrina into the terminal as far as security would allow. I knew, based on his tone of voice, that separating like that...with a barrier of security between them...had to have killed him. It's usually people in the armed services that have to deal with those types of goodbyes.

Their fairy-tale world had slipped back into reality. It was the one thing, over the last few days, they tried not to focus on even though they knew it was inevitable.

They stood there in front of travelers, vendors, workers and airport security personnel wandering around, clinging to each other as if they were conjoined twins. They glanced at the flight information display board, hoping for a delay in flight departure for Joplin...but no such luck. John held Sabrina tight in his arms as if she were about to be dragged away by guards to a place where he would never see her again.

Meanwhile, the line moving through security was getting longer. They kissed long and hard one more time before Sabrina grabbed the handle to her suitcase, looked into John's eyes, backed up and slowly turned away. John stood there, frozen in time. He stared after her until she finally made her way through the body scanner and beyond.

Twenty minutes later, Sabrina was putting her bag in the overhead compartment, fastening her seat belt and staring out of the small, oval window of the airplane. John climbed into his Jeep, despising the empty seat next to him.

Instead of exiting the short-term parking lot to head back to Coronado, John sat there peering out of the Jeep's windshield, up into the sky. He watched one plane after another lift off the runway and followed it until it disappeared.

There was no way for him to tell which flight was Sabrina's, but he sat there torturing himself just the same. As each plane took off, he felt as though his heart was breaking apart, piece-by-piece. Sabrina's plane sat on the tarmac waiting in line to lift off, her heart was breaking apart, piece-by-piece, as well.

Sabrina's plane finally taxied down the runway, lifted off and headed straight out over the ocean. When the plane made the hundred-and-eighty-degree turn to head back over shore and to the east, she peered down to the earth below. They were flying over the bridge leading over the bay to Coronado Island. Wondering if John's jet black Jeep was one in the line of many cars that now looked like a row of ants from that altitude, she glanced at the ankle bracelet he had given her and smiled.

At that point, a warm feeling came over her body. She recalled something she had read in an article a long time ago. The quote played out in her mind as if it were there just waiting to be resurrected for specifically this time in her life. 'If you love someone more than anything, then distance only matters to the mind, not to the heart.'

She laid her head back against the seat and closed her eyes. Her mind took her back to the night Skipper marched her to the table where John had his nose buried in some book about far-out places. She remembered the look on his face when he looked up at her and recalled how she felt at that moment. That was a moment when time stood still for both of them...and just think, I caused it to happen.

Anyhow, when Johnny-boy finally got back to the condo and walked through the door, he said he swore that he could smell the light, fresh scent of Sabrina's body mist lingering in the air. He said it was everywhere. Every room he entered, she was there in some way. He wanted it to remain permanent but he knew that, the moment he opened the door to the balcony, the ocean breeze would erase it forever...or at least until the time she would return to him.

He stood next to the fireplace, gazing at the porcelain sailboat on the mantle. His mind took him back to the exact moment at Skipper's, four days earlier, when he had looked up and she was there again, just as he had the first time he saw her standing in front of him with that unforgettable smile on her beautiful face. Up until that very moment, they were in separate states for over two months without a word or any inkling as to when, if ever, they would see each other again...and, yet, look what fate was able to accomplish.

The next thing that entered John's mind was the way she slowly lifted up her foot so he could clasp the ankle bracelet around her thin ankle and how smooth and warm her leg felt. He thought about the time they walked the historic district downtown, and it made him smile. The time they strolled the shoreline at Shelter Island made his heart seem light and joyful even though they were now miles apart.

He wandered into the bedroom and stared at the bed, which had been left untouched...just the way it was when they got out of it that morning. His mind was like a fountain, spewing thoughts and memories of how passionately they made love in that very bed...how their lips came together and seemed to only separate when they kissed each other in other places. John said that his head filled with everything they did at every moment.

John said that he made his way out the door leading to the balcony, stepped up to the railing and peered out towards the ocean. Moments later, he glanced at the two recliners and thought about the first time their bodies actually came together.

He took in a deep breath and, although the smell of the ocean was in the air, in his mind and senses, he could see, smell and feel Sabrina close to him. He could sense the wonderful fragrance coming from her hair the first time she moved past him onto the balcony.

Suddenly, John heard his cell phone ringing. For that split second, he had hopes that Sabrina was calling to tell him she had never boarded that plane...that she hungered so much for him, she would never go back to Joplin again. That wasn't the case, however. When John realized it was me on the other end of the line, the next thing I heard was, 'Damn it!'

I didn't take it personally, though. After hearing the first words that came from his mouth in a hopeful tone of voice, 'Sabrina,' how *could* I expect a warm greeting? It wouldn't take a rocket scientist to figure out how disappointed he was when he heard my voice on the other end. Talk about a reality check...that was a big one.

Although I knew that nothing I could say or do would change the way John was feeling, I let him know that I felt his pain and that I was there for him if he needed me. Initially, my call was to find out if Sabrina's plane left on time and to make sure that John wasn't contemplating a leap off his balcony. I never did bring up the balcony thing...I stayed true to the situation and played the role of the sympathetic uncle.

There was a point during that conversation that the only advice I could offer up was 'it would all work out in the end.' John had to process in his own mind how he was going to react to the separation over the next few days and beyond. He certainly didn't need me to dole out unprofessional advice that might derail him. John's a big boy, and he had to figure out on his own how to function without Sabrina around.

It was getting close to lunch, and I had to cut the conversation short. Even though John was still getting things off his mind and I had no problem being a sounding board, I had to get busy helping Sakae. Usually the day after Christmas gets real busy. People were wandering around Orange Ave. as if it were the last place on earth.

Little shops up and down the street were exchanging gifts that people received and didn't want...or selling stuff like crazy to people looking for the after-Christmas bargain...it was the same thing every year. Before hanging up, I told John that I hoped to see him later. I wasn't holding my breath, however. I figured he'd just stay home and sulk the rest of the day, waiting to hear from Sabrina once she landed in Joplin.

***

Shortly after John and I ended our call, he dialed Kate Sutter. He said it dawned on him that he hadn't called her on Christmas Day. Obviously, Sabrina had something to do with that. In addition to feeling despondent about Sabrina being gone, forgetting to call Kate made him feel even worse...that's all the poor boy needed was more depression to overcome. Calling Kate on Christmas Day was a tradition he swore he'd never break.

When John called the Galleria, Kate wasn't there. Michele, one of the girls working at the time, informed him that Kate had taken ill with some sort of bug and wouldn't be in until the next day. Kate was the type that, even on her deathbed, she'd figure out a way to get to the store. John decided to call her house.

John knew right away that Kate wasn't feeling good the moment she answered the phone.

John said, "Kate, Merry Christmas, late...how are you feeling? Michele said you were sick."

"A little under the weather, I'm afraid, John," Kate said. "There must be something going around. It's nothing to get concerned about...probably a cold or something. I'm feeling a little better today, thank God," she went on, coughing slightly, her throat sounding somewhat hoarse, "so don't worry about me. What about you? I missed hearing from you yesterday. Are you OK?"

"I'm fine, Kate," John said. "I just now remembered that I didn't call yesterday, and I'm so sorry for that. I feel terrible that I missed our yearly Christmas morning conversation. It's just that I was preoccupied with someone. The entire day just slipped away from me."

"Preoccupied with someone?" Kate said curiously. "Not Elizabeth?"

Kate knew all about the breakup with Elizabeth but was not aware that Sabrina slipped into the picture. Assuming that Elizabeth was the "someone" to whom John was referring somehow didn't seem logical to her.

"Elizabeth!" John replied, clearing his throat slightly. "Heavens no, Kate…not Elizabeth. I met a girl at Skipper's place and spent Christmas with her. When I first met her, she was visiting from Joplin, Missouri. Her name is Sabrina."

"Well, now, John…I'd like to hear about *her* sometime. I'm surprised that you didn't mention her to me before."

"To tell you the truth, Kate, she sort of caught me by surprise. I didn't expect it to turn into something."

"Something?" Kate said curiously. "That's interesting…Sabrina…hmm…pretty name…is she nice?"

"She's wonderful, Kate, and I *will* tell you about her soon," John said, as he flicked his eyes over to the sketch of the woman. "However," he went on, "I'd like to talk to you about something else. I don't want to keep you from resting, so will you be at the Galleria tomorrow?"

Kate said enthusiastically, "I hope so… call the store before you make your way over. If for some reason I'm not…you know where I live…you come here, OK?"

"Get better, and I'll see you tomorrow."

John kept glancing at his watch, desperately trying to will the hour hand to move faster. The five o'clock arrival time at Joplin Regional seemed days away, rather than hours, and the anticipation of hearing Sabrina's voice was driving him crazy. Hanging around his condo didn't help to make his situation any easier.

Chapter Thirty-seven

Without Sabrina's witty conversation, the place was too quiet. John's stomach growled from hunger. He and Sabrina hadn't eaten that much over the last few days and that, combined with all the "exercise" they experienced, if you get my drift, left him starving. He needed to get out…do something…go somewhere familiar, break away from where he was to make the time go by faster. I thought he'd jet over to my place, but that didn't happen.

John drove the Jeep over the bridge and headed straight for Filippi's Pizza Grotto in Little Italy. As usual, India Street around the lunch hour was very busy…people everywhere, strolling from restaurant to restaurant. Luckily, there was one parking spot left in Filippi's lot. The parking attendant, who knew John, was sitting on a high stool on the sidewalk with an oversize straw hat held in place with a string around his neck. He waved John up the concrete ramp and pointed to a spot in the back.

John decided to eat in instead of following his usual 'grab the pie and go' routine. When he walked through the door, he said there were people lined up past the deli cases…which stood on one side of the aisle with the pastas, breads and other specialty grocery items shipped directly from Italy on the other side. Just the smell of fresh deli meat and the balls of fresh cheeses hanging from ropes made customers feel like they were experiencing a vacation in Sicily. I was getting hungry just listening to John talk about it.

Other than a few shoppers waiting for Italian meats and cheeses to be sliced and bagged, most of the people in line were waiting to be seated at a table in the restaurant, which was located at the back of the building. Harriet, the day-shift manager, spotted John near the back of the line and waved him forward. Despite a few disgruntled looks, he squeezed through the line of people as if he had called hours ahead for a reservation…even though everyone knew they didn't take them.

Harriet, a long-time employee at Filippi's, liked John very much. Every time he came in, whether he ate in or took out one of their delicious pizzas, she treated him as family. I'll bet it seems to you that John has a lot of adjunct relatives…well, he does.

It was ten years ago, just before Billy Filippi passed away, that John gave him a painting of a gondola floating down a canal with an unforgettable, beautiful backdrop of Venice as a gift. That painting is one of the many paintings of Italy's picturesque shores and hillsides that hang on the vine-covered walls throughout the restaurant.

I knew Harriet myself from the old days. I even tried to date her years ago…hell of a looker back in the day. Big Billy Filippi, one of the four Filippi sons, made sure that the employees treated John like royalty anytime he wandered into the restaurant…and they never failed to do so.

Harriet gave John the usual hug before leading him to a secluded table way in the back. The small booth was in a corner surrounded by lattice which was intertwined with fake grapevines loaded with rubber grapes. Empty wine bottles hung precariously overhead. John always preferred to sit near the open kitchen where the aroma of pizzas and pasta cooking in the ovens wafted to the tables nearby. John said he was curious as to why she led him to a table in the back, after passing two small tables near the front. Moments later, he found out.

Harriet handed John the menu and warned him that Elizabeth was sitting on the other side of the restaurant. She said she was with some man she'd never seen before. John raised his head and glanced curiously in their direction; but with the restaurant as dark as it was, he couldn't spot them. With all the lattice work between the booths and the servers moving around with their trays, only Superman with x-ray vision would be able to see them.

John said, "Now I know why you put me at this table."

Harriet answered, "I took a guess and thought you might want to separate yourself from them."

Harriet knew that John and Elizabeth had split up. She thought it best to keep John away from that side of the restaurant and did the right thing. With Sabrina on John's mind, he didn't need or want any other distractions.

John said that, once he found out Elizabeth was in the building, he had second thoughts about eating in. He told the server when she took his order, that he had changed his mind and wanted his order changed to take-out instead.

As John waited for the box with the pepperoni pizza to show up at his table, he kept glancing at his watch as if that might make time fly.

Fifteen minutes later, Harriet walked up carrying the pizza and set it on the table. She smiled warmly and said 'This one's on the house.'

John got up from the table, kissed her on the cheek and made his way towards the front entrance. As he passed by the main wine rack, he spotted Elizabeth...who saw him at the same time. She was sitting in a small booth with... yeah...you guessed it...that Gary fella...'all business,' my ass.

When he told me he decided to leave the restaurant and not eat in, I got pissed at him. In my opinion, he should have stayed right there...at the restaurant. He should have eaten his pizza there at that table. I mean, why not? 'You're a free man' is what I said, rather harshly too, I might add. Why should he give a crap if she sees him there? It was over between them. I put my nose in it pretty darn hard about that...maybe a little too hard for John's liking.

After my rant, he offered his reasoning for leaving the restaurant. He told me that he'd had such a good time with Sabrina, he didn't want to let running into Elizabeth that afternoon ruin the high he'd been on over the last few days. I couldn't blame the man for that.

***

Still on a Sabrina countdown, John laid back on his sofa, the pizza box lying on the table in front of him with six of the eight slices untouched. As he stared at the ceiling, thinking about Sabrina and many other things, his brain churned like some machine spitting out product. The image of Elizabeth sitting in Filippi's with that guy slipped in with all the other stuff.

He said he shook his head several times to remove the image from his head but he couldn't help being curious about how long before their break-up she had been doing the mess-around. I didn't want to beat him down with harsh words again so, this time, I just became a good listener.

He reached for another slice of pizza before pushing himself off the sofa. He folded the big slice and took a huge bite off the end. Walking across the room to the work area, he gazed at the easel holding the canvas of the woman. After taking another bite, he switched his gaze to the unfinished painting of the schooner…then refocused again on the sketch of the woman. He closed his eyes and began to recall the image locked deep in his memory.

He glanced at his watch, then decided to kill some time and paint. For the next half hour, he lined up the materials he'd need before mixing the paint used to block the background of the canvas. With the proper sizing already applied and dried on the canvas, he was ready to paint.

He switched the magnifier light on and studied the photograph in the locket. With the basics of the portrait sketched in with a 2B pencil, he gently rubbed over the pencil marks, leaving just the faintest of lines.

He started applying paint with a scrubbing motion, working between the smaller brushes for the details then switching to a bigger brush for the larger areas. After he finished blocking the background, he began to block in the darkest darks, starting with the hair.

He glanced at his watch and was surprised that he'd been busy painting for at least two-and-a-half hours. He was disappointed that it was now five-thirty and he'd had no call from Sabrina. He said all kinds of scenarios were filling his head…even bad things that were hard to shake off. Just for starters, things like weather delays, missing a connection, or mechanical delays raced through his mind. When he mentioned this to me, he left out the less desirable scenarios.

He knew the exact scheduled arrival time of her flight into Joplin Regional, five o'clock. Knowing that, and the fact that it was now five-thirty, did not ease his anxiety. The expectation of Sabrina calling at any moment was the only thing holding him together.

John kept busy and made good progress on the painting. The work was serving two purposes. Get the painting ready to take to Kate's Galleria the next day…and make time go by quickly, even though he had lost track of how much time.

He referenced the photograph numerous times, flicking his eyes back to the canvas as he dry-brushed in the shadow lines and applied paint to the inner parts of the portrait while keeping the edges soft. John said, to his surprise, painting portraits was easier than doing paintings of boats on water, which required much more detail and background settings.

He narrowed his eyes, trying to make sure the hair next to the face was soft and somewhat blurred. He then took a dry brush and gently stroked over the lines to blend the edges. Two hours later, the woman in the photograph began to materialize on the canvas.

Adding highlights to the nose and the eyes created realism. Continuously shifting his eyes between the photograph and the painting, assessing tones, shades and finer detail, John worked determinedly until the painting was finished.

He got up from the stool, took two steps back, setting his feet flat on the floor. He closed his eyes, visualizing the image in his mind once more. He then opened his eyes and stared at his finished work. He was satisfied and convinced that he had it right.

John had become so engrossed in the portrait that time flew by...the sun had set and the only light in the house was the light situated directly over the canvas. The rest of the house was dark. He sat back down on the stool and studied the portrait for so long that he was in trance mode. This happened many times when he was laser-focused on a project.

It was now seven-thirty, and John still had not heard from Sabrina. Without the painting occupying his time, he began to panic. He said he paced the entire condo several times, moving through every room. He called, but Sabrina didn't answer her phone. It seemed strange to him that the message option didn't activate. John was at his wit's end.

When John called me, we had a house full of customers; it seemed like the busiest night ever. Sakae happened to be standing next to the phone at the end of the bar...then summoned me as if *she* was in a panic. I couldn't hear John very well over the noise and music. He rambled on so fast that, at first, I couldn't figure out what his problem was.

He kept saying 'Why hasn't Sabrina called?' over and over again. He actually wanted *me* to tell him why she hadn't called. Obviously, I had no way of knowing that answer. He needed someone to listen...and I couldn't at that moment. As I said, we were busy.

At the time there was only one thing I could say...'hang in there, Johnny-boy.' I told him there must be some logical reason why she hadn't called yet. I can still hear the panic in his voice when I think back to that night.

Anyway, I didn't hang up…I improvised. I stuck the phone to my ear, holding it there with my shoulder, while I mixed a drink for a testy customer. Suddenly, a moment later, I realized I was standing there holding a receiver against my ear with no one on the other end…John had hung up without saying another word. Now that really made me worry.

I grabbed the phone and looked at it curiously for a moment. At that point, what else could I do other than make my way to the end of the bar and set the phone back in its cradle? I just shook my head and went about tending bar, trying to convince myself that John would figure it all out and call back later with some good news.

I was wrong. John didn't call back with good news…he didn't call back at all! After he hung up on me, it was all John could do to maintain his sanity. Sitting there in the silence, staring at the walls, or standing out on his balcony wondering why she hadn't called just wasn't cutting it.

An hour later, around eight-thirty, John wandered into the pub. As I said, when he called that night, we were busy as hell. When he walked in, we were even busier. John stood at the end of the bar waiting for me to catch a break in the action…a look of despair on his face. I finished giving change to some guy that I had warned 'last call' after serving him more than three scotch-over-rocks during the last two hours…and then hurried over to the desperate-looking man standing at the end of the bar.

"The plane landed!" John said loudly. "I went to the airline website and…the plane landed!"

"That's good news," I replied as Sakae squeezed by and picked up an empty glass sitting in front of a woman with a sleeve tattoo. "Did she call?"

"Nope," he replied shaking his head.

"Did you call her?"

"Yep…five times. No answer."

I didn't know what to say. To tell you the truth, I was just as surprised as he was and now starting to wonder myself. "There has to be a good reason… otherwise she would have called," I said loudly.

Sakae rang the small bell at the other end of the bar, meaning I needed to fill a drink order. The bell was her idea some time ago, primarily because I shoot the shit too much with customers.

"Why wouldn't she call?" John asked, shaking his head again.

I could tell John wanted to start the whole conversation over again. Sakae rang the bell again, and I spun around quickly and stared at her even though I had an obligation to a customer. I turned back to John, who I knew was hurting, but there was nothing I could do to help at that point. It was me who was now in a quandary.

"Look, Johnny-boy," I said. "Don't freak out on me. I'd like to stay here, talk and worry about this with you…but, as you can see, we're busy…I've got to help Sakae. Why don't you sit down over there and I'll have Andrea or Sakae bring you something?"

I turned my back on him for a moment, and he was gone.

Chapter Thirty-eight

Five hours earlier

Around six o'clock, Sabrina walked out of the Joplin Regional Airport terminal and hailed the next taxi waiting for a fare. The driver put Sabrina's suitcase in the trunk of the car, pulled away from the curb and headed towards Neosho. The trip would be thirty minutes from the airport. Sabrina, exhausted from the long flight and lack of sleep over the last few days, could not wait to settle in back home.

It had been drizzling all day in Joplin. It was dark and cold out and the streets were damp and slick. The taxi driver, a hefty woman in her forties, was quick to make conversation--you know the type. Sometimes, you get in a cab and the driver never utters a word until a thank you for the tip, but not this one. From the minute they pulled away from the curb, she would not stop talking. She went about making small talk and asking questions, certain that her passenger wanted to participate.

"Travel far?" she asked, glancing at Sabrina through the rear-view mirror.

"San Diego," Sabrina replied, yawning as she gazed out the window at the streetlights reflecting off the damp blacktop. She yawned again and reached into her bag for her cell phone.

"San Diego!" the driver said, shaking her head. "I'd sure like to go to San Diego, but I just can't afford it...ya know what I'm saying?"

"I'm sure you'll get there someday," Sabrina said, trying to be cordial, praying for a break in the conversation, desperate to call John.

"It's been real cold here, ya know."

Sabrina sighed, "That's winter in Missouri for you."

"How was it in San Diego?"

"Nice."

Ten minutes into the trip, Sabrina started to dial John's number. The anticipation of hearing his voice excited her. At the same time, however, the driver got a call from dispatch and, the moment she reached for the hand microphone, it happened in a flash of sparks and shattered glass. A huge pickup, carrying bales of hay stacked in the bed covered with a tarp, broadsided the taxi as it went right through the red light. The accident was horrific, echoing as if it were an explosion in a wind tunnel.

The cab driver, focused on taking her call, misjudged the signal and crossed the intersection just after the light turned red. The driver of the pickup, traveling at the speed limit of forty-five miles per hour, realized at the last second that there would be impact and tried to swerve to the right, out of the way. His attempt at diverting his trajectory was futile, given the dampness and condition of the road.

The truck's left front end smashed directly into the middle frame, right-front passenger door and front fender of the taxi. The impact came within a millisecond of a direct hit on the rear door, centering the impact directly on Sabrina.

The taxi's right-front tire came apart and the wheel hub dragged on the blacktop, throwing sparks into the darkness like a Fourth of July fireworks show. The impact spun the taxi 180 degrees into a metal utility pole, causing gas to leak slowly from the hose attached to the mangled gas tank.

Two guys in a Tundra following the taxi (who, thankfully, happened to be off-duty firemen) skidded to a stop, jumped out of their vehicle and ran towards the mangled mess…which now had a small flame brewing under what was left of the crushed rear-end of the taxi. The bumper was hanging by a thread of twisted metal, and the trunk lid was wide open and badly creased.

The cab driver, although badly shaken, was able to vacate the vehicle on her own. Wobbling slightly on her legs, she limped around to the right side of the cab, threw her hands up to her head and screamed to whoever could hear her…"Passenger! There is a passenger in there!"

The rear door on Sabrina's side was buckled, but intact. Because of the impact and the severely bent frame, the window had shattered as Sabrina's head smashed against it. Meanwhile, the firefighters noticed the flames beneath the rear of the taxi.

One of the two men made an about-face and darted back to the Tundra to get the ten-pound fire extinguisher. The other off-duty fireman rushed to Sabrina's door and yanked hard to get it open. He yanked several times with all his strength until the door finally broke loose, causing a screeching metal-on-metal sound. Sabrina's unconscious body, still strapped in, fell limp towards the opening.

Meanwhile, the guy who had rushed back to the Tundra unhooked the metal strap that fastened the extinguisher to the inside running board of the truck and carried it back to the wreck as fast as he could. His friend reached in and unsnapped Sabrina's seatbelt. He carefully lifted her out of the car and quickly carried her several feet away to safety.

Seconds later, standing at a safe distance, the fireman pulled the pin and pointed the extinguisher horn just as the mangled wreck became a massive fireball. He jumped back just before the taxi exploded, causing flames and debris to shoot high into the sky.

Sabrina lay unconscious in the street, blood oozing from her head near the hair line just above her ear. The fireman, shielding her body with his, quickly took off his jacket and placed it underneath Sabrina's head as the blood trickled down the side of her cheek. A bystander called 911 and, within minutes, sirens were screaming down the road, getting louder by the second.

***

Obviously, John had no idea what was going on. It was now getting late. Sakae and I were cleaning up the pub when John called again. The only thing he knew was that he hadn't heard from Sabrina. In his mind, there was no explanation. He kept calling her phone, only to get some crazy sounds. I could tell he was in a panic, and I felt helpless to do anything.

He said that he called her office phone, but only got her voice mail. At this point, all those dreams of sunken boats and fighting for his life in the raging ocean seemed trivial and of no importance. He would rather be fighting to survive in a raging ocean than to believe Sabrina would not call after the wonderful time they had experienced together.

The only explanation that I could offer at the time was that Sabrina had had some time to think on that plane ride. She may have figured things were moving too fast between the two of them and, therefore, felt she needed to slow things down a bit…that she'd call in the morning. I knew it was a stretch when I suggested it, but I had to say something. As I expected, my rationale didn't help. John was a basket case, and that wasn't going to change until he heard from her.

***

Back in Joplin, the ambulance, fire trucks and police cars converged on the scene of the accident. The two off-duty firemen stepped aside and a paramedic dropped to one knee to assess the situation. He opened Sabrina's eyes and, using a small flashlight, could see her eyes reacting unequally.

He placed his index and middle finger to the side of Sabrina's neck where the artery passes close to the skin.

Her heart rate was dangerously low, but she was alive...still breathing. One paramedic carefully applied a neck brace while another examined her arms and legs for any visible injuries.

As they carefully lifted Sabrina onto a gurney, the police officers questioned the taxi driver as well as the driver of the pickup truck. No one at the scene had any idea who the victim was. Remnants of Sabrina's suitcase, her purse and cell phone were recovered in different locations around the scene...burnt to a crisp.

All the authorities could deduce as a result of questioning the taxi driver was that Sabrina had just flown in to Joplin International from San Diego. Within fifteen minutes of the paramedic's arrival, Sabrina was lying unconscious in a screaming ambulance, hooked up to oxygen and an intravenous drip, heading for Joplin Mercy.

Chapter Thirty-nine

With no call from Sabrina, John woke up the next morning with his head pounding. Little sleep and several more calls to Sabrina's phone with no response made it a night from hell…as if he hadn't had enough of those lately. I called him early and woke him up from what he said was finally a deep sleep. The phone ringing excited him until he realized who was calling. He was starting his day off as a continuation of the night before…waiting and wondering.

We talked for a while until he had to get moving. Sabrina hadn't called, and neither John nor I had a clue as to why. He said he was going to call her cell phone again, and I said I hoped she answered. That would solve at least one problem…knowing she was all right. Before we hung up, I told him to stop by Skipper's after he saw Kate, and I'd treat him to a tea and a hamburger. He didn't commit to it, but I knew he'd come at some point.

John called Sabrina's cell phone several more times but got nothing, not even a ring tone. He described it as mind-boggling and said, other than shaking and scratching his head after each call, he didn't know what else to do but wait and wonder.

John picked out the right-sized picture frame from several he had stored in a closet. He laid the frame on a piece of rug, so as not to scratch the front of it, and neatly nailed the canvas to the frame. Then he wrapped it in brown paper and tied it off.

It's a good thing he couldn't see the expression on my face when he told me, during the conversation we had that morning, that he was going to take the picture to the Galleria later that day. In my mind, displaying that picture in the

Galleria hoping to attract someone who might recognize the woman whose picture had been embedded in a lost locket for who-knows-how-many years was a million-to-one shot. On second thought, at least it gave the poor guy something to think about other than Sabrina…although, truth be told, a tsunami could hit the coast and he'd pay it little mind. Until Sabrina calls him, he was going to be a troubled man.

By the time John got his shit together, it was around ten o'clock in the morning. I was in the office preparing for the day and saw John's Jeep pull into one of the spots in back. He took the portrait out from the hatch compartment and walked away.

Kate was near the back of the store and smiled when she saw him. He put the picture down on the floor, leaning it against her desk.

"Where is my hug, Miss Kate?" John said, his arms stretched out wide.

Kate took a small step back and held up both hands. "I wish I could, John," Kate said. "Whatever I had, or still have for that matter, I certainly don't want to pass along to you or the girls in here. I don't *think* I'm contagious any more…but why take a chance? No hug today."

"This time, I'll let you get away with it," John said, smiling, "but I get a rain check…right?"

"Bank on it," Kate replied. "Now tell me about this picture. Is it something special?"

"I will tell you this much," John said, lifting it off the floor. "It's not a picture of a boat…but it is special. It's a portrait of a woman."

"Woman…?" Kate said, furrowing her brow. "Is it a picture of that someone you told me about yesterday? Are you expanding your portfolio?"

"Not really," John replied, removing the wrapping from around the frame. He placed the sixteen-by-twenty-four-inch painting on its edge at the corner of her desk. "I had a vision of her and…well…uh…I was compelled to paint her."

"It's really a beautiful portrait, John," Kate said, admiring the detail. "You should paint more of these, you know. With your natural ability, this proves that you can paint anything. With your name on it, this will sell fast. Who is the wom…wait a minute…what did you mean when you said you had a vision? Isn't this a real…living person?"

"Well, yes and no," John said in an apprehensive tone. "I'll only sell this portrait on one condition, Kate. Whoever wants it can only buy it if they recognize the woman."

Kate said, "OK… now you've got me confused. What is all this about?"

John set the frame back on the floor, leaned it against the desk and sat down in the leather armchair directly in front of Kate. He now had to revisit everything he shared with me, Sakae, Sabrina, and Ron King. Now we add one more to the list, Kate.

John spent the next thirty minutes talking while Kate listened. He knew it was a lot for Kate to take in. Although Kate was one of those people who are hard to read, the expressions on her face were telling. She was very interested in John's tale of the braided locket.

He started out by telling Kate about the locket he had found on the beach, which didn't stir up too much interest in Kate's mind. People find things on the beach all the time. The inscription and the picture of the woman seemed logical. What peaked her curiosity was when John started talking about dreams and fighting for his life in the ocean

The part that Kate found particularly interesting and strange was when John said he was walking along the ocean floor when he found Solitude One and then saw the ghostly figure of a girl in a flowing white gown. Although Kate tried like hell not to demonstrate the feeling of concern she had for John's state of mind, it wasn't easy. John, however, could recognize a level of doubt as her expressions were telling.

On the other hand, when John told her about Ron King and Solitude Two, that, in itself, was a different story altogether. Kate's mind opened up to the reality that inexplicable and strange things do, on occasion, occur...be it fate or mind-science or something perplexing that only God could orchestrate. She actually said that to him, which didn't make my case any easier.

"Whew!" Kate said, using her hand to wipe across her brow. "That's a hell of a story. I can tell this has been a lot for you to handle, John. I can't image what all this means, but the fact that you painted that portrait tells me there has got to be some explanation for these occurrences."

John had thought about the dreams, the locket, the inscription and the woman he'd just painted so many times that his mind was spent. He said that, although he had no choice but to tell Kate everything, he was sick and tired of talking about it. At the same time, however, he showed no disrespect to Kate and her thoughts about what he was telling her. Most of the time, he looked her straight in the eye.

After a while, however, John watched Kate's lips move but didn't really hear the words coming from her mouth. Sabrina was commanding his full attention. Althhough he didn't let on, he was feeling sick to his stomach. He couldn't stop thinking and worrying about Sabrina and why he hadn't heard from her. At that point, John said, the portrait, the story about it, and even his existence on this earth was secondary to Sabrina's well-being and his desire to be with her.

"So..." Kate said. "How can *I* help?"

John didn't answer. Kate looked at him funny. He was sitting across from her, his eyes glazed over. It was obvious to Kate that John was somewhere else besides in the chair directly in front of her.

"*John*?" Kate said softly. "John...are you OK?"

John blinked and gave his head a quick shake. "Huh? ...Oh...I'm sorry. What did you say?"

Kate smiled, "How can I help? You know...with the painting? And, John, really...are you alright?"

"Yes," John replied. "I suddenly became preoccupied with something else, and I'll tell you about that after we finish discussing this picture," he went on, tapping the top of the frame. "If you don't mind, Kate... I'd like to display the portrait in a conspicuous place for a while in hopes that someone inquires about it."

Kate said, "And if someone does...?"

"Then I'd like to be called right away. Michele or any of the others can reach me on my cell phone. Once I get a call, I will drop what I'm doing, get on my horse and get down here post haste.

"And what price do you want the painting to sell for?"

"If you don't mind, Kate," John said, "I don't want to sell it just yet. I'm hoping someone will recognize the woman and inquire about it."

"Well, in any event, I think it will easily go for three hundred," Kate said, "but anything for you. You can keep it in the Galleria as long as you wish. I'll instruct the ladies to be on the lookout. And as far as your story about the locket and the dreams, I won't share that with anyone unless you say it's OK," she continued in a voice now exuding a hint of concern. "I can tell something else is bothering you. I picked it up over the phone yesterday. So... now that we've discussed the portrait...what is troubling you? And about this girl you were with Christmas Day...?"

What John didn't know, while he was telling Kate all about Sabrina...how they met and the wonderful time they had spent together (with the exception of some of the personal things he shared with me), I had received a distressing call from Joplin.

As soon as I answered the phone, a stranger on the other end of the line said, "I'm sorry to bother you... but is this Skipper?"

I said, "Yes, this is he, and who is this?"

"It's Karla," she said, sniffling, sighing deeply.

Right then, my knees buckled. I knew something was terribly wrong.

"Is it Sabrina?" I asked nervously.

"She was in a terrible accident on the way home from the airport."

I paused and took a moment to process what she had just said...and she let me. My heart was in good shape, but my chest felt like it had collapsed with the news. I said nervously, "Is she... alive?"

"Yes, thank God," Karla replied, trying hard to keep it together for my sake. "She's been lying unconscious in Joplin Mercy Hospital since the accident."

I took in a deep breath and held it before asking, "Are you saying Sabrina is in a coma?"

"Well," Karla replied, "they are not sure...or at least they're not calling it a coma. She sustained some fairly severe trauma to her head. The good news is her vitals have now stabilized."

My conversation with Karla wasn't a long one but she did tell me that, after the accident, they had no idea who Sabrina was. The emergency response team got her out of the taxi just in time. She told me about Sabrina's suitcase, cell phone and bag--burned and scattered everywhere around the scene of the accident. That explained it all.

During the conversation Sabrina had had with Karla on Christmas Day, she said that she remembered Sabrina talking about yours truly and a pub called Skipper's in Coronado. She said she had no way of contacting John so she took a chance and looked up the number of Skipper's on the internet.

Before talking to John, I asked Karla if Sabrina had sustained any other injuries and she assured me that she hadn't, which gave me great relief. I asked her how they found out who Sabrina was. She said that, sometime the next morning, an attending nurse recognized Sabrina from a visit she had made to her Uncle Phil, who had had a stroke a few weeks earlier. I guess you could say that the nurse recognizing Sabrina was, pardon the pun…a stroke of luck.

Karla was calling me from the hospital. I told her I would get hold of John right away and break the news as gently as possible. I wrote Karla's contact number down and suggested John would be calling her very soon.

Forty

Breaking bad news isn't one of my strong suits. It is never pleasant, and I dread having to do it. It is always a matter of how you do it, though. The untimely death of Ginny was devastating to John. He went into a shell for what seemed like weeks before accepting the fact that his mother was gone. I feel certain that what I say and how I say it won't matter...it's going to crush the poor boy's heart, either way.

One thing I knew for sure, however...before telling John what happened, it was important for me to work through my own reaction to the situation. I needed to re-cover from my own distraught feelings first. It was going to be just as hard for me to tell him as it will be for him to hear it.

Sakae wondered why I was in the office instead of prepping the bar for the lunch crowd. She walked in and saw me sitting there with my head pressed into the palms of my hands. I explained the situation and, although she was shocked at the news, she was quick to remind me of one important thing...Sabrina was still alive...and that was good news. In some ways, Sakae is a lot like Sabrina, al-ways looking at the bright side of things.

I kept glancing out the door into the back lot. I didn't know if John would come through the pub after leaving the Galleria or just walk around the building to his car...either way I didn't want to miss him. I had to plant myself in my office until I laid eyes on him.

As you can imagine, all kinds of questions were swirl-ing around in my head...how to start the conversation was one. I began to doubt myself and wondered if I was the right person to give John the news. On the other hand, I had to tell him that Karla called. How could I do that and not tell him what she said? Now you see how conflicted I was about the whole thing.

I thought about just telling John to call Karla back and let her explain it all but decided that hearing it from a stranger would only make the news more difficult to receive. If not her, who else? Who was I kidding...it had to be me.

I convinced myself that I had to practice...formulate the right words. I actually said that to myself as I sat there sulking. Do I call his cell phone, or should I wait until he walks through the door? More questions needing answers. If I don't call and instead wait till he arrives, the pub might be busy...and then what do I do? Do you see what I was going through here?

All the questions were making my brain hurt. For a moment, I was convincing myself that I should see where his head was before I broke the news, but I quickly dismissed that idea. I needed to come up with the right approach...the time had to be right.

As you can see, I was really wrestling with the whole communication thing. Anybody other than Johnny-boy would have been no problem. It would be easier for me to tell a strange little boy his dog died. It may not be a good comparison but, honestly, that wouldn't compare with the angst I was going through about this situation.

I still hadn't moved from the chair. Sakae opened the door and stuck her head in for the third time in fifteen minutes. She knew what turmoil I was going through and must have felt sorry for me... otherwise she would have given me 'the look.' I nodded. It was my way of telling her I would be coming out soon.

What I really needed to do was rehearse...rehearse what I would say whether I saw him in person or had to tell him over the phone...whichever came first. It's almost as if

I was in a race and had no idea where the finish line was. I was a long way from being even remotely prepared.

I rehearsed phrases like...'John, I have bad news'...'John, I got a call from Karla and there has been an accident'...'John, Sabrina's been hurt but she's alive.' No matter which way I phrased it, nothing sounded good to me.

Well... as it turned out, I wasn't on a time clock. John didn't come back to get his Jeep for hours. After John finished up with Kate, and as he was walking back to the pub, a car honked twice to get his attention. At first, he said he paid no attention to it. After taking a few more steps, he heard a voice cry out.

"John! John Adler!"

John glanced over at a red Ford Edge as it double-parked...he didn't recognize the car. He peered through the open passenger-side window and recognized Ron King as the driver, so he stepped off the curb and made his way over.

"Ron?" John said, with a surprised look on his face.

"Yeah," Ron replied. "I happened to recognize you walking down the street...what great timing! Ever since the day you...uh...look, John, " Ron went on as he glanced up at the rear-view mirror and noticed an approaching car, "I have something I want to share with you and I can't do it here, double-parked in the middle of Orange Avenue. I'm on my way to the Marina to take Solitude Two out for a spin. If you're not doing anything for the next few hours, why don't you join me?"

John didn't hesitate. He opened the car door, slid into the seat and shook Ron's hand. "It's going to be cold out there," John said.

"Don't worry," Ron replied, pulling away from the curb. "I've got warm gear on board.

Ron King is a good-sized man, at least six-two in height. He wore a gray, bushy Fu Man-chu mustache that grew well below his upper lip, and he had a healthy crop of salt and pepper hair, sides cut short. When he put on his ball cap as they walked towards the dock, he reminded John of the actor, Wilfred Brimley...except not quite as old and less heavy.

Since both John and Ron knew how to sail, they inspected all the standing rigging—the wires and ropes that support the mast—including the turnbuckles and cotter pins securing the rigging to the hull. After trolling between the docks, out of the marina and into the bay leading out to the ocean, Ron checked the wind direction indictor attached to the top of the mast. He pointed the boat into the wind to make sure there was the least amount of wind resistance to raise the sail with the sail straight back.

John secured the bottom front (*tack*) of the mainsail and jib to their respective shackles on the boom and the bow of the boat. Ron yanked on the jib sheet, the side away from where the wind was coming, trimmed the mainsail and turned the boat slightly into the wind--maybe 60-75 degrees off the wind--and they were underway.

Suddenly, Sabrina came back into John's mind. He hadn't checked his cell phone since heading for the Galleria. He pulled the phone out of his pocket and immediately became angry with himself...the battery was completely dead. He'd used it so much the night before calling Sabrina's phone that he hadn't paid attention to the battery life. Ron noticed that John was acting strange, uptight.

"Seems like something's wrong, John?" Ron yelled, as the bow of the boat crashed against the large ocean swells and through the loud, whistling wind coming off the sails.

"I've been waiting for a call, and my phone has a dead battery!"

Ron pulled his cell phone loose from the holder attached to his belt and held it out in front of him. "Here," he yelled, "use mine."

"Don't know the number by heart," John replied in a loud voice. "It's programmed in mine, and I've got nothing."

"I'm sorry," Ron said loudly, the wind making it almost impossible to hear across the deck. "Do we need to turn back?"

John shook his head. "No...that's OK. I'll take care of it later. I'm anxious to hear what you wanted to talk to me about."

"In order to do that," Ron said, talking loudly through the strong cross wind. "We should heave to!"

Now John had me with that one. I had absolutely no knowledge of what the hell that meant... 'Heave to.' As he gave me a brief lesson on sailing, I got bored and asked him to cut to the chase. Basically, 'heave to' means to slow the boat into a controlled position without dropping sails so they could basically drift. Now I've explained it...that's what they did.

Once adrift, Ron said, "After you left my house, I got to thinking. I made calls to two of Steve's old friends," he continued, as he turned the rudder to keep the boat drifting toward the wind. "They were both with Steve at a nightclub the night before he took his boat out. Even though it was many years ago, one of them remembered something I thought to be interesting. He said my brother and two other guys were trying to convince a couple of good-looking chicks to go sailing with them."

"Did he know if they went?" John asked, anxiously.

"Unfortunately, no," Ron replied, shaking his head. "But he did say that one of the girls, college girls by the way, seemed interested.

"After finding that out, I wanted to find and tell you. I was ready to go to the gallery where I purchased your painting and ask if they could help me. If that didn't work, I would abuse my position and use government intelligence-gathering data to contact you," Ron continued with a wide grin. "And here we are."

While Ron was talking, John suddenly had this strange feeling. He said that the sensation only lasted a moment or two…just long enough to cause him to glance over at the coastline. He got the feeling that they might be sailing in the same area off the coast where he was the day he spotted the sailboat sitting on the ocean floor.

He kept the strange feeling to himself, but he glanced over the edge of the boat straight down into the water…it was dark and murky.

Chapter Forty-one

While John had a good time sailing out to the Point with Ron King, I'm not sure that the information Ron had for him did anything other than put more questions in his mind. Now that it seemed possible that one of those two girls did perhaps go sailing with Ron's brother, Steve; without real knowledge or facts to work with, there was nothing to do but wonder. The only thing that Ron's information provided was just another ambiguous piece to an unsolved mystery of the enigmatic locket.

It was about four-thirty when John came to the pub. I had to thank God for that one. It was the right time for him to walk in--between rush hours. When I spotted him, I took in a deep breath, exhaled slowly and began to prepare myself for being the bearer of bad news. Sakae, changing the 'specials' menu on the chalkboard off to the side of the entrance, spotted him as well and turned to get my attention. She gestured for me to stay calm.

"Where have you been, Johnny-boy?" I said as he made beeline around the other side of the bar towards my office.

"Sailing with Ron King," he replied, seeming to be in a hurry. "I'll have to tell you about it later, Uncle Skip. Right now, if you don't mind, I need to slip through your office and out to my car. My cell phone is dead, and I need to hook it up to the charger in the Jeep to use it."

When John made his way through my office and out the back door to his car. I went into the office and shut the door behind me. I watched as he leaned into the open door of the Jeep and fiddled around with the cord to the phone charger. I knew exactly what he was going to do…try Sabrina's phone again. I watched as he pressed buttons on the cell phone. I knew that making that call was futile, and it killed me.

I saw him shake his head in disgust, appearing very irritated. He tossed the phone attached to the cord down onto front seat, backed away from the Jeep, slammed the door and headed back in. I took in another deep breath. At that point, the rehearsing, thinking and pondering I had done earlier didn't help me a bit; I was searching again for the right words. That morning, the world slipped off its axis when Karla called me, and I had no idea how to set it right.

As soon as John walked through the door, he saw me point to the chair behind my old wooden desk. He stood there and looked at me curiously. I suggested he sit down. He angled his head as if to say, 'Is there something to this?' I couldn't hold back. There was no reason to, at this point. Any approach to communicating would have to do. I had to lay it out there quick…like ripping a bandage off a sore.

"Karla called me," I blurted out while trying like hell to maintain a calm look on my face.

At first, I could tell that John had no idea what or who I was talking about; but a millisecond later, he made the connection.

"Karla?" he said, narrowing his eyes and then widening them.

At that point, I didn't allow him to say anything else. I just went for the rest of it. "There was an accident, John. Sabrina is alive," I said, in a firm tone.

"Accident!" John interrupted as he shot to his feet. "Where…how…when?"

"Now calm down," I said, forcefully. "We can get through this. I told you that she was alive, so just let me explain!"

At that point, I was in total control of the situation; I had information that he didn't. John plopped back down in the chair as if his body was a limp sack of potatoes. Not knowing what else to do with himself, he started nervously running his hands through his hair.

There was no doubt in my mind that he wanted to pound his fist on the top of my desk or scream at the top of his lungs…but he didn't. I had to give the boy credit for maintaining his cool. Once I could tell he was ready, I started from the beginning.

I told him that I received a call from Karla around ten-thirty, shortly after he went to the Galleria. I explained how she was able to contact me and how the accident happened. I rushed through it intentionally, trying not to give John a chance to ask questions. I wanted to get it all out there first.

I explained everything I could about the accident, including the fact that an off-duty firefighter had pulled Sabrina out of the taxi just before it caught fire and blew up…and how lucky she was that the innocent bystander saved her life. That's when John dropped his shoulders and pressed his head deep into the palms of his hands.

I walked around my desk, stood next to him and placed a hand on his shoulder for comfort. I wanted him to calm a little before breaking the rest of the news. I told him to take a deep breath, and I did the same.

"When I talked to Karla this morning, she said Sabrina was unconscious from trauma to the head."

"I knew there had to be something else," John murmured. "What is it?" he went on as he lifted his face out from the palms of his hands and took in another deep breath. "Are you telling me that Sabrina is in a coma?"

He turned and looked up at me with a blank look as if I were Sabrina's doctor. I repeated exactly what Sakae told me. "The good news is that she is alive."

"What hospital?" John said softly.

"Let's see," I said reaching into my pocket for the paper. "I wrote it down when Karla told me…Joplin Mercy Hospital." I handed him the paper. "Karla's phone number is also on there. She told me to have you call her as soon as I made you aware of the situation."

John pushed the chair back away from the desk. I stepped aside and he rose from the chair. Without saying another word, he turned and made his way out the back door to his Jeep again. As he went to call Karla, I went back out to the bar and told Sakae it was over. She asked how it went, and I said I didn't know.

I told her what I said, and she was relieved it was over. I know *I* was relieved...at least for now, that is. For John's sake, all that we could hope for was Sabrina's recovery sooner than later. As I said before, he already had too much to worry about.

I couldn't stand the wait. Fifteen minutes had passed, and I was curious as to what new news Karla might have. I hurried back into my office and glanced out through the screen door, only to see John still sitting in the Jeep...still talking.

The call lasted a good half-hour. When John finally did walk back into the office, I was back out behind the bar preparing things for the dinner crowd that would likely be filing in within the next two hours.

John told me he kept his cool the whole time he was on the phone with Karla, another reason to be proud of him. He said it was as if Karla had been willing him to call. He said that she lit up as soon as she heard his voice, her tone changing from a somber pitch to a joyful tone in an instant, even with the subject matter at hand. She'd been sitting on pins and needles, waiting most of the day to hear from him.

There was no need for introduction, small talk or any of the politeness that might occur had they met before Sabrina's accident. There was only an apology from John for not getting in touch sooner. John said that the tone of the call could not have been more serious. At that point, Sakae and I wanted to know everything.

"Karla," John said softly. "Tell me everything—the truth... I can take it.

There was silence for a moment on Karla's end except for a muted sniffle. "She's hurt badly, John," she said, trying not to sob as she had been doing all day. "She's been unconscious ever since they pulled her from the taxi."

"And the doctor? What has he said about her prognosis?"

"Nothing yet, John," Karla replied, her voice low, slightly muffled as she blotted her nose with a tissue. "Sabrina sustained a gash to the side of her head. I heard the doctor tell Sabrina's uncle that she could be in a mild coma...but it was too early to tell."

"What about other injuries?"

"Thank God," Karla said sighing, "...nothing other than maybe a bruised shoulder and a facial laceration."

"Have you been able to see her?" John asked.

"Yes," she replied speaking more clearly. "I'm sitting next to her right now. With the exception of being kicked out every now and then by the nurses, I've been with her ever since we were informed about the accident this morning. Her Uncle Phil was here earlier, but he couldn't sit around any longer and went home...the stress was getting to him. The stroke he went through recently makes him tire easily. He went home to get some rest."

After a moment's pause, John asked curiously. "What do you mean 'you found out in the morning?"

"Didn't Skipper tell you that the taxi caught fire?"

"Yes," John replied. "But...?"

"Everything was burned," Karla said, interrupting. "Her suitcase, all the clothes in it, her cell phone..."

"Cell phone?" John broke in. "That's why I got nothing every time I called!"

"I called several times myself last night," Karla offered. "Sabrina was supposed to call me when she got home; and when she didn't call, I was in a state of panic all night."

"I know, Karla...you weren't the only one. It seems like I called Sabrina's phone a hundred times. So how did you find out she was in the hospital?"

"It's a strange thing," Karla replied. "She was brought in as a Jane Doe. It wasn't until this morning that a nurse recognized her. It happens that Sabrina visited her Uncle Phil here the day after she got back from working the Del Coronado project. That nurse put two and two together, and the hospital ended up calling Sabrina's uncle."

"Karla," John said in a serious tone. "You can't begin to know what strange things have been happening lately. Anyway," John continued, "I'm coming."

"Coming?" Karla replied.

"I'm going to get the first plane out...tonight. Can you recommend a hotel?"

"I have the key to Sabrina's house...you can stay there."

John chuckled. "Sounds great to me, but I'm not sure I could do that at this point."

"Based on the conversation I had with Sabrina when she called me from your house, I'll bet she wished you lived there."

"What about her mother and sister?"

"They are on their way from Florida."

Chapter Forty-two

John walked into the San Diego terminal at seven o'clock that night. It didn't matter that it was a Sunday night…there were lines of people everywhere…travelers heading home after Christmas. Waiting for his flight, scheduled to take off at nine o'clock, was making his skin crawl. He had feelings of impatience and apprehension all at the same time. I had offered, and even demanded at one point, that he eat something at my place before he left, but he was too upset about what had happened to Sabrina to eat anything.

Standing in line for the ticket he had purchased over the phone (which, in itself, was a miracle given it was the day after a holiday) felt strange. Everything around him seemed surreal. His mind was obviously playing off his anxieties and fear of flying. Just being in an airport had given him the creeps since that flight to Chicago years ago.

What seemed like millions of people scurrying around, dragging bags, chasing after kids and pulling carts with squeaking wheels…it was all one big blur. He shoved his ticket in his jacket pocket then, dragging his carry-on behind him, headed up the ramp towards security.

As he passed the concession, he smelled freshly-baked pizza. It was Sabarro's…not Filippi's…but it was going to have to do. He decided he couldn't hold off any longer. Going all day with no food in his stomach and then strapping himself into the seat of an airplane he didn't want to be on would make a potential flight from hell even worse.

While seated at a high table by the railing lining the ramp to security and the gates, John ate one of his two slices of pizza and thought about the people walking by. One of the things popping into his mind was they all had a story…but likely not as strange as his. They had no idea what was going on in his life, nor he in theirs.

Everyone seemed to be on their own mission…some carrying briefcases with deadlines to meet, others having to work the next day, and still others hating the fact that they had to leave their families for another year. He sat there shaking his head, worrying about the tragedy that had just happened to disrupt his life.

Here was John…a man who, just a few months ago, had not a care in the world. He had no one to report to and no place to go when he woke up in the morning. He had a fiancé who was hot and gorgeous (although a bit of a bitch), and a talent that many people only wished they had. He wondered how the people rushing around the airport looked at him--if they even looked at him at all. He wondered how many of them were having to see a **psychiatrist for *their* demons…John was thinking too much, if you ask me.**

As he took the last bite of pizza, he suddenly felt a tug on his pants leg. He looked down and there stood a little boy…no more than three years old, holding a small plastic sailboat…looking up at him and smiling. The little boy's mother quickly walked up and took the boy up into her arms.

"I'm sorry," she said. "Sometimes he's quick to get away from me."

"You don't have to apologize," John said smiling. "I was the same way at his age. I see he likes sailboats."

"He's got them all over his room…along with tons of other toys."

"He's a cute kid. Does he like to fly?"

"He's much better about it when his dad is with us. My husband's in the Navy…stationed here in San Diego. We spent Christmas with him."

"How neat is that?" John said, glancing at his watch. "Well… I guess I should get going. I need to psych myself out before I catch my plane."

"Aerophobia?"

"More than you know," John replied. "You and your boy have a safe flight. Nice talking to you," John went on, and then pulled up the handle of his carry-on. "My name is John."

"Don't worry about your flight," she said, smiling. "It's safer than driving, you know? It was nice meeting you, too…I'm Virginia."

You would think that things could not get any stranger…what are the odds…a little kid that likes sailboats with a mother named Virginia? Are you kidding me? John took his seat in first class. Good thing he could afford it; it was the only seat available when he booked. At least, with his anxiety, he could fly in comfort. I'll tell you, feeling the way John was feeling, if it were me, I would have taken immediate advantage of the free alcoholic beverages.

***

The flight wasn't as bad as John thought it would be. Other than the initial take-off, the plane flying out over the ocean before turning back towards the east, and some slight turbulence along the way, he said it was tolerable. Two hours in the air and John was fast asleep, leaning back in the soft, leather recliner. John hadn't had any dreams worth talking about for a few days. During the flight, however, it was as if he had taken some psychedelic drug.

He relived the entire sequence of nightmares all over again…the initial dream of fighting for his life in huge ocean swells…the dreams of being in the violent storm with punishing rain slapping him in the face and waves slamming on top of him, driving him under the water.

The voice of the girl crying out for help rang loud in his ears. With his eyes closed and his body calm, his mind was exploding with brain wave patterns shooting in every direction. Neither the flight attendant nor the passengers sitting near him had any clue as to the turmoil taking place his head.

He could see the mast of the sailboat ripped and torn, leaning sideways--the boat about to capsize. The image of him walking on the ocean floor and spotting the name 'Solitude One' was vivid. He could see the girl in the white flowing gown hovering over the boat, haunting him, her arms extended towards him.

He found himself standing in front of the mirror, witnessing the face of the woman melt away as the mist covering the mirror beaded up and slowly dripped down, distorting and eventually erasing the image. He said he could see himself from a distance, running along the shoreline, the breeze pushing against his face.

The next image that flashed through his mind was the heart-shaped locket…the braids embedded around its outside edge pulsating, emitting a glow that got brighter second by second. He was standing ankle-deep in the water staring at it slithering at the water's edge, growing in size the longer he gazed at it. The whole experience was a collage of pictures fading in and out, like images off a reel from an old super-eight camera.

The most disturbing images John saw while in that REM sleep were images of Sabrina looking out the window of the taxi when the truck plowed into it. The image of her being pulled from the vehicle, unconscious and lying in the street with blood seeping down her face, was horrifying.

The final image of the taxi exploding and going up in flames is what startled him awake. After blinking his eyes and shaking his head, he checked his watch. He had been in the air three hours; one leg of the flight complete.

A change of planes, and he was in the air again. This time, he was flying on a regional airline…no first class. The flight attendant handed out blankets. He took one, draped it over himself and fell asleep again. The next thing he knew, 'fasten your seat belts' rang out over the inter-communication system…they were on approach into Joplin.

John rented a car and drove fifteen minutes to the Hilton, the closest hotel to Joplin Mercy Hospital. He walked into his room, tossed his carry-on on top of the stand against the wall and went straight for the sink. He soaked a washcloth in cold water and pressed it against his face.

It was now very late, around one-thirty in the morning. Within fifteen minutes of checking into the hotel, he was heading to the hospital. As he drove down the dark street, the headlights of the few cars heading towards him appeared like starbursts against the damp road ahead. All he could think about was Sabrina.

He had no idea what to expect when he got there. The fact that visiting hours might be over didn't deter him…he was going to see Sabrina, no matter what. He was two blocks away when the neon sign high up on the building caught his eye, 'Joplin Mercy Hospital.' When he glanced back to the road, yards from the intersection, the yellow light was just switching to red.

He slammed on the brakes so hard that all four brakes locked and the car swerved and skidded to a stop just inside the crosswalk. He took a deep breath and steadied himself. The light seemed to take forever to change. He heard sirens coming from behind. He looked in the rear view mirror and saw an emergency response vehicle barreling down the road, colored lights flashing.

The traffic light in front of him suddenly switched to green, but too late for him to move his car through the intersection and to the right, so he just sat there right in the path of the flashing lights rushing towards him. As the ambulance maneuvered around his car, he couldn't help but think about how scared Sabrina must have felt strapped to a gurney in the back of a vehicle just like that…if she were awake at the time.

From the general parking area, John made his way into the lobby and up to a counter where a stout, older man wearing a security uniform sat behind a desk, doubling as a receptionist. He was sipping some very black coffee and reviewing a stack of paperwork. John noticed a plastic placard on the wall behind the desk. Visiting hours had ended at eight o'clock.

The man looked up at John with a curious look on his face. John said it didn't take but a second or two for the man to recognize the tired look of sheer desperation on his face. I'm sure that the security guard had seen the same look many times before.

"I just flew in from San Diego, sir," John said politely. "Can you please tell me what room Sabrina Harper is in?"

The man slowly put his coffee down on the desk and punched a few keys on the keypad in front of the screen before looking back at him. He smiled in a kindly manner and then said, "Fifth floor…502."

Chapter Forty-three

After taking the elevator to the fifth floor, John made his way down a wide, silent hallway looking for signs with a sequence of room numbers. He reached a small, empty waiting area with four upholstered armchairs and two dispensing machines--one for water and soft drinks and the other for candy bars and chips. On the wall next to a long corridor, he saw a sign with an arrow pointing to room numbers 475-525.

At the end of another corridor, he noticed an orderly dressed in gray pants and something similar to a pull-on scrub shirt. He pushed a cart with a large, cloth bag hanging from one side. White folded towels were stacked on top of the cart with various cleaning materials arranged on the two shelves below.

The employee pushed the cart through a set of double doors, which opened automatically as he approached. As John got closer, he could see a sign hanging from the ceiling above...'Intensive Care Unit (ICU).'

All of the sudden, the reality of it all hit John right between the eyes. He was about to encounter a situation which far outweighed any nightmare he'd had up until then. He had to confront the truth that he would soon be face-to-face with a woman who had become very special in his life as she lay unconscious in a hospital bed. He would look at her and wonder...if...and when she opens her eyes...would she know who he is? Would she see him as John or just one of many people surrounding her in an unfamiliar place that seemed strange and scary?

As John made his way toward the doors, he told me he was thinking the worst without even knowing Sabrina's real condition. He couldn't shake the bad thoughts invading his mind, no matter how hard he tried. He cringed inside thinking she might lose the memory of the short but wonderful time they had spent together.

He forced good thoughts into his mind, thoughts that quickly filled his head. He remembered how the scent of her hair filled his senses as she stepped by him onto the balcony that day and how they lay next to each other to keep warm. He thought about how they gazed into each other's eyes as they sat at the small table in Arrivederci's, sipping wine…and how the candlelight reflected off Sabrina's smooth, silky skin.

The sight of her beautiful face as she stood in front of his table at Skipper's that first time as he took his nose out of that sci-fi novel and saw her gazing at him--that moment was indelibly etched in his mind. He recoiled at the thought of her not remembering that wonderful night...the first time he laid eyes on her...the significance of which he had not yet been able to explain to her.

As he got closer to the double doors, he pictured her face in the dim light of his bedroom as they made passionate love for half the night, their bodies inseparable until morning…and the sight of her wearing his button-down shirt and panties as she fixed him her famous vegetable omelet.

Thinking of all these things had his heart pounding by the time the automatic double-doors leading into the ICU opened. Visiting hours had been over for hours. Karla had extended her welcome until the nurses finally insisted she go home.

Just because the security guard let him through, would someone else working on this floor insist that he leave before getting to see Sabrina? John didn't know what opposition he was going to be up against as he tried to see the girl he was so much in love with. The kid was on a mission, I tell you; and one way or the other, he WAS going to see her!

When he walked through the doors, a smell of freshly-brewed coffee was coming from a break room. Two nurses were getting their fix of caffeine to jumpstart the long night ahead. The area he walked into was oval-shaped, with doors all along the outside perimeter leading into private rooms. The inside area was mostly a huge nurses' station with rows of file cabinets and several computers lined up on the counters. Chairs and phones completed each work-station.

There were two nurses who looked to be in their middle thirties sitting together, chatting--one with long hair, the other short. A much younger looking nurse, perhaps a nurse's aide, sat a short distance away, fiddling with some papers.

One of the two nurses sitting together spotted John heading straight for them. She nudged the other nurse to get her attention. Since John already knew he was in violation of hospital rules regarding visiting hours, he quickly had to determine which of the nurses he would approach. He also had to have a compelling story. Persuading them to let him see Sabrina was his goal. He decided to take on the two nurses sitting together.

He noticed they both wore wedding rings. He hoped that that meant they were the sentimental, romantic type. As John stood at the counter, both nurses stared at him as if they were in a daze. Although he'd never admit it, because he's not vain in that way, that seems to be the effect he has on most women...no surprise there.

Even though he'd traveled for hours and sported a shade of stubble on his face, John was definitely eye candy to them. He gazed directly into their eyes. After an uncomfortable moment of flicking his eyes from one to the other, he said. "Good morning...my name is John Adler. I just flew in from San Diego. The woman that I'm going to marry was in a bad accident, and she is somewhere in this hospital, presumably still unconscious. Can you help me?"

While John was delivering what he thought was perfect justification, the two nurses couldn't sit still, squirming in their seats. They both subtly competed with each other for John's attention. One nurse asked for the name as the other scanned the list of patients.

"Room 502," John said smiling. "The person in the lobby said that was Sabrina's room number."

The nurses looked at each other, pointed in the same direction, and said in unison, "It's that way."

As they looked at each other awkwardly, the nurse with short hair took over. "Just follow the walkway around to the other side of this station and you'll run right into 502...on the left. One of us will be in later to check her vitals...oh," she continued, as she glanced again at Sabrina's paperwork, "you should be prepared. She *is* still unconscious."

Well, that wasn't difficult at all. John probably could have asked them for a steak and baked potato, and one of them would have rushed out to cook it. John made his way around the corridor to the other side of the station.

He said everything was quiet. So much so, that it gave him an eerie feeling. With the exception of one or two, all of the rooms he passed heading to 502 had the doors closed. Four-ninety-seven, four-ninety-eight, four-ninety-nine. He counted in his head. The closer he got to Sabrina's room, the more the little hairs on his back of his neck started to rise.

He wondered how many people in this section of the hospital would ever make it out alive. He said he dismissed that thought quickly. Sabrina was going to be one of them. He reached 502 and stood outside the door for a moment, preparing himself for whatever he would see when he walked through.

All he wanted to do was focus on Sabrina's beautiful face. He told me that he had decided, no matter what she looked like, he would see only the beauty in her.

I could tell by the look on Sakae's face as John was telling us this story that she wasn't going to take much more without breaking down. I took her hand and squeezed to comfort her. She quickly got up from the chair and hurried off to the restroom.

John hardly pushed on the door and it swung open easily; the room was dimly-lit. The bed was against the far wall and Sabrina lay motionless; her upper body slightly elevated. It was shocking to the point that John felt his stomach twist...not because of the way she looked but just because...

The top of her head down to her forehead was swathed in white bandages. Her face, swollen around her right eye, was the color purple. Her right shoulder, wrapped with some sort of thick padding underneath the bandages, looked twice as big as her left shoulder, and translucent tubes on poles fed medication into her veins. John said that he stood over Sabrina, feeling utterly helpless.

Chapter Forty-four

John blinked several times, trying to get orientated. The nurse with the long hair came walking into the room to check Sabrina's vitals.

John said, "How long have I been sleeping?"

"Not sure," she said, smiling. "You were sleeping when I made my rounds two hours ago.

Realizing he might be in the way of the nurse performing her duties, he quickly slid the chair he was sitting on a short distance away from the bed and stood by with his arms tightly folded while the nurse examined Sabrina's pupils. The nurse aimed the beam of a small flashlight on and off Sabrina's pupils.

John said it was painful to watch. Sabrina's head lay perfectly still, and her body was motionless. The nurse continued with the other routine duties he assumed she did for other patients as she made her rounds from room to room. John wanted to ask her a million questions but didn't know where to start or even if it was appropriate to do so.

"I can't thank you enough for letting me stay here with her," John said softly. "Am I breaking the rules by being here?"

The nurse inserted the ear pieces of the stethoscope snugly into her ears. "Only if I ask you to leave, and you resist," she replied with a grin.

As she checked Sabrina's blood pressure and pulse, John was compelled to ask, "Is everything good?"

The nurse looked at him and smiled, "Perfect."

The nurse went on about the business of taking readings from the other equipment riddled with little colored blinking lights, checking for any variations with previous readings. She checked the level of the fluid in the drip bag and lifted the blanket by Sabrina's feet just enough to feel for dampness before loosely tucking it back in between the mattress and the bed rail.

When she lifted the blanket, John caught a glimpse of the ankle bracelet. Seeing it still around her ankle sent warmth surging though his body.

When the nurse finished her business, she replaced the chart and started to leave the room. John said sheepishly, "Excuse me. Uh...before you go...do you think she will come out of this soon?"

"I'm not a doctor, you understand," she said compassionately, smiling, "but I've seen it happen time and time again."

John sighed deeply. "Thank you for saying that."

* * *

It was now seven in the morning. The night-duty nurses had left, and the next shift took over. The aroma of freshly-brewed coffee seeped through the slightly-cracked door into Sabrina's room. He stepped across the hallway and stood in front of an administrative assistant about to finish a phone conversation. Several other people, wearing hospital garb, were moving from room-to-room, carrying clipboards and pushing small carts. It was that time of the morning when the pace in a hospital begins to pick up.

"How can I help you?"

"I was wondering," John said, "Could I buy a cup of that coffee that smells so good?"

Two lights on the phone lit up before the woman could answer. She picked up the receiver, quickly placed the palm of her hand over the microphone and motioned to the right. She whispered, "Ten yards, that way. There's fresh coffee sitting on the shelf right behind the wall separating the desk and storage area...you can help yourself."

John, in his polite manner, mouthed 'thank you,' nodded his head and walked away. While pouring coffee into a paper cup, he faintly heard Sabrina's name mentioned. He quickly put the pot back on the hot-plate and made his way into the corridor and around towards Sabrina's room. Three ladies in street clothes were standing outside 502 talking to a nurse.

One of the three ladies was much older than the other two...she looked quite matronly. Her look was staid and dignified...an attractive, slightly graying, somewhat plump woman. She wore tan pants and a blouse with a light jacket over it. The collar was tucked under her hair, which just rested on her shoulders.

The other woman had similar features to Sabrina, although she looked a little older...maybe just into her forties. She stood a little shorter and had highlighted hair cut short with waved layers blended to a neck-hugging, tapered nape. She wore pants, sweater and two-inch heels...her shape was similar to Sabrina's as well. The third woman was thin as a rail, around thirty-six, and seemed ten feet tall but was probably about five eleven, in reality. Her hair was light brown, cut short with short spiky layers...very trendy.

If it weren't for John's ability to quickly recognize, remember and process things, he would have been standing in the middle of the four of them rather awkwardly. However, he remembered Sabrina describing Karla as being tall and thin.

"Karla?" John said softly, stepping up alongside of her.

All the ladies, with the exception of the nurse who had walked off just as John appeared, turned to look at him. Karla knew right away who it was.

"John!" Karla said excitedly before throwing her arms around his shoulders as if they were long-lost friends. "I wondered if you were able to get a flight out last night...until just now, when the nurse told us that you were actually here all night."

John turned slowly toward Sabrina's mother, "Yes, Karla, I was here all night," he said extending his hand and looking straight into Margaret's eyes. "And you're Sabrina's mother, Margaret. I'm John Adler…Sabrina's friend. I'm so sorry we had to meet under these difficult circumstances."

Margaret's eyes filled with tears. John said she tried like hell to put on a smile but, instead, broke down in his arms as if *she*, too, had known him forever. Heidi, Sabrina's sister, put a hand on her mother's shoulder, smiled at John and then said softly, "Hi, John…I'm Sabrina's sister, Heidi. Thank you for being here. Sabrina told us both all about you. She will be delighted when she wakes up and sees you."

It was distressing all around. They all loved the woman lying in that room. She had no idea what had happened to her two nights ago. She walked off that plane looking back at the wonderful time she had with John, and perhaps a wonderful time ahead…and in a blink…well…how does anyone know when this sort of thing might happen?

They walked into the room single file, with John leading the way, holding the door open. Once in the room, he stepped aside and so did Karla. Sabrina's mother and sister slowly went to the side of the bed. As soon as Sabrina's mother got close, she broke down again…but this time into Heidi's arms.

John walked back out to scavenge for two more chairs, since there were only two in the room. He spread out the chairs in a half-circle around the side of the bed and they all sat there silently…all the ladies holding tissues at the ready in their lap. John had to break the silence. He thought for sure that Karla would, but apparently she was out of character that morning.

John, positioned close to the head of the bed, rose from his chair and grabbed the safety rail with both hands. He leaned slightly down towards Sabrina.

"OK, Sabrina," he said in an even tone. "We are all here with you so you can open your eyes now."

Pausing for a moment, John leaned in closer…close enough to feel her warm breath again. "Please wake up, my darling," he whispered as he kissed her lips softly. As soon as their lips parted, just like in the movies, Sabrina's eyelids began to flutter…then slowly opened. They opened and closed several times as she turned her head towards all the machines situated on the right side of the bed. She was terrified at what she saw.

She had no idea where she was or why she was there. She looked around at all the electronic equipment and the clear tubes running from those skinny poles and shivered inside. John had his hand on her forearm and felt her body stiffen. Heidi and Karla rose from their chairs while Margaret remained still. She sat there sobbing tears of joy.

"Sabrina," John said softly. "It's OK…you are OK. You were in an accident, but you are OK."

Sabrina turned her head, saw John standing there, and smiled tiredly. Heidi moved up close to the rail. "You scared the hell out of me, little sis," she said with a warm smile. It was the only thing she could think of to say without breaking down.

Sabrina's mother managed to stand, move to the bedside and took Sabrina's hand. Karla quickly made her way out to the nurse's station to inform them that Sabrina was now awake.

"Hi, Mom," Sabrina said, her voice soft and cracking a bit.

"You came back to me, my little girl," Margaret said, weeping… "I prayed that you would."

Suddenly, there was chaos. Two nurses hurried into the room. One of the nurses, with a stethoscope hanging around her neck, lifted the chart off the hook and made a beeline for the head of the bed. The other nurse followed behind… pushing a small cart which she rolled towards the end of the bed as she instructed everyone to leave the room. Sabrina turned her head towards John as if to say, 'please don't leave.'

John leaned down and kissed her again. "I'll be right outside…we'll all be right outside until they finish. After that, we are back in here…OK?"

Sabrina slowly nodded, then closed her eyes again.

Chapter Forty-five

After John, Margaret, Heidi and Karla cleared out of the room, they stood single file near the wall so as not to get in the way of foot traffic and equipment moving through the corridor. Suddenly an older man, wearing scrubs with a stethoscope hanging from his neck, walked past and turned into 502.

Karla turned to look at John. "He's the doctor who saw her yesterday," she whispered. "He's a nice man. He explained to me and Sabrina's Uncle Phil everything that he thought was going on with Sabrina at the time."

After a few minutes, Heidi took Margaret the short distance to the waiting area. John and Karla leaned against the wall, anticipating the moment the doctor would walk out of the room.

"That girl in there loves you, you know," Karla said with a grin, softly nudging John's arm.

"I hope so," John replied, shoving his hands in his pockets, "Because I'm going to ask her to marry me."

Karla acted as if she would jump out of her skin when he broke that bit of news…something that he had decided on the spur of the moment. John couldn't wait to get back in that room to ask her. He felt confident that, even though the time they had spent together was short, she would say yes. A wise man once said…'Time is not relevant when it comes to two people meant to be together'.

John said, sighing anxiously, "I don't have a ring, Karla. Do you think it matters?"

Karla leaned her head back against the wall and smiled. "A ring…? Nah… Truthfully," she continued, "the beautiful ankle bracelet she is wearing will suffice for now,

I assure you. I saw it around her ankle yesterday. You did buy it for her, didn't you?"

"Yes."

"I knew it," she said, smiling at him. "Then the ankle bracelet will cement the deal."

It seemed like forever before the doctor walked out of the room, turned in John's direction and stopped. He carried a clipboard tucked between his arm and side while he was texting a message on a smart phone. One of the two nurses followed him out of the room and waited near the opening. John walked up to the doctor, waited until he was finished, and extended his hand. The doctor glanced briefly at the nurse and handed her the clipboard.

"Doctor," John said. "I'm John Adler. Sabrina's mother and sister are sitting in the waiting area, and I believe you met Karla, Sabrina's best friend, yesterday. We are all anxious to hear what you have to say."

The doctor was a short, portly man with dark hair graying at the temples who wore bifocal glasses in a thick frame. He smiled at Karla, and then reached for John's hand.

"I'm Doctor Jones...Carl Jones. Pleased to meet you. Why don't we walk down the hall and go see them now," he said in a gentle tone. "That way I can tell all of you at the same time about Sabrina's condition, and what I believe to be her prognosis."

There was no one else in the waiting area at the time. Heidi helped her mother up from the chair as Doctor Jones approached with John and Karla. After introductions, the doctor began to explain Sabrina's condition.

Now don't expect me to get all of the medical jargon correct. In essence, what John told me was this...Sabrina had experienced a severe blow that caused a gash on the side of her head and had lost quite a bit of blood as a result.

He said the MRI indicated Sabrina had a slight edema or, in simple terms, she had minor brain swelling. He explained that, normally, the blood to the wound would absorb into the body within a few days. He also said that usually, with an injury such as Sabrina's, patients don't tend to be unconscious for more than a few hours. The fact that Sabrina was unconscious for two days gave him pause, to some degree.

The doctor wanted to make sure Sabrina hadn't sustained some injuries other than those of which they were currently aware. He concluded by briefly explaining the physiological process that keeps a person conscious...the transfer of chemical signals from the brainstem to the cerebral hemispheres. The doctor wanted to be cautious, however, and run a few more tests just to make certain her brain functions were normal.

Other than all of the medical terms and jargon, he said Sabrina was a lucky woman. He was confident that Sabrina did not sustain any other significant injuries and, in time, she should be just fine.

John asked, "How long will Sabrina have to be here?"

"Let's see," he said, adjusting his glasses. "We'll run tests...keep her under observation for a few days...I'd say four more days, to be safe.

Everyone was relieved at the news. Four more days and John could take Sabrina home. John, Karla, Margaret and Heidi made their way back to 502. One nurse was still there, adjusting and resetting the equipment situated around Sabrina's bed. She finished up by wiping Sabrina's face with a warm, damp cloth. Before leaving, she made it clear that Sabrina needed to rest and that she could only have one visitor at a time for the rest of the day.

Margaret and Heidi had come from the airport straight to the hospital. John could see they were weary from the long, early flight from Florida. He suggested that they go to Sabrina's mother's house to rest and freshen up and that he would stay. There was no argument from any of them. Based on what the doctor said, they were all confident that

Sabrina was out of the woods and they could leave her in John's hands.

It was still early in the day. Karla wanted to be there when John popped the question to Sabrina but knew it wasn't her place and would have to get the scoop later. Besides, she volunteered to head straight to the office to inform Sabrina's Uncle Phil, who was involved in an important meeting, of the good news. Before leaving, Karla stopped short of the door opening, turned, glanced at Sabrina's mother and Heidi, winked at John, then gestured a thumbs up…they had a little secret.

***

Sabrina slept most of the day, only waking now and then. When she did, John was there holding her hand. John checked his watch. It was three-thirty. Sabrina had fallen asleep again so John decided to go downstairs to the cafeteria for a sandwich. That's when I got the call from him.

When John told me the good news, I immediately relayed the message to Sakae. We felt like celebrating. It was one-thirty in the afternoon when John called. The pub, packed to the rafters with a lunch crowd, prohibited us from doing that sort of thing. If it were not for that, I would have sneaked Sakae into the office and had my way with her.

I didn't like the fact that John was going to be away for a while…for how long, he couldn't predict. Four more days in the hospital…Sabrina goes home…John stays for who knows how long…the whole thing sucked. Sakae was hoping for another miracle…that John would bring Sabrina back to Coronado and they would live happily ever after in California. I think she missed the big tips John gives her for the free tea.

As John sat in the hospital cafeteria eating his chicken sandwich, he felt happy. The words from the doctor were music to his ears…'she should be just fine'. He gazed at the paintings hanging on the wall around the cafeteria. Although painting was his passion, Sabrina was the love of his life.

He'd been in Joplin for around thirteen hours and hadn't seen the light of day in the city where Sabrina grew up. Even though he wondered how long he would stay...it really didn't matter. He would stay as long as it took to get her back on her feet...until she was completely healed.

John had made up his mind that he would take this opportunity to convince Sabrina to come live in Coronado. He knew it wasn't going to be easy. Her career was there in Joplin. She was doing exactly what she loved...journalism...and he had to figure out a way around that important issue. She loved investigating and writing as much as he loved painting. John asked me if I thought that Sabrina could get a position with one of the papers or magazines in San Diego...maybe her uncle could help. My answer...I have no idea.

He knew that living all of her life in one place, the place where her mother lived, would come into play in his effort to convince her to relocate. He thought about how beautiful Coronado is and how much fun and happiness he could provide for her there, just off the sandy shoreline. He pictured them running on the beach just as the sun set or enjoying a glass of whatever as they sat on his balcony watching the waves crashing onto the beach.

He said that he would see to it that Sabrina visited Joplin whenever she wanted. She could bring her mother out any time she missed her enough. I would say that John's life has gone from mundane to complete confusion in a very short period, wouldn't you? There was one thing, however, that wasn't confusing to him...Sabrina. Whatever they decided to do, they would be doing it together...of that, he was certain.

Chapter Forty-six

Two days after Sabrina regained consciousness, she was moved from the intensive care unit into a room on the fourth floor. Between the time that it took the administrative staff to prepare the paperwork and the nurses to manage the transfer, John made a quick trip to the hotel to clean up and change clothes.

Sabrina didn't like the idea that John was staying at a hotel. She wanted him to stay at the house she had purchased just six months earlier in a newer section of Neosho. As much as John knew she wanted him to see her new house, the hotel, a short distance from the hospital, was much more convenient and kept him close.

Sabrina's recovery seemed to be swift. Other than the gash that took twelve stitches, and a slight headache, she felt close to normal. Following doctor's orders, Sabrina, wearing one of those unflattering hospital gowns that bothered her but not John, took short walks in the corridor three times a day, holding onto John's arm…a vital part of the rehabilitation regimen.

With the exception of feeling somewhat dizzy now and then, which made it difficult at times for Sabrina to maintain her balance, she was doing fine. According to the doctor, minor dizziness was common after such a severe blow to the head so they didn't worry much about it. John kept in touch with me, giving updates and assurances on Sabrina's status. Margaret and Heidi had visited three times after Sabrina moved out of intensive care, bringing her a pair of new slippers and homemade chicken-vegetable soup in two small plastic containers, enough for both of them. Sabrina's Uncle Phil stayed in touch by phone.

Karla and some of Sabrina's other friends popped in and out to see her, always bringing with them something of encouragement. Multi-colored bouquets of flowers and women's magazines took up the entire top of a medical supplies cabinet against the wall.

Although it wasn't the best of circumstances, given Sabrina's confinement to a hospital bed with nurses coming and going every other hour, everyone involved was optimistic.

It was just a matter of time before they would be looking in the rear-view mirror. The hospital would be just a fading memory. They would soon be on the way to Sabrina's new house, and she was excited to show it to him.

Speaking of Sabrina's house, a thought crossed my mind. She never mentioned the house to John during the time they spent together in Coronado. Here, they had conjured up an entire fairy-tale scenario. It was all about them being in love and *their* dream versus *his* dreams. The fairy tale never included a newly-purchased property or them living in Joplin.

I have a theory... does that surprise you? They talked about everything under the sun...including...let's say...some of their darkest secrets, which you might expect. That's what love-birds do. Sabrina's new house never entered the conversation ...so why not?

My theory is...and mind you, I see it as part of a big picture. Sakae sees it as me speculating too much. In any event, I think they blocked out anything that might keep them separated. Whether she lived in a new house, an old house, apartment or an igloo, she didn't want to bring it up...and I don't think, at the time, he would have wanted to know. Anyway, enough with the speculation for now.

While Sabrina was mildly medicated and peacefully sleeping, John slipped out of 502 and called me. He wanted some advice. Isn't that ironic? He was conflicted about what his approach should be when trying to convince Sabrina to sell her house and move to Coronado. After almost losing her as a result of that accident, John seemed to be in a state of confusion or just downright irrational...not thinking clearly. He actually thought that if he didn't take the time now to discuss it with her while she lay in that hospital bed, his chances of bring it up at a later date would somehow change things. I'll tell you...this poor kid was head-over-heels, out-of–his-mind in love. I guess I couldn't blame him for that, but John wanted it all at once...and now.

So John says to me... in a state of panic, I might add..."I love her, Uncle Skip. I'm going to ask her to marry me the first chance that seems right and, if it has to be in this hospital, well so-be-it."

I said, "You mean...while she is lying in a hospital bed?"

He said, "Hospital bed, hallway, on the moon...I don't care. I'm going to do it."

"Congratulations, Johnny-boy!" I said. "I approve."

"I'm going to tell her to sell her new house, quit her job at the magazine and fly home with me...you know...after a week or so, maybe...when she feels up to it. What do you think?"

Now it was time for my two cents. Boy, did I let him have it. "You're talking craziness here, Johnny boy! Are you hearing what you're saying?"

John was wound up as tight as a spring...I thought his mind would explode. He was emotionally out of control and grasping for straws. I guess he thought my response to that nonsense would be...'Great, go for it boy,' even though Sabrina had her own life and that life wasn't considered at all in his plan...yes, *his* plan. I wasn't about to let my thoughts go unspoken about this. After all, what are uncles good for if not to butt in? Besides...he asked me.

Based on my knowledge of Sabrina—and I'll have to admit the encounters were brief—she seemed smart, logical and reasonable. Now I *will* say this. I do believe Sabrina loves John dearly. However, Sabrina buying into a plan that bears no resemblance to levelheadedness…well, we have to conclude it just wasn't going to go John's way. It was just adding more chaos to an already untenable situation.

"Now listen here, Johnny-boy," I said firmly. "Sabrina's been through a lot over the last several days. Putting pressure like this on her now is not right, no matter how paranoid you are about being away from her. No matter how much you love her or how much you think she loves you, you have to get real here. Forget about her house and her job. Think about her mother, her friends…her whole life is centered in the Joplin area. Take my advice. Ratchet back two notches, and take it one day at a time."

John just listened. He didn't say anything. In itself, that was amazing to me. I thought for sure he'd give me his 'you've turned this into one of those Uncle Skip's come-to-Jesus talks'. Since he was giving me the opportunity, I kept at it. Oh…by the way, before I continue, I just want you to know that Sakae was listening to my end of the conversation, nodding in agreement the whole time with everything I was telling him.

"Here is what *I* suggest," I said calmly. "No matter if you do it now, do it tomorrow, or do it next week, I'm sure she'll say yes *whenever* you ask her to get married. So before you go off half-cocked and start making demands, make sure you discuss everything together… all the options. Talk with her about the things that directly affect the two of you ultimately living together, then…."

"You're right, Uncle Skip," John broke in. "What the heck am I thinking?"

"Wait a minute," I said. "I'm not finished."

"I know what to do now," he replied, in a sudden, confident tone of voice. "Thanks for listening. I'm glad we had this talk." The line went dead.

Chapter Forty-seven

In between interruptions from the nurses checking Sabrina's vitals and the machines, they talked and joked with each other. With John sitting in a chair and Sabrina lying back in the bed against a big white pillow, they spent the afternoon talking about all kinds of things.

They talked about the portrait of the woman and the fact that it was sitting on a shelf in Kate's Galleria. John was still hoping to get a nibble from anyone who might recognize the woman, taking him closer to finding Anna.

He told her about his sailing out in the ocean with Ron King on Solitude Two. He shared with her what Ron had said to him about his brother and his friend trying to persuade some girls in a nightclub to go sailing with them the night before Solitude One went down.

Sabrina was glad to hear that there had been no more strange dreams. She hoped that meant, at least for now, that burden was no longer on John...she figured that *her* current circumstance was burden enough for him right now.

It was nine o'clock in the evening, and John could see that Sabrina was getting tired. Her eyelids were getting heavy, most likely from the meds. He wanted her to go to sleep, but there was something important he wanted to do first.

Earlier, when John had gone downstairs to the cafeteria for sandwiches, he stopped by the little gift shop close to the chapel and bought a bright red rose. When he returned to the fourth floor, he asked the girl at the nurse's station to keep it for him. She took the rose, stuck it in a glass of water and put it on the lower counter.

Sabrina was falling asleep, and John was determined to do it right then. He pushed himself up from the chair, leaned over and kissed Sabrina on the lips.

"Don't go to sleep yet, my darling," he said softly. "I'll be back in a jiff."

It wasn't more than a minute before John walked back in with the rose in his hand. She saw him and smiled widely. As he stepped up to the side of the bed, Sabrina said, "John…what a beautiful…"

John quickly put his finger against her lips. "Shhh…don't say anything yet."

He fell to one knee, reached through the bed railing and took her by the hand. With his other hand, he held the rose up as if it was a torch at an Olympic ceremony and said. "Sabrina Harper…I love you more than life itself. That night you walked into my life changed me. I can't imagine my life without you in it. I want nothing more than to live the rest of my life with you. Will you marry me?"

Sabrina wasn't expecting that to happen, especially while lying in a hospital bed with a head full of stitches. It was awkward, but she loved it. Her heart pounded and her eyes filled with tears; it was the perfect moment. They were alone together…in the real world…not some fairy-tale world they had made up where time stood still. She wished that she was stronger so she could jump into his arms and press her lips against his and hold him tight…but the joy of hearing his proposal made up for not being able to do that.

"Yes…! Yes…! Yes!" Sabrina said as she wiped away a tear with a tissue she pulled from the box sitting on the over-the-bed table.

When John heard the first "yes," that's all it took. He got to his feet, laid the rose on the table in front of her and gazed deep into her eyes. "Thank you, Sabrina, for making me the happiest man in the world. No ring yet," he said with a smile. "Does it matter?"

Sabrina smiled back, "Matter...? Heck no. Nothing matters but this very moment. Besides," she added, "that means we get to do this all over again... *I'm* the luckiest *woman* alive."

The emotions that surfaced during those moments were no less exciting than an actual wedding ceremony. This was another part of this story that drove Sakae to break down in tears. I must admit...it even got to me a little. Anyhow, it wasn't long after John's memorable proposal that a nurse they had never seen before walked in, making her rounds. As usual, John moved aside. The nurse checked Sabrina's blood pressure. Using a small flashlight, she peered into Sabrina's pupils.

"Your blood pressure is a little high," she said as she removed the stethoscope from her ears.

"That man over there," Sabrina said, "just asked me to marry him."

"Well, then," the nurse said, smiling as she turned to John, "that explains it." There was a pause. "As exciting as this is, however," she went on looking at John, "you're wife-to-be should really try to get some sleep."

It wasn't long after the nurse left the room that Sabrina fell fast asleep.

***

Sabrina slept all night, straight through the nurses' rounds. John, on the other hand, said he was up and down all night. Even with the door closed to Sabrina's room, he could still hear the indistinct voices of the nurses talking at their stations, carts moving around on the linoleum floor and, every now and then, the faint sound of a siren penetrating the window as ambulances pulled up to the emergency landing off the street below.

Every time he heard a siren, he had visions of emergency medical technicians taking Sabrina out of an ambulance and rushing her through the emergency doors. He pictured her lying on a gurney while doctors and aides scurried around, wondering if she were going to make it…it pained him to think about it. It's a wonder the poor boy got any sleep at all.

He would doze off and wake up, then doze off and wake up again. It went on like that all night long. Every time he woke up, he'd check his watch; it seemed that time was standing still. He couldn't remember how many times he got out of the chair during the night and hovered over Sabrina's bed, checking on her, making sure she was still breathing.

Each time he checked on her, she was sleeping peacefully…and that's all that mattered. There were moments as he stood there under the dim light, watching her sleep, when he marveled at her natural beauty and wondered what dreams filled her head.

He wanted her thoughts to be about the two of them being together. He hoped that her mind was filled with thoughts of them and the time they would be spending together for eternity. Sounded a little corny to me…but Sakae thought it was sweet.

John moved his chair as close as he could, close enough to Sabrina that he could hear her breath. It made him think of the moment, two days earlier, when she woke up out of the dark state she was in as he kissed her lips…feeling once more her warm breath as it passed through her nose and brushed his cheek.

Once again, corny, but hey… John said the kiss reminded him of Sleeping Beauty when Prince Phillip kissed Princess Aurora to wake her and he intended to save that story and tell it to her on their wedding night.

The window in Sabrina's room was covered by heavy curtains, closed to the middle. After a long night, thin streaks of morning light seeped through the thin separation in the middle.

John sat there in the quiet, thinking. It would only be one more day before he could rescue Sabrina from that dreadful place. Suddenly, the door swung open…filling the room with light from the corridor. He glanced at his watch…eight o'clock in the morning. I guess when you're sleeping off and on all night, in the end, time sneaks up on you.

An older, heavy-set nurse with slightly graying, short hair walked in. She was wearing wire-framed bifocals and had a stethoscope hanging from her neck with the blood pressure cuff sticking out of one of the large pockets on her over-sized smock. She carried a plastic shot glass with pills inside in one hand and a cup of orange juice in the other hand. She put the pills and juice on the over-the-bed table near the end of the bed and went to the window.

"Sorry to disturb you," she said, grabbing each curtain in the middle and spreading her arms wide, letting more light into the room. "We get moving pretty early around here."

The nurse's rustling woke Sabrina out of a deep sleep. She pushed the over-the-bed table up toward Sabrina's chest then pressed the button to raise the head of the bed. "Good morning, young lady. How do you feel this morning?" she said as she handed over the juice and pills.

Sabrina swallowed the pills with the juice and turned to look at John, who was now standing, and smiled. "Other than a slight headache," she replied, "I feel wonderful, especially since my husband-to-be is here."

"Husband-to-be, huh?" the nurse said with a warm smile. The nurse inserted the ear-pieces of the stethoscope into her ears and wrapped the cuff around Sabrina's arm. She squeezed on the rubber bulb several times, and then took the reading. "Pressures a little high but should come down once you move around a little. Your breakfast should be coming in soon." She looked at John. "I can order an extra, if you'd like?"

John smiled wide. "Oh, no...don't bother. I'll get a muffin from the cafeteria later. But I will take a cup of that coffee that smells so good out there."

"You can help yourself," she said as she made her way out of the room.

They couldn't be happier. Sabrina had survived a terrible accident, John got on a plane without having a panic attack...and, on top of all of that, they got themselves engaged. In baseball terms, you would call that a triple play. I could be mistaken, but I think John might hold the world record for going from being disengaged to a new engagement in less than ninety days.

With the easy part done, the hard part was yet to come. What I mean by that is...where do they live and when do they do it? I'm sure, at that point, it was probably the furthest thing from their minds; they were as happy as campers in a wilderness.

They delivered Sabrina's breakfast, and John got his fresh coffee. He passed on the trip downstairs to get a muffin because he didn't want to leave her...so they talked non-stop for two hours. It's amazing what two people can have to talk about, even under the worst of circumstances.

It's called two-way communication...give-and-take... something John and Elizabeth couldn't do during the entire time they were together. John and Sabrina even tackled the subject of where they were going to live. According to John, it went like this.

"Where do you want to live?" John asked, as he kept his fingers crossed behind his back.

Sabrina didn't hesitate. "Coronado."

John...surprised and wide-eyed that she would come out with an answer so quickly...said, "What about your mother?"

Sabrina replied, "I don't know."

John said, "Are you sure about Coronado?"

"Yes."

Again, he said, "But what about your mother?"

"I don't know what to do about that."

"Has she ever been to Coronado?"

"Believe it or not…she's never been to California."

"That's good news. We'll get married in San Diego… she'll love it and want to stay."

"Married in San Diego? But I have a lot of friends here."

"How many do you think?"

"I don't know…I've never counted…but it has to be dozens. Let's see…my mother and my uncle…work friends, other acquaintances, high school and college friends I keep up with now and then. Throw their families in the mix, and it adds up quickly. How many do you have?"

"Let me think.   There's Skipper, Sakae, Kate, a few sailing buddies, a couple other owners of art galleries and a few friends I went to San Diego State with. After I add that up in my head…I guess it boils down to us getting married right here in Joplin."

Sabrina laughed. "Skipper will just have to shut the pub down for a few days," he continued, his voice serious. "But, Sabrina…I have to ask again…what do we do about your mother? I feel like I'm stealing you away from her. "

"I don't think she'll move out of Joplin, but she'll understand if I do…my sister did. Besides…we can bring her out to visit anytime she wants to come, especially in the summer. She usually goes to Florida in the summer, but now she'll have a choice."

"What about your job?"

Sabrina smiled warmly, shaking her head. "It's just a job, John."

"OK," John said rubbing his palms together. "We are making a lot of progress here. Shouldn't we be writing this stuff down?"

Sabrina chuckled and pointed to her head. "I've got it *all* right here."

John moved the over-the-bed table away. "Are you up for a walk? The nurse said you should move around a little."

"I'd love to go for a walk," she replied. "I just wish it were a walk around Shelter Island."

"Me, too," John said, as he moved his chair out of the way, lowered the safety rail and pressed the button to raise the head of the bed further.

Sabrina turned her body towards the side of the bed and hung her legs over the edge. John slipped the new slippers Margaret brought onto each foot and helped her slide off the bed. They went through that same routine every time they went for a walk.

Standing close, the tips of their feet almost touching, John put his hands on her arms just below her shoulders and she put her hands on his hips. Their eyes locked and their lips met. The kiss was warm and passionate. If the door to the room stood wide open, which it wasn't, they wouldn't have cared. As their lips came apart, Sabrina collapsed in his arms.

In a panic, John held on tightly to keep her from falling to the floor. Her eyes went shut, and her head fell to one side. John, *trying* to stay as calm as possible under the circumstances, lifted her up as far as he needed to get one arm situated under hers. He secured her body against his and reached for the button to summon the nurse.

"Help...! Help!" he yelled, holding her limp body between him and the bed, as he jabbed at the call button.

Chapter Forty-eight

Nurses came rushing in like the Calvary. One nurse took Sabrina by the legs while John held her steady. Another nurse quickly lowered the head of the bed. Two other nurses watched as John and the nurse lifted her lower body up onto the bed. Sabrina was unconscious.

John laid her head on the pillow and softly shook her shoulder in an attempt to wake her. He said her name twice, but there was no response... no flickering eyelids...no motion. One nurse told John in a firm voice to leave the room. Reluctantly, he backed out... not taking his eyes off what he could see of Sabrina's body with all the nurses now gathered around from one side of the bed to the other.

John paced back and forth in the corridor just outside the room, desperately hoping for one of the nurses to exit so he could corner her for information. John said he was scared to death that, this time, he would surely lose her. He racked his brain, trying to figure out what was wrong...a normal reaction for anyone in that situation, I suppose.

Suddenly he spotted someone in a white coat hurrying down the long corridor. It was Doctor Jones, resettling his glasses on his nose as the stethoscope swung from side-to-side on his neck. John's impulse was to stop him to ask what was going on, but he knew it would be futile as the doctor hadn't had a chance to assess the situation. One of the nurses rushed out of the room as the doctor went in.

"Is Sabrina awake?" John spat out as she hurried by.

The nurse didn't stop or even look at John. "Not yet," she said. She was carrying a vial of blood.

John became fidgety, shoving his hands in his pockets, pulling them out, then shoving them back in. He looked one way and then the other down the corridor as he paced in front of Sabrina's room, wondering when the door would open again.

John was now officially a basket case. His body started to tremble in fear. He said all he could do was keep repeating that Sabrina had to wake up and had to be all right. It was the only thing he could do to calm himself down, but that wasn't really working. He said he stopped pacing, stood in one spot near the room, and breathed deeply in and out.

Because Sabrina seemed perfectly fine the day before, Margaret and Heidi said they would not come by to see her until around one o'clock in the afternoon. Now, with this happening, John had an obligation to call them. He reached for his phone then realized he never put her relative's phone numbers into his contact list. Normally John would have covered that base. Chalk it up to all the chaos. He rushed to the counter and asked the administrative nurse to look up Sabrina's next-of-kin contacts, place a call to Sabrina's mother's number, and hand him the phone. The girl didn't hesitate...she called the number and quickly passed the receiver over the counter.

Heidi answered. "Heidi," he said nervously, "it's me, John."

"What is it, John?" she whispered. "What's happened to Sabrina?"

Margaret sensed that something was wrong. "What is it, dear?" she said. "Is it the hospital?"

"It's John," she said, glancing over at her mother.

"You better bring Margaret to the hospital...something has happened, and I don't know what it is, exactly. She fainted suddenly and the doctor is in with her now."

The look on Heidi's face terrified Margaret. Hands quivering, Margaret reached for the phone, but Heidi wouldn't allow it.

"We're on our way," Heidi said as she set the handset in its cradle.

John was now the loneliest person in the world. Although every instinct in his body was telling him to bust into that room, all he could do was wait. He stood against the wall, closed his eyes and lightly rapped the back of his head against it, a few light taps. He wasn't going to wait in any waiting area...he'd stand there all day if he had to. A helpful nurse brought water and handed it to him. He looked at her sheepishly and thanked her.

They were in Sabrina's room for at least half an hour. The doctor checked Sabrina's airway, breathing, and circulation...everything seemed normal. Sabrina's blood pressure was a little elevated and her pupils slightly dilated; but, overall, there seemed to be no cause for concern.

Doctor Jones walked out of the room with his clipboard and gently placed a hand on John's shoulder. He led John across the aisle, and laid the clipboard on the counter in front of a nurse sitting behind a computer. He instructed her to order a CT scan and notify him as soon as the results were complete. He then started making notations on the paper clipped to the board.

John had a million questions, but didn't ask one. He stood there...anxious for the doctor to finish making notes. Finally, after a few minutes, Doctor Jones removed his glasses, folded them and slipped them into the upper pocket of his white coat.

He looked at John with doctor's eyes. I didn't know what the hell that meant when John said it... I guess maybe sympathetic but serious? At that point, without having the needed test results, the doctor didn't know what caused Sabrina to relapse into unconsciousness. He said they were going to do another CT scan and that should provide some answers. I didn't like the way any of that sounded but didn't voice that to John at the time.

The doctor told John that Sabrina's physical reaction to the injury to the head seemed normal …with the exception that she was unconscious longer than they considered usual…but that that didn't mean too much.

The doctor went on to explain the brain's capability to restore some functions after substantial injury, which he said was a phenomenon called "plasticity" that is usually helped by rehabilitation. This all went right over John's head, and mine as well, as John tried to explain it to me. What John didn't want to hear him say, but which he did, was that they were moving Sabrina back to the ICU.

John watched as they wheeled Sabrina out of her room, her eyes still closed. He stood there with thoughts ricocheting around his brain as they pushed her down the corridor to the lab. It was now a waiting game. Waiting for the results of the scan, waiting to find out which ICU room she'd be in…and waiting for her to regain consciousness. As he stood there draped in a feeling of hopelessness…thinking that this nightmare was starting all over again…he felt a hand touch his shoulder. Margaret and Heidi stood behind him.

John put his arms around Sabrina's mother as Heidi stood by silently. "We were just getting ready to go for a short walk," John said, shifting his eyes between them, "and suddenly, Sabrina collapsed in my arms. The nurses responded quickly and helped me put her on the bed. I couldn't get her to respond to me. That's when a nurse instructed me to leave the room."

"Where is she now?" Heidi asked, her eyes expressing signs of fear.

"They are going to do a CT scan and then take her back to ICU."

It was as bad as it gets. Margaret broke down in tears and John almost had to carry her as he led her to the waiting area. Heidi could hardly steady herself but managed to pull herself together for the sake of her mother.

Chapter Forty-nine

John, Margaret and Heidi sat in the small waiting area near the ICU, awaiting some word about Sabrina's condition. John shot up from his chair every time someone even remotely resembling a doctor approached them. John said it seemed never-ending. The wait was unbearable, especially for Sabrina's mother.

It was while they were waiting for word that John stepped away, pulled his cell phone and called me with the bad news. As he explained the situation, his voice was very shaky. He tried to give me all the details quickly, knowing that word could come at any minute.

I glanced at Sakae, who was stacking a handful of napkins at the end of the bar. Based on what John told me, I became concerned that the result of this latest event might not turn out so well. However, I tried to calm him as best I could. Whatever the news was, I suggested he stay optimistic, especially in front of Sabrina's mother and sister.

Although John seldom went to church or read the Bible, he is a believer. It was his conviction that God has a plan for all things…that's what he remembered most from his mother's strong faith and his Catholic upbringing. He said Margaret and Heidi were both Christians.

When he stepped away from the waiting area to call me, Heidi and Sabrina's mother were holding each other's hands, praying in low voices, asking Jesus to intervene and heal Sabrina. I told him that praying sometimes relieves the personal burden of stress in situations like this and that I thought he ought to be saying a few "Our Father's" and "Hail Mary's" of his own.

It had been two hours since the nurses wheeled Sabrina down that long hallway when Doctor Jones finally walked through the double doors with a look on his face that you sometimes see in the movies when the news is not good.

Fortunately, each time John had seen Dr. Jones, although he was very cordial, his demeanor was never any different...so trying to predict what he was going to say was tricky. John stood up while Heidi and Margaret remained seated, Margaret clutching a wad of tissue in her hand.

The doctor removed his glasses from the bridge of his nose and stuffed them into his upper pocket, a gesture which seemed to be his normal routine before talking to them. Then, as if there were nothing out of the ordinary going on, he looked at them steadily and said, "Well...Sabrina is awake and resting."

John's knees buckled slightly. Margaret spat out a big sigh of relief. "Thank you, Lord!"

"This time, we performed a CT scan of her entire body. It revealed minor inflammation of her spinal cord, which is consistent with a severe whiplash...also called neck sprain or neck strain...it's an injury to the soft tissues of the neck. A disruption in her circulation caused by the swelling is what caused her to fall unconscious."

Margaret took more tissues out of her purse and handed some to Heidi...but Heidi was too shocked to tear up after hearing the words 'spinal cord.' While relieved that Sabrina was conscious, John worried about the next words that might come from the doctor's mouth.

Doctor Jones went on, "After reading the incident report, I believe that the initial impact of the accident did not cause her spinal problem so that leads me to believe that the momentum of the taxi hitting the pole did. Right now, she has limited feeling in her lower body. Severe extension injuries like that," he went on, smoothing down his coat, "could show up anytime and have this kind of short-term effect to the intervertebral discs."

After hearing that bit of news, anyone within fifty yards could hear Sabrina's mother cry out with grief. The doctor put his hand on Margaret's shoulder to calm her. "There is good news, Mrs. Harper," he said, in a compassionate, reserved tone of voice. "Take a deep breath and calm yourself. The scan showed minor but no sustainable damage to any of the nerves of the cervical spine that would indicate any lasting paralysis, so Sabrina *will* recover from this in time."

"Uh...pardon me, Doctor," John said politely. "Are you saying that, right now, Sabrina is unable to walk?"

"At this point, I don't even want her to try," he replied. "It's just that Sabrina's injury will require her to stay off her feet for a while. I suggest that you rent, uh, perhaps, a transport wheelchair. That kind of wheelchair, the transport type," he went on, "is not too cumbersome and she can be move around comfortably and easily. Once Sabrina is released from the hospital, she will need it to get around for a while."

"She'll be given leg exercises to do while lying in bed or sitting in a chair. The good news is that Sabrina is physically fit and that will help her get strong faster. Eventually," he went on, flicking his eyes between all three of them, "and it's hard to predict *exactly* when, Sabrina will be walking or jogging or doing anything else she was doing before the accident."

"Doctor...how long do you think my sister will be this way?" Heidi asked, looking up at him with puppy dog eyes.

"For most patients..." he said, taking a moment to formulate his answer. "Well...let me put it this way. As I said...Sabrina is a strong young lady and, under these circumstances, that's very helpful. The symptoms of this kind of injury usually subside in 2 to 4 weeks. We are going to keep her neck immobilized for several days using a halter. She should wear this at home as well...and..."

"At home?" Margaret said, interrupting unintentionally, her eyes opening wide. "When *can* she go home?"

"The exterior damage...meaning the wound to her head...is healing fine," he replied, lifting his glasses out of his pocket with one hand and tapping his other hand with them. "If she is stable over the next *few* days, then I'd say, oh...three or four more days. For now, however, **Sabrina will be on a** non-steroidal, anti-inflammatory drug. She will have heat therapy and be given range-of-motion exercises," he continued with a warm smile. "She will be fine, Mrs. Harper...I promise."

"Thank you, Doctor," John said. "Can we see her now?"

"She's back in room 502," he said. "You can see her at any time. Actually, my guess is she's waiting for you as we speak."

This was the second time over the last few days that Sakae and I got good news from John. The fact that Sabrina passed out in his arms was a setback, but she woke up again, and that's all that counted. There was more good news than bad coming from Joplin, including the marriage proposal, and that's a good thing. John said he even took my advice after our last conversation. He said his 'Our Father's' and 'Hail Mary's'...and got his prayers answered.

***

When John, Margaret and Heidi walked into 502, Sabrina was lying in the bed smiling and joking with a nurse. It's amazing how fast circumstances can change. Looking at Sabrina lying there wearing a neck halter and a smile on her face brought immediate comfort to Margaret and Heidi...not to mention what it did to bolster *John's* spirits.

As soon as the nurse took hold of the handle to the cart and pushed it out of the room, Margaret, with tears of joy running down her face, leaned over the bedrail, placed her hands gently on Sabrina's face and kissed her forehead.

"I'm fine, Mom," Sabrina said, softly, smiling. "Don't worry. How do you like this wretched thing they have around my neck...cute, isn't it?"

Heidi stepped up to the bed and took Sabrina by the hand. "You know, girl... I can't take much more of this. This is the second time in less than a week that you've scared the hell out of me...and, if you must know," she smiled, gently rubbing Sabrina's forearm, "that dog collar you're wearing is very becoming."

At that point, they all had a good chuckle. John said that he had lingered off to the side, waiting for Sabrina's mother and sister to provide an opening. He couldn't wait to slip in and show Sabrina how relieved he was that she came back to him for a second time. John moved to the foot of the bed, about the only position Sabrina would be able to look at him without straining. When he came into her view, she smiled widely and then gave him what he explained as a curious look.

"Well... John," she said evenly. "Did you tell them?"

Because of the emotional rollercoaster John had been on over the last few hours, it took some thinking to decipher what she meant. Margaret and Heidi turned to look at John before glancing at each other curiously. That's when it hit him like a ton of bricks. John shook his head from side to side. "With so much going on, I...uh...no, I didn't."

Sabrina didn't hesitate. "We are getting married!"

Well, I don't have to tell you what *that* news flash did for morale around that hospital bed. For the moment, all else seemed to be forgotten. The fact that Sabrina's ability to walk was questionable because of an accident caused by a cab driver who wasn't paying attention to the road was now trumped by great news.

By the way, if you ask me, that taxi driver must have squeaked through the safe driver's test by the skin of her teeth. Believe you me…I've seen, firsthand, how some cabbies decide that they have the right-of-way, no matter what. If I've seen it once, I've seen it a thousand times. I've put people who had too much to drink in taxis. Sometimes, I watch the cab drive off and wonder if it might have been safer to let the drinker drive home. I'm not saying all cabbies are like that…I'm just saying…

Hearing the news about the engagement, Margaret's emotions went off on another high. Heidi hugged John, thanked him for being there, and told him that she couldn't wait to have him as a brother-in-law. John was already feeling like a member of the family…even though he had yet to pass the 'Uncle Phil test.'

It was late in the afternoon. All things were pretty much back to normal, so Margaret and Heidi decided to go home. Scheduled to catch a plane back to Florida the next morning, Heidi finally felt comfortable enough to take the flight. She made Sabrina promise, however, that there would be no more surprises before she left…or after, for that matter.

It was back to Sabrina and John spending quiet time together…the rollercoaster ride over for now and, hopefully, forever. Even though some difficulties lie ahead over the next few weeks, given the doctor's prognosis, they felt the worst was over.

A nurse brought in a bowl of fruit and some yogurt and set it on the over-the-bed table. She rolled the table up close to Sabrina before leaving the room. They were both starving…but not for fruit and yogurt. After all that had happened, they were starving for each other.

Sabrina said, "Why don't we pretend we are sitting in Arrivederci's over a plate of chicken Caesar salad, sipping wine?"

"I like that idea," John said as he picked up the fork, stabbed a piece of cantaloupe and held it up in front of Sabrina's lips.

Sabrina smiled, opened her mouth and said, "I could get used to this, but I'd rather it be a big strawberry."

Now, you see what I mean about Sabrina. Nothing has changed. She sat at the bar cracking jokes the first time I laid eyes on her, and she is still doing it under these conditions.

The second piece of fruit John stabbed with the fork *was* a strawberry… although he wouldn't elucidate Sabrina's method of eating it…that was something I just had to picture in my mind. It wasn't easy to do either…visualizing her with that halter around her neck.

Suddenly, the phone on the stand next to the bed rang. Once John picked it up, Karla's voice rang out on the other end as if she was using a megaphone. Sabrina could hear her even with the phone pressed against John's ear. Sabrina's mother got everything started with the call to the magazine. First, the news about Sabrina's setback and then she broke the news to Phil about their engagement. Phil then spread the news around the office, leaving out the part about Sabrina's relapse, of course. Why spoil good news with bad? I would have done the same thing. The more I hear about Sabrina's Uncle Phil the more I like him. While Karla was spewing her excitement about the engagement into John's ear, he handed the phone to Sabrina.

Sabrina looked at John and her eyes widened; she couldn't get a word in edgewise. About five minutes into a one-sided conversation, Sabrina was able to explain how John proposed. That set Karla off again. Sabrina looked at John once more and shook her head. At that point, John knew that in some way, Karla, was going to play a major role in planning the wedding…beginning with that phone call.

Chapter Fifty

The next three days went fast. Hospital personnel had moved Sabrina out of ICU for the second time…this time for good. She had therapy three times a day. John watched intently as the therapist worked Sabrina's lower body. With Sabrina flat on her back, the therapist worked one leg at a time. She slowly pushed Sabrina's legs up towards her torso, bending her knees. With Sabrina's legs straight, she made her point her toes towards her head and then the opposite way. She helped Sabrina roll on her side and extended her leg upward to different levels. She rolled her to the other side, repeating the process. John was now a quasi-certified therapist by virtue of visual expertise…at least, that's what *he* proclaimed.

During those three days, there were times when John felt very comfortable leaving Sabrina, especially when she had visitors in the room. In addition to going to the hotel once a day to change and such, he made a trip to Candice Healthcare Equipment Rental to rent a transport wheelchair, which fit neatly in the trunk of his rental car.

Although it was extremely cold in Missouri, he even mustered up enough courage to jog for an hour around the unfamiliar neighborhoods of Joplin. Doctor Jones made several visits and seemed pleased each time he read the notes the nurses had made on Sabrina's chart. He said the same thing every time…which John found more and more comforting…'She's making good progress.'

John and Sabrina were ecstatic when they were told that one more day in the hospital would be her last…Doctor Jones had given the release order. Sabrina made arrangements with Karla to pick up Margaret and come to the hospital. The next morning, John transferred Sabrina, still in the hospital-provided gown but wearing her heavy wool coat, from the hospital wheelchair into Karla's car. They followed John to the airport to return the rental car and drove together to Sabrina's house. It was nice to hear that things were finally coming together.

***

A week had passed since John wheeled Sabrina in through the front door of her house. I have to admire what Johnny-boy did. He checked out of the Hilton that same day and immediately took on the role of a part-time care-giver.

It wasn't easy, but John had help. Margaret was at the house most of the time during the day and early evenings, managing lunches and dinners and other things that needed to be done for Sabrina. Sabrina was finally showing pro-gress. The regiment of therapy, allowed her to finally ditch the dreaded neck halter.

It was late Saturday afternoon, a brisk but sunny day. The girls...meaning Karla, Margaret and Sabrina...were talking and laughing in the open living area as if the acci-dent had never happened. John sat at the oval table in a nook surrounded by bay windows in the kitchen, working on his laptop. John said just hearing the ladies chat it up helped to erase any fear or doubt he had that Sabrina was well on the way to recovery.

As John checked his sales and inventory levels on the gallery websites, he periodically glanced out the window at Sabrina's nicely landscaped backyard. Even though the landscape was very nice, the green lawn, cement walkways, and variety of bushes lining the block perimeter wall were no match for the view from the balcony of his condo in Coronado.

John's mind wandered. Inventory levels didn't mean much at that point. He thought about how nice it would be if he and Sabrina were, at that very moment, standing together on the balcony looking out towards the ocean admiring the golden sunset. He recalled the last time they were together there. Sabrina had made a comment that was etched in his mind. 'I could stay here forever'.

Until now, John's mind had been preoccupied with so many different challenges that this was really the first time he had to think about being home. As much as he liked Sabrina's house, it was a far cry from living near the ocean…and it was great to know that Sabrina agreed with him. Everything John was saying was music to our ears, Sakae and me. First the engagement and then finding out that Sabrina agreed to live in Coronado. Let's move on. Because John is such a popular artist with a huge fan base in San Diego, the gallery websites revealed that inventory was quickly diminishing at all of them, which meant he needed to start painting again soon. Being away from Coronado and his studio for two weeks straight had put him behind the power curve. This was something he didn't want Sabrina to know. She would feel bad and try to convince him to go back home to paint, and she would follow. I'll tell you…wild horses couldn't drag him away from Joplin until Sabrina went with him. Sabrina got tired early that evening. They were in bed by nine, thankful that another day had passed and that, tomorrow, Sabrina would be stronger than she had been the previous day.

The rain was heavy, the wind fierce. John was in the middle of it, fighting to keep his head above water. Once again, huge ocean swells were battering him. He could see the mast of the sailboat, ripped and torn, leaning sideways-- the boat about to capsize. The storm was charged with thunder and lightning, and John was taking in more water than air, gasping with every movement of his body. The ocean swells capped and curved into giant white waves crashing down on him, burying him under tons of foamy water…plunging him beneath the dark water's surface.

In the midst of it all, he could hear someone yelling...crying out for help. "HELP ME!! HELP ME!! HELP...."

"W-H-O-'S O-U-T T-H-E-R-E!!" John yelled at the top of his lungs. The voice rang out again, echoing all around him from what seemed to be far off in the distance.

"HELP!! HELP ME!! HELP...."

Suddenly, he found himself wandering along the ocean bottom again...scanning, searching. Through the mass of marine life surrounding him, he noticed, in the distance, the obscure wreck of a sailing vessel, a portion of which was buried under the sediment. As he made his way closer, he could see the mast and boom leaning almost parallel to the ocean floor, the headsail torn and shredded, moving, flowing with the sea current.

Through the murky water and algae, he could scarcely make out the name painted on the boat...'Solitude One.' The image of a skull and the remnants of chest bones filled his head. The image of a girl in a white flowing gown hovering horizontally over the boat...reaching out for him...was flickering like a silent movie in front of his eyes. Suddenly, the girl's body turned horizontal and began floating towards the ocean's surface until it slowly vanished from sight.

John woke up, plagued once again by the recurring dreams. The dream made him uneasy, unsure of where he was. He shook his head to rid it of the cobwebs and propped himself up on one elbow.

Reality set in as he realized that Sabrina wasn't lying next to him...the wheelchair was folded and still positioned near the wall, exactly where he left it the night before. He panicked as he quickly pushed himself out of bed and hurried out of the bedroom. He heard a noise coming from the kitchen. It was Sabrina, standing over the stove, cooking.

Amazed and panicky all mixed in the same emotion, he spat out, "Sabrina, what in God's name are you doing?

Standing…no wheelchair? Are you sure you should be doing this yet?"

"Calm down, darling," she replied with a smile that was reassuring. "I woke up this morning feeling stronger than ever. You were sleeping so peacefully, I didn't want to wake you," she continued as she picked up the spatula and shoved it under the omelet cooking in the pan. "I wanted to surprise you with my world-famous vegetable omelet. After all, you've been making me breakfast every morning since I left the hospital. I thought it was time that I return the favor."

John knelt down on one knee next to her, put his hand on her right leg and ran it from her ankle up to the top of her thigh, then stood up and gazed into her eyes. "Which leg did you feel my hands touching?"

Sabrina flirtatiously batted her eyelashes and replied, grinning, "The right…would you like to try the left?"

Well, according to John, with the exception of the stitches that the doctor said would disappear after her hair grows out completely around the wound, everything seemed as though it was back to normal. They sat at the table eating breakfast as John told her he had another dream.

He said this dream was very different from the others…different in the sense that it wasn't just one dream…it was a compilation of all the dreams John had had previously. The one difference, however, was the girl in the white flowing gown was now ascending towards the surface of the water.

In Sakae's faith, that was some sort of a sign. She tried to convince me that the girl floating towards the surface *was* the sign, the impetus that allowed Sabrina to stand and walk. Now I'm not a believer in those ancient beliefs, but who in the hell am I to judge?

Chapter Fifty-one

I was working at the pub when I spied Kate Sutter walking in - you know, John's Galleria-owner friend. She often walked down to the pub to buy a chicken sandwich, but truth was, it had been a long time since she had been in here. I told her what had happened to Sabrina and that John was with her in Missouri looking after her. She had been wondering why she hadn't seen or heard from him in a while. She had recent news about the portrait of the woman he left in her Galleria and seemed upset about it. She also told me that she had misplaced John's cell phone number.

John told me he had left the portrait with her so I asked what was wrong only because whatever news she had about it was of interest to me as well. I assured Kate that I would communicate whatever she wanted to John the next time he checked in with me. In any event, she seemed upset about the whole matter.

My prodding didn't work, however. She didn't have all the details and was adamant about me not saying anything until she spoke with him first.

Meanwhile, in Missouri, John made sure that Sabrina's recovery was maintained at a slow and steady pace, just as the doctor ordered. The relapse she had at Joplin Mercy tore him and everyone else up, and he wanted to insure that there was no chance of that happening again.

Over the next few days, they took short walks around the neighborhood. John continued Sabrina's leg exercises, which invariably ended up with them making passionate love. If you ask me, that was the real reason that John made her keep exercising. When I voiced my opinion about that to Sakae, she slapped me across the shoulder with a damp bar towel. So that you know…I was only joking.

***

John said they took drives around Joplin, had dinner at Margaret's house, and met Karla for lunch at Club 609. They told Karla about John's dreams, and she became so immersed in the whole thing that you would think she was the one doing the dreaming. What Karla, Margaret or Sabrina's Uncle Phil did not know yet was all the discussion John and Sabrina had had about where they were going to live after they got married. It *was* official…they were going to live in Coronado.

John drove Sabrina into downtown Joplin to meet with her Uncle Phil. Although Sabrina was the happiest girl in the world, telling her uncle that she was quitting the magazine and moving west was one of the hardest things she had to do. The next hardest thing would be to tell her mother.

She cautioned her uncle…who was happy about the engagement but not about the news of Sabrina leaving Joplin…not to say anything just yet to anyone else. She would have told her best friend, Karla, if it weren't for the fact that Karla would have had the news all over town in a matter of minutes…likely before Sabrina's mother and uncle found out. You know the mouth on that woman; it just keeps flapping.

John waited in the car while Sabrina met with her Uncle Phil. Karla had just come back from lunch and noticed Sabrina in Phil's office. She couldn't stand not knowing the subject matter. Karla, however, being a fairly insightful person, had inklings about what was going on…a sneaking suspicion. It had been obvious to Karla that Sabrina really liked Coronado and she remembered Sabrina mentioning to her that John would never leave Coronado during their conversation when Sabrina was with John over the Christmas holiday.

Sabrina told John that Karla was peeking over the top of her cubicle every two minutes, peering into her uncle's office. Finally, after bobbing up and down like a bobber tied to a fishing line, Karla saw Sabrina stand, her uncle stand, and then watched as they hugged each other as if they were saying goodbye forever.

Karla pulled a box of tissue from her desk drawer in preparation. When Sabrina walked out of Phil's office, she went straight for Karla's desk to break the news. After that, the other coworkers all gathered around. Although things were going to change drastically around the office with Sabrina gone, the vote of confidence for what lay ahead and congratulations regarding her engagement were overwhelming.

Actually, it wasn't all bad news...Sabrina moving to Coronado. Sabrina was still going to work for the magazine, only remotely. Sabrina didn't think about it at the time...but her uncle did. Writing human-interest stories does not necessarily require the writer be located in any one place...doing research along with some traveling can be accomplished almost anywhere. Sabrina would be writing for the magazine from her home base in Coronado, John's place.

John was excited when Sabrina made it back to the car and told him what her uncle suggested. Sabrina could now continue to do what she loved to do but she would be doing it from home. The first phase of communication was complete...now came the tough part. It was time for them to head off to Sabrina's mother's house...breaking the news to her would be much harder.

When they walked up the steps to the house, they could smell the delicious aroma from the roast Sabrina's mother had cooking in the slow cooker. Margaret was talking long distance to Heidi when they walked in. Sabrina figured she could now kill two birds with one stone.

John blew a kiss to Margaret and sat down in a chair next to a small gas fireplace. Sabrina sat on the couch next to her mother and asked for the phone. Sabrina switched the phone to speaker. John said the conversation started with Heidi asking Sabrina how she felt. Even though they had been talking to each other every day, this new topic of discussion…Sabrina living in Coronado…had yet to surface.

Sabrina laid the phone down on the coffee table in front of them and rubbed her palms together as if she were making a strategic move in a chess match. She placed a hand on her mother's knee and said, "John and I have made some decisions over the last few days, and we are definitely getting married here in Joplin. However…"

Margaret let out a deep sigh of relief as she reached over and hugged Sabrina before smiling warmly at John. Before Sabrina could get back on track, Heidi said, "I know the rest, little sis. You and John are going to live in California…right?"

Sabrina looked at John and then at her mother before nodding her head. "Yes…but…"

"That's OK, Sabrina," Heidi said evenly. "Mom and I have already talked about this…and especially over last day or two. Mom has decided to live in Florida. The weather is much better here, especially in the winter. So now there are two houses to sell in Joplin…won't that be fun?"

John saw Sabrina's face turn from a look of anguish to delight. She wasn't expecting this outcome…Margaret was as calm as a cucumber. Apparently… unbeknownst to Sabrina, they had talked about Sabrina's mother moving to Florida in the past, even before John and Sabrina met.

They didn't want to tell Sabrina until her mother was ready. The severe winters started the discussion and, with John now in the picture, it was going to make the transition easier. Actually, John said that Sabrina told him that she was going to bring it up herself because of Margaret's developing arthritis problems…good timing for all, I guess.

Sabrina was happy. John could see it in her eyes. What to do about leaving her mother in Joplin was a big concern to her. *This is another thing working out in my favor…I mean in everybody's favor.*

"You know, Mom," Sabrina said smiling, "you can come and visit us in Coronado any time you want."

"Now wait just a darn minute," Heidi said, chuckling on the other end of the line. "What about me? I like California."

"Yes!" Sabrina replied excitedly, looking at John. "We have three bedrooms."

John was happy just to sit there and not say anything. He was witnessing what was going to be his family and loving it. Suddenly, his cell phone rang. He pulled it from his pocket, recognized who was calling and answered.

"Kate?"

Chapter Fifty-two

While Sabrina and her mother talked to Heidi in Florida, John stepped into another room to take the call from Kate. As he did so, it dawned on him that he had not talked to her for at least two weeks, which was very unusual. The feeling of guilt John had about not calling Christmas Day suddenly came upon him again.

"Hi, John," Kate said. "I happened to see Skipper yesterday. He told me the news about Sabrina…how is she doing?"

"It hasn't been an easy two weeks for her, Kate, but she's recovering quite well from the accident. Uh… listen…Kate… I'm sorry I haven't called but…"

"John…please," Kate broke in. "I can't blame you…you've been preoccupied. The most important thing right now is that Sabrina survived what was, according to Skipper, a horrific crash."

"It was terrible, Kate…I can't tell you," John said. "For a time there, it was really touch and go. I didn't know for sure if she'd make it. She was in a coma for a few days, woke up, and then had a relapse."

"Well, I must admit," Kate said, "the minute Skipper told me that you managed to get onto an airplane…I figured the situation had to be serious."

John chuckled. "I would have strapped myself onto a rocket ship to get here if I had to…that's how much I love this woman, Kate."

"Hmm…" Kate said in a warm-sounding voice. "It seems as though you've met the perfect girl this time, huh?"

"Hold onto your seat, Kate," John replied. "I asked her to marry me while she was lying in a hospital bed with bandages on her head and wearing a neck brace. Kind of romantic, don't you think?"

"Well..." Kate said, chuckling lightly. "*That's* a proposal to remember. You guys can tell your grandkids about it one day."

John laughed. "There's more," John said excitedly. "Sabrina has agreed to leave Joplin and live in Coronado once we get married."

"I sure love hearing all this good news," Kate said, coughing lightly. "I hope you two will let me have my good friend who does a wonderful...I mean, he takes really great wedding pictures. If you don't mind, it could be my contribution to the bride and groom." Kate waited for a response, but there was a long pause instead. "John?" she said curiously. "Are you still there?"

"Yes...Kate...I'm here," John replied, taking a moment, pondering what he would say next. "Uh...it would be great to have your friend take pictures. However...and Skipper doesn't know this yet...we have decided to get married in Joplin."

"Oh...I see...hmm," Kate said. "Well, then... I guess I'll just have to find another way to contribute if I'm flying to Joplin for the wedding."

"Just having you here will be more than enough."

After a brief pause in the conversation, Kate said, coughing again, "John, *I* have news as well...unfortunately, it's not near as good as the news you just gave me."

Just hearing Kate say that made John flinch. He said that things had been going so well over the last few days; he couldn't take hearing any more *bad* news. "What...? Are *you* all right, Kate? Is something wrong? When I saw you last, you weren't feeling well...and you still have a cough."

"That's just it, John," Kate began to explain. "It wasn't long after you left the Galleria that morning that I went back home to rest and, wouldn't you know, I had to stay there for a week. I wasn't really feeling up to par and probably shouldn't have gone back to the work so soon in the first place. Whatever bug I picked up must have bit the hell out of me again. My doctor friend stopped by to check on me…gave me some pills, and insisted that I stay in bed."

"Well…" John said, "how about now? Are you up and around, Kate?"

"Yes…I am, thank God. But it took a while…must be my age," she sniffed. "I was sure miserable… I'll tell you that. It was *some* flu bug. Anyway, here is the bad part…and I didn't know this until two days ago…it's about the portrait of the woman you painted…it's gone."

"Gone..?"

"Yes, John," Kate replied. "It was inadvertently sold."

There was a long pause on John's end of the line. He tried to process in his mind what Kate had said…but only confusion set in. "I don't understand, Kate," he said. "But it…uh…it wasn't for sale."

"I know, John," she said. "And I'm so very sorry that it happened. There's no one to blame but me. Because I was ill…I never had a meeting with the girls to explain the plan. By the time I got back to the Galleria, it had been sold."

"But it had no price?"

"Well…Michele thinks that one of the small pricing tent tags we use instead of stickers so that frames aren't marked up may have been inadvertently moved over in front of the portrait. I talked to the girl who sold it…she just started working part-time for us a week ago. Anyway, she says that some middle-aged woman came in the store and was amazed at how much the portrait of the woman looked like her aunt…and she had to have it. She paid $300 cash and walked out with it."

"Did the girl get her name?"

"I'm afraid not, John. Listen, dear… I'm truly sorry about this. I hope you'll forgive me."

I guess I could not blame Kate for not sharing that piece of information with me; she really didn't have all the facts. Secondly, if I had tried to explain it, I would have confused the man more. Anyhow, after John hung up with Kate, he called me…but he saved that bit of news for last.

John and I talked as the conversation in the next room between Sabrina, her Mom and Heidi went on. I must say, I was delighted to hear that Sabrina's mother presented no obstacle to the two of them living in Coronado. After my last conversation with John, I was concerned as to how that might play out.

The fact that her mother was moving to Florida seemed almost divine intervention. I was not happy, however, about a wedding in Joplin, Missouri…that knocked me for a loop. A place is a place, I guess, and I had to live with it.

What does it really matter, anyway? I would stand up for Johnny-boy in Alaska, if necessary…and he knew it. Close the pub for a few days...no big deal. It would still be there when we got back. Besides, when I told Sakae, she was happy. She was looking forward to a vacation. Joplin, Missouri, wasn't Hawaii…but so what? It was a vacation, nonetheless.

Now this thing about the portrait was disturbing. I mean…what now? I guess…if John never had one more stinking dream about sunken boats, buried bones and a floating girl in a white gown, the whole thing would be moot…it wouldn't matter, would it? But he did.

John could have taken his $300, less Kate's commission, and banked it. The problem is…the damn dreams just kept on coming. When I told Sakae that the portrait sold and how it happened, she said it was another sign of some sort—whatever!

We put the painting out of our mind. Sakae and I were pleased that Sabrina was recovering nicely. Unfortunately, there was a lot left for those two kids to figure out. All of that made me wonder…when *would* I see Johnny-boy again? At some point, I knew John would be coming home. The million-dollar question was, however, when?

There was Sabrina's house to contend with, and now, her mother's house had to go on the market. They had to sell the furniture…or move it…and who knows what else…all of that takes time. One thing Sakae and I knew for sure…all of this was pushing *our* marriage further into the future. I still haven't told John about that.

***

When we hung up, John strolled back into the living area where Sabrina and her mother were just ending the call with Heidi. Without hesitating, he went straight for Margaret, kissed her on the cheek then went back to sit in the chair next to the fireplace. It didn't take long for Sabrina to recognize that something was bothering him; he had this dazed and confused look on his face.

Sabrina said, "What is it, John? Is everything all right? I heard you say 'Kate' when you answered that call… is *she* OK?"

John just stared at her. Deep thought was the best way to describe what she saw in his facial expression. The only thing he could hear at that point was his subconscious reminding him of what Kate had said. 'The woman was amazed at how much the portrait of the woman looked like her aunt.'

"The portrait…" he mumbled, shaking his head slightly, "…the portrait was sold."

"Sold?" Sabrina said as she got up from the couch and made her way over to him, planting herself on the arm of the chair. "How could that be?"

"Oh…" John replied, nodding. "It will be alright."

"But…how? You said you told Kate it wasn't for sale. You even told her some of the story…didn't you?"

"Kate became very ill right after I gave it to her and was confined to bed...so she never got the word out to the sales people in the Galleria. According to Kate, there was some mix-up with pricing tags. And listen to this," he went on, sighing deeply, "it was sold to some lady who said the picture of the woman looked just like someone she knew...her aunt."

That news took all the air out of Sabrina. "Did they get the lady's name?" Sabrina said, sighing deeply.

"I asked the same question and, unfortunately, the answer to that is 'no.'"

"What now?" Sabrina said, putting her hand on John's shoulder.

"I guess we'll have to figure something out when we get back to Coronado."

Now Margaret didn't know anything about what her daughter and son-in-law-to-be were talking about. The way they went on about Kate and the portrait, it was as if she wasn't in the room. To be fair about it, they had to explain the whole story to her. Actually, John said, Sabrina's mother enjoyed the story. Apparently, she is an avid reader of fiction novels.

Chapter Fifty-three

John said he could hardly move after the spread Margaret put on the dinner table that night. He had stuffed himself with roast, mashed potatoes, the best tasting asparagus he'd ever eaten, and a mixed green salad with ranch dressing that was out of this world.

They got back to Sabrina's house just before the rain started coming down in buckets. John lit up the gas fireplace while Sabrina slipped out of the pants and sweater she wore and into lounging pajamas. They had decided that morning that they would get started with the work of coordinating everything they had to accomplish before the wedding. After that, they could start planning for the wedding.

Now that Sabrina's mother was moving to Florida, it added more to the equation...the whole thing was going to be a delicate dance. First on the priority list was setting a date for the wedding or, at the least, picking the month.

"Let's see," Sabrina said, snuggling up next to John on the couch near the fire. "When should we have the wedding?"

"Yesterday," John replied, smiling as he planted a kiss on her forehead.

"OK..." Sabrina said, softly digging her fingers into his ribs. "Are you saying that we should resurrect the H.G. Wells time machine, set it for yesterday with Las Vegas coordinates and grab a quickie ceremony in one of those, you know...Elvis chapels?"

"I get it," John said, chuckling loudly. "I guess that means you want to have a serious dialogue about this now, right?"

"Well, I was just thinking," Sabrina replied as she sat straight up on the couch, folded her legs into a lotus position beneath her, and looked into his eyes. "Consider this," she went on in a serious tone of voice. "You've been away from your studio now for over two weeks. I know how you miss your painting...and you need to paint. Besides, there are people counting on you. I know that you miss Skipper, and the beach and the marina. I also know that what happened with the portrait really hit you hard...I could tell it when you walked back into the room at my Mom's house after your conversation with Kate."

John said, "You summed it up pretty well, with only one exception. You left out what really matters most...you didn't mention how much I love you."

Sabrina smiled softly. At that point, how could they possibly have a serious discussion about anything? She put one arm around John's neck and, with the other, began to unbutton his shirt from the top down. She rubbed her hand along his chest, feeling the taut, tight brawny structure...all the while gazing deeply into his eyes. He gently placed his hand underneath the back of her silky pajama top and pressed his lips against hers...they kissed passionately, tongues entwined.

He slowly moved his hand up to her neck between the shoulder blades and began running his fingers down the small of her back until her skin quivered. He moved his hand down until he felt her soft and silky-smooth leg. She felt a tingling sensation run through her body. She leaned her head back against the top of the couch, taunting him...begging him to kiss the side of her neck. He gently laid her down on the couch, slipped off her pajama bottoms and began to go down, ever so slowly, caressing and kissing her.

OK...I can't do it anymore. I can't take what little he told me and explain all the details of that situation. This is where you have to use your own imagination again. So let's skip what would have been the next two hours and continue with what happened after.

Oh… If you must know, there is just one more little tidbit of info. John said they ended up on the rug lying in front of the fireplace on the couch cushions. Sabrina tried to get them back on track to discuss wedding plans, but the only thing John wanted to do was to lie there and relive in his mind the previous two hours.

"Now, come on, John," Sabrina said, nudging him for the third time. "We do need to put our heads together and make some decisions here. If we don't get something accomplished soon, we'll end up doing what we just did every time we start talking about the subject."

John sighed deeply. "I wouldn't mind that one bit."

"See…" Sabrina said, with a deep sigh, laying her head back on the cushion out of frustration, "ugh..."

"OK…" John said, propping himself up on one elbow. "I know…but I just can't help it… it's what you do to me."

Sabrina stared into his eyes, shook a finger at him and smiled. "Ah…ha," she said, narrowing her eyes. "You're doing it again, aren't you…? You're trying to distract me."

John sat up and held his hands in the air. "I give up," he said, chuckling loudly. "Let's make a plan…or at least we'll get started with one. You go first, Sabrina. Then I'll go, and then you go again, and together we should be able to devise something."

"Now that's a start," she replied, sitting up. She thought for a moment. "OK…I got it…let's go to Coronado."

"What?" John said, creasing his brow. "Yes…that's in the plan somewhere…but something has to come first, doesn't it?"

"Agreed," Sabrina said nodding…thinking. "I'll call my realtor, the one who sold me this house. I'll tell her she has two listings…this house and my mother's. I'll tell her to get started right away and *then* we'll go to Coronado."

"OK…alright…that's good…that's a start."

"Good," Sabrina said. "We are making progress. Do you want to take over now?"

John said, "Uh...I think you have this well in hand...you keep on going."

Sabrina stood up, picked up one of the cushions, placed it back on the couch and sat on it. "Alright...see what you think about this..."

OK...now that all the lovey-dovey stuff is over, old Skipper can take it from here. That gal, Sabrina, really does have her shit together. She laid out a plan...with a little input from John...which I must admit fit perfectly into their situation.

You already know the first part...they contact the realtor. After that, they decided on March for the wedding as the weather would be nicer by then in Joplin...problem number two solved. They figured, however, it would take some time for the realtor to get the process started, you know... all of the listing details, getting signs on the houses, starting up the advertising process, etc. John told me that it wouldn't be long and they would be flying back to Coronado, which Sakae and I thought was great news.

Devising the rest of the plan would depend upon how fast the houses moved...and the prospects on that weren't very encouraging. The average time it takes to sell a house in Joplin was 4 to 6 months. The bottom line, however, was that there really wasn't that much of a hurry to do anything, with the exception of moving Margaret to Florida.

The fact is...John needed to get back home to start painting again. Sabrina was supportive of that, and the galleries were screaming for his artwork. On top of all that, John needed to figure out what he was going to do about that damn portrait...as if there was anything he could do, at this point, other than paint another one and hope for the best. I was hoping he'd just forget about it.

Chapter Fifty-four

Two weeks later

Sabrina's head wound was almost undetectable, the houses in Joplin had *for sale* signs in the yards and John was painting again. Sabrina was working on a story featuring the Old Globe Theater in North Park, a theater built in 1935 with a most interesting past. She decided it would be smart to write about some of the historical venues around San Diego since she was here...her Uncle Phil agreed.

They were taking advantage of every moment of their time together before Sabrina had to fly back to Joplin. Heidi planned to fly to Joplin from Florida as well. The two of them had to help pack Margaret's house and figure out what they were going to do with most of the furniture, once the house sold. They decided all the stuff their mother had accumulated over the years would never fit into the small townhouse Margaret intended to buy in Florida, which was a stone's-throw from where Heidi lived.

When John wasn't sketching at the marina and Sabrina wasn't working on her human-interest piece, they took in all the sights and sounds of San Diego. John was familiarizing Sabrina with the San Diego area with a vengeance. They went to the zoo and the historical museums (which is where she got the idea to write about the Old Globe Theater). They went to Old Town and ate authentic Mexican food. They spent time driving around Del Mar and even had a picnic in Balboa Park...and on and on and on.

John hasn't made his way to the pub in the afternoons after sketching like he used to...and I miss that. The simple fact that Sabrina is working out of his condo would explain it. It seems that Johnny-boy would rather spend time with her instead of me...go figure.

Now don't get me wrong...it's not that I'm complaining, you see. It's just that I was used to seeing Johnny-boy almost every afternoon before all this started. Since they have been together, only seeing John on those days when Sabrina was out doing interviews for her column kind of sucked...besides...Sakae wasn't scoring his tips. It does put a smile on our faces when we see them together, however. Sakae and I were thrilled to have our Johnny-boy back in town. Sabrina was cooking a lot, and I didn't blame them for eating in most of the time. I guess that's what young lovers do.

Now listen to this. It was kind of awkward and funny at the same time. One night, when John and Sabrina were sitting at John's table, Elizabeth walked in. She didn't even glance at the table where *they* used to sit together but came straight for the bar to see me.

My back was to the front of the bar and when I heard her voice from behind..."Hi, Skipper...long time no see"...I almost swallowed the toothpick I had in my mouth. When I turned to face her, I pretended to be delighted to see her...which, of course, I really wasn't. I surreptitiously glanced at the table where John and Sabrina were talking it up...they had no idea that Elizabeth had walked in.

"To what do I owe *this* pleasure, Elizabeth?" I said.

"Well, first, Skipper," she said, sounding somewhat sincere, "I'm sorry I haven't been in to see you...you know...besides being busy at the firm, I thought it would be awkward if I ran into, you know, John, and perhaps the new girlfriend who was at his place the night I returned some of his stuff. Anyway," she went on as she took a small felt-covered box from her bag and put it on top of the bar in front of me. "I've decided to give the ring back. My friends tell me it is bad luck to keep it."

"First off, Elizabeth," I said, keeping her attention focused on me. "I'm not superstitious so I wouldn't know about those things. But if you want to give it back...I'll be happy to deliver it to John or..." I went on, pointing over at the table, "you can give it to him yourself."

I thought it might be a little risky doing that, but I was fairly certain she'd hand it over quickly and skedaddle out before John saw her...which she did. It would actually have been embarrassing for her, and she knew it. It was priceless, however, seeing the look on her face when she glanced at the table and saw them sitting together. Maybe I should call this place the Priceless Inn, instead of Skipper's. Later that night when I told Sakae what I did, she said I was just being vindictive...I didn't see it that way.

As soon as Elizabeth cleared out and after I mixed a few drinks for which Sakae had been waiting patiently, I made my way to John's table. There was no need for me to be timid or secretive about giving him the box in front of Sabrina. Knowing Sabrina's attitude about things, it would be like water running off a duck's back, so-to-speak.

I laid the ring on the table in front of John. He looked at me as if...well, to tell you the truth, I didn't analyze the look. All I did was say 'here.' He didn't know what it was at first, and Sabrina just sat there, waiting for him to react. Before John opened the box, I thought I'd soften the situation and tell a little white lie.

I said, "It's the engagement ring. Elizabeth wanted me to give it back to you...so I'm giving it back."

With a look of confusion on his face, John said, "Uh...how did you get it?"

"She came in a few days ago and asked me to get it to you. I had forgotten about it until now."

Basically, I didn't give John a chance to ask any more questions. I told them I was busy and quickly made my way back to the bar. Luckily, Sakae rang the bell at the same time I said I was busy.

John and Sabrina both stared at the ring box. Then Sabrina said, holding out her hand, "May I?"

John shrugged and handed it to her. Sabrina smiled as she opened it. John said the moment was somewhat awkward.

"It's a beautiful ring, John," she said, gazing at the diamond sparkling under the dim overhead light. "That was very nice of her to give it back," she continued as she closed the box and handed it back to him. "Most women don't."

"I suppose," John said, slipping it into his pocket.

"Actually," Sabrina said, somewhat anxiously, "this is good timing, don't you think?"

"Good timing?"

"Yes," Sabrina replied. "Remember...? Tomorrow is the day we decided to look for *my* ring. You can sell that one back, or return it, or whatever...then we can pick one out for me."

John said he didn't like that idea. He struggled finding a response, and I'm sure you'll remember why. He bought Sabrina's ankle bracelet at the same jewelry store.

"If it's all the same to you, Sabrina," he said, reaching across the table for her hand. "I'd rather return it another time. I don't want to associate picking out a ring for you with the one in my pocket."

Well...I think John was pretty quick on his feet with that one. I'm not sure it would have made a difference to Sabrina, however. I don't see her as the jealous type. She probably would have laughed off the coincidence.

Chapter Fifty-five

It was around one o'clock in the afternoon. John and Sabrina sat in a quiet Red Sails Inn restaurant on Shelter Island Drive eating caesar salads and sharing a shrimp cocktail. Sabrina couldn't take her eyes off the channel-set, princess-cut diamond engagement ring John bought for her at Daniel's Jewelers in Mission Valley earlier that day... same jewelry store, different location.

John told me Sabrina's ring cost a hair over four grand. The ring fit her finger perfectly right out of the glass case. Although Sabrina loved it, she thought it was a little pricy, but he insisted she have it.

Just to contrast the difference between Sabrina and Elizabeth...Elizabeth's engagement ring cost fifteen grand. It was some sort of hand-engraved solitaire with a diamond that weighed over two carats. She bragged about it and openly flashed it to all her friends.

Sabrina's ring, a mere 0.72 carats, cost just over four grand. There you have it. You see the difference? Flashy, Sabrina is not. As a matter of fact, Sakae had to ask Sabrina if she could look at it. I would take Sabrina's modest way of thinking over Elizabeth's need to be 'noticed-by-everyone, everywhere-she-went' kind of attitude anytime.

After they finished lunch, they drove out to the Island, sat on John's favorite bench and watched the boats move in and out of the harbor. It was breezy on the Island that day, but they didn't mind...they were dressed for it.

John said just sitting there alongside Sabrina made him feel whole again. Forget about all the bad things that happened up to that point. Forget about the weird dreams, the breakup with Elizabeth and the accident that almost took

Sabrina's life. It was a perfect day. According to John, as far as the two of them were concerned, every day going forward would be the same…perfect.

As they watched the palms on the many trees lining the Island's shoreline blow in the cross winds and the seagulls fighting to fly against the wind high overhead, there was a serenity that made them thankful they were together. For the first time, Sabrina wanted to talk about that terrible night when, in a split second, her world went dark. It was so painful for John to even think about, he insisted that she put it out of her mind…but even then, she wouldn't.

"I have to talk about it, John," she said, laying her head on his shoulder, grasping the sleeve of his light jacket tightly. "I waited to talk about this because I didn't want you to have anything else to worry about…you know what I mean," she went on in a soft voice. "Up until now, I figured that the dreams you have had to contend with were enough for you to handle. I didn't want to pile on my burdens. At night, after you are sleeping soundly, I've been lying there next to your warm body, catching a chill just thinking about how close I came to losing you. It's not so much the accident itself that haunts me. It's the mere fact that things can happen so quickly to change our lives. Those things can sometimes be out of our control, and it scares me."

John lifted his arm up and placed it over her shoulder to comfort her. "Now you listen to me, my love," he said. "We are here, together, right now, and I won't ever allow anything that's within my control to change that. You are the best thing that ever happened to me. Before I met you, even when I thought my life was heading in the right direction, it was going absolutely nowhere. Now my life finally has purpose…I have you in my life, Sabrina…and I thank God for that."

Sabrina gazed at John with teary eyes. "When I was sitting in that wheelchair, there were many times I couldn't help but think about never being able to get up, even walk again…and what that might mean. I couldn't help thinking," she went on, as she blotted the corner of her eye with the sleeve of her sweater, "would you still love me?"

John moved off the bench to settle on his knees before her and gently placed his hands on her lower thighs. "I love you more than life itself. Do you remember what I said when I proposed to you while you were lying in that hospital bed?"

"Every word of it," Sabrina said, leaning forward, putting her hands on his cheeks. "You said that you were so blessed to have met me and that you would be honored to marry me."

"What else, Sabrina?" John asked taking her hands in his. "I said…I want nothing more than to live the rest of my life with you and that meant under all circumstances…do you understand me?"

Sabrina took in a deep breath, then exhaled. She nodded slightly, "Yes."

John rose up to sit next to her again, pressed his lips against hers softly. A moment later, as he looked directly into her eyes, he said, "And you should know something else, my darling Sabrina. No matter what happens in this crazy world that we live in…whatever dreams that I have or whatever your thoughts might be…whatever…I will love you until the last breath leaves my body." He kissed her again.

Yes…you guessed it…Sakae sat there crying like a baby when John told us what happened that day on Shelter Island. I really have to go back to what I said before…someone should make a movie about this story.

A bit later, just as they were driving back to Coronado…John's cell phone rang. It was Michele from the Galleria.

Chapter Fifty-six

Now this is the part of John's story that had me believing in things like spherical aberrations, fairy tales and maybe even ghosts. What I'm about to tell you is not only a departure from probability, but something that may change the way you think of dreams and what dreams really mean.

John and Sabrina drove straight to the Galleria. They rushed through the doorway as if they were first in line at Macy's at the stroke of midnight on Black Friday. Michele was standing at the check-out counter and motioned towards the back. Kate and a lady claiming to be related to the woman John had painted were sitting on the antique sofa.

Kate and the woman…who appeared to be in her mid-to-late fifties, wearing a nice pair of straight-cut dark pants that hit mid-calf, a colorful turtleneck sweater and a pair of comfy dress heels…stood up as John and Sabrina approached. John noticed the portrait leaning against the left side of the sofa.

Kate smiled at John as he kissed her on the cheek. She looked at Sabrina and marveled at how beautiful she was. She quickly wrapped her arms around Sabrina's shoulders and hugged her as if she were some close relative she hadn't seen for a long time. John said that, for a moment, it was a little uncomfortable for him. The person he wanted so badly to meet stood by, quietly smiling, until Kate was finished giving Sabrina the over-the-top warm greeting.

OH, I'm sorry," Kate said, turning to the woman. "I got so wrapped up in meeting John's fiancée that I'm ignoring people. Mrs. Hargrove," she went on, recovering quickly, "this is John Adler. He painted the picture of your aunt."

How did Kate know the painting was a portrait of the lady's aunt? I'll tell you how. As soon as the lady walked into the Galleria earlier in the day, she had introduced herself as the niece of the woman whose portrait she had recently purchased.

The other reason is this Hargrove lady had pulled an old picture of her aunt out of her bag and compared it to the likeness of the woman in the portrait. The resemblance was uncanny...like the woman, herself, could have posed for John while he painted it.

John offered his hand, and Mrs. Hargrove accepted graciously. He then introduced Sabrina. "It's hard for me to explain how surprised I am," John said, openly showing his exhilaration. "I don't quite know where to start but..."

Mrs. Hargrove interrupted. "Let me try, John," she said, "...that is... if you don't mind me doing so."

"Oh...not at all, Mrs. Hargrove..."

"First of all," she said with a warm smile. "My name is Lois...Lois Hargrove...and I would be happy if you called me Lois."

John smiled. "Thank you for that. I will," he replied. "I have a feeling we both have a lot to talk about."

Mrs. Hargrove handed John the picture she had shown to Kate. John studied it for the longest time. In the picture, the woman John was so familiar with was standing next to a young girl in a cap and gown, a high school graduation. Although mostly covered by clothing, John could see the chain and a portion of the locket around the woman's neck. At that moment, everything associated with his dreams... the monstrous waves driving him beneath the ocean's wrath, the boat stuck in the sediment, the skull and bones in the hull of the boat, the girl in the white flowing gown, the image of *that* woman in his mirror became real. How everything happened and why *John* was chosen would no doubt always remain a mystery. But now, at this time, it all became reality.

"What is the woman's name? John asked, continuing to stare at the photo.

"Hazel Slater," Mrs. Hargrove replied.

Suddenly, a curious look came across John's face. The thought crossed his mind that it wasn't the name of "Anna" as was on the locket. Things all of a sudden seemed even more confusing.

Kate had one of her workers bring two chairs up next to the sofa, one for Sabrina and one for John. I like the name Lois, but I would prefer to use Mrs. Hargrove as I tell this story. Mrs. Hargrove said she lived in Carlsbad. She and her husband travel to Coronado now and then. They stay overnight at a Cherokee Lodge bed and breakfast a block away from downtown Coronado so they can enjoy the fine restaurants and small historic-type shops.

She said that her husband thought it silly for her to drive the distance to Coronado to explore something that would probably turn out to be just a coincidence…the likeness between the portrait and her aunt. She went on to say that the reason she purchased the portrait in the first place was because the portrait of the woman so much resembled the aunt that she loved so dearly. She said that it bugged her day after day, and the curiosity became too much to bear.

"I just had to find out," Mrs. Hargrove said, looking at John. "Exactly how did you come about painting her?"

John paused, thought about her question for a while and then glanced at Sabrina, who gave him a nod. She was silently telling him that this is what he was hoping for…possibly a way to find out once and for all if all those dreams really meant anything. John took a deep breath. They all sat there staring at him as if they were getting ready to watch the beginning of an Oscar-winning movie.

"I found a locket," John finally said. "And then there were some dreams."

I guess there was no other way for John to put it other than just come out with it…no way to sugar-coat the beginning of what he was about to say. John said Mrs. Hargrove had this look on her face that made him want to crawl under a rock. Sabrina could tell and reached her hand across and placed it on John's forearm. When she did that, it automatically had a calming effect on him.

That's when John took another breath and told the story straight from the beginning…starting with the day he was sailing and his boat went adrift. Next, it was the dream about fighting for his life in the ocean in the middle of a storm. He told her about the subsequent dreams. From John's viewpoint, it wasn't hard to tell about each dream as each situation was still so vivid and locked in his brain.

John told her all the things that happened, including the Solitude One and Two stories. He told her about meeting a man whose brother was lost at sea on Solitude One with some others, who were unidentified. Her eyes widened when John got to the part about walking along the ocean floor and seeing a girl in a white flowing gown hovering over the sunken sailboat.

Each one of them was on the edge of their seats as he told them how he saw remnants of a skeleton buried in the sandy sentiment inside the boat's hull. Sabrina sat there, expressionless. She had heard John talk about the scary details of that dream before and was just as into it as the others who were hearing him tell it for the first time.

When John told me he intentionally held out telling Mrs. Hargrove about finding the locket, I understood why. He thought that the sequence of events would make more sense if he laid out the unbelievable things first, without disclosing that he saw the image of the woman he painted in his bathroom mirror, that is. He wanted to begin the second part of the story with finding the locket and then let that lead to the portrait of the woman.

Mrs. Hargrove said, sighing deeply, "John...I must say that that is a very interesting story. It's almost like I've been listening to a fictional book on tape, but how does this have anything to do with this portrait of my aunt?"

Three workers were milling close by, listening to John tell his tale. One of the gals even brought small bottles of water for each of them. It's a wonder she didn't make popcorn, too.

John started telling Mrs. Hargrove about finding the locket. When he described the locket as being a gold braided locket, that's when Mrs. Hargrove almost came off the sofa.

"My aunt gave a locket like that to my cousin, Anna!" she proclaimed. "Do you have it with you?"

John, Sabrina and Kate looked at each other in amazement. I almost fell out of my chair when John told me what Mrs. Hargrove said. The locket was lying in the key dish at his condo so he couldn't produce it.

"I don't have it with me, but could you describe it to me?" John said anxiously.

Mrs. Hargrove said, "I most certainly can. I was jealous when my aunt gave it to Anna."

John looked at Sabrina, she looked at him, and Kate looked at all three of them.

Chapter Fifty-seven

When the words came out of Mrs. Hargrove's mouth, John, Sabrina and Kate were stunned. I only wish that Sakae and I could have been right there when she said it. Knowing Mrs. Hargrove's aunt had given the same kind of locket to a daughter named Anna seemed to legitimize things. It answered some of the questions that had been burning in John's mind over the last three months.

I presume there is a possibility it could all be just a strange coincidence. However, there may be another explanation...such as God using John as a conduit to right something that went terribly wrong years ago. A young girl was lost and never found. I'm not saying that God makes mistakes, but could it be, in this case, He made one and was now making it right, so to speak?

Once John described to Mrs. Hargrove what he found that afternoon on the beach, she wept. She seemed certain that John did have Anna's locket, especially because of the inscription inside. Although it was important to know about the locket, there were still questions that needed answers. Mrs. Hargrove had the answers to some of them.

As everyone sat there in amazement, John reached over to the end of the sofa and picked the portrait up off the floor. He set it on his knee, pointing it towards Mrs. Hargrove.

"Now, Lois," John said, "are you telling me that this is a portrait of your aunt?"

"Yes," she replied. "I'm certain of it now more than ever."

John said, "And you said your aunt's name is Hazel Slater?"

"Yes," she replied, her eyes fixed on the portrait."

"And Hazel had a daughter named Anna, your cousin?" John said flatly.

"Yes," Lois replied. "She went missing over thirty years ago."

John was grilling Mrs. Hargrove as if he were a prosecutor gleaning information from a key witness under oath. I'm sure John didn't want to come off that way but, in his mind, there was no other way to get the information he needed.

"And where is your aunt living now, if you don't mind my asking?" John said, as he set the portrait down and leaned it against his chair."

"Virginia Beach," Mrs. Hargrove replied. "She is in a rest home. She is eighty-two. Hazel had a stroke three months ago and has been in a coma ever since. We don't think she will make it much longer."

At that point, emotions were running high. Kate took a tissue from a box sitting on the table next to the sofa and handed it to Sabrina, who had tears in her eyes, then took one for herself. Mrs. Hargrove told them that Hazel had a terrible breakdown shortly after her daughter went missing and never really recovered from it. By the way, it sure seems strange that things started happening three months ago...Hazel has a stroke and John finds the locket.

She said that Hazel's husband took a sabbatical for three months at the time Anna went missing, flew to San Diego and searched for Anna until he became ill himself. He died ten years ago... they say of a broken heart. Tell me...how much more heartbreaking can a story get?

Mrs. Hargrove said, "My aunt always told me that she would never leave this earth until she found out what had happened to her darling Anna."

John leaned forward in his chair and said in a compassionate tone, "I'm really sorry, Mrs. Hargrove, but I am convinced that Anna drowned out there on the ocean along with three other people...I'm sure of it. No one had any idea that Anna innocently went sailing that day on Solitude One with three people she had met just the night before."

Kate suddenly broke silence and said, "No one knew where to look for her...she just vanished into thin air," she continued as she blotted a tear from the corner of her eye. "That is so sad...and it is terrible that, after all these years, her mother will never know what happened to her daughter."

Out of the blue, John said, "I have Anna's locket and, for some reason, I feel I'm supposed to give it to Hazel, personally. Lois," he went on as he reached over and gripped her hand, "would you mind giving me the name and address of the rest home where Hazel is staying. I want to get there before it is too late."

Mrs. Hargrove reached into her bag and took out a card from inside a small pouch. "Here, John," she said, handing him the card. "I always keep one with me. I will drive back to Carlsbad and give my husband the news. We can fly into Norfolk tomorrow, a day earlier than we had planned. When we go, we stay at the Double Tree...I recommend it."

By now, emotions were running very high...that seems to happen a lot in this story. Kate piped in. "If no one minds," she said, hailing Michele over to where they were sitting, "I have to be there with all of you. If I don't go, I'll start having dreams of my own...do you mind, John? Sabrina? I will have Michele make our arrangements, if that's OK."

Sabrina looked at John and then at Kate. "Please do, Kate," Sabrina responded. "This is going to be the most compassionate thing anyone could do at this point for that poor woman who has suffered for so long...and I don't think any of us should miss it. And if Hazel is not awake at the time we get there, well, we can just hope for a miracle."

***

John and Sabrina came bursting through the door at Skipper's. John couldn't wait to tell me and Sakae what had happened. Sakae broke out in tears as she listened; and I, like a man, fought to hold back. While John and Sabrina were beaming like children on a ride at Disneyland, it dawned on me the significance of what just happened.

Who in Heaven's name would ever believe this story? I wouldn't even tell Joseph Navarra this one. All he would do is grab a pen, a prescription pad and prescribe me one hell of a remedy to stabilize my mind. I guess I *could*, every now and then, spin the tale around the bar…however, I'd have to make sure the customers down a few first. I could get away with it then, I'm sure.

Sakae…well, she wanted to go with the rest of the clan to Virginia. We both knew that wasn't possible. Not only did she run the floor, she was the pub 'keeper of the peace.' Michele, Kate's assistant, called John with the flight and hotel details just before they were about to leave the pub. I have to say, I was happy everything turned out the way it did. There was now a chance that John could focus on what was real in his life, once and for all.

The next afternoon, John, Sabrina and Kate were on a flight to Norfolk, Virginia, to meet up with Mrs. Hargrove and her husband, who had caught an earlier flight out of John Wayne Airport.

Chapter Fifty-eight

The Golden Living Nursing Home – Lynn Shores was a beautiful facility located near Lynnhaven Bay. John, Sabrina and Kate entered the lobby and were greeted by a skilled nurse who had been expecting them. Mrs. Hargrove and her husband, Bruce, sat in Hazel's private room next to her bed. It was the second time they had visited since she had slipped into a coma three months earlier.

The nurse led John, Sabrina and Kate into an elevator which took them to the second floor. John said he developed a fluttery feeling in his stomach as the elevator door opened. Sabrina could tell that he was nervous. He reached into his pocket for the third time since entering the facility to make sure the locket was still there. That, alone, shows you how nervous Johnny-boy was.

They stepped out of the elevator into a carpeted hallway. The nurse led them past several open doorways...no numbers, just name plates on the wall next to each room. Elderly Residents lay in beds. Some of them were watching TV, some were sleeping, and some they could hear moaning softly...the last place I'd want to be. John said Mrs. Hargrove was Hazel's only living relative, so the five of them were the only ones there.

When they walked into Hazel's room, Mrs. Hargrove introduced her husband. John looked at Hazel as she lay there motionless with her eyes closed, and he immediately sensed that they had made it just in time. When Mrs. Hargrove said that Hazel might not make it much longer, John didn't interpret that to mean just a day or so.

Hazel was lying on her back, hooked up to what they told John was a BiPAP machine...with a mask covering her nose and mouth, her neck expanding and contracting with each breath forced into her.

Before the nurse left the room, she assured Mrs. Hargrove that Hazel was not on life support…the BiPAP was primarily to keep her comfortable. Hospice had taken over a few days earlier and administered a slow morphine drip into her arm to make sure she was not in any pain. Her heart rate was hardly registering on the monitor near the head of her bed.

Now this is where this story goes way out there. Although, at the time, there were five people in that room, only one witnessed the entire event…John. Sabrina and Kate stood to the side while Mrs. Hargrove and her husband were seated near the bed. John stepped up next to the railing of the bed and gazed at Hazel lying there peacefully. He said that, suddenly, the same feeling he had on the beach when he found the locket rushed through his body. He turned to look at Sabrina, who smiled and nodded her head.

John reached into his pocket for the last time and pulled out the gold chain and locket. Hazel's right hand lay on top the blanket just above her stomach, next to her heart; her other hand lay at her side. John gently lifted her right hand, placed the locket on her body and laid her hand down on top of it.

Mrs. Hargrove had a handful of tissues and began to cry; Bruce put his arm around her for comfort. Kate took a tissue out of her purse and handed Sabrina a few as she began to weep. Suddenly, everyone in the room let out this quiet, incredulous gasp. Hazel slowly opened her eyes.

John, who was closest to her, didn't know what to do and moved back a step. Hazel's eyes stared intently towards the foot of the bed; there was Anna standing right before her. Bruce got up from his chair and hurried out to the hallway to find someone. That's when John saw her. It *was* Anna…in a white flowing gown, in the form of a silhouette, almost transparent, hovering in mid-air over the foot of Hazel's bed. Sabrina saw the look of stunned amazement on John's face, but didn't know why.

"What is it, John?" she said softly.

John didn't speak. He stepped forward and put the palm of his hand on top of Hazel's hand, the one covering the locket. He felt Hazel's hand close around the locket. Moments later, the silhouette of Anna rose towards the ceiling and slowly vanished into thin air. Hazel's eyes began to close just as a nurse came rushing in with Bruce. John moved over to stand by Sabrina and Kate as the nurse felt for a pulse. The nurse switched off the BiPAP machine, and for a moment, all was quiet. She turned to look at everyone and said, "I'm sorry for your loss." Hazel was no longer breathing. The nurse took a clipboard attached to the end of the bed, looked at the clock on the wall and made note of the time of death.

John stepped over to Mrs. Hargrove and said, "Did you see her?"

"I saw my aunt open her eyes…if that's what you mean, John," she replied, still in a state of shock.

John turned to each of them, shifting his gaze from one to the next. "Did you see Anna? Sabrina?" Sabrina shook her head. "Kate…did you see her?" Kate shook her head.

At that point, the room was still. John didn't know what to make of it. He was sure, as he stood there, that Anna was in that room and then rose up only to vanish in thin air, just like in his dream. He paused a moment and took in a deep breath before turning to Mrs. Hargrove once more with a warm smile.

"Your aunt finally found her daughter," he said, sighing happily. "Anna was here in the room with us, and Hazel saw her. I'm sure of it; I saw her, too."

Epilogue

Time passed. John and Sabrina's wedding was unforgettable. It took place in Old Kinderhook, in Camdenton, Missouri, located on the shore of the Lake of the Ozarks amid lush green hillsides and magnificent trees. Those in attendance marveled at how beautiful Sabrina looked, standing under the huge, white gazebo. I stood next to John as his best man, thinking back to that mischievous twelve-year-old boy sneaking into the Chinese restaurant with a pigeon in a brown paper bag.

Karla stood next to Sabrina as her maid of honor, and Uncle Phil gave Sabrina to John. It was a match made in heaven.

***

The streets were crowded, just the way I like it. Sakae was beautiful and smiling, from the minute we walked into the Elvis Wedding Chapel in Las Vegas…and all through the time we partied into the wee hours of the night. I wanted to wear a black wig and sideburns for the memorable occasion…but Sakae, John and Sabrina thought it would be a little over the top, even for me, so I wore my captain's hat instead. That was about as formal as I would get.

John and Sabrina had one hundred people attend their wedding, and we had a total of ten. I guarantee you, however, that my wedding in Vegas was much more fun. I would never say that to John and Sabrina, however.

Seven years later

Life was good. We were getting older, but who was counting. John, Sabrina and little Johnny-boy, Jr. came in for lunch one day and headed straight for their table. We were busy…but not too busy that I couldn't spend time with my extended family. I went to their table and sat down next to little Johnny, Jr. John and Sabrina had a funny look on their face. Little Johnny reached under his chair, grabbed a brown paper bag, placed it in the middle of the table and let go. I looked at John, he looked at me, and I looked at Sabrina. We all looked at each other. The bag began to move…and we all broke out laughing….

Meet our Author

Michael Livolsi

Michael J. Livolsi, a former singer/songwriter, was born in Brooklyn, New York, in 1945. He spent his early years in San Diego, California, and moonlighted for several years as a singer in nightclubs. For the last thirty-seven years, he has lived in Arizona. Michael earned certifications in Human Resource Management and Business Management at Arizona State College of Business while working for a major aerospace corporation. During his tenure in aerospace, he held various positions including an eighteen year stint in Human Resource Management and ten years in Sales which provided him the opportunity to travel to several countries around the globe. Married for forty-seven years and a proud grandfather, Michael is now retired. His interests include music, exercise and enjoying quality time with his four children and eight grandchildren. Michael has always loved to tell stories and others have loved to listen. Being a writer of fiction since his retirement has brought him great joy and excitement, especially when the late hours of work writing are rewarded with the memorable endings to his novels. Michael has written three novels. His first novel *"Hidden Purpose"* is a captivating thriller-love story. His second novel a wonderful romantic fantasy of adventure and the third novel "*The Braided Locket*" a romantic mystery that shares some of the author's real life personal experiences has motivated him to press on and continue writing the many stories that are still evolving in his mind.